"You Can't Leave Me Like This!"

"No?" He laughed. "Morag, *mon minou*, you are a paradox of words. I do not believe you know what it is you want."

"Oh, yes I do! I want . . . I want you . . . to . . ." Her face reddened, flushed with desire, and she stopped as she saw his smug look. How could she even contemplate such an action, here in her grandmother's home? "I want you to forget about marrying me. I want you to go back to France."

"Is that so?"

He leaned over her again as his hand, on her knee, reached up to the smoothness of her thighs . . . as she strained against him . . . with her arms about his neck, kissing him for all her worth.

"Tell me you will marry me," he whispered, biting her ear gently, driving her further insane.

"No!"

"*Sang dieu*, Morag. You are a stubborn little wench. Go on, say it. 'Tis nothing disgraceful to love a man. Say that you want me."

"You are a fiend and a blackmailer," she cried as the waves of warmth swept over her. She gasped for breath as the heat increased to an unbearable level, barely letting her think.

Dear Reader:

We trust you will enjoy this Richard Gallen romance. We plan to bring you more of the best in both contemporary and historical romantic fiction with four exciting new titles each month.

We'd like your help.

We value your suggestions and opinions. They will help us to publish the kind of romances you want to read. Please send us your comments, or just let us know which Richard Gallen romances you have especially enjoyed. Write to the address below. We're looking forward to hearing from you!

Happy reading!

Judy Sullivan
Richard Gallen Books
8-10 West 36th St.
New York, N.Y. 10018

This Bitter Ecstasy

SERITA STEVENS

PUBLISHED BY RICHARD GALLEN BOOKS
Distributed by POCKET BOOKS

A RICHARD GALLEN BOOKS *Original* publication

Distributed by
POCKET BOOKS, a Simon & Schuster division of
GULF & WESTERN CORPORATION
1230 Avenue of the Americas, New York, N.Y. 10020

ISBN: 0-671-43055-6

First Pocket Books printing May, 1981

10 9 8 7 6 5 4 3 2 1

RICHARD GALLEN and colophon are trademarks
of Simon & Schuster and Richard Gallen & Co., Inc.

Printed in the U.S.A.

This Bitter Ecstasy

Chapter One

HER GREEN SILK dress rustled as Morag Elliot leaned over to peer nervously back down the dark tunnel she had hurried through. Yes, the carriage was still there. She wondered if the driver had guessed where she was going. She hoped not. Maman would be terribly upset if word got about the French court that Marie Thérèse was using a love potion to win the Marquis!

Shrugging off that anxiety, Morag continued walking rapidly along the narrow street, her wooden pattens clattering on the cobblestones. The winter wind seemed sharper here. Shivering, she pulled her fur cloak closer about her. An auburn wave of hair escaped, framing her face, as her slender white hand clasped a scented linen kerchief to her face. God's wounds! She wrinkled her small nose in disgust. 'Twas no wonder Maman—and King Louis himself—hated the city!

Morag peered into the gloom. The creaking signs outside the shops here always gave her the shivers, as if this January cold weren't bad enough. The chemist's couldn't be much further now.

" 'Odsblud!" Morag murmured. "You'd think the woman would have her shop closer to the street."

After all, it wasn't as if the chemist were a true Frenchie. In truth, she had escaped to the city at the same time Morag and her mother had. But then "Madame Le Blanc," as she was known, hadn't had the luck to court connections. She was also doing something that, if the King were to learn of it, would force her out of her home in exile. Ever since Madame de Montespan's involvement, the King had been particularly harsh on the witches.

"God's death!" Morag stepped aside, just in time to avoid a bucket of slops coming down on her. Pressing the handkerchief to her nostrils, she walked faster, hating the fog that surrounded her and made visibility so difficult. She knew she shouldn't curse so. Maman didn't like it, but her father had always encouraged Morag's freedom of expression and had been amused when the Scots temper she had inherited from him flared like fresh-lit gun powder. It was only here, at the French court, that Maman insisted that Morag act the lady, that she use carriages or ride sidesaddle, that she dance and mince words like the rest.

Tears sprang into Morag's large green eyes. She wished Papa were still alive. She had always felt so safe and warm with him. Papa had always told her what a "bonnie lass" she was, that she must never forget the royal blood which flowed in her veins. Though many a year had passed since King Jamie I had made love to her great-grandmother Margaret, Morag had never wearied of hearing the tale.

"One day, lass, ye'll find a man who'll love ye with a passion, just like Meg and the King," Papa had said.

Morag sniffled, recalling her reply:

"I shall never love anyone as I do you, Papa. I would rather be a nun than risk that."

But Andrew Elliot had laughed. "Nay, lass. 'Twill happen one day, mark my words. 'Tis my only wish to see it so and to meet the man who'll tame my little daughter." Morag had responded, green eyes snapping, "Then you'll have to live forever, Papa, for no man will ever tame me!" and had ridden away from him as fast as her horse would carry her.

The creaking of the sign above her brought her thoughts back to the present. But Papa hadn't lived forever; he hadn't even lived the year out. Morag wiped the tears from her eyes.

It had been such a senseless duel that had killed Andrew Elliot. He had been defending King James II's honor, his friends told her and Maman. He had died for the Stuart cause. Not that it had done much good, Morag thought bitterly. James and his family had fled the country secretly, forcing all the remaining Catholics to follow suit or feel the rage of the Dutch Protestants.

Because of her father's devotion to the deposed King, Morag and her mother had been welcomed into the English court at Saint-Germain-en-Laye. With her French-gypsy blood, her black eyes snapping with as much vitality as when she had left France twenty years before, Marie Thérèse Elliot soon captured the hearts of several French nobles. She and her pretty daughter were ensconced in a tiny room in Versailles, and Marie gamed for their livelihood.

Morag turned abruptly, thinking she had heard steps behind her. Her heart pounded. She saw no one, but this foggy area was infamous for its crimes.

Quickening her steps, she reached the chemist's and entered the shop. She paused a moment, leaning

3

against the door, as the bell jangled. The strong scent of cloves and other spices assailed her, bringing tears to her eyes. As her sight adjusted to the dim light, she saw two yellowish eyes peering at her.

"Madame Le Blanc?" Morag's voice trembled. She gasped then, as the eyes moved rapidly: the cat had jumped back onto a crude table.

"Well? Oi ain't got all day."

Morag turned toward a low-beamed door. The shriveled old woman there cast a baleful eye on her visitor. Morag realized that the witch-woman, or chemist as the hag chose to be called, was not much bigger than she was. From where Morag stood, she could see a human skeleton standing in the back room. Her green eyes widened and the old woman, realizing what Morag had seen, stepped into the girl's line of vision.

"Well? Ye be from court?" she demanded.

Morag nodded. Nervously, she shoved the hood of her cloak back; her hair fell in auburn waves about her face. She was determined not to let the witch know how frightened she was. When she spoke, she forced herself to keep her voice calm.

"I've come for a potion . . . for Madame Elliot."

"Elliot?" The woman sniffed, as if scenting the air about Morag; or perhaps she was smelling the street. Whatever it was, she nodded. She seemed to know what was wanted.

"Ye'll wait, miss?"

Morag nodded and glanced about the room as the woman disappeared. The shop wasn't much different from chemists she had visited in London. Glass bottles of all colors and shapes lined the shelves, glimmering in the dim light of the single candle that the woman had left. Morag tried not to look into the shadows that

4

played about the room. Sinking into a cane chair, she closed her eyes.

Why, of all men, was Maman so determined to win Quentin Adam Sauvage, the Marquis d'Angeau? He was a libertine and a boor, half-Indian and complete barbarian. Of course, the man was wealthy, he was one of Louis' favorites, and his uncle, the Duke du Lauzun, was also a favorite. But he was also younger than Marié Thérèse by several years, had reportedly slept with nearly every woman at court, and was rumored to have an Indian wife somewhere in America.

There were other wealthy nobles at court. Why couldn't Maman have chosen someone else? Morag shivered. That man, that half-savage, made her uneasy—the way he stared at her with those hooded gray eyes and half-smiled, as if he were mocking her. As if . . . as if . . . She blocked the thought, nauseated. The other girls who served the Princess de Conti were always giggling and whispering such things, but Morag refused to listen to their lewd talk. She knew the others made fun of her for not having had a man yet, but Morag refused to be baited. Oh, how she wished Maman would let her join a convent! But Marie Thérèse would not hear of it.

The witch-woman emerged from the back. The cat meowed, jumping from the table onto the old woman's shoulder.

"Is that the potion?" Morag asked, seeing the vial of yellow-green liquid in the woman's hands.

"For love, yes, miss. 'Tis indeed that."

Morag hoped she didn't show how uneasy she felt. The stuff looked vile. How would Maman ever get the Marquis to drink that? Well, Morag shrugged, digging into her reticule, that was Maman's problem.

5

Withdrawing a gold louis, she handed it to the old woman, who bit the coin and nodded.

"'Tis potent stuff, m'girl. Oi suggest, if'n it's not for ye, ye'd best seal it well." The witch laughed as she handed over the vial.

"Yes, yes, I will take care it remains sealed," Morag said impatiently. Anxious to leave the place, she tucked the vial into her reticule and turned toward the door. As she did, she heard the rumble of thunder. A storm was coming.

"Wait, m'girl. Wait . . . don't ye want yer fortune told?"

"I . . ." Morag glanced toward the door. Maman was expecting her return with the potion, and the *carrosse* that Marie Thérèse had borrowed from the Marquis waited at the head of the alley.

"They usually do," the old woman whined.

The chill wind blew under the door, raising gooseflesh on Morag's arms. She had a sudden premonition that whatever this hag told her would come true, and she wasn't sure that she wanted to hear it. Her hand was on the door.

But the old woman was not so easily put off. "Oi'll not charge ye, m'girl. Yer mam's a good customer."

The thunder rumbled again, sending shivers up Morag's spine. She should get back to the carriage before the storm broke.

"Will it take long?"

Madame Le Blanc shrugged. "'Tis not fer me to know, 'tis the spirit within me. 'Twill depend on wot Oi see. Well?"

Slowly, Morag nodded. Her curiosity had conquered her fear.

The woman smiled and beckoned for Morag to follow her into the back room. Morag stared at the skeleton, fascinated. It was gruesome, but it was harmless, wasn't it? Hesitantly, she reached out to touch it, then jumped away with a gasp as a gust of air rattled the bones.

The witch cackled. "Don't let it scare ye, miss. It's 'ow we'll all end up one day. Giv' over yer 'and, dearie. Let us see."

Reluctantly, Morag presented her hand to the woman, who turned it, palm up, toward the light. "Ah, yes, ye got the courage 'n Oi'd say ye'll need it. Ye got danger 'n there."

"In where?" Morag stared at Madame Le Blanc, her green eyes large in her elfin face.

"Yer life, lovely. Here now." The old woman's eyes seemed to glaze over. "There is a ring, a black onyx ring . . . beware." Morag felt the blood drain from her face. The Marquis had such a ring!

The woman dropped Morag's hand then.

"Did you see anything more about the ring?" Morag asked.

The hag shook her head. "Did Oi disturb ye?"

"No, of course not."

"Oi can't 'elp what comes. Here now, lovely, let's us do them cards. Mayhap they'll tell us more."

Morag nodded, watching the woman shuffle the cards. These didn't look at all like the ones Maman used in *hoca;* the strange figures on them made Morag uneasy.

Silently, she watched as the cards were laid out on the table. A dark face in one card looked almost like the Devil himself.

"Who's that?"

"'E?" Madame Le Blanc pointed to the card and shrugged. "Oi don' know as yet, but 'e's a real one, Oi kin tell ye that."

7

"A real one?"

"A real man, lovely, 'oever 'e is. 'E's virile an' dark 'aired, an' a dangerous man t' cross, but Oi see ye crossin' 'im more 'n once. Do ye know such a one?"

Morag swallowed hard and shook her head.

"Me bones tell me 'e's the owner of the ring. 'Ere . . . " The old woman placed another card next to this one. "Ah, yes, lovely. Whether ye will or no, this man'll 'ave a great influence 'pon yer life. But," she pointed to a similar card, which had come up next, "ye'll 'ave t' be careful, lovely. There's two of 'em, two dark men. Both'll bring ye pain 'n trouble." She clucked her tongue.

Morag's thoughts raced as she tried to recall all the dark-haired men at court. There were a number of them who had offered for Maman and for her. There was Maman's other lover, Jean Baptiste . . . but the name Quentin Sauvage kept returning to her. He was that first man, she was sure. He was as dark as any man could possibly be, and he did have a hold over her through Maman. She shivered, thinking of his dark hairy arms, folded across his broad chest, that irritating half-smile of his. Yes, she would definitely stay away from him.

Rain began to strike the roof. Morag remembered the *carrosse* and driver waiting in the street. Abruptly, she stood.

"Ye don't want t' know more?"

Morag shook her head. "Another time, perhaps. I must leave."

The woman shrugged. "Jist remember, lovely. Fortune 'n fate canna be fought. Ye'll 'ave long journeys ahead in your life, 'less ye stay clear o' those men."

But Morag was no longer listening. She brushed past the skeleton. A bay leaf dropped from the herbs hanging from the ceiling rafters. It floated down past her in slow motion as she reached the door. Thinking it an omen of some kind, Morag turned.

"Thank you, Madame Le Blanc, I—"

The woman nodded. "No need t' say more, lovely. Oi likes the looks o' ye. Jist remember t' ave the courage. It's in ye."

Morag left the shop, clutching her reticule containing the vial for her mother. Cold rain pelted her. She pulled the fur hood over her head and began to run, her wooden pattens echoing eerily as they struck the cobblestones.

The Marquis' servant, Botemps, grunted a greeting as she entered the carriage. "Mademoiselle Morag—"

Morag glared at him. "I believe your master is waiting? I suggest you drive off—now."

The servant touched his cap, nodding. The gnome-like little man was always respectful to her, but Morag could not look at him without thinking of his master. Already, the Marquis had too much control over her life. She wished Maman had never taken up with him. It was *his* carriage they used; *his* money which bought her clothes, which fed her when she and Maman did not attend the balls, which paid Elise, their maid; *his* influence which allowed them to live at court. His influence, too, had got Morag permission to use the royal library and to wander about the royal menagerie at leisure. Disgust rose in her like bile as she remembered the day permission had been granted. It had been after she had returned to their rooms unexpectedly. The sight of her mother naked with that heathen sprawled on top of her, his slim, hard buttocks gyrating, had so astonished Morag that she had gasped, drawing attention to herself and a curse from the Marquis.

It had been days before Morag could shut that scene

from her mind. Even now, it embarrassed her to think of it. Nervously, she glanced about the carriage. This would be her first time alone with the man since walking in on him and her mother.

Thunder rolled again, and Morag shivered. A yawn escaped her. God's wounds, she was tired. If only Maman wouldn't insist that she attend all the balls. If only she would be reasonable and allow her to join Queen Mary's convent.

Morag bit her lower lip, torn by mixed emotions. She most certainly did not want Quentin Adam Sauvage for a stepfather, but Maman had told her that if the potion did not work, if the Marquis did not propose marriage, she had plans to marry Morag off.

No doubt it was that heathen who had put Maman up to it. Not that he knew of her mother's plans to wed him, but Morag knew for a fact that he had pointed out to Marie Thérèse that it was time for her daughter to have a husband.

A husband, indeed! Morag bit her lower lip thoughtfully. Maman had changed since she had met the Marquis. Never before had she insisted that Morag attend those ridiculous balls and games. Never before had Maman, in all of Morag's eighteen years, talked of marriage, or forced her daughter to do what she truly did not want to do. But of late, Maman had been threatening marriage more and more.

No, Morag decided, she must never marry. She shivered as the wind rocked the coach; she could never do *that* with a man. Just seeing her mother and *that* man had been enough to sicken her for life.

Mayhap, if Maman did marry the Marquis, she would allow Morag to return to England. It was true that they had left the country because of King William, because of their Catholic faith, but Morag had a desire to see her father's family, to know what a real family was like. Even if the Elliots had remained Protestant, even if they had cut Papa off for marrying a Catholic, surely they would not deny his daughter the chance to meet them?

The *carrosse* slowed. She realized they must be near the Palais Royal, where the Marquis d'Angeau had his hotel. She closed her eyes momentarily. It would serve the man right if Maman did marry him. With her passion for games, she would go through his fortune in a matter of weeks!

As the coach stopped, Morag leaned out. Seeing the open gate of the hotel's *porte cochère*, she called: "Botemps!"

"Yes, Mademoiselle?" The man jumped down.

Morag pursed her lips. "Tell his lordship I do not care to come in. I wish to return to Maman at once. If his lordship is not ready to leave, mayhap he will agree to let me go on back to court alone. After all, he rode his horse here, didn't he?"

"Yes, Mademoiselle."

"Then there is no reason why he cannot ride back." Her voice sounded more confident than she felt.

The servant nodded as the rain hit his balding head. "Yes, Mademoiselle."

Morag took a deep breath, watching Botemps disappear into the hotel. She hoped he would not be long. She also hoped that the Marquis would allow her to go on ahead without him. It was asking quite a lot when it was raining but, after all, the man had been raised with the Indians.

The coach door flew open. Startled, Morag glanced up to see her mother's lover framed in the dim gray light of the rain-darkened afternoon sky.

"What is this insolent nonsense about returning to

court alone? Since when do I take orders from a chit like you, and how dare you try to appropriate my carriage!" The gray eyes flashed angry sparks at her. "You come into the hotel this instant—I want an explanation of where you've been."

"No," Morag said stubbornly. He must not learn what her mother had commissioned her to buy. "I'm going home! I'm not answerable to you for my comings and goings."

"Damn you, girl, you're answerable when you're using my carriage!" Quentin Sauvage reached into the coach and his strong fingers grasped her wrist like a vise. "Now come into the house, where it's warm and dry, instead of sitting out here in that wet cloak that looks like a mangy cur!"

"How dare you talk to me like that!" Morag flashed back. "I'll sit in my wet cloak if I choose to, and I hope I take a chill and die! I'd rather be dead than think of my mother with—with a half-breed savage like you!"

He slapped her so hard that the blood rushed to her face. "You're a little hellcat. Someone should teach you a lesson."

"'Twill not be the likes of a . . . a bastard like you."

He slapped her again, not quite as hard as the first time. For a moment she quieted. He was an animal, a heathen Indian! Why, it was rumored that he didn't even attend chapel, although he had been educated by the Jesuits. Of course, being one of Louis' favorites—though God only knew why—he got away with it. Morag gritted her teeth, vowing that Sauvage would pay for this humiliation—for his whole evil being. She thought of the card in her fortune. Aye, there was no doubt: he was the Devil's spawn.

She heard him say, "I'm only trying to take care of

you, Morag." His arm was firmly about her as he escorted her toward the door of his hotel. "Botemps, you will come to us in the drawing room, after you have changed your clothing."

"Very good, sir."

Forcing herself to behave with dignity, she shrugged him off and walked ahead of him into the hotel. As mansions went, this was a modest one, but big enough for a bachelor of his standing. At the stairs, she paused. Usually the hotels had their drawing rooms on the second floor, but she had learned that the Marquis D'Angeau did not always follow custom.

He came up behind her. "Yes, go on. It's the first door at the top."

Well, at least he was sane in that respect. It would have been foolish to have the drawing room on the first floor, so close to all those disgusting street smells.

Silently, she walked into the room with its large ceiling-to-floor windows and mahogany wainscotting. She sank down into a soft velvet chair that faced the clear windows. Behind her, she could hear the Marquis moving about.

He came forward and placed a drink on the stand next to her, but she ignored it. A perfume filled her nostrils, sweet and heavy. Another woman? Probably. She forced herself to think of other things; tried to control her trembling.

She had been at the hotel before, with Maman, but never had she been alone with the Marquis, or any other man. Frightened, she remembered what the other girls always talked about, what men were prone to do with unprotected women. She remembered Quentin Sauvage's reputation and the disgusting scene she had witnessed with Maman. If only Botemps would hurry back; but would he protect her from his master?

13

Hands twisting in her lap, she glanced about the elegantly-furnished room. Tapestries of woodland scenes, of Louis XIV's victories and of Grecian myths covered the walls. Polished walnut sideboards and benches rested on a Turkish rug with a geometric design. Firelight sparkled off the crystal chandelier. *Why didn't he speak? What was he going to do with her?*

Finally, she turned toward him. He was standing by the marble mantel holding a drink. She didn't like the cynical way he was staring at her. Abruptly, she turned back toward the window. Her hand trembled as she reached for the glass of sherry beside her. Slowly, she sipped it, feeling the warmth flow into her veins.

"Well, are you calmer now?"

She refused to answer. Instead, she stood. Whirling about to face him, she had to grasp the edge of the chair for support. Perhaps she had drunk the sherry too fast. The warm glow filled her whole body, and she felt oddly lightheaded. She struggled to find the right words. "As soon . . . as soon as your servant comes, I should like to leave. If . . . if you don't mind, that is."

"Ah, but I do mind." He was watching her intently. It unnerved her. "Why were you at the chemist's today?" So Botemps had told him where she had gone!

He folded his arms over his chest and waited for her to continue. When she didn't, he said "Your mother gave me to understand that she needed the carriage for a matter of great importance, but she would not tell me what it was. Nor did she say that she would be sending you into that neighborhood alone, without a male servant for protection. Fortunately, Botemps kept his eye on you."

Morag shrugged, feeling her heart pound. She wet

her lips nervously, praying that she would not betray
Maman.

"My mother needed medicine for a headache."

His arms were still folded across his chest, like a
statue. "Why couldn't Doctor Fouberg prepare your
mother something?"

She thought quickly. "Maman has used this before.
She wanted something that she knew would work."
Morag shrugged in what she hoped was a casual man-
ner. "Am I to judge my own mother?"

"No." He dropped his arms and then strode toward
her. She tried to back out of his reach, but it was too
late. "But had I known where you were going, I would
not have allowed it." His hand touched her shoulder;
the gold signet ring with the black onyx center felt cold
against her skin. She stiffened, remembering Madam
Le Blanc's warning. Inside, she trembled with fear of
him, but her back was straight and her eyes flashed.

Her chin jutted out defiantly. "If that is the case,
then I am glad you did not know!"

His hand remained on her shoulder. "Let me see
tthe vial."

"Why?"

"I am curious to see what magnificent medicine you
have been sold." He gave a soft laugh, as if he knew
what it was she had, as if the touch of her skin told
him everything.

She inhaled deeply. Her stomach tightened as she
removed the vial from her reticule. Maman would kill
her if Quentin Sauvage found out. Worse yet, she
would force Morag to marry—probably Madame de
Montespan's nephew, that horrid creature.

The Marquis took the bottle from her and opened
it. He sniffed, glancing at her quizzically. Her heart
hammered. Would he know?

"There seems nothing unusual about it." He sealed the vial, returning it to her. "I should think that Fouberg could have done as well, but—" he shrugged, "it is done. Nevertheless," his hand rested on her shoulder with mock affection, "I shall have to speak to Marie about allowing you to wander about Paris on your own."

"That is not necessary. I—" Why was he looking at her in that strange way?

The sound of the door closing below made him drop his hand. Her sigh of relief was audible. A smile crossed his face. "If you thought I was going to rape you, my little hellcat, you needn't have worried."

"I thought nothing of the kind." She was outraged. "I'm merely relieved to have your clammy hand off me."

"Is that so?" His brows rose.

"Of course that is so! Would I lie to you?"

"Would you?" The laughter in his voice made her furious. He crossed the room to pull the silken bell-cord. Botemps appeared.

"Sir?"

"Botemps, the young lady will be returning to her mother's now. I will accompany her."

"You wish to take your books?" Botemps asked.

The Marquis nodded.

Morag's eyes widened. It was one thing to use the royal library, but it was quite another to actually own books oneself.

"And, Botemps . . . ?" The servant paused at the door.

"You'll bring another cape for Mademoiselle Elliot. Hers is still wet."

"I need nothing from you," Morag said tightly. Her

16

eyes flashed and her fingers tightened on the chair where she stood.

"My dear little Morag, while you are with me, I am responsible to your mother for you." He turned back to his servant. "Get the cloak, Botemps."

The man hurried away.

Morag tried to keep her voice even. "Monsieur le Marquis, no one is responsible for me. Least of all you!"

Why was he smiling like that? He folded his arms over his chest, watching her with horrid sleepy eyes that seemed to absorb everything.

"You know, Morag, the Indians I grew up with had much the same philosophy. One is responsible only for one's self. But then, of course, one must take the consequences for what one does."

The Indians! How dare he compare her to a savage!

She was about to speak again when Botemps appeared with a fur cloak of smooth white sable, far superior to the one that had been ruined by the rain. He handed it to d'Angeau. Unaccountably, Morag shivered as the Marquis approached. She tried to control her trembling as he placed the cloak gently about her shoulders. Reluctantly, she had to admit that she had been cold and wet and that she did need it, but it was humiliating to be always taking things from him.

A tantalizing perfume rose from the garment, enveloping her. Thinking to embarrass him, she sniffed the elusive scent and asked sweetly, "Pray, sir, whom was the cloak made for?"

He glanced at Botemps, who was waiting at the door for them. In a conspiratorial whisper, he said "My dear little Morag, you must promise not to tell your mother . . ."

Morag flushed. At last she would learn something

that might persuade Maman against this creature. "Of course I promise."

"The cloak was made for . . . your mother."

Morag's jaw sagged for an instant. Quickly, she closed it.

"You made a fool out of me!"

The mocking smile lit up his gray eyes. "I did only what you asked, Mademoiselle." He held out his hand. "Are you ready to return to Versailles now?"

Ignoring his hand, she strode past him. There was nothing to do but return in the coach with him. But somehow, she vowed, she would have her revenge.

Passing through the *porte cochère,* Morag vowed that this evening, before she went to the ball, she would light a candle to St. Jude, patron of impossible causes, praying that she get satisfaction from this odious man.

Chapter Two

MORAG SAT SILENT as the coach joggled along the rutted roads to Versailles. The cold seeped through to her bones, yet she refused to wear the fur. Her skin tingled with the cold and with an awareness of d'Angeau's presence as he dozed beside her, his muscular arms folded across his chest, his dark curls falling forward.

Glancing surreptitiously at him, she suspected that he only feigned sleep, that he was staring at her from under those heavy lids with eyes that could be bored one moment and alive with discomforting scrutiny the next. Was it true, what they said, that living with the Indians had taught him how to read minds? She shifted uncomfortably. Closing her eyes, she tried to shut him out.

Exhaustion overwhelmed her. Without further hesitation she pulled the fur cloak about her, hating herself for giving in. She had to admit that it was warm. Her head nodded slightly as she relaxed.

Her companion stirred and Morag jerked her head upright, her heart lurching from the sudden transition. She waited a moment. The rhythm of his breathing seemed steady enough. Perhaps he was asleep, perhaps she could close her eyes after all . . . just for a few moments.

Her mind wandered to the past. She thought of her father, of the way he had held her when she had been a wee girl, of the warm protectiveness of his arms.

The lurching carriage, as the horses stumbled in a rain-filled hole, forced her awake. The wind seemed to be buffeting them from side to side. She grimaced then, realizing that Quentin's arm was around her.

"Are you all right?" he asked.

"Don't touch me!" She jerked away as if scorched. Beneath the cloak, her fists clenched into tense balls.

"Very well." He sat back calmly, eyeing her. Obviously, he was enjoying her discomfort. "I was only concerned about your not getting hurt. That was a rather nasty plunge there, and this wind doesn't help matters."

"I don't care. I would rather fall, than be saved by the likes of you."

That damned cynical smile curled his lips. "What are the likes of me, Morag?"

Confused, she stammered, "Someone . . . someone who goes about with different women. Who . . . who doesn't care a farthing for their hearts or their feelings. Someone who . . . who uses women."

"Oh? Are you saying that I don't care for your Maman? That I use her?"

"No!" She reddened. "I don't know." She swallowed hard. Then, as her dislike of him propelled her thoughts, she added, "It's not unknown that you've made a number of conquests at the court, Maman included. Why, I've even heard that you and Queen Mary—"

She stopped. The pulses at her temples were throbbing. She shouldn't be talking to him like this.

"Yes, go on."

"I just know that I don't want you—or any other man—touching me." She scooted over to the far side of the swaying coach, catching her cloak. Frustrated, she tugged at it as he watched. Damn his eyes!

The smile played on his lips. "Some man will eventually touch you, *ma petite*. I warrant, when he does, you'll not find it such an awful experience. Your Maman certainly doesn't."

"Don't talk like that!" She put her hands to her ears, wrinkling her nose. When she saw that he would be silent, she dropped her hands to her lap, clasping them to avoid showing her nervousness. She was ashamed of the way her voice betrayed her. "You're wrong. No one will touch me, if I have my way. I intend to join the nuns at Saint Cyr, or some other convent."

His right brow raised. "Do you now? That would be a waste."

Unconsciously, she frowned. He touched his hand gently to her chin, sending a shock through her system.

"Come, *mignonne,* don't look so defeated. You will find some way to have your revenge on me."

Her eyes widened. "How did you know . . .?"

He took his hand away. "I know my women."

Her chin went up. "I am not one of your women! Nor do I ever intend to be. When you and Maman—" She stopped short.

"You were about to say?"

"Nothing." She stared out of the carriage window, watching the rain splatter. The town of Versailles

21

loomed in the distance, with its fine red and gray stone buildings; they were nearly at court.

Thankful that he did not pursue the subject, she averted her eyes from him for the remainder of the journey.

Marie Thérèse Elliot was resting on the lounge in the rooms she shared with her daughter when Morag burst in. Languidly, Marie raised her head and frowned at her.

"Oh, it's you, Morag, *ma chère*. What took so long? Did you get the potion?"

"Yes, Maman." She sank down on the chaise. "The driver took an inordinately long time, and then we had to stop for the Marquis."

"Oh!" Marie Thérèse sat upright, her rose damask gown opened slightly, revealing heaving breasts. "Did Quentin return with you?"

Morag pursed her lips and nodded. She fingered the silver-gilded post on the lounge.

"You didn't tell him anything?"

"Do you take me for a dunce?" She shot a glance at her mother. "Of course not."

Marie Thérèse sank back down on the pillows and sighed. "That's good. I know sometimes you allow your tongue to get the better of you, just like your father. Give me the vial, Morag. Oh, I do hope this will work!"

There was a pause as Marie Thérèse reached over for a sweetmeat on the side table.

"You know, dearest, I do wish you would be more reasonable and consider marriage. After all, you are almost eighteen. Why, I was married to your Papa when I was a wee . . . fifteen."

Morag pouted. "Obviously, you are different than me, Maman. I told you, I do not want to marry anyone. I wish to join the sisters." She reached for her sewing.

Marie Thérèse gave an exaggerated sigh. "Oh, what a bother you are, child. What am I to do with you, Morag? Marriage . . . it is . . . the way of the world. We women are made for men."

"No!" Tears sparkled in Morag's green eyes as she sucked the finger she had just pricked. "You promised me if I obtained the potion for you—"

Marie Thérèse frowned. "Hush! Don't you know that there are spies everywhere? Lower your voice!"

Morag swallowed her tears, aware of the tightness in her throat. "Maman, you promised me."

"I promised that you would not have to marry . . . yet. I did not say never." Again, she sighed. "Dear heart, it isn't as bad as you fear, but . . . very well, we will drop the subject for now."

Morag's throat ached, but she managed to say, "Thank you, Maman." She brushed the tears from her eyes.

Marie Thérèse watched her daughter sewing. "*Ma petite,* I hope you are not doing what I think."

"No, Maman." Morag kept her eyes on the material in her hands. "I am not mending anything."

"Good. You know I have told you often enough that that is a servant's job, and you are not a servant. You are the granddaughter of an English lord, and you have a great future, *mon coeur*. One that does not involve such drudgery."

Marie Thérèse swung her bare feet over the side of the chaise and quickly slipped into furred slippers as she tied her robe. "But if you are not mending, pray, dearest, what are you doing?"

Morag bit her lip, glancing up now to meet her

mother's eyes. "I have made myself a costume for tonight's ball."

Marie Thérèse's eyes widened. "Made yourself *what?*"

"A costume."

Pretty frown-lines appeared about Marie Thérèse's blue eyes. "*Ma foi!* Morag, that is not done. Why, in holy name—Quentin had costumes made for both of us. Quite nice ones, too, you must admit."

"Yes, Maman. The costumes are quite nice." Morag continued sewing, her face hot.

"But, my love, then why—why are you ruining your beautiful hands with such folly?"

Morag folded away the patchwork skirt she had been working on. "Because I am sick of accepting charity from your lover." She went to sit next to her mother.

"Oh, *ma petite*," Marie Thérèse said, her arm about her daughter, "You know it's only for a short time. Soon he will support you, and it will not be charity."

Morag's jaw jutted out. She glared at her mother. "I don't want that either. I hate the Marquis d'Angeau."

"Morag!" Marie Thérèse's eyes darted to the faded green silk of the walls, to the carved door. "I tell you, you must lower your voice. There are spies—"

"He knows how I feel."

"Oh, Morag, you didn't! Oh, *ma petite,* you have ruined—"

"No, I haven't," Morag said ruefully. "I'm sure nothing I say could change his mind about you."

"Did he tell you?"

Morag flushed. "No, but it's not hard to guess."

"Oh, Morag, *mon coeur,*" Marie Thérèse's slender hands went to her daughter's shoulders. "I wish you could like him. After all, if my plans succeed, he will soon be your papa."

"No one will ever be my papa but Papa."

Marie Thérèse gave a shrug. "Well, he will still have the obligation and right to help me direct you . . ."

"Maman, please, must we talk about this now?" Morag left the couch and stood by the window. Desperately, she searched for another subject. "Isn't Nicole due to arrive today? Will she be here in time for the ball?"

Marie Thérèse yawned and stretched her arms. "I suppose. I must say, I think it rather tiresome of my brother Charles to foist his daughter off on me like that. Especially when I have you to be concerned about. It's just like Charles, though. Do you know, when I married your father he would have nothing at all to do with me? But now that I am at court, well, that's a different matter. Now it's 'dearest sister' and 'my sweetest Marie Thérèse.'"

"Tell me more about Cousin Nicole." Morag turned from the window.

"Oh," Marie Thérèse signed, "there isn't much to tell. She's your age. No, perhaps she's a year younger. I believe she is about your size. I hope she has brought along a decent wardrobe. I've trouble enough as it is trying to find clothes for you."

"But what is she like? Does she read? Is she religious?"

"Pooh! Who cares about that? All I care is that she be no competition for you. Indeed, I fear if she is anything like her father, your suitors will fast disappear."

"Then good riddance to them!" Morag cried. She nodded toward the window. "The rain has stopped. I am going for a walk by the canals. Send Elise to find me when Nicole comes."

25

Marie Thérèse nodded and sank back languidly onto her pillow.

The costume ball was one of the leading attractions of the carnival season. As with all the grand balls at Versailles, the gallery was divided into three parts. Two balustrades were decorated with Gobelin tapestries; there was a center area for dancing, a stage for Louis XIV and his wife, the plump Madame de Maintenon, to sit on. They would be flanked by all the ambassadors and Princes currently at the court. A small amphitheater held the orchestra, which included two dozen violins, a half-dozen oboes and a half-dozen flutes.

As usual, Morag was impressed with the show of wealth—the massive amount of gold and silver in the trappings, in the clothes, in the furniture, and on the floors—and the vivid splashes of color of the varied silks, satins, gauzes, linens, lawns, hollands and every other conceivable fabric worn by the guests. How could she not be awed after having been raised in semi-poverty—always wondering if Papa would be able to collect on his gambling and if they would eat that night?

Someone opened a balcony door, creating a light breeze, and the flames of the four thousand wax lights about the room flickered, causing the gold to shimmer and rainbows to play among the crystals of the chandeliers.

The Duchess d'Aubin appeared wearing black velvet trimmed with gold lace. Diamonds dotted her costume carelessly. Only the headdress told Morag that the woman fancied herself a Princess from the Dark Ages. The outfit was easily worth ten thousand *pistoles*, far more money than Morag had ever had. She took a deep breath as the Duchess of Savoy, a guest from the English court at Saint-Germain-en-Laye, followed in a gown of silver tissue, a small crown of diamonds in her hair. Her wrinkled face had been painted with rouge, and she looked like an ancient trollop. Morag didn't know what she pretended to be, and didn't care.

Nevertheless, she now wished that she had taken Maman's advice and worn the velvet Breese "peasant" outfit with the yellow cloth cuffs and collar and the black Venetian lace, which the Marquis had selected. But it was too late. She had put on the Scottish maid's costume she had sewed herself and given Cousin Nicole the other.

Well, what did she care that she was underdressed? She hadn't wanted to come to the ball anyway. A few quiet hours in the chapel would have appealed to her more, but she had promised Maman and so she had come . . . for a few hours, anyway.

The Marquis d'Angeau was announced, with Madame Elliot.

Morag glanced up briefly. She had to admit that Maman looked lovely in the fuchsia silk with the pear-studded bodice, her curls, as dark as her lover's, arranged in the latest fashion. She was supposed to be a gypsy Queen, but though there was gypsy blood in her, tonight Marie Thérèse hardly looked bohemian.

Quentin Sauvage, standing next to his mistress, was completely covered by a black cape. His black curls had been tied back tightly and resembled a cropped head. Morag couldn't guess what he represented. She flushed as d'Angeau glanced in her direction and smiled. He didn't seem upset that she hadn't worn his costume; she had hoped he would be.

Deciding not to remain in the same room with him, Morag wandered into the outer room, searching for her cousin. Where was Nicole? The King would be here soon, and no one came in after His Highness. It just wasn't done.

Morag couldn't say that she had been pleased to meet her cousin. Nicole, with her blonde curls and china-doll blue eyes, seemed as vapid and flighty as the rest of the females at court. Oh, how Morag longed for the peace of the convent! If only she could convince Maman.

She became aware of a small group of whisperers, who glanced at her and became silent as she approached. Morag flushed. She knew that they were gossiping about Maman and the Marquis. Holding her head high, she walked by them.

They didn't wait long to continue their conversation.

"He's almost always at the *petite levée* to help the King dress. They say His Highness positively dotes on him."

"And I heard," said another, "that he killed his mistress in the colonies. Jealousy, I'm sure."

Morag slowed her pace. Obviously, they were talking about Quentin Sauvage. The name suited him. He *was* a savage. Morag didn't doubt that he had murdered his mistress . . . and others as well.

She knew, too, that his boyhood days with the Indians had served him well. If he wanted to, he could be as quiet as death. It was said that he could elude even Louis' ever-present Swiss guards. If so, it was no wonder so many married women at court craved him for a lover.

She heard another woman in the gossiping group comment, with a giggle, "She's been through so many hands that she's slightly soiled by now. He'll tire of her soon enough. I wonder what he sees in her?"

Morag clenched her fists. Well, let them wonder—

the idiots. Did they have nothing better to talk about? She hurried away before she could say something she would be sorry for.

There was still no sign of Nicole. Morag stopped. She had come to the tables laden with the richest and rarest blossoms, all coaxed from the hothouses of the court, and exotic fruits. The sideboards, too, were covered—soups, pastries, fish, fowl—delicacies to tempt any palate.

She became aware of a sudden silence. The King was coming. Morag hurried back into the main room. It wouldn't do for her to be absent. Despite the vast number of courtiers, Louis always seemed to notice when someone was missing.

Everyone looked expectantly toward the glass doors as Louis entered with his wife. Even at fifty, the Sun King cut an impressive figure in his red velvet coat with the gold Venetian lace. Peering into his eyeglass, he spun about on his famous red-heeled shoes. He seemed to be looking for someone.

Then his face broke into a smile that creased his double chins. "Ah, Quentin."

Everyone turned to glance at the Marquis d'Angeau. "Come close, boy."

Quentin Sauvage sauntered forward with the easy grace of a panther.

Louis frowned. "Turn." He waved his hand as he switched his inlaid cane from one side to the other.

Quentin obeyed. The black cape flared.

Louis was puzzled. "Pray, Quentin, tell me what you are supposed to be?"

A slow smile softened the bronzed features. "This is not my costume, Your Highness. If you will permit . . . ?"

Louis nodded. "Yes, yes. Go on."

With a tug at the neck-cord, Quentin dropped his cape to the floor and folded his arms across his chest. Men gaped with astonishment and ladies gasped. Louis' mouth fell open as his fat-pocketed eyes took in the lean oiled figure before him. D'Angeau's muscular body bore only a square of leather covering his manhood.

"Mon Dieu!" Then Louis chuckled, slapping Quentin on the back. *"Merveilleux!* An Indian! Yes, I adore it."

The room buzzed with conversation. The King tapped his walking stick once. Silence resumed. With his cane, Louis lifted the black cape from the floor, as if it were a dead animal. Quentin took it from the walking stick and, with a slight bow, retreated into the crowd.

Head erect, cane forward, Louis continued toward the dais. The silence remained absolute until the King, along with Madame de Maintenon, reached the top. Smiling in Quentin's direction, Louis sank onto his throne and lowered his cane.

Trained to fall in, the nobles immediately took their places as the music began for a lively *branle*.

Morag hung on the edge of the crowd, watching. She—and others—were still astonished that the Marquis d'Angeau would dare come almost naked and, most astonishing of all, that the King should simply smile and permit him to carry on. It would have served the man right to have been banished from the court for such a stunt. Yet, she couldn't help but stare.

"Pardon, Mademoiselle Scottish maid . . ."

Morag turned abruptly. The Duc du Maine, Louis' favorite illegitimate son, stood beside her dressed in a black cassock.

"Yes?" She pretended not to know him, though his

30

slightly effeminate features betrayed him, just as her coppery curls betrayed her.

"This dance, Mademoiselle?" He extended a slender white hand.

Morag sucked her lower lip slightly. She disliked Louis August, Madame de Montespan's natural son. She had seen the cruel way he beat his horses and servants, how he ignored people of lesser rank unless he wanted to use them. He was a year younger than Morag, but already his reputation with women far outweighed d'Angeau's.

"Well?" There was laughter in his immature voice. "Mademoiselle, if it is my costume which puts you off, let me assure you that even the clergy— though they profess to be married to the Church—do not denounce women." He grinned, showing teeth stained yellow with snuff. "The black coat can hide a great many mysteries—" he lowered his voice—"and pleasant surprises."

Morag didn't like to think about this thinly-veiled hint, but she knew she would have to accept him.

She nodded. He grasped her hand tightly with a vicious grip that hurt. She wanted to cry out, but a side glance at him told her that she had best not. She was thankful that there was minimal physical contact in this dance.

When the music ended, Morag breathed a sigh of relief. She had done her duty, dancing with the Duc du Maine. One, maybe two more dances—the lively gavotte and then the more sedate minuet—after that she would be free to retire.

Before she could move out of Maine's reach, the doors to the hall opened once more. Morag stared. She couldn't believe that Nicole had come—now, after Louis.

Then she gasped. Yes, her cousin was wearing the costume that the Marquis d'Angeau had given Morag, but only part of it. Morag's eyes widened when she realized that Nicole, like Quentin Sauvage, was practically naked. She had taken the black sheath of Venetian lace that had covered the peasant dress and placed it over a simple black gauze.

The silence in the room was deafening as Louis held up his cane and beckoned Nicole forward. People glanced at Marie Thérèse's flushed face, at Morag, and then at Nicole, as the blonde girl, smiling graciously, walked slowly up to the dais.

Morag's heart was in her throat as Nicole passed her. Anyone could see the girl's nipples through the gauze. What in the world was her cousin doing? The Duc du Maine tightened his grip on Morag's arm, while he stared, unabashed, at Nicole's offering.

At the throne, Nicole Le Martin curtseyed low, showing off the white-dusted tops of her ample breasts— as if not a thing were wrong.

"You'll pardon me, Your Highness," Nicole lowered her eyes demurely, "but I am just come to stay with my dearest Aunt Elliot. I was so tired that, though I had meant to rest but a moment, I found myself asleep. Yet I was determined to come to see the grandest of Kings and partake of his pleasures." She smiled at Louis then; Madame de Maintenon frowned. "Pray, Your Highness, I hope you will forgive your humblest servant."

Louis grunted and nodded, unable to take his eyes off the girl. "*Bienvenu,* Mademoiselle. I hope you will enjoy your stay here."

Raising and lowering his cane again, he signaled for the gavotte to begin.

Morag took advantage of Maine's leering fascination

with Nicole. Freeing herself from his grasp, she hurried to the safety of gold-gilt chairs against the red damask walls. A moment later, Nicole joined her.

"You must be mad, Nicole! Whatever possessed you?"

Nicole Le Martin smiled. She stretched her slender white arms out, straining the thinly-sewn seams of her gown so that her red nipples seemed about to burst through the lace.

"What possessed me, Cousin? Why, the desire for a little adventure. After all, that's why I'm here . . . for adventure and to catch a husband. Besides, I'm not the only one with daring." She pointed to Quentin Sauvage. "What's that fine stallion's name? The one dancing with Aunt Marie." She licked her lips. "I dare say he gives a good ride."

Morag grimaced. She found it hard to believe that Nicole was younger than she was. "I wouldn't know about those things."

"Wouldn't know?" Nicole shot her a sideways glance. "You've lived at court for nearly a year! What? Are you planning to become a nun?"

Morag swallowed hard. "As a matter of fact, I am."

"Oh, what rot! You don't know what you're missing!" Nicole added in a conspiratorial whisper, "Besides, Cousin, even if you were a nun, it wouldn't make much difference. They're not all as straight-laced as you might think." She giggled.

"Stop!" Morag whispered, horrified. "Stop! Isn't anything sacred? You sound as bad as . . . him." She gestured toward the Duc du Maine who, gavotting with another partner, had been leering in their direction.

"*Ma foi!* You are strange!"

Morag blushed and stood. "I must get some air. Excuse me."

33

Pulling her shawl closer about her, she escaped from the overheated room onto the balcony. The chill winter air felt good against her perspiring body. She wouldn't be able to stay out here long, but at least it served as a momentary respite.

Morag was surprised at the sound of footsteps behind her. Before she could turn, her shoulder was gripped tightly. She was spun about to feel the wet lips of the Duc du Maine crushing hers.

Aghast, she pushed him away, trying to control her revulsion. "Please, Your Grace . . ."

"*Mon coeur,* I love you. I desire you. Do you know you are beautiful, even without all the jewels of the others? You are a jewel yourself, Mademoiselle Elliot. What would you have one do?" His hand tightened on her wrist.

"Please, Your Grace! You are hurting me." Tears were in her eyes.

"Then let me stop hurting you." His voice dropped. "Let me pleasure you. Let me show you how pain and pleasure mingle to heighten the senses. You won't regret it."

Her throat was dry. She wanted to tell him that she wanted no one. She wanted someone to come and help her.

As d'Angeau stepped out onto the terrace, she sighed with relief. For once, she was glad to see the man.

"Ah, Maine! So there you are!" The Marquis grasped Maine's shoulder firmly. "Your father is looking for you. He wants you to dance the minuet with Madame."

Maine frowned. Dropping Morag's wrist, he jabbed a finger into the air. "One day, d'Angeau, you will go too far." Spinning on his heels, he re-entered the ball-room.

Gingerly, Morag touched her wrist, thankful that Maine was gone.

"Did he hurt you?"

She shook her head. Not wanting Quentin Sauvage to see her tears, she turned to look out at the canals. All the pulses in her body seemed to vibrate as he stood behind her.

He gently touched her bare shooulder near her neck. She felt the onyx fleur-de-lis ring—a gift from Louis—against her skin.

"If he hurt you, let me know. I can control him."

Morag shrugged, staring out at the canals and the gardens. Just this morning jonquils had bloomed, almost as naturally as if they were growing from the soil. This evening, Louis had replaced them with jasmine.

"What is there to control? He's but a boy."

"In years, perhaps. But his mentality is not a boy's. He thinks like a man—a man who has been hurt and wishes to hurt others."

"Why should he hurt me? I've done nothing to him."

"You entice him. You may still think like a girl, Morag, but your body is that of a woman."

There was silence for a moment. He remained behind her. She closed her eyes, listening to the music. Except for the painful throbbing in her wrist, she could almost feel safe here, as if d'Angeau were a shield between her and the others. But no—her eyes flew open—that was ridiculous. He was as much a part of the scene as Maman and Maine and Nicole.

"Shouldn't you go in? You'll catch cold in such skimpy clothes."

He laughed. "My dear little Morag, I have worn less

35

in more severe weather than this. You don't have to concern yourself with me."

"And you, sir," she raised her head still higher but continued to stare into the darkness of the gardens, "don't have to concern yourself with me."

"Morag, turn around. Look at me."

She took a deep breath and spun about to face him. His gaze was direct, challenging. His cool gray eyes seemed to rake her as they traveled from her trim shapely ankles, adorned in white silk stockings, up past her skirts to her narrow waist, which she had cinched with a burgundy sash, to the swell of her bosom, which peeped out over a demure square neckline, then down the voluminous sleeves to her hands clutched in front of her.

A warm flush crept up her face as he scrutinized her. Was he going to say something about her not wearing his dress?

"You made the outfit yourself?"

Swallowing hard, she nodded.

"I like it. Better even than the one I sent. The simplicity complements your beauty, Morag, much better than jewels and diamonds."

An embarrassed pleasure overwhelmed her feeling of anger. His hand touched her chin gently and he tilted her head up. She jerked away.

"Oh, Morag!" He gave a low laugh, passing a knuckle along the fragile bone of her cheek. "Do you know that your eyes seem almost golden under the moon?"

She was shivering from the chill, from his touch. "You, sir, are no gentleman. At least, the Duke—"

Her voice broke as his fingers continued to trace a molten path down her neck and finally rested on her left shoulder.

"Did I ever claim to be a gentleman? You yourself

36

have told me that I'm a barbarian. An Indian. Come here, Morag." He reached out to pull her to him.

She turned her head away, recognizing that lustful look in his eyes.

"You disgusting coxcomb! You think just because you prance about, showing yourself, that all women will fall at your feet. If I told Maman—"

A low laugh rumbled from his chest. "Ah, Morag, I'm transported to have won your heart."

Humiliated and angry, she broke away, hearing her sleeve rip as she escaped from the terrace and onto the promenade, toward the forest near the orangery.

After a moment, she stopped running. She was in the groves now. Thank goodness he hadn't followed her. Leaning against a tree, she paused to catch her breath. Even from here she could see the moon's glimmer on the copper cupolas and hear the music of the ball. There seemed no escape. The masses of statuary and fountains surrounded her, a constant reminder of where she was. A sob escaped her.

"Lord, I hate that man!" What did he want of her? Why did he torment her so? She glanced down at her ripped sleeve and grimaced. She couldn't return to the ball, not like this. She'd be damned if she would provide food for more gossip.

Sighing, she turned toward the pavilion and the rooms she shared with Maman. Once there, she lit the candle and ruefully glanced about at the curtained bed for Maman, the lounge by the windows, the small but ornate dressing table. To Morag, everything here was tinged with shame. They owed their presence to Quentin Sauvage. If not for him, for his influence, they would still be living in the garret at the inn in town. She thought about Quentin's luxurious Versailles mansion on Rue de la Chausu de Clagny, just outside the palace gates. How Maman would love to be there as his wife! How Morag would hate it!

She undressed quickly, then slipped into bed. Pulling the covers over her head, she thought of Quentin Sauvage and how much she hated him.

Chapter Three

THE APRIL RAIN depressed Morag; a glum feeling rested heavily on her heart. She sat by the window with an open book of verse in her lap, unread. Normally, she would be out walking no matter what the weather, but these past few days she had been tense and edgy.

Carnival was over. Lent had already passed. Morag, for one, was glad that the number of balls, gamings, operas and concerts had diminished, though they hadn't stopped altogether. Louis thought too much of his courtiers to do that. His philosophy was: the busier they were with diversions, the less mischief they would get into. Morag was sure he was right. Besides, there were still several foreign ambassadors in attendance at court. Louis liked the ambassadors to see the extravagant activity at the French court, liked to have them report to their respective governments about the careless luxuries of the Sun King. He hoped to intimidate them. Usually, he succeeded. But it wasn't so much the frenetic round of partying that upset Morag; it was her mother—and her cousin.

39

Within a week of coming to court, Nicole had made it clear that, no matter whom else she might bed—be it the Duc du Maine or the King himself—she intended to have Quentin Sauvage. Already, she had moved out of the Elliots' rooms and, using those doll-like looks that belied her scheming intelligence, installed herself in rooms next to the Chevalier d'Effiant.

Morag knew that Maman was worried. Though Marie Thérèse had said nothing to her daughter, the potion obviously hadn't worked, or was slow in working. Reluctant to let Quentin out of her sight, Marie spent her waking hours either with the Marquis alone, or at gambling—neither of which pleased Morag.

If only the Marquis would propose, perhaps Maman would forget about Morag's marrying. All men were goats. If only Maman would let her speak to Madame de Maintenon!

The King's wife had shown a liking for Morag when she had visited the school at Saint Cyr. If she were told how much Morag wanted to return to the community there, Morag was sure the Queen would encourage it. But getting to talk with Madame was a problem in itself.

The ormulu clock struck two. No doubt the King and his wife would be at their midday meal now. Where was Maman . . . with the Marquis? Or perhaps she was arranging some distasteful alliance for her daughter.

Morag closed her book with a defiant bang. If she waited too long, it would be too late. She would try to see the King's wife today. Meanwhile—she glanced at the tray that Elise had brought up and pushed it away—meanwhile, she would walk to the menagerie and see the ostrich that had been injured yesterday.

Taking one of Maman's capes from the chest, she

slipped it over her shoulders. Rain or not, she must leave the room before she suffocated.

Quentin Sauvage shifted slightly in bed, as he absently toyed with his mistress's dark curls. Her breathing was steady, her head resting on his hairy chest. Unexpectedly, he thought of Morag, resting accidentally against him on the journey from Paris in his coach.

Well, it was only natural for him to think of her! She would, after all, be his daughter, once he married Marie Thérèse—if he married her. For some reason, that idea did not sit well with him today. Perhaps he was having second thoughts. But he was a man of his word; he had offered and she had accepted.

Marie stirred, as if knowing that he was thinking of her. Quentin knew that Marie didn't love him, that her real reason for desiring the marriage was support for herself and Morag, yet Quentin didn't mind. He couldn't say that he loved Marie Thérèse either. Oh, of course he was fond of her, and it would be convenient to be married, to have someone to see to his daily needs, but did he want to be shackled with a daughter like Morag? More important, could he curb Marie's gambling?

Probably, if they left court, but the only other place he wanted to go was home—to the house in Ville Marie, New France, or to his mother's tribe.

His thoughts wandered to Morning Flower then. She had been a good wife, once she had got over her initial Huron aversion to his Mohawk blood. He missed her. If he had ever loved anyone, it had been Morning Flower. His hatred for the English flamed then, as he thought of her senseless death. One day soon, his

41

chance for revenge would come. Meanwhile, he would remain at court.

He glanced over at his claret jerkin and suede knee-coat; they would look ludicrous to the tribe. He had no doubts that he could shed his court ways and return to the life of the Indians with the ease of a chameleon, but he doubted if Marie Thérèse—despite her protestations that she would go wherever he wished—would like that life. Then he thought of Morag again. Yes, she would fit in, probably better than she did at court!

Lazily, Marie Thérèse sat up, stretching her arms. "Oh, I'm hungry."

She kissed him, mewing with satisfaction. "Has it stopped raining? Can we eat in the garden?"

Quentin laughed softly. His mistress was like a child who had been told it could have anything in the box, no matter what the cost.

"Yes, my pet, we can eat in the garden."

"Good. And we must make our plans."

"Plans?"

"Our wedding plans." Her eagerness raised her voice slightly.

Quentin shrugged "What is there to discuss? We will be married when I am ready to marry. I think Morag should be given time to adjust to the situation." He had moved from the bed and begun to dress.

"*Mon Dieu*, Quentin. Morag is almost nineteen. It is time she realized that she cannot have everything her way. In fact, I have been far too lenient with her. I'll be glad for your hand in controlling her. If she dislikes—"

Seeing her alarm, Quentin bent and kissed her brow gently.

"Marie," his hand was on her shoulder. "I don't believe your daughter hates me as much as she claims to. It's only natural that she's afraid I will take the place of her father. And seeing your life as it's been . . ." He shrugged.

"What's wrong with my life?" Marie pulled her robe on, watching as he finished dressing, wondering why he hadn't called his valet. There seemed no sense in doing something for yourself if you could have others do it.

"Nothing. Do you plan to marry her off soon?"

Marie flushed and shrugged. "Most probably. I haven't yet decided who."

"My precious, I hazard a guess that the number of your lovers has made Morag fear . . ."

"What has that to do with anything? I've only enjoyed myself. I've done nothing to make Morag fear men."

"Well, it seems to me that your daughter was a great deal protected by her father. That she wants no man except one who can equal him."

"That was Andrew's fault. I told him—" Marie paused, realizing that she sounded shrewish. "Quentin, *mon amour,* when Morag is married she will be happy."

"Perhaps. If she marries the right man, that is. Your daughter needs someone . . . someone who will initiate her gently. I don't believe any of the dandies here can do that."

Marie Thérèse inhaled sharply. "Quentin, my heart, if I did not know better, I would say you were in love with my daughter and not with me." She gave a nervous laugh.

Quentin's eyes narrowed. "Let us say that I understand her nature. After all, if I am to help you guide her, I will need some love for her, will I not?"

Marie Thérèse nodded.

"I shouldn't worry about losing me, my love. At least, not to someone as inexperienced as your daughter." He laughed. "Come. Let us eat now. Later, while you have the masseuse oil that delicious body of yours, I will seek out Morag." They walked through the connecting rooms to the rotunda-like drawing room.

"Oh, Quentin, is that necessary? I'm sure the child already knows. You know how quickly gossip is passed at court."

Quentin frowned. "I know." He led her down the few steps toward the garden patio where lunch had been set, sheltered from the light rain. "But I think it's important that she hear it from one of us."

Having seen to Marie's comfort, Quentin left the mansion and walked down the wide avenue to the Place d'Armes, entering the Cour Royale through the open blue and gold gates that divided the palace from the town. He strolled across the main outer courtyard, passing the remodeled office buildings to his right and left.

He paused a moment before mounting the five shallow steps that would take him to the inner courtyard, the Cour de Marbe. This had been the château's original yard, but now it was paved with red, white and black marble flagstone. The sun was fully out now, warming the air after the rain. If he knew Morag, she would not have stayed in the pavilion rooms a moment longer than necessary.

Instinct told him that the girl would be at the menagerie. He had noticed that she favored the ostrich; perhaps she recognized a kindred spirit. He wondered if he would be able to help Morag lift her head out of the sand. He caught himself, wondering what in God's name had possessed him to think that.

More purposefully, he continued on in the direction of Saint Cyr, passing the corner where vividly-colored birds sang on their perches in gilded-domed aviares. In a moment, he entered the cool château, skirting through the colonnade of red marble columns. The afternoon hush was upon the building, as many of the court indulged themselves in post-luncheon entertainments.

Coming out into the fresh air again on the far side, he saw that Louis had added still another statue of white marble and gilded lead to his group of Apollo. The god was shown here surging from the waters, his chariot drawn by two magnificent steeds. Next to him his mother, Latona, also faced the waters. Quentin paused to examine the new addition. As Jupiter's mistress, Latona had been forced to flee from the anger of her lover's wife, Juno. When she had paused to quench her thirst at a pool, Latona had been kept from drinking by a crowd of malignant country people, who had thrown stones and handfuls of earth into the water near her face. Praying to Jupiter for help and revenge, Latona had found her tormentors turned into frogs.

Quentin admired the way Marsy had depicted the myth, with Latona and her children looking toward the sky for help, while around her the tormentors—of which the new piece was one—had already been transformed into frogs, spouting water into the basin, or were in the process of metamorphosis. It wasn't hard to see why Louis liked this myth: the lesson of vengeance wreaked on those who dared malign a royal mistress. It was too bad more people didn't learn from myths, Quentin thought, as he stroked the smooth stone.

The menagerie wasn't far now. He wondered how Morag would take the news of her mother's coming marriage. He hoped that she would be happy, that she would be amenable to his guidance.

The road toward Saint Cyr and the animal house was lined with tall cypresses, many of which hid entrances to grottos for the "entertainment" of the nobles. When he had first arrived at court, Quentin had thought it rather distasteful to have seduction so open; but having lived here—and having all too often stumbled on the King or one of his sons—Quentin had soon learned the ways of court. Now he himself used the grottos for his occasional dalliances.

A high-pitched whistle startled him. He glanced up to see the Duc du Maine coming toward him. The young Duke imitated his father by wearing a tall plumed hat with a red feather and red silk ribbons— some of which were now undone—in his black curls. He also wore an elaborate Venetian lace collar over an embroidered jerkin of blue, gold and silver. A knee-length coat of gold brocade enriched with diamonds was followed by red hose and shoes ornamented with huge satin bows, the high heels a different color from the uppers and toes. It was hard to believe that this foppishly dressed gentleman was only seventeen; harder still to believe that he was as cruel and haughty as he was reputed to be. He was so much more handsome than his chubby legitimate brother, the Dauphin.

As they drew near each other, Quentin realized that Maine was going to ignore him. Purposely, he stopped and placed his hand on the young man's shoulder.

Maine halted, aghast that anyone would have the audacity to stop him if he did not want to be stopped. His eyes narrowed as he stared down at Quentin's well-formed hand, and then haughtily let his gaze travel up the arm to meet Quentin's eyes. It was a moment before Maine could swallow his anger and speak.

"You wanted something, d'Angeau? I am not accustomed—"he jabbed his forefinger into the air in front of Quentin—"to being stopped."

Quentin dropped his hand. With mock humility he said, "Your pardon, Your Grace. I am looking for Mademoiselle Elliot. Have you seen her?"

"Who?"

"Mademoiselle Elliot—Morag Elliot."

"Oh, your whore's daughter. That redheaded chit." Maine sneered. "What if I have?"

Quentin controlled his temper. "Is she by the menagerie?"

"Perhaps." He began to move on.

Again, Quentin stopped him.

"If you touch me once more, d'Angeau . . ."

"Just tell me if you've seen her."

The Duke's upper lip curled. "Yes, I've seen her, by God." He gave a laugh. "Yes, I've seen her."

Quentin tightened his grip. "So help me, Maine, if you've harmed the girl—"

"Guard!"

Magically, one of the ubiquitous Swiss guards appeared in the forest. Quentin dropped his hand; he was a favorite, but so was Maine. If Louis had to choose between the two of them, Quentin had no doubt it would be the Duke.

"Sir?" The guard clicked his heels.

"Nothing, soldier." Maine grinned. "Just seeing if you were alert."

"Yes, Your Grace." The guard melted back into the forest shadows.

Maine shrugged his shoulders as Henri, his valet,

hurried up from behind to brush the "dirt" off. The Duke walked on a few steps and then turned.

"Rest assured, Quentin Sauvage, the chit is untouched by me—at the moment. But I suggest you hurry to the menagerie before she and her cousin tear each other's hair out." He paused, glancing at Henri, who had moved up ahead to wait for him. "I suggest you teach that wench some manners, d'Angeau. If it's beyond you, I'd be more than happy to take a hand."

Quentin snorted in response. "I think that's a matter for Morag and her mother to decide."

"Just so," Maine commented. "Her mother and her papa." Laughing, he continued on his way as Quentin hurried down the path.

Next to the Grotte de Thétis, with its underground cave lined with pebbles and shells, Morag liked the menagerie best. Except for the caretaker, there was seldom anyone with the animals. She enjoyed helping Eugène take care of them—all of them—including the birds that Louis kept: the cockatoos, parrots, toucans, birds of paradise, lorikeets, flamingoes, pelicans, herons, and the ostriches, which were her favorites.

Approaching the six-sided compound, Morag was conscious of the silence about her. It seemed strange, almost as if someone had muffled the animals. There were other creatures here besides the birds, and Louis was constantly adding more. For now he had two camels, four leopards, a lion and even a hefty elephant. As she let herself into the cavernous grotto, she wondered where Eugène was; he usually came forward to greet her.

A sound startled her. Cautiously she glanced about. Visitors entered here at their own risk. Although one could see the animals better from this level, one was also subject to jokers. It was here, below the rails, that the pipes for the flowing waters ran. Even the King himself had been known to turn the icy water jets on, drenching the unsuspecting.

Morag's heels echoed on the stone floor. "Eugène?" She wondered if the ostrich would like the piece of meat she had saved for him.

She was aware of her heart beating as she stood listening, trying to identify a new sound: laughter, high-pitched male laughter. Morag shivered, not liking the way it vibrated against the walls of the grotto.

"Eugène? Are you hurt?"

The laughter was followed by a low moan . . . someone in pain? Surely, no one would be using the menagerie for a trysting place; there were so many other places to go.

"Is someone here? Are you hurt?"

She turned about, seeing nothing. The moaning was louder now. Yes, it did seem as if someone were in pain. But why the laughter? Goosebumps appeared on her flesh.

She advanced further into the grotto, her heart beating faster. If someone were hurt, what could she do?

Morag's thoughts were abruptly altered when her cousin Nicole stepped out from behind a rock. Her hair hung loose, her skirts and hose were twisted, and there were marks—scratches—on her fair shoulders and neck.

"Nicole! What's happened? Are you hurt?"

Nicole glared at her, tilting back her head abruptly as she attempted to fasten a sleeve. "Hurt? No, Cousin, I am not hurt."

"But those marks . . . that was you moaning just now, wasn't it?"

"What if it was?" Nicole shrugged as footsteps echoed on the rocks above. "Does it matter? You've interrupted it now."

"But . . . who?"

Nicole began to retie her ribbons. "You really are an innocent, aren't you? Someone should take you in hand and show you how to enjoy yourself. Then perhaps you'd not be bursting in others."

Morag's eyes widened and she blushed. She realized now what had happened. "I . . . I'm sorry . . ." She began to back away. "I only came to see the ostrich—"

"You can stay if you want to now, Cousin. I don't give a damn. But if you bother your maman and her lover this way, it's no wonder it took him so long to declare himself."

"What do you mean? Has the Marquis . . .?" Morag's throat closed.

Nicole ignored her cousin's confusion. "Truly, I cannot fancy Quentin with a wife. There is a savagery about him that would make him an uncomfortable companion for a woman." She licked her lips with familiarity. "But perhaps your maman likes it. I know I do."

"When did the Marquis . . .?" Morag stopped. "I heard nothing at Mass today. He must have told you himself."

"Oh, Morag, you dunce! It's all over court. Are you in such a world of your own that you've heard nothing? Of course, just because he's planning to marry doesn't mean that I intend to give him up. After all, a man like Quentin needs variety."

"Nicole, tell me. Was he here?" Morag's heart pounded. "Have you and he . . .?"

"Why, I do believe you are jealous, Cousin." Nicole

gave a low laugh. "Don't be. You're a little innocent. Someone as simple as you could never please Quentin's diverse tastes. Do you want to know what we do? Shall I tell you how he undresses me, how he rams his manhood into me, how—"

"Don't! Stop!" Morag cried, holding her hands to her ears.

Nicole was laughing harder now. "You really should have the experience, dearest Cousin. The pain and the pleasure when a man enters you." She licked her lips. "But then, of course, you'll know soon enough. I hear that you are to be married."

"You're lying!" Morag flew at her. "Maman would have told me —"

Suddenly a heavy hand seized her shoulder and she was pulled away from her cousin.

"You!" She struggled as she saw Quentin. "So you didn't leave after all. Were you waiting for me?"

He pinned her arms to her sides. "I don't know what's happened between you two, but I think you should leave, Nicole."

"Gladly." The blonde retreated. "Thank you, Quentin dear. By the by, congratulations."

He nodded curtly, still holding Morag, who had stopped struggling but continued to glare at the pair of them.

Morag felt the pressure on her arms ease as Quentin released her. Without looking at him, she said, "Is it true?"

"What? About your mother and me? Yes, Morag, it's true."

"Why didn't I know, then? Why didn't Maman come to tell me?"

"Your mother is busy at the moment."

"So she sent you. Did she think I would dislike it less if you told me?"

"Perhaps . . ."

"Well, you're wrong. But there's nothing I can do about it, is there?"

"No, Morag, there isn't. Your mother and I are to be married . . ."

"When?"

"We haven't made any decision on that yet."

"So there's still time for you to change your mind." He smiled. "Do you think I will?"

"Nicole said—"

"I wouldn't pay any attention to what your cousin says."

"Oh, you mean you haven't slept with her?"

He leaned back against a rock, his gray eyes hooded as he watched Morag. "Did she say I had?"

Morag sucked in her breath. "Yes." She flushed. "She also said that Maman plans to marry me off. Is that true?"

"If it is, your mother hasn't mentioned anything to me, but I should think it's time for you to consider—"

"I suppose you would use your influence with Louis to force me into marriage even if I didn't want it." Tears sparkled in her eyes.

"No, Morag, I have no plans to force anything on you."

She was astonished at the look of tenderness in his eyes. Dare she ask him? Her hand trembled as she brushed a loose curl out of her eyes. She was acutely aware of the tension between them.

"Would you help me then? Would you ask Madame de Maintenon if I may join the sisters? You could. I mean, she would listen to you. At least . . . the King would. I would be ever so grateful. I . . . I would do anything you asked. I—"

He jumped forward, yanking her to one side as a snake slithered by. "Get out of the way, Morag."

Her eyes widened. "Where?"

"Up on the rocks." He put his arms about her waist and swung her up as the reptile raised its head, swaying dangerously.

"Look out!" Morag cried.

Quentin turned just in time, side-stepping the creature's strike. He circled the snake, throwing his plumed hat to one side. The reptile turned toward the distraction. Quentin, his gray eyes narrowed, swooped down and, with a wild cry, caught the snake by its neck just below the head.

"Be careful!" Morag cried, watching the snake thrash about.

"Don't worry, *mignonne*, I know how to handle my friend here. Just let me put him back in his box, then I'll get you down."

She nodded, watching with relief as he disappeared for a moment.

"The cage was purposely opened," he said, coming back to her.

"My cousin?"

"No doubt. Come down." He held out his arms.

Her skirts flew up momentarily when she jumped. He grasped her firmly, easing her to the ground. She remembered the momentary feeling of safety she had experienced with him the night of the ball.

"Are you all right?"

She nodded, but her heart beat uncomfortably. A sudden desire to remain in his arms overwhelmed her. In a small voice, she asked, "Will . . . will you hold me just a bit longer?"

With a questioning look, he pulled her to him.

They stood like that for a moment. Morag felt warm. Perhaps she could accept him as her papa. She closed her eyes, wondering if he would kiss her.

Frustrated, she opened her eyes, realizing that Quentin didn't intend to kiss her. She was about to pull away when the fountains about them came alive, spraying them with ice-cold water.

"What the—" Quentin glanced up as Morag jerked away. The rocks above were empty.

"Nicole?"

He narrowed his eyes. "It could have been." But he thought of Louis, who was also fond of practical jokes . . . and of Louis' bastard son.

He took Morag's hand. "I think we should leave before anything else happens."

"But the ostrich . . ."

"You are drenched, Morag. Your mother won't be happy if I allow you to become ill."

She clenched her fists as she followed him. She had no right to be disappointed, but she did have every right to hate him. He should have let Maman tell her.

Within minutes, they had reached the top of the grotto. If Nicole had been there, there was no sign of her now.

"Well, will you help me to join the sisters?" Morag asked, reminding him of what they had been discussing when the snake appeared.

"No, Morag. I will not resign you to a life of protective custody unless you are sure that's what you want."

"But I am sure! I'm positive!" she cried, tugging angrily at her wet dress, which clung uncomfortably to her body.

He turned to her again. She was aware of his staring,

aware that her erect nipples could be seen through the soaked silk of her dress. She hated him again, hated him for the strange feeling he aroused in her.

His cool fingers touched her cheek. "When you are sure of your decision, Morag, we'll talk again, but for now . . ." he gently turned her in the direction of her pavilion, ". . . you'll have your maid dry your clothes."

He placed his damp coat over her. "It may not dry you, but at least it will cover you from other prying eyes."

She flushed and he gave her a gentle push forward.

"Oh, I almost forgot, my dear. Your mother wants you at the amusements tonight."

"And if I don't wish to come?"

"I suggest you do."

She stood there for a moment until he disappeared in the opposite direction, silently as an Indian. Then she pulled his coat about her and ran to her room.

Chapter Four

MORAG DIDN'T UNDERSTAND what had possessed her. She hated Quentin . . . why should she want him to kiss her? He was going to marry her mother! He was going to be her father!

Desperately pushing the thoughts away, she plunged into the hot tub that Elise had prepared for her. She flushed, thinking how she must have looked with her wet clothes clinging to her. It had been Nicole who had drenched them, she was sure of it.

Closing her eyes, She tried to squash the fear that had risen in her. What if what Nicole had said were true? What if Maman had already arranged a marriage for her?

A sob caught in her throat. No, Maman wouldn't have done that. Not without asking her. Nicole had to be lying.

Perhaps if she were polite to Quentin tonight, he would relent and speak to Madame de Maintenon for her. Quentin . . . her heartbeat quickened. She had actually thought of him by his Christian name! Yes, she supposed she had better get used to doing that.

Maybe, if she showed Maman that she no longer objected to the alliance . . . ? She grabbed the warm towel, rubbing her slender body until it turned pink.

As she approached the reception rooms of Versailles, Morag realized that it was Monday. Louis would be holding a *jour d'appartement* this evening, allowing all to gather in his drawing room. She paused a moment on the path, listening to the bells ring. It was nearly six. The music would be starting soon. She lifted her three skirts, her cloak scarcely touching the ground as she ran. Until she had wrung a promise from the Marquis that he would speak with Madame de Maintenon, she would have to keep Maman happy.

Breathless, she reached the gold inlaid doors of the apartments and paused. The music had started. Well, if the King hadn't arrived yet . . . She glanced toward the next room where Louis' throne was. It was here that one of the chorales would sing Lully's concert. No, they hadn't begun yet; it was all right. Smoothing her modest skirt of green brocade, she entered the room and glanced about.

Where were Maman and the Marquis?

Turning, she saw Henri, the Duc du Maine's servant, standing near a small door. His large round head, twice the width of his narrow body, made him look like one of the funny men from the carnival. Morag felt sorry for him, but she did not like him. She realized then that he was motioning to her.

She didn't like the way he looked at her but, curious, she reluctantly moved toward him.

He was, she realized then, standing by the antechamber used for billiards. As she approached, she could see that card games were being held in the billiard room.

I might have known, she thought, passing Henri with a curt nod. She hoped that the Marquis would be able to exercise some influence over Maman's gambling; so far, it seemed, he only joined her.

Entering the room, she paused and quickly curtsied, seeing the King seated by the windows without his throne—indeed, without ceremony of any kind. He smiled at her and nodded, giving her permission to advance to the tables where a hushed whisper emphasized the seriousness of the players.

D'Angeau glanced up briefly from his cards. His eyes seemed to smile at her as he motioned for her to take the chair behind her mother.

Morag sat down. Marie Thérèse had been too engrossed to see her daughter, but Morag couldn't help noticing how lovely Maman looked in the blue and silver dress, her pretty dark curls clustered back over her ears as she concentrated on the game. Next to her, the Marquis d'Angeau struck an equally interesting figure, in his blue holland jerkin lined with red to show that he was a court favorite.

Her cousin Nicole was also at the table, holding her cards tightly in her hand, leaning forward seductively to expose a generous portion of powdered bosom. Morag winced as she saw her cousin's hand stray to the bony knee of the Duc du Maine, seated beside her.

They were playing *hoca*, Morag knew. The game was her mother's favorite, but each player had his own rules. Probably they were using Maine's now.

She realized then that the Marquis was staring at her. Did he guess that she had been thinking about him earlier? She flushed and hoped not.

Morag watched as a new hand was dealt. "Maman, why . . . ?"

Marie Thérèse glanced up quickly, shooting a stern look at her daughter. She seemed only now to have become aware of her presence. "Morag, be a good child and bring me a supper plate."

As Morag stood and started across the room, Nicole called after her: "You can bring me one too."

Spinning about, Morag favored her cousin with a glare. "I am sorry, dearest Cousin, I can only manage one. You'll have to wait your turn or go yourself."

"Oh, I can wait," Nicole responded lightly. "I can wait as long as necessary."

Morag clenched her fists as she left the room. Why did she let that girl goad her? She should just ignore her. After all, it was Maman's problem if Nicole wanted Quentin. Morag had nothing to do with that . . . or did she?

As with every supper night, the tables had been laid with wines, soups and special creations of the chef. Tonight, he had fashioned a cake to resemble the statue of Apollo out near the canals. Morag paused to admire it. It was truly a work of art.

Bringing the plate back to her mother, Morag saw that Quentin had paused in his card-playing and was eyeing Maine warily.

"What is it, d'Angeau? Had enough tonight?"

"Of your playing? Yes, I have."

Maine stood abruptly and Henri entered the room. "Are you accusing me of something, d'Angeau?"

Quentin's lips tightened into a grim smile. "I never accuse anyone without proof, but one might suspect someone who is so quick to take offense."

Maine's pasty forehead, beaded with sweat, glistened in the shimmering candlelight. He sat down abruptly.

With a worried look, Marie Thérèse turned to Quentin. "Dearest heart . . ."

"Marie, I believe you've had enough of the cards for this evening."

"Oh, no! Not just yet. I've but one more round and I shall recoup my losses. I am sure of it, *mon cher*. Please. If you don't wish to stay, take Morag out for me. I shall join you in the dancing presently."

The tension in the air made Morag's heart seem to beat faster. She didn't know about cards, but she wouldn't put it past Maine to cheat. Still, how could Quentin prove it?

"Please, *mon coeur*," her mother pleaded. "One or two rounds at most . . ."

Quentin touched her shoulder lightly. "Very well, one round, Marie. Just remember, you only have fifty *pistoles* left for the remainder of the week, and tonight is but Monday."

"Fifty! You said I might have a thousand *pistoles!*"

"For the week, *ma chère*." His mouth was grim. "You've already used nine hundred and fifty tonight."

Marie Thérèse shrugged. "Well, what of it? I'm aware of the limit you have placed on me but, Quentin, my love, you have little to worry about. I shall win it back. I know it."

Quentin glanced at Maine. "I hope so." He gently touched Morag's elbow, leading her from the room.

Once outside in the sweet night air, with the tinkle of the fountains and the music of the hidden players stationed along the canal surrounding them, the pair paused for a moment.

"Well, shall we go to the concert?" Quentin asked.

Morag thought a moment, conscious of being alone

with him, of her pulses pounding. No one else was in sight. Why was she feeling so strange? Nerves probably. She didn't like being alone with her mother's lover. She didn't trust him—her face warmed—or was it herself that she didn't trust? No, that was silly! She was going to be a nun, a faithful nun, but she needed his help. What better time to ask him again than now?

Swallowing hard, she shook her head. "If you don't mind, I would like to walk to the orangery first, before we join the others."

"The orangery, is it?" What was he reading into her words? Should she explain to him now? No, it must wait. She wanted to be sure that they were alone, that there would be no spies to tell Maman.

He laced his arm through hers and she shivered.

"Cold?"

Morag shook her head but, nevertheless, he removed his coat and placed it about her shoulders.

"Thank you," she said quietly.

He nodded, and they continued walking.

The orangery was deserted, quiet. The blossoms smelled so sweet. Morag sat down on a white wrought-iron chair facing a fountain. It was warmer here. She shrugged off Quentin's coat, glad that he remained standing away from her, but not glad of the way he slouched lazily against a tree, watching her.

After a long moment of silence, he spoke. "Well, Morag, what's wrong?" His voice seemed to resonate in the air about her.

She crushed a blossom she had picked between her finger and thumb, the heady scent wafted to her nostrils.

"It's about this afternoon. About what my cousin said . . ." She paused. He was watching her, towering over her, making her feel uncomfortable. "Nicole said

. . . she said that Maman had already arranged a marriage for me.''

"But I told you then that Marie Thérèse hasn't told me anything about it.''

Morag wished he wouldn't stare at her so. "I thought . . . perhaps . . . Maman had left it to you to tell me, as she—''

"I assure you, *mignonne,* that is not the case. And it was not for lack of courage that your mother did not tell you of our marriage, that I was the one to speak to you this afternoon.'' He sat down next to her.

"No?'' She inched her body away from his. "Well, it doesn't matter who says I am to marry, because I won't . . . at least . . . not if you help me.''

A smile played on his lips. "How am I to do that?''

Morag turned toward him then eagerly, hoping against hope that she detected sympathy in his voice. "You are a favorite of the King, my lord . . . You could ask him to void any marriage contract Maman might make.'' She moved closer to him, forgetting herself. "You could ask Madame to help me find a place with one of the orders, my lord . . .''

He was still smiling. "My name is Quentin, Morag. Not my lord, sir, or d'Angeau, but Quentin.''

She blushed.

"Shall I spell it for you?''

"No . . . Quentin.'' His name brought a strange taste to her mouth.

"Good.'' His hand was on her shoulder. "Now, about your request . . .''

His mouth swooped down hard on hers, forcing her lips apart savagely as he thrust his tongue between them, kissing her hungrily. No longer meeting resistance, he continued to kiss her, more gently this time. She felt giddy as his hands moved down across the valley of her breasts, gently touching her erect nipples beneath her gown. Moaning softly, she began to tremble, forgetting where she was, until he broke away, smiling.

Gasping for breath, Morag stood. "You . . . you vile creature! What was the meaning of that? I am going to be your daughter. I—"

"But you aren't my daughter yet, Morag. Now you're just a very attractive but innocent girl." He took her by the wrist to prevent her escape. "No . . . don't leave until you hear me out."

She stiffened, but remained where she was.

"You're not meant for the solitary life of a nun. I should think about your response a moment ago."

Shame flooded her. "I didn't—"

"Oh, but you did." He dropped her hand.

"I don't know anything about responding to stolen kisses! But I do know that I hate you, and I always will." With that, she ran from the orangery.

Quentin wondered if he should go after her; it wasn't safe for a young girl to be running about the grounds alone at night. But, he reasoned, she would probably go straight back to the pavilion rooms.

With an easy motion, he moved away from the bench. It was time he rejoined Marie who, he felt sure, was still at the gaming table.

Quentin was right. As he re-entered the billiard room, passing Maine's manservant, he saw by the number of cards in Marie Thérèse's hand that they had just started another round.

"*Chérie*," he placed a hand on Marie's smooth shoulder, "I believe there is an opera about to start."

"Not now, Quentin, love." She shrugged him off. "I must finish this."

"It looks as if you have just begun. I believe you can quit now, if you like."

"No."

Maine chuckled. "Your fiancée doesn't wish to leave the game until she has recouped her losses."

"Oh?" Quentin sank into the empty chair beside Marie Thérèse, watching her intent expression as she studied the cards. "How much have you lost, *chérie*?"

"Not much," Marie Thérèse shrugged. She played a knave on the table, licked her lips, and bid. "One hundred crowns."

Maine covered the knave with a king. "Five hundred crowns." His voice was high-pitched with tension; it almost sounded as if he were laughing. "Match it—if you can."

"How much do you owe him, Marie?" Quentin's hand gripped her shoulder.

"I told you. Not much."

"No, two thousand *pistoles* is not much," Maine said, "unless you are unable to pay."

"Two thousand! *Nom de Dieu!*" Quentin cried, pulling Marie Thérèse to her feet. Her cards fluttered to the table.

"Now look what you've done!" She glared at him. "I had two kings. I could have won this round."

Quentin glanced at Maine. "I doubt that."

"And what is that supposed to mean, d'Angeau?"

"Whatever you wish it to mean, Your Grace." He took Marie Thérèse roughly by the elbow. "Come, Marie. Your gambling is at an end for this evening."

Maine rose too. "Aren't you planning to pay your debts, *ma chère*?"

"Yes . . . yes, of course." She glanced at Quentin

64

and paused. "Later . . . I mean. I can't very well pay you at the moment, but—"

"But I can." Disdainfully, the Marquis withdrew four coins from his pocket and threw them on the table. "Now come along, *chérie*."

Reluctantly, Marie Thérèse allowed him to lead her briskly out of the room and along the path in the palace gardens.

It was only a week later that Marie Thérèse told her daughter, "Well, pet, it is all arranged."

"What is arranged?" Morag put down her hair brush. She watched in the mirror as Elise twisted her hair back and off her shoulders as she liked it. True, it wasn't the most fashionable arrangement, but it suited her when she went riding, as she planned to do this morning.

"Why, the wedding." Marie Thérèse shrugged, daintily sipping her morning chocolate.

Morag pursed her lips and nervously smoothed the green holland riding skirt. "You mean, your wedding?"

"No, pet, yours." Marie Thérèse stretched languidly. "I have arranged for you to marry the Comte de Lalande's youngest son."

"What! Maman, you *promised* me . . ."

"Hush, love. I promised only that I would wait a bit, but my dearest, times are hard."

"Hard? Maman, you are to marry d'Angeau. He'll provide for you."

Marie Thérèse shook her head, clucking.

"What do you mean? You *are* going to marry him?"

Marie Thérèse shrugged. "Oh, I shall marry him,

chérie, but the man is tighter with his money now that we are engaged."

"And you need money for your cards! You are disgusting!"

"*Chérie!* Don't take on so. After the first few times, you will relish the moment when he penetrates you."

"I won't! I won't even let the man touch me!" Tears stood in her eyes. "Maman, how could you do this to me?" She sniffled, taking the handkerchief which Elise handed her. "How much did the Comte pay you for me?" The words stuck in her throat, but she had to know.

"Does it really matter, pet?" Marie Thérèse carelessly poured more chocolate into her cup. "You carry on as if it's your death warrant I've signed."

"It is! How much did you get?"

Marie Thérèse shrugged. "The usual, five thousand *pistoles.* I was a fool . . . he is desperate for you. I could have got more, but a bargain is a bargain."

"Yes, Maman, you *are* a fool, because you'll have to pay it all back. I shall never marry the son of that disgusting old Comte. If I do not join the sisters, then I shall kill myself."

"Morag, calm yourself!"

Ignoring her mother's cry, Morag sobbed, "You have ruined me!" Running from the room, she slammed the door behind her.

Anger continued to build in Morag as she approached the royal stables. "Damn him! Damn that d'Angeau!" It was his fault. If he would give Maman the money she wanted . . . she might have known that he would be her downfall.

The day was excessively sultry, as Morag led Flame out of the stall. As she had confided to her cousin

Nicole, Flame was her favorite mount, because he was wilder and more savage than the other horses. He would make her forget the scene in the bedroom with Maman—if anything could.

As she took the reins, she remembered that not only was this Quentin's horse, but that the riding habit she wore was his gift—and he was the cause of her problems! Would she never be free of the man? She pulled on the reins, pursing her lips as she led the horse out of the yard. Her body still burned with the shame of her response to his kiss. It was inconceivable that she had ever wanted it.

Furious with herself and with him, she nudged the horse into a fast trot. Not many people were about yet and that was good. She hated to ride with too many people watching. With another nudge, she began to gallop toward the early morning mists, which still hung low on the fields. Now was the best time to ride, when everything was fresh, before the sun began to wilt the leaves. Probably it would rain later today, but that didn't really spoil her plans. She would not return to Maman until very late. Perhaps if she were caught in a storm, if she became ill . . . yes, that would solve everything.

Leaning forward, she whispered to the animal: "Faster, boy. I want to feel the wind in my hair and on my face."

The horse acknowledged with a snort, and soon the pair were speeding along the paths, southward, away from the palace, from the town, from all that Morag hated. Her hair slapped at her face but she felt exhilarated, alive for the first time in days.

Morag wasn't the only rider out that morning. From a distance, the Marquis d'Angeau and the Duc du

Maine rested their horses under a tree, while their eyes followed Morag's race across the fields.

Quentin was amused at the way Maine had sought him out these past few days. He had known the boy was after something and now, watching the Duke's face as Morag flew past, his suspicions were confirmed.

"A pretty child, yes?" Maine said.

"A child, yes. I should think you would like them more experienced, Maine. I know I do."

A smile cracked the pasty face. "Inexperience is good sometimes, my friend. It's nice to teach them what you want. Why do you grimace? Have you no desire for the chit? No liking? She will be your daughter, after all."

Quentin shrugged, his eyes narrowing. "If I marry Marie Thérèse, yes, Morag will be my daughter but . . . no, Maine, I have no desire for the girl."

"Ah, well. It doesn't matter. I fear neither of us will have the opportunity to teach her pleasure. She is to marry young Lalande." Maine laughed. "Or hasn't your dearest Marie informed you of her bargain? Quite a coup she made. Perhaps my cousin—"

He was cut short by a scream from Morag. Without pausing to excuse himself, Quentin swung into his saddle and rode furiously toward her.

As he approached, he could see that the reins were dragging loose. The little fool. She shouldn't be riding Flame if she couldn't control him. Morag screamed again, clinging to the horse's mane. She didn't understand what had happened. Everything had been fine until they began to gallop, and then, suddenly, the reins had come loose in her hands. Frantically, she had tried to control the horse, to slow him, but Flame was no longer obeying her. Morag shut her eyes fearfully, realizing that in a moment the horse would be charging into the trees.

She scarcely heard Quentin's shrill whistle, nor was she prepared for the way the horse suddenly slowed, then turned and trotted meekly to where Quentin waited on Thunder.

Catching her breath, Morag sat upright again in the saddle, trying to compose herself.

"Are you all right, Morag?"

"I—I'm fine," she said, aware that her voice quivered and that her hand clutched the saddle horn. He would have to be the one to rescue her! "How—how did you do that?"

He gave a casual shrug. "Something I learned with the Indians."

"Oh." She could think of nothing else to say.

"Why were you riding so recklessly? I ought to swaddle you, child! If you can't control the horse, you shouldn't ride him."

"I can control him just fine." She tried to stop the tears that suddenly filled her eyes. "I can control him fine—when the reins aren't broken." She swallowed hard. "I suppose you expect me to thank you."

"You could." He dismounted and held out his arms to help her down.

"I've no need of your assistance."

They dueled with their eyes for a moment before he said, "You appeared to need it before. I don't think you should ride Flame back, but I do suggest you reach some shelter before the storm breaks. Take my mount."

Unable to tolerate his show of concern, she said, "Are his reins to be cut too? Though mind, I can't understand why, if you went to all that trouble, you would bother to save me. You must have known I would be too upset to check everything, after what happened this morning.''

His hand stopped on Flame's head where he had been stroking the horse's nose; the animal snorted.

"Oh? What happened this morning?"

She took a deep breath, hating him more every minute. "I'm sure you know well. After all, weren't you and Maman party to selling me to that pitiful creature, Louis de Lalande? I'm surprised you let Maman make such a poor bargain. Why, she tells me that she's been offered as much as ten thousand for me! She—''

"Morag!" He swung her down off the horse then, startling her into silence. His hands remained on her waist, as he looked into her eyes. "My dear little cat, I don't mind taking the blame for what I have done, but not for what I have not done. I had nothing to do with this arrangement of your mother's. Nor—'' he thoughtfully picked up the cut ends of the reins, his eyes narrowing—"with this.''

Thunder rolled across the sky. They both glanced up.

"Now, if you've calmed down a bit, I suggest that you take Thunder back to the stables on Rue de La Chausu de Clagny. It's nearest. You will instruct Botemps that your Maman and I will be joining you there for breakfast shortly.''

"So early? What if I don't want to?''

"If you wish my help in the matter of your marriage, you will do as I say, Mademoiselle.''

She flushed and reluctantly allowed him to give her a hand up onto the horse he had been riding. Gently, he tapped the animal's rump.

"I will see you soon, *mignonne*.''

"No hurry,'' she retorted. Taking the horse's reins from him, she turned back toward the town.

Chapter Five

MARLY. IT WAS the height of favoritism to be invited
to join Louis there. The Marquis d'Angeau had gone
a number of times, but for the first time the King's
invitation had been extended to include Marie Thérèse
and Morag.

Morag was happy to be getting away from Versailles,
even if it was only for a week, happy not to see the
Comte's son leering at her. God, he made her sick—
almost as sick as Quentin Sauvage did, staring at her
with those hooded eyes of his.

She had been positive, the day he had stopped her
runaway horse, that he would help her, that he was as
horrified as she that Maman had sold her. But the only
thing he had seemed angry about when he confronted
Maman later, was she had asked so little.

"Surely, you can do better than that, *mon amour*."

Marie Thérèse had shrugged. Glancing at her daughter, she said, "True, she is a beauty, but everyone at
court knows she has a temper and a sharp tongue."

"If I am such a shrew, then no one should want

me at all. You should let me join the sisters. You should—"

Quentin had taken hold of her arm. "Morag, calm yourself. Your Maman has your best interests at heart."

"I wonder!" She had jerked away. Though Marie Thérèse called after her, she had continued to run. Thank goodness the rain had stopped by then. She hid the rest of the day with the animals. By sunset, Maman had left the pavilion—her blasted gaming again—and Morag had returned to cry herself to sleep.

Nothing more had been said since that day about her marriage. But to hope that it might be canceled was something Morag feared was too great even for Saint Jude. Yet it did seem to have been postponed.

Whatever was happening, Morag was pleased to learn of the trip to Marly.

The estate of Marly was an open marshy place surrounded by woodland; it had a commanding view of the Seine. The château itself had been built on a rise that faced south, toward the river. In front, the land was terraced with neat rows of trees and ornamented by a series of artificial lakes. On the other side of the lakes was a row of evenly-spaced identical pavilions—six on either side. They were joined to each other by lines of perigolas.

Morag's first view had been obstructed by the banked-up terrace that concealed the château from the road. Once she had passed that, her first impression was of extraordinary, brilliant color. More than Versailles, Marly was Louis' private showplace. The balustrades and window frames of the château and surrounding buildings were brightly gilded; the statues in the gardens had been painted. The birds, animals and flowers that decorated the glistening fountains were surrounded by the deep and varied green of nature. Taking a deep breath of the sweet soft air, Morag wished she could appreciate the perfection more, that she didn't have to worry about what Maman might be planning for her.

Their room, just above Quentin's, was in the third pavilion. All twelve pavilions, she discovered, were divided into small apartments—one above the other— connected by an oval staircase. The rooms were paneled and draped in crimson satin. Each had been provided with all that a guest might need—down to the nightshirt and hairbrush. Besides these apartments, the main château had twelve others, four of which were permanently reserved for the royal family.

Maine would be in one of those, Morag realized. She wondered if he had Nicole with him. She had seen little of her cousin except for occasional glimpses at the *divertissements,* but the less Morag saw of Nicole, the better. She did know that her cousin was, or had been, Maine's mistress. The Duke had a habit of quickly tiring of his women.

Having settled in, they were received by Louis in the huge octagonal salon, which took up most of the inner core of the château. It was a large and confusing room, with numerous windows that allowed in the fresh air which Louis loved. Morag realized that the room could also be quite cold and drafty. She didn't envy people who came here for the winter holidays.

Louis informed them that there were to be games during and after the concert for those who wished to play.

Marie Thérèse smiled at the King as he said, "My dearest, I do hope that your pretty head won't be too full of music and dance. My son would like you at his table tonight. I am told your game of *hoca* is utterly delightful and devious."

Bowing, Marie Thérèse said, "I am only a mere player, Your Majesty. My game is nothing compared to yours but," she smiled into Maine's narrow face, "I should be happy to provide entertainment for His Grace."

"Quentin?" The King asked expectantly.

"No, Your Excellency. I don't believe I'll game tonight. I would rather enjoy the grounds, if you don't mind."

The King glanced at Marie Thérèse and then back at Quentin. "Yes, of course."

Maine glanced at Morag, who flushed under his stare. "Where will you be, *chérie?* The games or the gardens?"

Morag curtseyed. "The gardens, Your Grace. I know nothing of cards."

"Nothing of cards!" Louis was astounded. "Quentin? Is that true? Your fiancée's daughter knows nothing of cards? How refreshing. How very refreshing. I dare say, though, that should be remedied."

Quentin stepped up beside Morag. She could feel his presence without turning. "Your Excellency, I believe her mother's gaming is quite enough for both of us."

It was Marie Thérèse's turn to blush.

"*Hmm.* Yes." Louis raised his monocle to stare at the dark-haired beauty with the gypsy blood. "Your debts are . . ."

"Minimal, Your Majesty, And with the luck of Apollo—and the blessing of the Great King—I shall recoup my loss tonight."

"Well," Louis shrugged, "it is as you wish, my dears. As you wish."

Marie Thérèse slipped her arm through Quentin's as they bowed back into the crowd, whispering, "How dare you insult me like that! Reminding the King of my debts."

Quentin frowned. "If you consider the truth an insult, my dearest Marie, then we've much to learn of each other. Perhaps . . ."

"Oh, Quentin, I was only joking. Of course I know you meant no harm. I do rather get carried away with my gaming. In fact, I would be delighted if you would occupy my daughter while I . . ." she shrugged.

"I will not go with him, Maman. I will return to the rooms."

"What? Alone?" Marie Thérèse raised her brows. After a pause, she said, "Well, you will come with me to the games, then. The King is right. It's time you learned something about cards."

Morag frowned. She supposed it was better to be with Maman than risk a repeat of that other night at Versailles with the Marquis. Reluctantly, she followed her mother into the Duc du Maine's salon, where the gaming would take place. She knew that once her mother became engrossed in the cards, it would be an easy matter to slip away; then she would be free to explore the beautiful gardens on her own.

Each of the private apartments, Morag realized, was furnished and decorated in different colors. Maine's rooms had been done in a gaudy purple silk that shimmered with the many lights of the candles.

She took a seat near the wall, feeling uneasy as bugs flew past and singed their wings on the candle flames. The way Maine was staring at her—the way his servant, Henri, was grinning—it was almost as if Maine were planning something . . . but what? As far as she knew, she was still promised to the Duke's cousin. Not that there would be any chance of marriage with Maine, in any case. *Mon Dieu!* The man was a Prince of the blood. She wished now, though, that Nicole had been invited to Marly.

Glancing away from Maine, she folded her hands, watching anxiously as her mother laid out the first card. As Morag suspected, Marie Thérèse soon became involved in the cards and never noticed when her daughter slipped out of the room. Neither did Maine, for that matter. Both were intent on their playing. It pained Morag, the way Maman was losing so heavily and betting so recklessly. Perhaps she should find Quentin and tell him.

She changed her mind, though, as she reached the gardens. The Marquis had plenty of money. He could take care of Maman's debts. If he really cared about her mother, he would have stayed at the gaming to watch her.

Like most guests at Marly, Morag was enchanted with the secluded little arbors and their seats that were available for talking, intrigue, or just sitting and watching the fountains play over the statues as Morag did. A full moon reflected on the waters, making the spray seem almost silver.

There seemed no one else about. Only twenty guests had come to Marly this time. Maman and Maine were playing cards; others were too, she was sure. Then there were the concerts and the opera.

She inhaled the heavy perfume of the flowers. It was lovely to be alone in the world, to pretend not to have any cares.

She began to walk. The carefully-designed path led past the cascades through the woods and to open spaces beyond. Tomorrow a game of pall-mall would be played there. That she would enjoy. Hitting the wooden ball through the iron ring was more stimulating that sitting inside playing cards.

Turning south, she found herself at a delicately-wrought iron balustrade topped by the twin horse design of Antoine Congésor. Beyond that, Morag could just make out the roofs of Saint Germain. She stood there for a moment. Queen Mary would be in chapel tonight, saying a prayer for her husband.

Morag had heard little news of King James since he had left for Ireland last year, but she knew that things were not going well. Indeed, the Duke du Lauzun, Quentin's uncle, had just been sent over with a transport of two thousand men to assist the King in his battles. She hoped that he would win Ireland, that he would triumph over William and they could all return to England.

Briefly, she wondered how her father's family had fared. Andrew had been heartbroken, she knew, when his brother Donald, for reasons of family interest, had cut off all communication with him. But then, Andrew had gone against the family and turned Catholic to marry Marie Thérèse. She wondered what the Elliots were like, if she would ever meet them, if she would ever return to England again. Oh, how she longed to have a real family—aunts, uncles, cousins—not like Nicole but real cousins, with whom she could talk. A tear slid down her cheek. Would things be different when Maman married the Marquis? No, he had no family, and he certainly wasn't the family type.

As she continued to gaze toward Saint Germain, she wondered if Mama and Papa had been happy together, if her father had felt the alienation from his family worthwhile.

She shivered, remembering the quarrels over money, remembering Maman's tears. Was it any wonder she feared marriage? She wished she could believe that her parents had been as devotedly in love as Maman said. But Morag remembered the all-too-frequent visits of the dressmaker's son. Seeing how her mother behaved here at court, Morag wondered if the dressmaker's son had been Maman's lover. What was it Maman said? Variety made for love? Yes, that was it. Apparently, even King James thought so; he was said to have many mistresses, despite Queen Mary's tears.

At the card table, Marie Thérèse's luck was no better than it had been for the past month. Something had to change soon, she was sure of it. She stared at the cards in her hand and frowned. What should she do? Within the last half hour, she had lost two thousand *pistoles:* the total sum that Quentin had left her. She didn't dare ask him for more. Yet how could she stop now? She was so positive that her luck would turn—maybe even with the next hand.

Maine broke into her thoughts. There were just the two of them now; the others at the table had given up. By the pile of coins in front of him, Maine was the obvious winner.

"Well, Marie Thérèse, what do you do? Just sit there? Or do you play?"

"*Mon Dieu!* Is that a question? Of course I play."

"Well, this next question is more difficult. With what do you play, *chérie?* You have already lost what you had. You owe me five thousand *pistoles* now."

"I know. I know. You will be paid, Your Grace."

"Will I? Your fiancé was not too happy about paying me last time."

"I will pay you, I promise. Just deal the cards."

"No, *chérie.* Not yet. I have a proposition."

Marie Thérèse stared at him, her eyes bright. "What?"

Maine licked his lips. "I will stake you double of what you have lost."

"And what do you get in return?"

"Your daughter."

Marie Thérèse's eyes widened. "To marry?"

Maine laughed. "Come, *chérie,* that is not possible. No, I only want to . . . initiate her. I believe she has not yet experienced the joys of a man?"

Marie Thérèse frowned. "No, she has not, but—"

"If you win this hand, I will give you ten thousand *pistoles.*"

Marie Thérèse whistled softly under her breath. She pursed her lips, like her daughter. "And if I lose, you get Morag?"

He nodded.

"I could say yes . . . but, Your Grace," she paused, desperately trying to think of some other way of paying him, knowing how furious Quentin would be when he found out—if he found out. "My daughter is very headstrong and temperamental."

"All the better." He laughed, a high-pitched laugh that made Marie Thérèse nervous. "I like women with spirit. It increases the pleasure a hundredfold, my dear. Have you ever tried being strapped down?"

Marie Thérèse's lips were dry. She shook her head.

"Ah, I should give your lover some instruction. It makes the meeting so much more enjoyable."

"For you . . . or for her, Your Grace?"

Maine looked blank for a moment. "Why, both, I imagine. I've never had any complaints."

Marie Thérèse swallowed hard. "No, I don't imagine you have."

"Well? Do you continue to play?"

Her luck would change—it had to! Think of how many games she could play with ten thousand *pistoles!* She already had a king and a queen in her hand. If the rest of the cards should fall . . .

"Very well, Your Grace, I accept your proposition."

She glanced up to see his smile of triumph. Remembering then what Quentin had said, she added, "I doubt that you will win, Your Grace, but if you should, you *will* be gentle with Morag . . . at first, I mean?"

Maine chuckled. "*Chérie,* as I told you, no woman has ever complained of my methods." His cold hand folded over hers.

"Henri! Get me pen and ink."

"Yes, Your Grace." Henri bowed away from the table.

"Is that necessary, Your Grace?" Marie Thérèse's voice quivered. For just a fleeting moment, she wondered if she shouldn't refuse Maine's offer.

"Of course it's necessary. Not that I don't trust you, *chérie,* but it is better this way."

Marie took a deep breath. "What if Morag refuses?"

Maine shrugged. "Then you will have to persuade her. If necessary," he grinned, "I am sure you can purchase something . . . an aphrodisiac, perhaps—" he paused, "from your friend, Madame Le Blanc!"

So he knew about that! Marie Thérèse flushed.

"You might also put a mild sedative in her wine. We can arrange to have dinner one night, all of us. Then you and your lover will leave me and mine."

Marie Thérèse swallowed hard. "You seem to have it all planned."

"It has been on my mind for some time now. Of course, if your daughter agrees, there will be no need of any of that, but—" he smiled as Henri brought the pen and paper—"I rather think a little something might add to her enjoyment."

He was silent a moment while he wrote—Marie Thérèse was acutely aware of the pen scratching the surface of the paper—then he handed the sheet to her.

She read it quickly. "You write that you want Morag for your mistress for one year, or until you tire of her. One year is a long time, Your Grace. Until you tire of her is even longer." Marie Thérèse glanced up.

"But I may tire of her after one week, or one month." He shrugged. "I have been known to do that. If Mademoiselle Morag is a quick learner—"

"Nevertheless, I think—if I win—the amount should be twenty thousand. I assumed that you would want her only for one night, perhaps two, or possibly even a week, Your Grace, but certainly not a year."

"Very well. I can be generous. I will give you twenty-five thousand *pistoles,* provided we surprise Morag and you permit me unlimited access to your daughter."

Marie Thérèse sucked in her breath. "My lord, that is most . . . gracious of you."

He glanced up at Henri, who immediately hurried forth with fresh parchment and a new supply of ink.

As the quill scratched the surface, Marie Thérèse had thought suddenly of Andrew—how handsome he had been when they had first met, how tender and skillful his lovemaking had been, how he had gone away with her when they found Morag was due. What would happen to Morag if she became pregnant? Maine wouldn't marry her; he couldn't.

Marie Thérèse picked up her cards again. She wouldn't think of that; she was going to win this hand, so it didn't matter what she signed.

"Have you finished, Your Grace?"

"Anxious to get to the cards, are you?"

Marie Thérèse nodded.

"Good." He handed her the paper. "Here. Sign. Then we shall get on with it."

Marie took the quill from his bony hand.

"As you wish, my lord."

Chapter Six

MORAG SAT BY the grand canal, breathing deeply, watching the sun rise over the tree tops outside Versailles. Perhaps a ride in one of the gondolas would soothe her. She glanced about and changed her mind. It was quiet here. If she took the boat, she would have to row herself; she couldn't see any servants about. Not that she couldn't manage, but at the moment she just wanted to think.

Ever since they had returned from Marly last week, Maman had made a concerted effort to be kinder to her and more understanding. Morag couldn't help but ask herself why. It was nothing she could point to, and she was glad of her mother's company, but since Maman was engaged to Quentin Sauvage, it seemed strange that she would want to spend time with her daughter instead of her fiancé.

She wondered too about Quentin. From being overly attentive to her, he had suddenly become quite cold and distant. Not that she cared, but it did make her wonder.

The invitation for tonight also disturbed her. Maman

had often been invited to Maine's rooms for gaming and Quentin usually accompanied her, but Morag couldn't fathom why this time Maine had invited her. She wondered if Nicole would be there. She had heard that the Duke had tired of her cousin, that she was now with the Prince de Conti.

Maman had told her that the dinner tonight was in honor of His Grace's cat's birthday! It seemed strange that a cat would be honored, but then, Maine *was* strange. Perhaps she had misjudged him, perhaps he wasn't as cruel to animals as she had heard. Well, she would go; she had promised Maman that she would. But when the gaming began, she would sneak out as she usually did.

Her stomach growled hungrily. Sighing, she stood. The sun was already up. Smoothing her pale green dress, she started back toward the pavilion.

Marie Thérèse paced the floor as the ormolu clock struck half-past eight. Where was Morag? She should have been back for the morning chocolate by now. Marie Thérèse didn't like Morag's morning walks; they made her nervous—more so since they had returned from Marly. Did the girl know what had happened at the château? Had she any idea what was going to happen this night? Marie continued to pace, ignoring the maid. It would be just like Quentin to tell Morag, out of spite. Why, he might even help her to leave the court!

Damn the man! She should never have confided in him. Indeed, she probably wouldn't have, if he hadn't returned to Maine's rooms searching for her that night. Marie Thérèse still didn't understand how she could have lost, considering the cards she had held. Nor did she understand why Quentin had been so furious with her. Making love was a fact of life; it was time Morag learned something about it. Perhaps, once she was deflowered, she would be more understanding of Marie Thérèse. Perhaps, once she learned how much it could pleasure her, Morag wouldn't be so averse to marriage. Yes, one day soon, her daughter would thank her.

She clenched her fists, looking very much like Morag. Now that Quentin no longer wished to marry her, she had no choice but to see Morag well-married. Maine had promised that he would see that she was well taken care of—once he tired of her.

Where *was* Morag? Marie Thérèse shook her head slowly, staring out of the window at the fountains and the forests. She still couldn't believe that Quentin would quit her over such a silly thing. Perhaps, after tonight was over, after Morag had lain with Maine, Quentin would understand and come back to her. Marie Thérèse was sure that he couldn't stay away from her long, despite the fact that he was now bedding her niece.

The door opoened. Marie Thérèse ran to embrace her daughter. "*Ma chère,* where were you?"

"Maman, what's wrong with you? You're white as a ghost. You know I often go walking in the morning. You were sound asleep."

"I know, I know, pet, but I get worried when I wake and don't see you."

"And how do you think I feel when I wake and don't see you for days on end? Even knowing that you are with the Marquis doesn't make it easier."

"Oh, my poor pet. I never thought you might worry about me. You never said so before." She motioned for Elise to pour the chocolate. "Don't let's argue, my love. I want this to be a good day."

Morag shrugged. "Why should this day be different from any other?" She sat down by the small table and frowned at her mother. "Will the Marquis be at Maine's party tonight?"

Marie Thérèse didn't answer. Morag glanced up. Her mother sucked in her lower lip and shrugged. "He was invited, I know that, but whether he will come . . ."

"Maman, has something happened between you and the Marquis? You seem to spend very little time with him now and—" Morag paused. "I often see him walking with other women."

"You mean, you see him with Nicole," Marie Thérèse said dryly.

Morag flushed. "Well, yes, sometimes."

Her mother shrugged. "Men will be men, my love."

"But are you still going to marry him? Even though he spends so much time with others?"

Her mother laughed artificially. "My dearest daughter, I've told you—variety adds spice to life. It is good to know a number of different people, to experience each in a different way. Quentin understands this as well as I do. That is why we get along so well."

"But are you going to marry him?"

"Of course." Marie sipped her chocolate. "Why? Has he . . . said anything to you?"

"No." Morag pushed away her breakfast, suddenly losing her appetite. "In fact, he's been rather distant ever since we returned from Marly."

"Oh? Is that all? I shouldn't worry, pet."

"Have you quarreled with him?"

Her mother flushed.

"You have. About your gaming?"

Marie Thérèse nodded.

"Oh, Maman! After you schemed to get him to propose and sent me to the chemist and all—"

Her mother bent and kissed Morag's forehead. "Don't worry, my love. Quentin's just sulking now. I dare say he'll recover soon."

Morag frowned. "I hope so." She flushed too, then, wondering if her mother might misunderstand her. "For your sake, I mean."

Morag was surprised at how tense her mother seemed to be that morning. Rather than spend time with any of her lovers, Maman had insisted that they go to Paris as soon as they had finished their breakfast.

"You need some new clothes, my pet."

Marie Thérèse dropped Morag at the dressmaker's, explaining that she had some errands of her own to run, but would join her daughter shortly. Apparently, Maman had arranged with Madame de Courtan beforehand about her wardrobe, but Morag was sure there must be some mistake. The gowns that the dressmaker showed her were far too immodest. But when Marie Thérèse returned in the late afternoon, she sided with the dressmaker against her daughter.

Morag protested. "But I don't want such a low neckline, Maman! Nor do I want something as bare as this silver tissue."

Her mother shrugged. "I make the decisions, *chérie*. It is time you appeared in something more alluring. You are an attractive girl and—"

"And I don't wish to parade my body like Nicole."

Marie Thérèse's mouth tightened into a thin line. "What you wish is not important. You will have that silver tissue. You will wear it tonight."

"And pray, how can I manage that? We have barely an hour to return to Versailles."

"We will not be returning to court tonight."

Morag felt her heart skip a beat. Why this should upset her, she didn't know, but she sensed that something was wrong.

"But . . . I thought we were invited to Maine's tonight?"

"Yes, we are. Here in Paris." Marie Thérèse sat down beside her daughter. "So you see, there will be plenty of time for Madame de Courtan to fix the dress." She waved the dressmaker's maid away. "Morag, you look pale. Is something wrong, pet?"

Morag shook her head slowly. Why she should suddenly think of Quentin Sauvage she didn't know, but he was her first thought. "I . . . I thought that the Marquis would be there . . ."

"What does he matter?" Her mother looked at her closely. "You dislike the man. Maine will be there So will Jean Baptiste."

Morag frowned. "Maman, isn't it possible for me to return to court? I mean, I'm not really necessary for your evening's entertainment. Once the cards come out, you will ignore me anyway."

Marie Thérèse leaned forward and kissed her daughter's head. "My precious child! I promise, I will not ignore you tonight. There will be no cards. Only a musicale, a supper and then, if you wish, we will leave."

Morag sighed. There seemed nothing to do but agree. She only wished that her mother had made it clear earlier that they were to stay in Paris; perhaps she could have found an excuse not to come. Now she was trapped.

"You will enjoy yourself, pet. You'll see." Marie

rang the bell for the maid and ordered some wine. "A bit of wine will put you more in the mood to enjoy this evening's entertainment."

Morag sighed. "Very well."

Turning away from Morag for just a moment, Marie Thérèse poured a generous amount of clear white wine into the goblet.

Morag looked dubiously at the glass. "So much?"

"Go ahead, pet. Drink it. It will make you feel better."

Shrugging, Morag did as she was told. The wine had a mellow flavor. Her mother was right; it was the best wine she had ever tasted.

Within minutes after draining the glass, a warm glow spread over Morag. Her whole body seemed flushed, but what bothered her most was an unusual tingling she felt between her legs and at her nipples.

"More wine, pet?"

Morag shook her head. Her voice when she spoke, was unusually thick: "No, Maman . . . not now."

"Well, then, Madame de Courtan has kindly arranged for us to have rooms to rest in while she alters your dress. I suppose we ought to go up."

Morag nodded. Her head seemed unusually heavy. "Yes, I'd like a bath." Perhaps that would ease these strange sensations she was feeling.

By the time Maine's carriage called for them at half-past eight, Morag felt, if anything, worse. Despite the four more glasses of wine Maman had given her, she was tense. The silver tissue dress, which barely concealed her nipples, seemed to scratch her at the most delicate places. Would she never be rid of this awful feeling of irritation?

Getting into the carriage, the sensation was so unbearable that she wanted to tear the dress off, let the air soothe her naked body. Oh, why had she let Maman buy the awful thing?

Maine's mansion was not far from the gardens in the Saint-Germain district. A number of nobles had hotels here; the area was far more pleasing than the old Palais Royal where d'Angeau lived. Maine's mansion was more lavishly furnished than d'Angeau's, but Morag took an immediate dislike to the place.

She and her mother were greeted by Henri, who led them to the drawing-room door and paused there. Morag heard Maine's high-pitched laughter and she recognized Jean Baptiste's voice. The irritation of the silver dress flushed through her again. If only she could do something to relieve that awful sensation! She glanced at the pictures on the wall, trying to recognize the scenes. Why was her vision so blurred? Why did she have so much trouble concentrating?

Henri was bowing and smirking. "Pardon me, Madame Elliot, Mademoiselle Morag, I almost forgot—His Grace wishes that you disrobe."

Glancing at her mother, Morag saw that she was holding something white and shimmering. It looked like a large satin sheet.

"Maman, what . . ."

"It is a toga, pet. Didn't you hear what Henri said?"

Morag shook her head. She felt as if she were floating, as if her feet had no sensation. Had she drunk too much wine?

"Really, Morag, why don't you listen? His Grace wants us to take off our clothes and put on these togas. It's in keeping with the musicale."

"Oh," Morag said blankly. "Take off my clothes?"

The flushed heat about her breasts was making her nipples palpitate.

She realized suddenly that they were in a private room. One of Maine's maids must have undressed her, though Morag didn't remember it. She glanced at her mother. Marie Thérèse was already wearing one of the white satin togas, which had been pulled so tight about her youthful body that her nipples showed.

Morag swallowed hard, trying to understand what was happening.

As the maid wrapped the smooth cool satin about her, she brushed Morag's nipple. It had obviously been an accident, because the maid had quickly pulled away. Embarrassed, Morag didn't say anything as a flush spread over her body. Her whole body felt hot and tense; she realized, with horror, that she had liked the girl's touching her.

Morag's mouth went dry and she tried to swallow.

"What's wrong with me, Maman? Why do I feel— why are you staring at me like that?"

Marie Thérèse kissed her daughter's forehead. "Nothing, pet. You look fine." Her eyes glistened with tears—or was that Morag's imagination? "Why, dearest, do you feel ill?"

"Yes . . . no . . . I don't know. I . . . I feel strange."

"Strange? How so?"

Morag flushed. How could she explain it to Maman? Between her legs, Morag was beginning to feel a funny wet sensation and an ache.

"Here, pet." Marie Thérèse handed her daughter a goblet of wine. "Drink this and you'll feel better. I'm sure it's just nerves."

"Nerves?"

"Yes. After all, you've never worn a toga before, have you?"

Morag shook her head, or thought she did. She drained the glass.

If anything, the wine increased the horrid aching feeling, the feeling of unreality.

The nagging doubts left Morag momentarily when she saw that there were already several other women in the drawing room. That was good; it was too much bother to worry. Maman was right—the wine had made her feel better.

Maine's high-pitched voice summoned them over to the couch where he lay. He wore a toga of royal purple satin, attached at the shoulder with a gaudy gold and diamond clasp. The servant girl above him stood bare-breasted, feeding him grapes. Morag's eyes widened, and she felt the stirring of unease. She should get out of here; she should . . .

She gripped her mother's upper arm so that Marie Thérèse turned. "Maman . . ." Morag began, as fear rose in her. She wanted to ask her mother to take her back to court, or at least to the dressmaker's—anywhere but here. But if Marie Thérèse recognized her daughter's terror, she made no response.

Morag had the feeling, however, that something had passed between Maine and her mother, for suddenly the Duke dismissed the servant girl.

"Excuse me for not rising, ladies." He smiled at them, revealing snuff-stained teeth. "If you will take your places, the musicale can begin."

Morag found herself pressed onto the couch beside the Duke. Surely, Maman should be sitting there. Her bemused brain warned her that something wasn't right. Yet she accepted more wine, barely tasting its tartness, and leaned back against the pillows, not really caring if she rose again or not. It would be all right, she told herself, as a servant came to raise her legs up on the couch. After all, it was only a musicale, and Maman had promised they would leave after dinner.

The servant lit some thick purple candles near her head. Their light sputtered and went out, leaving a glowing wick. Morag was about to tell the man, but the low soft music had already begun. It was an Eastern melody, she heard someone whisper. The voice seemed to come from above her . . . or was it to her right? She couldn't tell.

How warm the room was! She was aware now of a heavy sweet smell that seemed to come from the glowing purple candles . . . and of that strange aching irritation between her legs and about her breasts. Her mouth was horribly dry.

Had she asked for more wine? She didn't remember, but her goblet was full again and she drank greedily. Two more candles glowed on the stage. A girl wearing only a blue gauze veil came out. The music quickened as she began to dance faster and faster. Morag could not seem to take her eyes off the girl, off the jewels shimmering in her navel and on her bare breasts. Vaguely, she was aware of Maine's hand on her leg. She didn't move; she wanted to, but she couldn't. Her own nature was fighting her as she felt his hand creeping up like a spider, felt the warmth suffusing her increase as Maine's hand reached under the folds of her toga. Oh, God . . . what was happening to her? She wanted to scream, but no sound came.

Then, suddenly, Maine removed his hand. She must have moved or done something, but she wasn't aware of it. Where was Maman? Why hadn't her mother seen or done anything?

Morag's eyes felt heavy. She closed them with relief,

trying to will away the annoying warmth, trying to move. Aware of a sudden silence in the room, she opened her eyes again. How had the candles gone down so fast? Where was Maman . . . Jean Baptiste and the others? She glanced over to the couch where Maine had been.

"I will be with you in one moment, Morag, my precious. I know you are anxious for me, but there are a few preliminaries."

Her heart pounded. Maine was standing over her to her right and his toga was gone. His skinny hairless body glimmered eerily in the dim light. She gasped in horror, jerked out of her lassitude by the shock. The blood seemed to pour rapidly through her veins when she heard Maine laugh.

"Don't worry, my precious, you'll enjoy it. I promised d'Angeau that I would be gentle . . . the first time."

D'Angeau! Had he made arrangements for this evening? Of course! That explained why he had been so distant of late; why he and Maman had quarreled, why he wasn't there, but . . . where was Maman? What had Maine done with her?

Tears sparkled in Morag's eyes. She watched, powerless to react, as Maine opened her toga, exposing her rounded breasts, her flat stomach and the tuft of red hair.

His long bony hand tweaked her breast. She moaned, feeling both pain and heat flood her. Her mind was numb; she was only vaguely aware of her struggle, of more pain as Maine alternately pinched and stroked her, his hands moving down her body past her hips and resting on her mound.

"You will forget the pain, my pet. You will think only of the pleasure. I will teach you to respond with this . . . to crave only this." He laughed, pulling at her hairs gently and spreading her grove as he rubbed her.

She groaned then, as his fingers violated her. She strained, trying to push him out, feeling her wetness and the heat increasing, barely aware of his comments:

"Good. Good, my precious."

Her whole body flushed with agony . . . and desire. It couldn't be happening, she told herself. She couldn't let Maine have his way with her—or let Quentin know he had been right. She must fight. She must. . . .

Maine had moved away from her suddenly. She heard him speaking to someone . . . Henri? Or perhaps it was Quentin after all, come to witness her shame. Slowly, with a deep breath, she willed her head to turn. Chains! Maine was holding chains in his hands!

With a supreme effort, Morag raised her hand, clutching the glass of wine she had been holding. Whatever the consequences, she must escape from here. She must get away . . .

Maine approached her again, a smile stretching his thin lips taut as he devoured her exposed beauty. He didn't notice the glass in her hand, or realize that she had begun to revive—regaining some of her capacity to resist—until, concentrating with all her might, she threw the wine in his face.

The next few moments were like a nightmare. Unsure of herself, of her legs, Morag stumbled from the couch. Clutching at the open toga, her feet bare, she ran from the drawing room and down the stairs. Maine was coming after her. She saw the door below, unbolted. She had to escape . . . had to! If she stayed, Maine would find her and chain her and take her. Oh . . . where was Maman?

Dizzily, Morag grabbed at the rail, falling as she ran down the stairs. Numbly, she realized that she had twisted her foot, but she must get out of there. A servant passed and Morag drew quickly into a doorway. She realized then that Maine probably wouldn't come after her, naked as he was, but would send someone else. Somehow she focused on the belt of her toga hanging loose at her side, and fastened it.

The commotion upstairs told her that Maine assumed that she was still in the house. It would be foolish, she knew, to go out into the night dressed as she was, but more foolish to remain here. Whatever drug he had given her, she realized, was beginning to wear off as activity forced her heart to beat faster.

She had reached the door when she heard Henri cry: "There she is!"

Not waiting for more, Morag flung open the heavy door. The cool air helped to revive her more as she ran down the steps and through the courtyard. Thank God the gate was open!

Morag crossed herself and took a deep breath. Then she made a dash for it.

She ran, having no idea where she was going, knowing only that she must escape.

After a few breathless minutes, she paused. She could smell the river and the tanneries. She shivered, and suddenly became aware that her feet hurt. Her head swam and she leaned back against the wall, letting the tears fall down her cheeks. Where could she go? She had no idea where Maman was—probably still at Maine's, and Morag could not go back there.

Taking a deep breath, she tried to remember where the dressmaker's was . . . over the river near the Palais Royal, wasn't it? Hearing footsteps somewhere behind her, she began to run again, gritting her teeth against the pain in her feet, heading toward the bridge. A full moon shone upon the waters of the Seine.

Breathless, Morag crossed the river. It must have been over an hour since she had left Maine; at least, it seemed that long. It was a mild night, but whether it was the drug or her scanty clothing, Morag was thoroughly chilled. Her hair hung loose about her face. She brushed it back and rubbed her arms, trying to warm them.

She ran blindly down one street and then another until she heard the sound of a carriage behind her. Thinking that it was Maine coming after her, Morag ducked into a doorway. The carriage approached and Morag's breath quickened. She recognized the vehicle—it was d'Angeau's. She realized then, glancing up, that she was on the Rue St. Augustin, near his hotel.

Thinking only of her fear of Maine, of her desire to be warm and safe again, she called out as the coach rumbled by. But the *carrosse* continued on.

Crying, stumbling, Morag followed it, watching as it passed through the *porte cochère* of d'Angeau's hotel. Running, she reached the gate just as it closed.

"Let me in!" she cried. "Please . . . Monsieur le Marquis . . . Quentin! Please . . . let me in!" She continued to pound on the gate, sobbing, her tangled auburn waves falling into her eyes. He must help her! He must let her in!

Suddenly, the gate opened and Botemps stood before her. "Be on your way, wench. We want none of the likes of you—"

"Please!" She cried, "Please . . . let me in. I must see—"

Quentin loomed behind his manservant. "What is it, Botemps? What is the commotion? *Mon Dieu!* Morag!"

Quickly, he wrapped his cape about her and swooped her up in his arms. "Botemps, get me some hot water, some bandages and blankets. Mademoiselle Elliot has been hurt, it seems."

."Yes, my lord." The startled servant quickly disappeared to do the Marquis' bidding.

Gently, Quentin carried Morag up the stairs and placed her on the couch in the drawing room. The painting of Louis on his horse looked down on her. Morag found that she could not stop sobbing, could not stop shaking. Forgetting everything but the safe comfort of his arms, she wept with exhaustion and relief.

She tried to tell him what had happened, but her sobs choked her. Only the words "Maine" and "chains" were distinguishable.

"Quiet, *mignonne*. We'll soon have you feeling better."

He handed her a glass of brandy, which Botemps had poured. Remembering the drugged wine, Morag shook her head violently, pushing the brandy away, unable to explain as her sobs continued.

"My dear . . . come. You need something to warm you quickly. You also need something to take away the sting when we wash your cuts." He held the glass to her lips. "*Mignonne* . . . drink."

Sniffling, she sipped slowly at the brandy. He was right. Her feet stung terribly as Quentin directed Botemps to wash the cuts and then mix and apply a salve. Morag gritted her teeth, trying desperately not to cry out, digging her nails into Quentin's arms.

The brandy was taking effect. She was glad that she had thought to come here, glad that Quentin Sauvage was holding her securely.

The sound of the bell ringing below jarred her, brought goosebumps to her skin. Wide-eyed, she looked at Quentin. It was Maine, she was sure of it. They had found her; they would drag her back.

The memory of Maine's pale hairless body flashed before her, and nausea rose in her. She would rather die than submit to that man; she clung to Sauvage. Downstairs, the bell at the gate rang again.

"My lord—?" Botemps appeared.

"Answer it, Botemps, but if it is any of Maine's household, say only that I am asleep. Then come back up to me."

"Very good, sir." The servant clicked his heels and spun about.

"Please," Morag begged, "don't let him touch me. Don't —"

"Maine won't harm you, *mignonne*." He pried her fingers from his arm.

"But you don't understand . . ."

"I do, little one, I assure you." He poured her more brandy. "Here . . . take a bit more. It will relax you. Perhaps I had better go down to deal with them."

She clung to him. "You will come back?"

Quentin smiled. Was he laughing at her? She searched his face desperately. No, it wasn't that. Gently, he touched her cheek. "You needn't fear, *chérie*."

He left the room then, leaving Morag feeling cold and lonely.

She realized that her cheek was warm where he had touched her, and her whole body seemed to quiver with a tension that she did not understand. Numbly, she drained the brandy he had given her. He wouldn't betray her—she was sure of that.

The door crashed open and Maine stood there, framed by a red cloak. He had obviously dressed hurriedly, for the ruffles in his shirt were awry, and he wore no jerkin.

"I thought I would find you here." He laughed.

Dazed with fear, Morag began to back away. Her hand reached out frantically behind her, searching for something to defend herself with, but there was nothing.

"No, my precious, you aren't going to escape me this time. Henri is keeping your friend d'Angeau well-occcupied downstairs."

"He . . . he didn't see you?"

"Do you think he would have let me in if he had? He knows what I want. It was all settled, my pretty red-haired wench: you are to be my mistress. Once I have deflowered you, you will thank me."

No words came from Morag. She shook her head slowly from side to side, her green eyes huge in her pale elfin face. Then her groping hand found something on the desk: a small knife for sharpening a quill.

Her voice quivered: "If you come any closer, I . . . I will kill you."

"With that?" Maine sneered and advanced on her. "No, my precious, I paid good money for you, and I—"

"You what, Maine?" Quentin Sauvage stood in the doorway, his arms folded ominously across his chest.

Maine whirled around. "That fool Henri! Can't he do anything right?"

"I wouldn't blame him. It was just obvious that he was taking too long." Quentin jerked his head and Botemps entered, holding a pistol. "Your man is downstairs, under guard. I suggest you both leave—now."

"Well, and I suggest that I do not. You're getting too big for your own good, d'Angeau!"

Quentin laughed. "Maybe so, Your Grace, but this is my home and I do not want you here."

But Maine made no move to go. "This girl is mine." He jerked his head toward Morag. "I paid—"

"You paid nothing, Your Grace. I am afraid you made a bad bargain. Now, I repeat: leave my home. You have done enough damage for one night."

Reluctantly, with a last angry glance at Morag, Maine left the room.

Quentin shut the door behind him. "You can drop the knife now, Morag."

She swallowed hard. "Is he truly gone? He won't come back?" She seemed paralyzed.

Quentin stepped forward and pried the knife from her stiff fingers. "He's gone, *mignonne*. You can trust me. He'll not hurt you."

Her small face crumpled and the tears streamed down. She was scarcely aware of her toga falling open, of Quentin carrying her to the couch. Only the safe warmth of his arms about her broke into her consciousness, as she cried on his shoulder. Her whole body seemed to tremble. She had been so afraid in that last moment, so sure that Maine would force her . . . that he would make her do that hideous thing.

When she felt Quentin's lips brush her forehead, her eyelids, her neck, she quieted. It felt so natural for her to be with him, to have him hold her, so good when he touched her.

"Morag," he whispered her name tenderly, "my little Morag."

Desire flamed in her, more intense than ever. She didn't—she couldn't—move away, not even when his hand slowly began to draw a circle about her pink-tipped nipple and traveled downward, feathering her body gently with delicious chills, coming to rest upon her mound as he gently massaged her into ecstasy. She strained against him, not wanting him to stop. It was almost what Maine had done; yet, she thought dizzily, this was different. This was . . . right. Some stranger seemed to have taken over her body. She was aware of nothing but the warm pressure of Quentin's lips, and of his hands as he stroked her, inflaming her desire more than the drugged wine could ever have done.

Her arms reached out about his neck and she pulled him toward her. Her whole body throbbed with the need for him as, gingerly, she touched his swollen manhood through his breeches.

"Morag," he whispered, kissing her ear, "don't."

She shook her head. Her huge green eyes stared up at him solemnly from beneath a tumble of auburn waves. "I . . . I want to."

She closed her eyes then, as she continued to touch him. It was impossible to stop, to think, as her lips again met his. She knew that this was what she had wanted and yearned for. The warmth of his lips swept her deeper into a tunnel of ecstasy. It was time, she thought, only vaguely aware of what she was doing, time to find out what it was that Nicole, Maman and the others thought so wonderful. It was time for Quentin to discover that she wasn't a child.

He licked her ear, making her moan softly. Her toga was completely off now; Quentin, too, had shed his clothes, without her being aware of it. He fondled her breasts, kissed her artfully, as his hand reached between her legs and paused.

A groan came from deep within her as she felt his pressure. The frustration and desire was unlike anything she had ever felt before. But as she felt his hardness and maleness against her, she resisted for just a moment . . . not rejection, but the pause of some wild thing breaking within her. With his knee, he spread her thighs.

Her body writhed with the first plunge and she dug her nails into his back. As the tempo increased, the heat in her was almost unbearable. Morag knew then; she understood what Maman meant. This was what it was to be a woman. A heady feeling engulfed her. She felt a rapturous glow, as wave after wave of delight engulfed her. His swift thrusts were follwed by a final plunge, and at last he rested motionless on top of her. All Morag could hear was his jagged breathing in her ear, as she savored the fullness of feeling.

Gently, he kissed her lids and brow. "I am sorry, *mignonne*. I did not expect that to happen." He rolled off her and brushed a curl from her cheek. "You should have told me you were untouched, Morag."

"Would it have mattered?" She bit back the tears, unable to think or move. Forgetting that she had encouraged him, she said, "You were determined to have me. You . . . you are vile." Flushing, she pulled the bedcover over her, now acutely aware of her nakedness, of the man beside her. How could she ever go into a convent, after what she had experienced this night?

He kissed her tenderly on the mouth. "I did not mean to hurt you, *mignonne*." His hand brushed her nipples. "What's done is done. I will tell your mother that it was none of your doing."

"I don't care what you tell her. I—" she strained away from him, trying to douse the fire of his touch had rekindled in her, but in a moment, desire had its way. She submitted to him one more time, feeling him take her to a still higher plane of fulfillment. This time, when he had done, she fell asleep in his arms.

The knock on the door came shortly after. Quentin moved, careful not to wake Morag.

"Yes, Botemps, what is it?"

"You'll pardon me, my lord, but Mademoiselle Le Martin wonders when you will be joining her."

Dieu! He had forgotten Nicole!

Glancing at Morag's red-gold hair fanned over his arm, he replied, "Tell her I will be with her momentarily."

Chapter Seven

MORAG STRETCHED HER slender limbs. For a moment, she felt wonderful. Then, chilled, she pulled the heavy brocade bedcover about her, aware of the pain in her feet and of the silence in the room as the ormulu clock ticked the seconds away. Her heart beat faster when she realized that she was alone. Somewhere bells were ringing; it was noon. Her head ached and she closed her eyes again, recalling all that had happened.

Had she really "given" herself to that man? She realized that someone—Quentin—had carried her to the bed, a huge double bed. It must have been he who covered her. Compared to her cot at the pavilion, this bed made her feel lost and insignificant, as if what had happened the night before was also insignifcant. Well, perhaps it was—to him, but not to her. How many other women had shared this bed with him?

Above her was a mural: an allegorical version of Louis as Apollo. Morag stared, fascinated, trying to block the feelings of last night.

She sat up slowly, wondering where she was. Her whole body flushed with shame as she recalled each vivid detail of their lovemaking. How could she have acted in such a wanton manner? What must he think of her for having surrendered so easily? Tears of mortification sparkled in her green eyes.

"Damn him!" She curled her small hand into a fist and pounded the bed. If he cared about her . . . She wiped her eyes impatiently and looked about her.

The room was obviously a man's. Dark green satin covered the walls; the furniture was of an attractive light wood. Perhaps his nature was not as somber as she had thought. Well, no, she had never really thought of Quentin as somber, and last night . . . last night he had shown her still another side of himself.

Morag's face burned. She had to admit that she had been wrong, that despite the pain of his first entry, the experience had ultimately been pleasurable. Would it have been the same with Maine? With anyone? Morag shuddered, thinking of Maine's spindly white body. No, she doubted it.

Her head swam and she lay back in the feather bed, closing her eyes again. The bed drapes moved in response to a breeze from the open window.

Morag swallowed hard. What would happen to her now? She had been so sure of her desire to join the sisters, but after what had transpired, how could she? Perhaps Quentin would marry her . . . No! How could she think such a thing? Maman would be furious. But . . . Maman was no longer engaged to him.

A sound startled her. Morag realized that someone was knocking on the door. Quickly, she made sure that she was covered. She didn't want Quentin to see her naked in the daylight.

"Yes, come in."

Disappointment filled Morag when a young maid tiptoed in; her stiff white apron crackled as she curtsyed awkwardly. "I . . . I heard you moving, Mademoiselle. I . . . did you wish your breakfast?" Obviously, the girl was new to service.

Morag nodded. "Where is the Marquis?"

"Oh, he is gone, Mademoiselle."

"Gone?"

Morag leaped from the bed, forgetting her nakedness, yelping with pain as her feet touched the floor. Jumping back into the feather bed, she covered herself once more, gritting her teeth against the pain.

"Pray, where did the Marquis go?"

"Oh, he and the Mademoiselle Le Martin returned to court early this morning." The maid brought over a basin of steaming water to help Morag wash.

Nicole! Nicole had been here last night? Furious, Morag pushed the basin away, splashing the girl. "I don't want that now! I want to know about Mademoiselle Le Martin and the Marquis."

The girl flushed. "What . . . what do you want to know, Mademoiselle?"

"How long was she here? When did she come? When—?"

"I am sorry, Mademoiselle." The girl shifted unhappily from foot to foot. "I do not know. Let me help you dress, Mademoiselle, and perhaps Monsieur Botemps can tell you."

Aware that her head and feet were throbbing more painfully than before, Morag nodded. She wanted to cry. How could she have thought that she meant anything to the man other than a quick conquest! Shame flooded her when she remembered how she had thrown herself at him. She still didn't understand why; it was all so confusing.

"Mademoiselle, you are crying! You are in pain?"

Morag's throat hurt. She nodded. Yes, she was in

pain . . . because of her own stupidity. She took the cloth which the maid handed her and blew her nose. The maid slipped a warm robe over her naked shoulders.

Vaguely, she heard the girl say: "I will get Monsieur Botemps. He will speak to you."

Morag nodded, relieved that the girl had gone. She lay back again and closed her eyes, whimpering softly.

"Mademoiselle?"

Abruptly, Morag sat up as Botemps approached the bed.

"Where is your master?" she asked, her green eyes narrowing. She hoped he couldn't tell that she had been crying.

At least the man had the goodness to avert his eyes. "He is not here at the moment, Mademoiselle. Is there something you wish?"

"When will he return?" Her voice cracked.

Botemps shrugged. "That I cannot tell you. I do not know my lord's intention."

"But why didn't you go with him?"

"My lord left me to see to your care, Mademoiselle."

"My care? My care!" her voice rose. "The de'il take him!" Her Scots' intonation increased as her anger grew.

Botemps frowned at the display of emotion. "My lord said it would be necessary for you to remain in bed for several days."

"'Tis enough, mon! I'm not some soft French miss as frae court. I'm Scots!" Her eyes blazed.

"My lord d'Angeau said that you are in no condition to walk. He left word that you are to be cared for until he returns."

Struggling to gain control of herself, Morag declared,

"Weel, when the man returns, he winna find me here. Get the carriage for me, Botemps."

"My lord has taken—"

"Then get me something else, mon! A horse. I winna stay here a minute mar than necessary."

"You will pardon me, Mademoiselle, but if you truly plan to leave, you will need some clothes."

"Then stop your foolish fussing and get me some!"

"I believe my lord returned to court to obtain—"

"I'll not be storied, mon!" She was shouting. "He's gone back with my cousin, Nicole, and you know it! He doesn't plan to return for me. He doesn't give a damn about me!" She threw the basin by the bedside across the room. Water dripped from the satin bed curtains, from the walls and from Botemps' clothes.

Impassively, he picked the basin up. "Is Mademoiselle finished?"

Morag pouted. "Yes, I am."

He placed the basin back on the bedside. "If Mademoiselle wishes to leave . . .?"

"That I do."

"I believe, Mademoiselle, that I can find you a dress." He paused. "It is one of your cousin's."

Throwing the basin had somehow calmed her. Her voice was more subdued when she said, "Very well, Botemps, bring it."

Nicole's dress, which the maid brought to Morag, was a deceptively simple holland of deep blue, but it had been cut nearly to the navel, and when it was laced, it made the most of Morag's alabaster breasts.

"Is there nothing but this?" She frowned, not disliking the image in the mirror, yet perturbed.

"I don't know, Mademoiselle." The maid blushed. "Monsieur Botemps just handed it to me and—"

"Oh, never mind," Morag said, irritated. Her feet

were throbbing terribly. If only she could crawl back into bed, go back to sleep. She would love to forget these past few horrid hours.

Biting her lip, she pulled on a teal satin slipper and heard the bell clang downstairs. Even before Botemps knocked, Morag's heartbeat had quickened with fear and panic. The hair on the nape of her neck rose as she recognized the high-pitched voice of the caller: Maine. She bit her lip, drawing blood, as she glanced about the room. There was no place to hide; nowhere to run.

Maine burst in as he had last night. His hose and scarlet doublet, both embroidered with gold, emphasized the sallowness of his complexion. His crushed velvet cape of royal purple was streaked with a scarlet that matched the red feather in his deep blue hat.

"So, your lover has left you."

Morag stiffened. "If you are referring to the Marquis, he is not my lover. He . . . he merely treated my cuts last night."

"Oh, really, Morag! Do you take me for a ninny?" When he sank down on the bed his cape flared out, like a peacock showing its fine feathers. Henri had entered the room now, holding a pistol on Botemps.

Morag glanced up in alarm. "Just a precaution, my precious," Maine said. He grabbed one of her feet, touching her cuts gently. "You know, this needn't have happened if you had been sensible last night."

She grimaced, not looking at him.

His hand rested on her knee. She was aware of his eyes on her breasts, of his hand moving up her skirt. Still, she did not move.

"Monsieur le Duc!" Botemps tried to come forward and was rewarded with a crack on the skull. He fell unconscious to the floor.

110

"Did you have to do that?" Morag cried out, horrified, as Maine put a hand out to hold her back. Henri shrugged and glanced at his master.

"I trust you enjoyed your first experience," Maine said. "Was d'Angeau gentle?"

She stiffened as Henri's pistol swung toward her. Flushing, she said, "I tell you, nothing happened." There was a pause as Maine's hand moved further up her skirt.

"Your Grace!" she gasped, as he slipped his hand between her legs.

He laughed, watching her face color. "Ah, perhaps the drug is still working."

"So . . . so you did put something into my wine."

"Of course. In fact, it was d'Angeau's own creation."

She gasped. "He . . . he gave it to you?"

Maine chortled. "Who else? He tells me it is very effective with the Indian maidens—he uses it quite often. Why else do you think he is so popular with the ladies at court?"

Maine ran a hand over the tops of her breasts. "I paid good money for your services, my dear, and I will not let d'Angeau cheat me of you."

Botemps groaned and stirred slightly.

"And . . . and what if I do not wish to be your mistress, Your Grace?" Morag jerked away from him.

"Oh, but you will."

He nodded toward Henri, who kicked Botemps, drawing another groan from the man. "What you see here will happen to your friend, d'Angeau."

Morag swallowed hard. "What do I care about him?"

Maine shrugged. "Perhaps nothing, but your Maman does. They are to be married, isn't that so?"

111

Morag pressed her lips together in a painfully thin line. "Aye, that is what she hopes." Her heart was hammering now. "But I cannot believe Your Grace would be so vile as to—"

The slap stung her cheek. She blinked with astonishment and pain. Maine's dark wig had slipped with the force of his blow, and Morag began to laugh hysterically, as Henri hurried forward to adjust his master's wig and dab the sweat delicately from his brow.

Maine's grip on her wrist was like a vise. "If you are done with your merriment, my precious, we will go."

"Go?"

This time Maine laughed; it was like a wild hyena's cry. "Surely, you did not think I would take you here? We are going back to my hotel."

"But, Maman—"

He raised his nose haughtily, snapped his fingers and Henri hurried forward with snuff.

"Your Maman," Maine said in his nasal tone, "has already been made aware of the situation. She will be well compensated, have no fear on that account, my precious."

"And . . . if I do not go with you?"

Henri cocked the pistol and held it inches from Botemps' head.

"He dies. This instant. D'Angeau will have a slower and more painful death. And your Maman . . ."

Morag stared at the unconscious man on the floor. A shiver ran through her; she felt cold and sick.

"My precious, do not make the mistake of underestimating me. While it is true that I am younger than you—" his hand cupped her chin roughly and forced her to look at him, "I know a good deal more of life and have power. I am the King's bastard, but I am his favorite bastard. When I want something done, it will be done."

With a wave of his bony hand, he signaled Henri. For such a dwarfed body, the man was surprisingly strong, Morag realized, as he picked her up.

"It is your own fault that your feet are cut, my precious, but we will put that to our advantage, won't we Henri?"

"Yes, Your Grace."

Morag could feel the vibrations as the ugly little man took one last look at Botemps, lying motionless on the floor. At least he was still breathing. She wondered what he would tell Quentin.

Chapter Eight

MAINE'S HOTEL WAS as grand as she remembered it from the night before. Morag, her feet throbbing, was only barely aware that the crimson room with its gold-framed mirrors in the ceiling was next to the room where she and Maman had changed into the togas.

She stumbled toward the bed Henri indicated to her and sank thankfully into the soft feather comforter, closing her eyes. She heard Maine order breakfast for her. Mayhap he wouldn't be so bad, if he was concerned enough for her welfare to do that.

She sat up and opened her eyes. A maid was standing by the bed, staring at her.

"Is something the matter?" Morag asked.

"You ain't no beauty, not with all that red har. Why, you're just a chit. My tiddies 'er bigger than yers. Can't see why he wants *you*."

Morag realized that the girl was jealous. No doubt she shared Maine's bed when no one else was about.

"I don't know either," Morag told her. "In fact, if you want to do me a favor, you'll help me escape."

The girl sucked in her cheeks. "Might be a favor to

you, but not to me. I ain't getting his dander up. His Grace ain't one t'toy with when he is angry." She pushed a cup of steaming chocolate toward Morag. "Go on . . . drink up. I ain't got all day."

Morag drank the chocolate. Almost immediately, she was aware of a ringing in her ears and of a tingling sensation all over her body, especially at her nipples. The wetness was back in her groin, and a growing warmth flooded her, making her forget the throbbing pain in her feet.

"The chocolate . . ." Her tongue seemed fuzzy, her vision blurred.

The girl laughed again. "What d'you think? Of course . . . His Grace gave you a little something in it. He always do—the first time. Heightens the pleasure, he said. I use it meself sometimes."

The girl undressed her none too gently and lifted Morag's legs back up on the bed.

Morag, her head swimming, heard the chains clanking and felt the cold metal bracelets clapped onto her ankles and wrists, but had no will to fight. Nothing could help her now. She closed her eyes, trying not to think of the future, and felt the girl fanning her gently, causing wave after wave of sensation to flood her.

Maine entered the room now. She couldn't see him, but she sensed his presence, and then felt his clammy touch as he came forward to stroke the silky area between her thighs. She moaned, hating herself for responding.

"Good, Michelle, my dear. Good job. You shall be rewarded tonight."

"Thank you kindly, Yer Grace."

Morag was conscious of the door shutting and felt mildly relieved that the girl had gone, but nothing seemed to relieve the tension she was going through now.

Maine's fingers invaded her and she gave a small scream of pain.

"You're a little liar, Morag, my precious. If you are still a virgin, then I am a fool. Did you think to fool me? I want an answer, Morag." He began to pinch her.

She wanted to answer but no words would come, only gasps of pain. She closed her eyes to hide the tears. It had not been her fault, what had happened with Quentin. Maine had told her himself that the Marquis had given him the drug he had used on her. It was *his* fault.

She swallowed, the nausea rising in her throat, as Maine took her. He would pay for this, she vowed. Quentin Adam Sauvage would pay . . .

By week's end, Morag thought she must have experienced every humiliation a man could possibly inflict on a woman. Drugged, exhausted from Maine's brutal treatment of her, she could not fight him. Besides, what was the sense? Actually, she found herself almost looking forward to his visits—not for any sexual pleasure, but for the drug which numbed her mind and blurred the pain.

He would tire of her soon, Morag thought, if only she could remain passive. But the drug wouldn't allow her to do that. She couldn't think beyond it, couldn't fathom what her life would be like free of Maine.

On the eighth day of her abduction, Maine entered

the room fully dressed. Hesitant, Morag rose to greet him. She was no longer chained down now.

Maine laughed. "Ah, I see we have you trained at last. But much as I would like to pleasure you today, my precious, I fear we must return to court."

"To . . . Versailles?"

Maine nodded. "My papa wishes to see me."

"And me?" Her voice was hoarse, her pulses pounding. Oh, she needed that drink.

He snapped his long fingers and Michelle came in, with a new dress for Morag. "I believe this should fit you. Of course you'll come with me, precious. Do you think I could leave your lovely body alone for that long? Papa might want me for several days. But there's time yet before we go." He shoved her back toward the bed.

"Wait!" Morag cried, hating herself. She saw Maine's triumphant smirk.

"Oh, yes, your drink."

Michelle handed her a glass and Morag drank greedily. As the drug took over, she closed her eyes and waited for the inevitable. She shut out Maine's groans of pleasure, thinking of the court . . . of how she would have her revenge on Quentin Adam Sauvage.

She wasn't surprised to find herself placed in the ivory boudoir adjoining Maine's rooms, but she was surprised that neither Maman nor Quentin came to see her.

Maine had warned her that it would go the worse for Quentin and her mother if she relayed any of his threats to them. She had promised that she would not; she had thought that at least Maman would be concerned enough to come and see her.

117

Hurt, Morag decided that her mother didn't care what happened to her. That Marie Thérèse might be responsible for her present situation never entered her mind; Quentin was the one she blamed. Maine had said that the Marquis had given him the drug and his blessing. But even if he hadn't, even if Maine lied, it was still d'Angeau's fault, Morag reasoned irrationally. If he hadn't been so eager to run back to the court with Nicole, if he had stayed with Morag that morning, then Maine could never have abducted her.

She paced the ivory satin room, kicking irritably at the furniture, wringing her hands. Her head ached; the sedative Maine had given her had dulled the pain, but it hadn't given her the glorious glow of her usual drug.

Miserable, she sank into the chair by the window and glanced out across the path. The Swiss guard—a big burly fellow with a red face—stood there. Did Maine really think she would try to escape? Didn't he realize how much she needed that drug now? It was scarcely two weeks since she had first taken it, yet Morag found she could not think without it.

Digging her nails into the side of the satin chair, she screwed her small face up, watching the guard. Yes, it was different here at court than it had been at the hotel. But though Maine allowed her to walk in the grounds, nothing seemed the same—not the canals, not the orangery, not the animals. Even the ostrich had died.

Besides, she felt uncomfortable—wearing clothes, being outside. She felt that everyone was staring at her, whispering. God, she hated Maine—and Quentin Sauvage too. If *he* hadn't given Maine the drug in the first place . . .

Her thoughts propelled her from the chair, and she

began to pace again. If Maine wouldn't give her the drug, then she would get it from Quentin. He would be sure to have a supply. Besides, it was time she took her revenge on the Marquis. Today! She pounded her clenched fist into her palm. Today she would wreck his house as he had wrecked her life. She would make him sorry for what he had done to her.

Without thinking, she lifted a glass of wine to her lips; then, remembering the sedative, stopped. No, she must keep her wits about her. She glanced out as the guard shifted position. Was there enough in the glass to sedate him so she could escape?

Perhaps he wouldn't drink. Perhaps he knew that Maine drugged her liquor . . . no, Maine would tell no one that, especially not a lowly Swiss guard.

Rapping on the window, Morag smiled and motioned to the man. He seemed reluctant to respond. Gritting her teeth, she bared her breasts slightly and smiled again, more seductively this time. It wasn't something she would have done two weeks before . . . what was she coming to? Well, there was no time to think about that now. She must get the drug before she went mad.

The guard licked his lips and glanced about, probably to make certain that neither Maine nor Henri were about. Then he came toward her.

Morag discovered that the stupid man knew no English or French. It took several charades before he seemed to understand that she wanted him to drink with her. Smiling, he swallowed one glass of wine and then another.

Morag watched warily, wondering why the huge burly man wasn't falling asleep. She poured him another glass and another, all the while smiling and pretending to drink her own wine. The guard growled suddenly and shook his head. He lunged at her; she evaded his grasp with a shriek. Astonished, Morag watched him right himself, sway and fall onto the floor with a thud.

She caught her breath and bent to check his pulse. Yes, he was alive. Satisfied, she grabbed a shawl to cover her telltale red hair and ran from the room.

If the past few days were any indication, Maine would be gaming now. He would not come to see her until later that night. Even if he did come that afternoon, she doubted that it would be for several hours yet. There was plenty of time for her to reach d'Angeau's mansion, get the drug, and return to her room.

Morag was breathless when she reached the drive in front of the Marquis' mansion. She paused, wondering if he were there, wondering how to get in. She had made no plans. All she knew was that she wanted the drug and wanted to destroy something of value to him—anything that would hurt him. But now that she was here, she had no idea how to proceed.

A woman's laughter startled her. Maman? Nicole? Morag peeped through the shrubbery and the iron gate which created the semi-privacy of the gardens. No, it wasn't either of them but one of the maids—and Botemps!

For a moment, she was shocked. Botemps had seemed so disapproving, so much like those Puritan friends of her father's, but then, she realized, anyone in the service of the Marquis would not be prudish.

Morag breathed a sigh of relief. If Botemps was in the garden with the maid, then the Marquis was obviously not at home. For a few moments more, she watched and waited, glad when Botemps and the woman went toward the house. She had already realized that if she wanted to gain secret entrance, she must climb the gate.

With a hasty glance around, Morag tied her dress up around her waist. Taking a deep breath, she seized the rail. Slowly, painfully, she inched her way up.

After what seemed an age, she peered over the top of the gate. Cautiously, she slipped her leg over—and jumped. Hitting the ground, she rolled over, grimacing and trying not to cry out. Her whole body smarted with the pain. But she must continue—and quickly. The court was coming alive after *petit coucher*. Time was running out.

Standing up, Morag wiped her tears on her torn sleeve. God only knew what Quentin would do if he found her there; she didn't know whom she hated or feared more—the Marquis or Maine.

The silence of the house was nerve-wracking. It seemed to press about her as she slipped quickly inside and upstairs to the drawing room. Quickly, she glanced about, haphazardly throwing open a drawer here and pushing aside a tapestry there. Nothing. The glass reflected a bedraggled image, but she didn't care. She must find that drug. Pausing, she tried to remember where Quentin's room was. It was there, she reasoned, that she was most likely to find what she sought.

The soft Turkish carpet muffled her steps. She kicked off her shoes, trying to soothe the pain in her ankles, and did not bother to pick them up.

The next room, another parlor—this one lined with mirrors—was empty. She glanced about, hearing voices from below. Who was it . . . the servants? She stepped lightly over the threshold. It wouldn't do to be discovered now. The mirrors seemed to shimmer as they reflected the light from the crystal chandeliers.

Her hand touched the door of the next room gingerly. The voices from below seemed to ring in her ears and mingle with the pounding of her blood. This was his room, she thought, seeing the muted greens and browns; it had to be. It was strong and masculine, so different from Maine's bright purples and crimsons.

Fear sat in her stomach like a coiled snake until she dared to exhale and step forward. Her hands trembled as she yanked open the drawers. Nothing. Throwing clothes and books onto the floor savagely, she no longer cared about not making any noise. Not a vial or a powder or a paper. Furious, she picked up a smooth Chinese vase and smashed it against the wall. Perhaps this wasn't his room after all?

Her eyes caught sight of a smooth brown leather case sitting on the bedstand. Her heart jumped to her throat. The drug? Would he keep it there? On second thought, even if it didn't contain the drug, it was obviously something of value to him, something she could destroy.

Her nose sniffed the warm oil of the case. The softness of the material was oddly familiar; her heart pounded as she touched it. Yes, it had to be something of value to him; it was well cared for and obviously treasured.

The gold clasp came apart easily when she found it and the case opened. Her breath caught in her throat, and the case dropped from her hands. She stared down at it. Lying in a bed of red velvet were her father's flintlocks.

Tears came to her eyes as she bent down to retrieve them. These were the dueling pistols he had used, the ones that had misfired on the day of his death. Shaking like a leaf, she picked one up. With the firm weight of the gun in her hand, memories of her father flooded back to her, choking her. *Oh, Papa!* She wiped the tears from her eyes with a dirty sleeve. How had that devil, Quentin Sauvage, come by her father's guns?

The sound of someone treading on a loose board startled her. She turned quickly to see him standing there. She raised the pistol and pointed it at him.

"Hello, Morag." He gave her a questioning look. "What brings you here?" He stepped forward, eyeing the clothes and books which she had tossed about the room. Bending, he picked up a piece of the broken vase, and then stared at the guns in her hand.

"Don't you dare come any closer! These are my father's pistols, and I know how to use them. I shall shoot you if you move." She cocked a pistol, giving him a tremulous smile. "I intend to shoot you anyway."

"Oh?" He stepped closer. His arms hung loose at his sides as he stared at her, trying to assess the situation.

"I said, don't take another step." Her hand shook as she jerked the gun upward, so it pointed toward his head. "Ye're daft for moving, mon!"

"Morag," he held his hand out in a gesture of appeasement, "I am unarmed, and also confused. If you plan to kill me—"he shrugged—"so be it. But I think you owe me the courtesy of an explanation."

"I owe you nothing, you devil! Not after what's happened." She kept the gun pointed at him.

"Morag." His voice was soft. "Very well, *mignonne*, I shan't move."

She took a deep breath and waited.

"Morag, I know those guns are your father's. You

may have them, if you like. Had I known, when Marie Thérèse gave them to me—"

Her hand wavered for an instant. "Maman gave them to you? She gave you my father's pistols? They're mine! Father promised them to me!" Hysteria rose in her voice, getting the better of her. "'Twill go ill wi' ye for lying, mon."

He shrugged. "Ask your mother. That, in fact, was how she and I met."

"What?" Her eyes widened, puzzled.

"*Mignonne*, she lost them to me at cards. They were part payment."

Morag felt the color drain from her face. She realized that he was probably telling the truth. Her mother would do anything for her gaming—even sell Papa's pistols.

"Well, even if that is so, you had no right . . . no reason to—"

"To—what?"

Tears blurred her vision as she struggled to continue to hold the gun straight. "To . . . to ruin me. To ruin . . . my future . . . my plans." She sensed rather than saw him move. "I said, dinna ye move!" Her voice rose. "Ye had no right t'destroy me!"

"Morag, *mignonne*, you exaggerate. I—"

"Nae, I do not." The gun wavered in her hand. "If it hadn't been for you, the Duc du Maine . . ."

"Now, listen to me, my dear girl. If any blame is to be laid for ruining your future, the fault lies with yourself. The wedding plans your mother made are destroyed. You are no longer of any value to the Comte de Lalande. You didn't have to go with Maine when he returned, but I have it that you went quite willingly."

"Willingly!" She choked, then remembered that he knew nothing about Maine's threats.

He had advanced now without her realizing it. One hand rested on the gun, the other on her shoulder. She realized that it was no use fighting him.

She began to cry; her whole body trembled. Her defenses suddenly crumbled and her pert chin sagged. She found that she no longer craved the drug, that all she wanted was the safety and protection of someone's arms, to forget . . . to forget . . .

"Morag, you did go with Maine willingly?"

She bit her lip. Let him think what he wanted. She could not endanger her mother's life. "Aye, of course I did." She wiped her eyes with her sleeve. "You think just because you were the first, you should be the only one." She tried to move away but he stared at her, continuing to hold her.

"My dear little cat, if I had known what a Pandora's box I would open, I would not have tried to save you from Maine and your mother."

"What do you mean?" She stared at him. "Maine and . . . Maman?"

His hands were on her neck now forcing her head up to look into his face. "Hasn't your lover told you?"

She shook her head slowly; her eyes didn't leave his face. "His Grace . . . the Duke said . . ."

"Did he blame me for having a hand in it?"

She swallowed hard. "Aye, he said . . . you gave him the drug that . . . that made me stay with him. I . . . I came today because . . . because—"

"Because you wanted more of it?"

She nodded.

Quentin's eyes narrowed. He brushed a stray curl from her face. "I see. So you wanted to kill me for that?"

Again, swallowing hard, she nodded.

"Yet you went with him willingly that day without the drug. And why did you refuse to see me, *mignonne?* I would have told you the truth, that it was not I who obtained the drug, who gave you to Maine."

She opened her mouth to protest just as someone knocked lightly on the door.

"Come in." Quentin's eyes did not leave her elfin face.

Botemps stepped into the room. "Excuse me, sir, but—" He stopped, seeing Morag. His mouth gaped open like a fish.

"My lord, I didn't know anyone was with you. I . . . " The servant was uneasy. "Sir, I saw you come in alone. If you'll pardon me, how did Mademoiselle Elliot get in?"

Quentin's gaze remained steadily on Morag; he saw her blush. "That is something Mademoiselle and I must discuss, Botemps. Be so good as to bring us some sherry."

Botemps nodded, reddening as he quickly turned to leave. "Very good, my lord."

Quentin waited until he had gone. "How *did* you get in, Morag?"

Pink suffused her face once more. "Over the gate."

"The gate?" The amused twinkle in his eyes made her want to slap him. "You must have been very determined to do that. My gate is the highest in the town." His hand remained on her shoulder; it was impossible for her to move.

Before she could protest, he had pulled her to him, kissing her roughly, then gently—butterfly kisses to her temples, her throat. Unable to resist, she melted into his arms as her fires—for all of Maine's cruelty—refused to be extinguished.

His hand touched her breast ever so lightly, but brushing one of her most recently acquired welts. She jerked away, tears in her eyes. Men! They were all the same!

"*Mignonne*." His voice revealed his concern as he tried to draw her back into his arms. "What is wrong?"

She held him off. "Nothing."

Botemps knocked and entered with the sherry. Quentin nodded toward a small table. "Put it there. I will ring if I need anything else." He stood looking at Morag questioningly until Botemps had left the room again, then he poured her a sherry.

"Here. Drink this."

She gulped it down and then sank to her knees, oblivious of him as she began to cry again. All of it—the wedding plans, Maman, Quentin, the drug, Maine, Papa's guns—all of it accumulated in the pit of her stomach. She continued to sob loudly.

Quentin sank down next to her. His arms went about her protectively and he began to rock her. "Morag," he whispered, his lips brushing her hair. "*Mignonne*, if I hurt you just now, I am sorry."

She shook her head, still sobbing, trying—unsuccessfully—to speak, to explain to him that it was one thing to tolerate a monster like Maine but quite another to realize that she wanted a man—actually wanted him—but was afraid because of the pain, because . . .

"Give me some of the drug," she whispered hoarsely.

"Even if I had it, I'd not give it to you."

Her lips quivered. Tears poured afresh. He held her silently to him, quieting her sobs.

Not until she felt the cool air on her body did she realize that he had undressed her.

"My dear Morag," he whispered, blowing softly into

127

her ear and nibbling the lobe gently. He touched her breast. "I will not hurt you."

He kissed her deeply; she felt both desire and revulsion at his touch.

"You've been hurt, my little cat. I am sorry for that." He stroked her hair, lulling her fears. "But I believe that if you are ever to trust a man again—to experience the joy of love again—you must allow yourself to forget."

"Forget?" She sobbed. "How can I forget? I—"

"Shh. Don't worry about Maine, *mignonne*. He will not harm you again."

"You don't understand." Tears shimmered in her emerald eyes.

"Did he threaten to hurt me? Your mother?"

Sniffling, she nodded, feeling the hairs of his chest against her cheek.

"He won't." Quentin's hand slid gently down her body, inflaming her. "Let me enter you, *mignonne*. I will be kind."

He kissed her again, his hand on her mound. Her nerves peaked with pleasure and excitement, with the acute awarness of their naked bodies. She nodded, closing her eyes tightly so that she would not think of Maine.

"No. Open your eyes, little one. I want you to see my face. I want you to remember me for this moment."

Reluctantly, she did as he asked; his swollen member seared as he eased into her.

For just that second, she gasped, as Maine's pasty face superimposed itself over Quentin's in her mind.

"No!" she cried and tried to roll away from him, but Quentin held her fast. He moved in her, faster and faster, and finally surrender took over as she realized that she could again feel the delight that he had shown her on that first night.

She moaned softly as Quentin kissed her bruised breasts, his tongue teasing her nipples. Their pleasure peaked, meeting her icy fear and melting it. Her passion matched his as he held her, soothed her . . . and brought her to completion.

Chapter Nine

IN THE *CARROSSE,* returning to court, Morag leaned her head against Quentin. She was lost in her thoughts, trying to recapture the pleasure of that afternoon, to forget the pain of the past weeks, to forget her distrust. It all seemed so perfect, so lovely. She could even imagine for that moment that Maine, Nicole and Maman had disappeared, that she and Quentin were the only ones left in the world.

She was amazed at her feelings. Just hours ago, she had hated this man with a passion. Now she would do anything to remain in his arms. Since he was no longer to marry her mother . . .

Then, as Quentin greeted the guard at the palace gate, the thought died. Morag grimaced, realizing that nothing had really changed. Simpleton, she thought, pulling away from him. He was just another man seeking his pleasure. He didn't love her—or he would have told her so. Besides, if it wasn't her mother, then it was Nicole. Morag remembered all too clearly how her cousin had taunted her: she *was* an innocent.

She tried to swallow her tears as she asked, "What . . . what will happen now?"

"Now, *mignonne?*" He glanced quizzically at her. "Now we will take you back to your rooms."

"Just like that?" She was aghast, her worst fears confirmed.

Quentin shrugged. "I shall speak to Maine, of course."

"Oh, of course." The emptiness flooded her like a giant wave, drowning the flicker of hope, leaving her breathless. No, he would never marry her. Her hatred of him rekindled.

They climbed out of the carriage near Maine's rooms. The place was silent. No guard was about, no candles had been lit. Had Maine come and found her gone?

She paused, sucking in her breath. It was past the dinner hour, and he usually came to visit her before then. Fear knotted her stomach. She waited for Quentin to catch up to her, trying to control her trembling.

"I suggest that you go in first, Morag."

"But—"

"Go on. I will follow."

She glared at him. So he was a coward after all! She might have known. Anyone who would take advantage of her defenselessness!

"Ye needn't follow, mon. Morag Elliot can take care o' herself."

"Really?"

"Really." She wet her lips, aware only of the contempt she felt for him.

The door to the delicate ivory boudoir, her prison, was open slightly, but the room was dark. Had she left it that way when she had fled? She thought not, but

if the Swiss guard were still unconscious on the floor
. . . well, she had managed him once, she would again.

At the entrance, she paused. The sweet heavy odor
of Maine's musk perfume haunted the air. No doubt
about it, he had been here. Her heart hammered. What
had he done when he found her gone?

Licking dry lips, Morag stepped into the room,
nearly stumbling over a large object in the middle of
the floor. Something wet touched her as she righted
herself. Cursing, she groped for the candle in the Bac-
carat crystal holder. She lighted it carefully, shielding
it from the draft.

Only then did she glance down. She gasped and
stared. Yes, it had been the Swiss guard she had
tripped over. Morag clutched the candle and bent to
look at him with morbid fascination. His throat had
been cut; the wide mouth of the wound gaped open
like a scream, still oozing blood.

She shut her eyes and backed into a chair, too weak
to stand.

"So you've come back, eh? Where did you go, my
precious?"

Morag's eyes popped open; the old nauseating fear
choked her. Maine sat in the semi-darkness, his thin
legs dangling over the arm of a guilt chair. There was
a glass of red wine in his hand. He put it to his lips as
he smiled at her.

"You . . . you killed him?"

"Don't be concerned, my precious. He was only a
stupid Swiss. There are plenty more where he came
from."

"But . . . you murdered him. Why?" Her mind was
numb. She wanted to stand but she couldn't; she knew
her legs wouldn't hold her.

"Isn't it obvious?" His voice rose an octave. He swung his legs about and stood. "Some wine, Morag?"

She shook her head, chilled with the death about her.

"Well, I shall have another glass. It was deuced boring waiting here for you. Where did you go?"

Morag shook her head, unable to speak.

"Stand up."

Biting her lip, Morag shook her head.

"Stand up, I said."

She shook her head again, dizzily, praying for some way out.

"Henri!"

There was no answer.

"Henri! Where is that blasted man?" Maine strode to the door. Morag forced herself to move toward the window, away from the body. Grasping the window sill desperately, she prayed for someone to pass. She would cry for help. She would not be abused again, not—A sound behind her made her turn.

Henri entered stiffly. Behind him was Quentin, with a sword at the servant's neck.

"I might have known," Maine sneered. "Did you have her today, d'Angeau? No, you needn't answer. That's too bad. You ruined her training. Well," Maine shrugged, "we will just have to begin all over again."

"I think not, Your Grace."

Quentin jabbed Henri with the sword, at the same time tightening his left arm about the man's thick neck.

"Please, Your Grace." Henri wheezed.

Maine snorted. "You think I care about him, d'Angeau? Kill him, if you wish."

He crossed the room quickly to Morag before she could move. His hand tore the green gown from her

133

body, ripping it down the center, exposing her white skin and pink-tipped breasts.

"Morag Elliot is mine. Bought and paid for until I tire of her. I can get another servant easily." He glanced at Quentin and saw the Marquis' jaw tighten.

"Leave the girl alone," Quentin pressed the sword tip into Henri's neck, drawing blood.

"Please, Your Grace," the dwarf begged.

"Very well, d'Angeau, I will fight you for her."

"No!" Morag cried.

"D'Angeau?"

Quentin nodded, releasing Henri, who fell to the ground at Maine's feet.

Maine kicked him. "Get up, you lout. Fetch my sword."

The servant ran from the room.

"We fight 'til the death, eh, d'Angeau? Winner takes Mademoiselle Elliott. Agreed?"

Grimly, Quentin nodded, as Henri returned with his master's foil.

"Not that, you dunce! My rapier—the thin one." He grinned, licking lips with enjoyment. "I intend to run d'Angeau through, not once but a dozen times."

Quentin shrugged and threw his coat over to Morag. "Put that on, *mignonne*. I don't want to be distracted during the fight."

Morag slipped into the black jerkin, tying it with trembling fingers. She wanted to plead with them to stop. It wasn't that she especially cared about either man, but she hated the idea of blood being shed over her. The death of the Swiss guard was quite enough.

"I trust you'll not object if I leave the country after your death, Maine." Quentin tapped his blade on his wrist, testing it. "I would hate to languish in the Bastille for shedding your blood."

Maine laughed sharply. "You'll not go anywhere but to the grave. However, seeing that you are one of Papa's favorites, no doubt I had better think about a journey of a few days or so." He took the rapier from Henri and immediately lunged, catching Quentin off-guard.

D'Angeau sprang back quickly, his own sword now in place. He had no illusions about his adversary: Maine was out for blood and would use every conceivable trick.

The pair danced about the room, jumping over the dead Swiss, over the furniture, their swords clashing loudly.

"Your footwork is excellent, d'Angeau," Maine commented, trying to back his opponent into a corner. "Better than one would expect from a heathen." He lunged again, and took Quentin's parry as their swords hit each other with a deafening clang.

Morag watched, her heart in her mouth. Her eyes widened with alarm as Maine seemed to score a coup; she saw the silver steel flash through Quentin's vest.

But the Marquis responded with a circular parry, throwing Maine off balance for a moment.

The pair were moving faster now. The clash of swords seemed to echo Morag's heartbeat.

"You are an excellent adversary," Quentin complimented as Maine leaped forward, barely missing him. "I regret that I will have to kill you." He thrust forward and missed, but quickly regained his balance.

Morag followed each movement as the men climbed onto the bed. The mattress sagged, crying out with their weight. Quentin bounded off, alighting between the bed and the chair as Maine slashed the curtain behind him to ribbons. They were near her now. Morag tried to back away but there seemed to be nowhere to go. Holding her breath, she squeezed around the huge bed.

Even to her inexperienced eye, Maine seemed to be tiring. Quentin apparently saw it too. Wishing to end the affair quickly, he made a terrible lunge at Maine, who parried his thrust and glided like a serpent under Quentin's blade, the point of his sword touching the Marquis' neck. Disgusted with himself, Quentin dropped his weapon.

"You are at my mercy now, d'Angeau. Shall I kill you?"

Quentin's eyes narrowed. "If you expect me to plead for my life, Maine, you're mistaken."

"Am I?" The blade cut Quentin's skin, drawing blood.

Not a muscle moved in the Marquis' face, but Morag screamed.

The sound distracted Maine just for that necessary second; Quentin's knee came up and out, catching the Duke in the groin.

The Duke howled with pain, doubling up as Quentin grabbed his sword again. Morag crossed herself, as the fight continued.

But Quentin's blow had defeated Maine. Within moments, he was at the Marquis' mercy, pinned to the bed, his flowered waistcoat falling open.

"It's not fair," Maine whined. "I would have had you just now but for her. It's not fair."

"I'll let you up on condition that you leave Morag alone."

"So you can have her?"

"No, so she can choose her own lovers—in her own time."

"I want another fight. I want—"

136

Quentin pressed his sword tip none too gently into Maine's skin. The young Duke squirmed.

"Oh, very well. I shall leave her alone—if you do."

"Agreed." Quentin sheathed his sword.

Glaring at him, Maine stood. "Henri! Where the devil are you?"

The dwarf hurried forward to brush the dust off his master's jerkin and coat. "I hope you're satisfied," Maine screeched at him, his voice higher than ever. "Do you see what I've given up for you? Now you must find me another virgin to train. You must—"

"Yes, Your Grace. Of course, Your Grace," Henri said, dancing about him.

At the door, Maine turned to Morag. "I trust you won't mind leaving the rooms tonight. Your Maman, I'm sure, will welcome your company."

Morag flushed and nodded.

"Well, d'Angeau, are you coming? You said you'd not have her either."

"No, Maine, I won't have her, but—if you don't object—I would like to see her safely to her mother's."

Maine frowned. "Oh, very well. Henri!"

"Yes, Your Grace?"

Maine jabbed his toe into the body of the Swiss guard. "Remove him!" With that, he left the room.

Leaving her to change her dress and gather her things together, Quentin went off to order a sedan chair for Morag. She was glad of that; it was only a short distance to Maman's rooms—just across the courtyard—but after all that had happened, Morag didn't think she could walk.

Within moments, the chair stopped. Quentin got out, but Morag hesitated. She was sure Maman would hate her—for having been with Quentin, for having gone with Maine, for everything that had happened.

"Come, *mignonne*." Quentin took her hand. "It is time you saw your mother."

She swallowed hard. "Please . . . mayn't I stay with you this night? I—" She hated herself for pleading with him.

"No, Morag, not this night."

"Oh, I see. You have other company this evening." She fought back tears and saw him smile at her through her blurred vision. God's death, she hated him! Well, the Devil take him! Clenching her fist, she scrambled out of the chair. "Well, go on, then. Go back to your mistress! I don't need you. I'm not afraid of my mother—I'm not afraid of anyone!" She pushed past him and ran to her mother's rooms.

Marie Thérèse was sitting at her dressing table, watching Elise in the mirror as the maid fixed her hair. The candles in the clay sticks flickered with the breeze as the door opened.

"*Mon Dieu!* Morag" She jumped up, embracing her daughter. "So, now you are a woman, you have come to see your old Maman. You come to tell me how much you enjoy life? Yes?"

"Enjoy . . . life?"

Marie Thérèse flicked the lace of her wrist. "Life or love, whatever you wish to call it. It is a lovely experience, is it not?"

Morag stared at her mother coldly, realizing that what Maine and Quentin had said was true. "No, it is not lovely."

"*Mon coeur*, you disappoint me. Well, never mind, it will get better. Is the Duke at cards tonight?"

"I really don't know, Maman." She slipped from her mother's arms and sank down on the feather bed.

"Well, we'll have a visit for a moment. Jean Baptiste—"

"Are you seeing him tonight?"

"Tonight? Yes, I see Jean Baptiste tonight and most nights."

"And what of the Marquis d'Angeau?" Morag swallowed hard. "Have you lost all love for him?"

Marie Thérèse shrugged. "He is otherwise occupied. But do not worry, my heart. He will come back to me. Variety is the spice of life." She stared at her daughter a moment. Morag continued to keep her eyes averted, watching the movement of the curtains in the evening breeze.

Marie returned to her chair, motioning for Elise to continue dressing her hair. "I'm sorry that you do not enjoy yourself, my pet."

"Are you?" Morag's head jerked around and her voice raised. "Maman, how was it that Maine and I were left alone in that room?"

"Why, it was part of the plan." Marie Thérèse adjusted the strap of her gown. In the mirror she saw Morag's shocked face. "Oh, my dearest heart, surely you do not hold that against me? I tell you, it will get better very shortly. I am confident."

"Did you go to the chemist's that day while I was at the dressmaker's?"

Marie Thérèse shrugged. "Dearest, you were quite nervous. Maine suggested that you would need something . . ."

"And so you obliged him. How much did you owe him, Maman?"

Marie Thérèse flushed. "That is not fair, Morag. I did it for you, for your future. He promised me that once he tired of you, he would arrange a good marriage."

"Yet my going with him destroyed the marriage plans you had already made for me."

"Pshaw!" Marie Thérèse flicked her wrist lace again as she tossed a curl over her shoulder. "The Comte's son was not good enough for you. Now that you have been with the Duc du Maine—"

Morag sank down on the bed again. Her head throbbed. "Oh, Maman!" Tears stained her face.

Marie Thérèse went to her daughter, putting her arms about the slender trembling shoulders. "Do not take on so, pet. It would have come sooner or later. It—"

"I am no longer with Maine, Maman." Morag's voice was husky with emotion. "He has asked me to leave his rooms." She wiped her eyes on her sleeve.

"Oh, Morag, what did you do? I knew you would ruin it! That is why I gave you the drug."

"It was not I who ruined it." Morag's voice rose to a hysterical pitch.

"No?"

Morag remembered then that her mother knew nothing about her and Quentin.

"Morag, my pet, tell me. What happened? I must know. I must—"

"You must do nothing, Maman. Nothing happened. We did not suit each other." There was a sour taste in Morag's mouth. She fingered the bedspread nervously.

"Oh, bosh! What is there to suit? Maine is a man and you are a woman. It just needs more time."

"No, Maman. There is to be no more time. He . . . tired of me."

Marie Thérèse stared at her a moment and then shrugged. "Ah, well, such is life. Did he say anything about setting you up with another man?"

Morag was tight-lipped. "He said nothing, Maman."

"Well, then, I shall have to speak to him. He cannot make promises and then throw my daughter off as if she were spoiled meat."

"No! You'll not speak to him!"

Marie Thérèse glanced questioningly at her. "Morag, you are not—no, it hasn't been a month. You wouldn't know yet even if you were. Well, tomorrow, we will go to Paris. I will get something from Madame le Blanc. We must see that your union has no fruit."

Morag nodded stiffly. She had never thought of that. To have a baby! Would it be Maine's or Quentin's? It did not matter. She did not want either man's child.

"Maman, I am . . . sorry . . ." she sniffled. "What will happen to me now, Maman?"

Marie Thérèse patted her daughter's head. "I will consider that in the morning. Meanwhile, I must be prepared when Jean Baptiste comes." She took up her shawl. "I should not worry though, love. Now that you are experienced, we shall easily find a man who will appreciate your charms."

Chapter Ten

THE POTION MAMAN obtained from Madame Le Blanc made Morag ill, but it was just as well. She wanted to see no one and was content to remain in the rooms. Even after she had recovered though, Morag was reluctant to venture forth. After all that had happened, not even the loveliness of the spring flowers could lure her out.

Two weeks after her daughter's return to her rooms, Marie Thérèse burst in on her with shining eyes. "I have done it, *mon coeur!*"

"What have you done, Maman?" Morag asked, looking up from the book on her lap. Fear began to creep up from her stomach, chilling her arms so that the hairs stood on end. Had Maman arranged another marriage for her? Her hands trembled as she put her book down.

"I have Quentin back—I have won him."

"Won him?"

"From your cousin. We are to be married next week. Are you not pleased?"

Morag gripped her chair, trying to hide her shock. "Yes, Maman. Of course I am pleased. It's only that . . ."

Her mind went blank. Now, of all times, she must not tell Maman what had happened between her and Quentin. Her anger rose. God's death, she hated that devil! The audacity of the man—to marry her mother after—But she had only been a toy to him. Swallowing her anger, she tried to smile, but her mother saw that something was wrong.

"What is it, Morag, my pet?"

Anger and disgust drained from her then. Quentin was what her mother wanted. At least, if they were married, Maman would not be so concerned with her future, so anxious to find her a husband or a wealthy lover.

" 'Tis nothing, Maman. I wish you the greatest happiness." Morag rose and embraced her mother, wishing that she really meant what she said.

"Thank you, my love." Marie Thérèse kissed her. "Quentin asked about you, you know."

"Did he now?" *Bastard!*

Marie Thérèse put her arm about her daughter. "Tonight you will come to the concerts with us. We will all celebrate."

"I don't wish to go."

"Pet! I thought you had got over that childish resentment."

"Well, I haven't."

"Then why were you so upset when Quentin and I broke off our engagement?"

"Because . . ." She groped for words but could not

143

find them. "Oh, very well. I will come with you to-night."

"Good. Now," Marie Thérèse pulled the cord for the maid, "we will have something to eat, *mon coeur,* and I will tell you how I beat your cousin at her own game."

That afternoon, unable to bear the silence of the rooms while her mother slept, Morag slipped out. She remembered the last time she had gone to the menagerie in the afternoon, but she doubted that she would see Quentin there today. Anyway, it didn't matter. She had to see the animals, had to say goodbye to them; Morag had decided that once her mother was married next week, she would leave court.

She would return to England, to her father's people. Perhaps there, where no one knew of her past, she could join a convent. King James was still in Ireland. There were always troops and supplies being sent over. Somehow, she would find a way to cross the channel. Even if she had to go to Ireland first, she would get to England.

Hearing her name called, Morag paused and turned to see Nicole approaching.

"Going to meet your lover, Morag?"

Morag flushed. "I am going to see the animals."

"A likely story!" Nicole's eyes narrowed. "You know that he's not going to stay with your mother, no matter what he might say."

"Who?"

"Don't be daft, Scots girl." Her cousin tried to mimic Morag's accent. "I'm speaking of Quentin Adam Sauvage. He told me himself that he is marrying her only because of the money."

144

THIS BITTER ECSTASY

Nicole laughed savagely. "It seems that your mother finally got lucky at cards. She beat Quentin at *hoca* twice running. He owed her ten thousand *pistoles.*"

"So? He has money. Why didn't he just pay?"

Nicole shrugged. "All I know is that he is marrying your mother because of it, but if you think he'll remain with her long—"

"Of course he will."

Nicole's eyes seemed to dance with the sunlight. "What a simple fool you are. Quentin Adam Sauvage loves me. He will continue to sleep with me no matter whom he marries."

"I don't believe you."

"No? Ask him. I spent the night with him before your maman came to gamble."

She smiled. "When your mother had gone, I slipped back into his bed. He's magnificent. But then, I believe you know . . .?"

Morag was aghast. She recalled the night of her first "experience." He must have gone to Nicole right after that too.

Laughing, Nicole ran from her toward the woods. Morag stood looking after her, clenching her fist. She had no doubt that it was Quentin her cousin was hurrying to meet. Perhaps she should return to her mother and ask for the truth. But . . . how did her cousin know of the marriage, when it hadn't been announced yet?

Morag turned away from the path to the menagerie. The best place for her now was the chapel. She would confess her sins and her fears to Pére de Choise. The King's confessor had expressed a fondness for her. If she talked with him, she would no doubt feel better.

But Morag's confessor disappointed her. Instead of

145

encouraging her to go on hoping for a convent life, he told her that she must direct her thoughts now toward marriage.

"It is the role of woman, my child."

Morag protested and left the confessor's cubicle. Somehow, somewhere she would find safety.

Marie Thérèse awoke and stretched, hearing the knock on her door.

"Yes. Who is it?" She pulled her robe about her.

"It's me, Aunt Elliott. I must speak to you."

Marie Thérèse frowned. "What do you wish to speak about, Nicole?"

"Your marriage," the girl answered. "I cannot talk through a closed door."

Marie Thérèse tied the robe and quickly brushed her hair. The chit was probably jealous. Probably she would tell of her affair with Quentin—not that it didn't bother Marie, but she most certainly would not let her brother's daughter see that.

"Aunt Elliott . . .?"

"Yes, Nicole, I am coming. One moment." Marie sighed and sipped some wine to fortify herself before she opened the door.

Nicole Le Martin looked the picture of innocence: her blonde curls piled about her head, her blue eyes shining, the lace of her high-necked gown perfectly ruffled against her smooth skin.

"Hello, Aunt Elliot."

Marie Thérèse frowned. "Call me Marie, Nicole, please."

"Oh, I am sorry, Aunt . . . Marie." The girl smiled. "Yes, I guess being reminded of your age and of the fact that you are my aunt when we have shared the same lover *would* make you feel rather strange.''

Marie Thérèse pressed her lips together, trying not to lose her temper. She moved back to the lounge and sat down.

Nicole's eyes widened. ''Doesn't it bother you, Marie, that Quentin prefers my younger, firmer body to yours?''

''You don't know that he does.'' Marie's nostrils flared. Her hands trembled as she poured some more wine.

''Oh, but I do know.'' Nicole watched her aunt intently. ''Here—'' She leaned over, taking the decanter from her. ''Let me do that.''

The pair of them struggled silently for the glass, unitl Marie Thérèse finally released it. What did it matter; let the child pour.

Nicole smiled. ''I believe I'll have some too.'' She glanced about. ''Have you another glass?''

Marie Thérèse began to rise.

''No. Sit. I'll get it. You need your strength.''

''I'm not decrepit yet, Nicole!'' Marie snapped.

''No.'' The girl laughed. ''Not yet. Still,'' her back was to Marie Thérèse, ''did you know you have another rival . . . besides me, I mean?'' Nicole turned, handing her aunt a full glass of wine.

''Oh?'' Marie's tight grip on the stem of the glass betrayed her feelings.

''Yes, you do . . . *we* do.''

Marie Thérèse forced herself to smile, showing Nicole that she didn't believe her. Sniffing the wine, she inhaled and sipped.

''Your daughter.''

Marie Thérèse nearly choked on the wine. She began to cough.

"Careful, Aunt." Nicole seized the glass and patted her aunt on the back. "You don't believe me, do you?"

Marie Thérèse stared at her.

"Here. Take your wine, but drink it slowly this time, Aunt." Nicole handed back the glass and picked up her own again. "It's true. Haven't you noticed the way she looks at him?"

"Don't be ridiculous, Nicole. Let's be honest. We two are the only immediate contenders for Quentin's interest, and of the pair of us, it's obvious that he prefers me."

"Is it?" Nicole's voice had risen slightly. "We both know that he's marrying you only because of the money. That if you hadn't ruined him with your gaming when you were first engaged—"

"Oh, bosh!"

Nicole stood and refilled her aunt's glass as well as her own.

"Anyway, that's not what I'm here about now. Why do you think Maine dropped Morag?"

Marie Thérèse shrugged and took an unladylike gulp of her wine.

"He didn't tire of her, as she probably told you."

"Then why . . .?"

"He and Quentin dueled over her. She had been sleeping with our lover. They both wanted her."

Marie Thérèse stood, suddenly feeling the effect of the wine. "I don't believe you!"

"It's true," Nicole said, watching her closely.

"But . . . why, then, is he marrying me?"

"I'd say because he wants to be near her. She won't have him, so—"

"What rot!" Marie Thérèse shook her head slightly, trying to clear her brain and her blurred vision.

"It's not, Aunt. Anyway it doesn't matter."

148

"Why not?" Marie Thérèse became aware of a strange numbness creeping up her legs, her arms. She sank back onto the lounge and tried to focus on her niece.

"Because he isn't going to marry you."

"What?" Marie Thérèse blinked her eyes and shook her head in confusion. "What did you say?"

"I said," Nicole bent and kissed her aunt's forehead, "that you are getting too old, dear Aunt. In fact, you are aging by the minute. He will never marry you, Marie Thérèse Le Martin."

"Elliot! My name is Elliot!" Marie Thérèse cried.

"Is it? Did you really marry Uncle Andrew?"

Marie Thérèse's eyes were wide with terror. Her blood seemed to rush through her body like a tidal wave, yet she could no longer feel her hands, could not speak.

"My cousin is a bastard, isn't she? That's why you're in such a hurry to marry her off. That's why you daren't return to England."

Marie Thérèse could only whisper: "The . . . wine. You . . . put—"

"Oh, do you want more wine?" Nicole poured her aunt another glass, but Marie Thérèse's hand could not hold it. The goblet crashed to the floor, splattering its contents over the white wool carpet, staining it.

"Dear me, look at that." Nicole clapped her hands to her mouth. "Oh, Aunt, I am sorry . . . truly I am. But, you see, I am going to marry the Marquis d'Angeau, not you."

Marie Thérèse could only stare at her niece as the girl moved toward the door.

"Don't worry." Nicole paused. "The discomfort won't last much longer. I'll give your love to Papa when I see him. Oh, and don't worry about your daughter, either. I'll see that she's well taken care of.''

The door slammed behind her.

Tears welled up in Marie Thérèse's eyes and rolled down her cheeks as she sat there helpless. It was all her fault. Oh, poor Morag. Poor, poor Morag . . . .

Chapter Eleven

AT HER MOTHER'S graveside, Morag felt numb. Everyone said that Maman had poisoned herself because of d'Angeau. No one believed Morag when she said that Quentin and her mother were about to marry. Even Nicole denied any knowledge of it. The Marquis himself was not there to say yea or nay.

With a sick feeling, Morag felt the dull drizzle of rain on her face. Only *he* could have wanted her mother dead. The lout hadn't even stayed around for Maman's funeral.

Nauseated, Morag remembered how she had fled to d'Angeau's mansion after finding her mother's body, only to learn from Botemps that the house was being closed. The Marquis had suddenly been commanded by the King to join his uncle's forces in Ireland. William had been crowned King of England in a mock ceremony, and every effort was to be made to assist James. Botemps himself was returning to his family outside Rouen. The Marquis would be supplied with another servant in Dublin.

"But he . . . he was to marry—" She stopped. "When . . . when did he learn of this command?"

"Why, only this morning, Mademoiselle. I believe he saw your mother just after."

The bile rose in her throat as the nasty taste of suspicion grew. "Yes . . . I believe he did." She turned on her heel, leaving Botemps gazing after her in bewilderment.

Morag sought out her confessor again. Without revealing her suspicions, she told him of her sorrow. It was he who arranged for the funeral.

Morag had expected her cousin to gloat; instead Nicole sympathetically had invited Morag to stay with her.

"After all, Cousin, I am sure you would not want so many reminders of your mother about you. Besides, you'll have to vacate the rooms anyway, now that the Marquis has gone off."

Morag nodded. "Will he die in Ireland, do you think?"

Nicole's eyes widened. "You sound as if you hope he will."

"I do. He killed my mother."

"You *saw* him kill your mother?" Nicole inhaled sharply.

"Not actually do it, but—" Morag flushed. "Well, he left court just after, didn't he? He must have wanted to avoid something."

Nicole nodded. "Yes. You're probably right, dear heart. It is a good thing for both of us that we did not get too involved with that man." She put her arms about her cousin. "I will probably be leaving court myself shortly, but you are welcome to stay with me until you can find yourself a protector."

Morag shuddered. She didn't want a . . . protector.

She didn't even want to leave her mother's rooms, but she knew that—alone as she was—she would have to do something.

"Thank you, Nicole. It seems I have misjudged you."

The days passed, one blurred into another. For two weeks after her mother's death, Morag continued to sleep poorly, to grieve.

Lying awake on the cot in Nicole's rooms, she listened to the sound of the court. She wanted to participate, to forget everything, yet just being at the gaming, at the concerts, made her remember. She knew that she would soon have to find another place to stay— Nicole had made it clear again only this evening that she wanted privacy for entertaining. Actually, the arrangement was uncomfortable for both of them. With the Marquis gone, her cousin had taken up with not only the Comte Lelande but his son as well! Morag was amazed at Nicole's choice of men and said so, but the girl had just smiled and said: "The pleasure is the same, all the same, dear Cousin. Handsome face or not, all that matters is what is below. Besides, the Count gives me nice things. They both do."

It wasn't even dark yet. Realizing that she would never be able to sleep until she had come to some decision, Morag rose from the cot and dressed in a striped silk riding costume. A ride would help her sort things out; at least, it always had in the past.

At the stable, she saw that both of Quentin's horses were gone. It was just as well; she wouldn't have wanted to ride either of them anyway. Glancing about, she selected a mount which Louis kept for his guests. The King, she was sure, would not mind if she borrowed it, since almost everyone was at the gaming tonight. Besides, she had ridden the animal before. Mounting the horse, she trotted down the forest path.

Morag gave the horse his head. The ground was slippery from the recent rains, but the animal was steady. Bypassing town, they re-entered the forest. Morag didn't really know where the horse was going. She thought she knew all the possible paths about the palace, yet these woods did not look familiar. Well, what did it matter, as long as she found some place to be alone to think.

She had only five hundred crowns to her name, scarcely enough to rent a room in the overpriced town, let alone make her way to the coast. She would need quite a bit more to book passage for England, especially with a war going on.

The horse paused at the edge of a clearing overshadowed by giant firs. Morag felt her skin prickle; she stared at the huge boulder in the center of the clearing. Just where was she? The green lichen on the rock seemed to stand out ominously. She didn't know why she should feel so frightened. Perhaps it was because everything was so quiet. Morag could hear no birds, no rustle of animals in the undergrowth, no breath of wind in the trees. Or perhaps it was because the horse refused to budge.

Dismounting, she tried to encourage the animal to move across the clearing; the path continued on the other side. The horse would not stir. Frustrated, she glanced again at the rock. Chills prickled her skin and her heart was beating fast. This was ridiculous. It was an ordinary rock. Yet the flesh continued to creep on her upper arms and neck.

Fighting her fear, she took a step forward. The horse pulled back. Nerves tense, Morag looped the bridle over a tree branch and boldy crossed the clearing to the giant stone. The horse snorted, pawing the ground, as Morag inched closer to the rock. It was larger than she had thought. Standing beside it, she saw a hollow in the center that formed a natural water basin. Something glittered in the pool of rainwater.

A chill passed through Morag. It was a ring, a ring of onyx and gold fleur-de-lis . . . like the one Quentin Sauvage wore, like the one the fortune teller had described.

Her mouth dry, Morag stretched out her hand to pick it up, but recoiled almost instantly and glanced about. She had the feeling of being watched—watched by someone evil—but no one was about.

Steeling herself, she plunged her hand into the water. There were two items in the slimy basin. Morag could barely control the sickness which rose in her throat. There was the ring and . . . there was her mother's locket. Both items were covered by a brown slime that could only be dried blood.

Unable to control herself now, Morag turned away, throwing the ring and locket on the ground, seeing the locket chain curl about the ring. The blood drained from Morag's face, and she realized that she could stay there no longer.

Dizzily, she began to run . . . only to find herself falling. In that moment, sprawled on the ground near the boulder, Morag had a flash of insight. She saw Quentin Adam Sauvage, naked, walking about the boulder, praying to his native gods. What else did she need to know?

With a force beyond her usual power, Morag propelled herself up and forward. Grabbing the horse's bridle, she dragged the animal after her and ran from the clearing, stumbling over roots and stones. Only when she reached the familiar stream, did she pause. Gasping for breath, taking great gulps of air, she realized that she should have taken her mother's locket. Well, she would not go back there now.

Remounting the horse, she vowed that her mother's death would not go unavenged. There was only one person who could manage that, who hated Quentin as much as she did . . . Louis Auguste, Duc du Maine.

By the time she had reached Nicole's rooms again, Morag was calmer. She dressed with care, dousing herself liberally with Maine's favorite scent, staring grimly into the mirror at the silver tissue dress. Yes, tonight she would go to the Duke and make the arrangements with him. What happened to her wouldn't matter, as long as that devil suffered. Yes, then she would be happy. Oh, yes, she thought as the maid fixed her hair, then she would be happy indeed.

With one last glance in the mirror, she gulped down her glass of wine and turned away.

Morag realized that Maine was probably already at the amusements. If she wanted to speak to him, she would have to seek him out there. She hadn't been to the gaming since Maman's death, but she knew that if she didn't find Maine that evening, her courage would fail. She walked quickly toward the card room. The mock tournament had ended but, knowing Maine, she was sure he would be gambling the evening long. She wondered whom he played with now that Marie Thérèse was gone . . .

Anguish stabbed her heart. Her mother would be avenged—no matter what it cost her.

Her stomach tightened with sick apprehension as she entered the brightly-lit rooms, searching for the

Duke. What if he refused her? But, of course, he wouldn't. After all that had happened, he must hate d'Angeau as much as she did.

Resolutely, she jerked her head up, looking like a small defiant candle, her hair the color of flame as the multitude of lights played on it. She had seen the Duc du Maine now, and knew from the way his eyes glazed over that he had seen her.

Forcing herself to smile, she approached him as he dealt for himself and three others. "Good evening, Your Grace."

He turned; his thin lips curled upward briefly and he nodded.

She swallowed hard. He wasn't making this easy for her. "I . . . I must speak with you."

"Oh?" He glanced at Henri, who immediately brought over a box of snuff. The servant ogled her openly and Morag flushed.

"Yes, Morag?" Maine yawned and continued to deal. "What did you want?" His painted face seemed to shimmer in the candlelight.

"To . . . to talk. I—"

"You know I made a promise—" he turned his head toward her briefly—"that I dare not break."

"But," she flushed, "he can't hold you to it now. He . . . he isn't here."

Maine's lip curled slightly. "Is that so?" He pulled in the coins he had won and glanced again at Henri, who nodded slightly. Surely, Morag thought, he had known of d'Angeau's departure? After all, it was already two weeks.

"What did you wish to speak to me about, Morag?"

She was uncomfortably aware that the others seated at the table were listening avidly. "If you please, I must speak to you alone, Your Grace."

157

To her relief—and surprise—he swept his hand over the table, clearing the other players away. It seemed they knew Maine's reputation and did not protest. If he wanted to be alone, then it was best to leave him alone.

Morag remained standing until Maine motioned for her to sit.

"Some wine?"

She shook her head.

He smirked. "It's not drugged, my precious. After all, you came to me of your own accord tonight."

Morag pursed her lips then, and nodded. She took the glass he handed her and sipped slowly.

"It's good."

"I know it's good. It's my private stock. What is it you want, Morag? Do you miss our little romps, eh?" He laughed, his thin lips a red slash in his white-painted face.

"No . . . I mean . . . yes, of course, I do." She pushed herself up in the chair, trying to appear interested. "But that isn't why I wanted to speak with you."

"No?" He filled her glass again.

Morag drank, knowing she needed the false courage.

"We have a mutual problem. Someone . . . someone we both dislike."

"Is that so?"

Morag nodded. She gulped down more of the wine, feeling a heady glow.

"Yes. It's so . . . the Marquis D'Angeau."

"Oh, come now, Morag." He motioned Henri over and took a pinch of snuff in each nostril. "If you hate the fellow so much, why did you run to him?"

Morag closed her eyes against the memory of finding her father's pistols. She clenched her fist, remembering how the devil Sauvage had taken advantage of her weakness. "Because . . . because I wanted to speak to him."

"But you did more than speak to him, my precious, eh?" Maine's face loomed so close to hers that she could smell the stale wine on his breath.

"I . . . I want him to suffer for . . . for what he did."

"Do you now?" Maine idly picked up a card, a knave of hearts. He crushed it, folding it about his bony index finger.

"What do you say, Henri? Can we oblige Mademoiselle Elliot?"

Henri giggled. "We can, Your Grace. Indeed, I think we can."

Maine nodded, his attention on Morag's heaving white breasts, which peaked above the silver tissue gown.

"It will cost you, of course, my dear."

She refused to meet his gaze until his hand touched her knee. Then, licking dry lips, Morag lifted her green eyes to his. "I would think, after the insult you suffered, you would be most happy to comply with my wishes, Your Grace." She was amazed at how firm her own voice was.

"Oh, I am. I am. But murder is a serious business." He shrugged. "What will you pay, Morag?"

Her eyes were steady now. "You know that I've nothing to pay you with."

"Oh, but you do." He took her slender hand, kissing her wrist, chilling her to the marrow.

"It is you who will have to pay for that, Your Grace."

"What?" He stared at her.

She spoke firmly now, her green eyes flashing. "Indeed, you never paid Maman for me, did you?"

Maine's mouth sagged open.

"I will agree to be your mistress again if you make d'Angeau suffer, and if you pay me five hundred *pistoles* for each time you . . . use me." There, she had said it. Relief flooded her as she saw Maine smile.

"Two hundred."

"Five hundred, or I find someone else. The Marquis has other enemies at court."

"True, true," Maine nodded, "but none with my connections." His thin nail stroked her arm to her elbow. "You drive a hard bargain. Very well, my precious, five hundred it is. We begin tonight, yes?"

Morag took a deep breath then and nodded. "Very well. Tonight. When . . . when will I know about . . . d'Angeau?"

Maine glanced to Henri. "Your lover will be dead within three months, my precious."

The scent of his sweet perfume was making her sick. Swallowing hard, she said, "Then I will stay with you for three months."

160

Chapter Twelve

A DEAFENING ROAR arose from the Paris streets as thousands of Frenchmen lit bonfires and cheered. Rag dummies hung in the square, crude likenesses of William III about to be burned in effigy.

Morag watched the scene in amazement from the window in the relative safety of Maine's plum silk drawing room. Turning, she stared into the ivory painting of the Chinese vase. The smooth glaze reminded her of King Louis' garden house, with its colored porcelain tiles lining the windows and its constantly chirping caged bird.

She sat down gingerly on the Chinese brocade lounge. Thank goodness the three months with Maine were almost up, and she sould soon be free.

She hadn't heard about Quentin's death yet, but she imagined she would shortly. At least on that score, Maine could be trusted, since his hatred of the Marquis matched hers.

Morag closed her eyes. Blocking out the cries of the crowd in the streets below, she mentally counted her money. Maine had been honest with that too. He had given her the five hundred she had asked each time he had used her and now she had ten thousand *pistoles* of her own. The humiliation she had endured made her sick. But, in less than a week, she would be free to find some way across to England, to her father's family.

A light knock on the door startled her. Morag sat up straight, heart pounding. She never knew when Maine would come . . . or what he would demand.

"Yes?" Her voice trembled.

The maid, Michelle, walked in.

"Yes, what is it?" Morag winced at the way the girl looked at her.

The girl grinned, sensing Morag's discomfort. "There is a woman, a beautiful woman, to see you."

"Who?"

"She says she is yer cousin."

"Nicole!'"

"*Oui*. Shall I show her in?"

Morag nodded. She hadn't seen Nicole since the day she had left her cousin's rooms, the day she had found the ring and the locket in the woods and known what she must do.

Nervously, she stood and walked toward the window as another cheer went up from the crowd. Whatever Nicole wanted, it must be important for her cousin to have ventured out into the streets today. Morag pursed her lips; her instincts told her that Nicole Le Martin's visit had something to do with Quentin.

Nicole burst into the room, her yellow curls bouncing. "*Mon Dieu!* What a crush! Phew!" She held her nose. "I cannot see why the fools should be so happy about William's death. James is a fool."

"Don't say that! My father died for him." Morag took a step toward her.

Nicole shrugged. "The English King is a fool, and so are you, Cousin."

Morag blinked. "Why do you say that? Why am I a fool?"

Nicole laughed. "Because you are here." She waved her hand and glanced about Maine's luxurious drawing room.

"If you mean because the Duke is about to be married—"

Nicole laughed again and Morag gritted her teeth. "No, dear Cousin, no one expects Maine—or any other man at court—to be a faithful husband. No, you are a fool, dear little Cousin, because you allow Maine to dupe you. He is taking advantage of you."

Morag tightened her grip on her fan. "If you mean my being with him—"

"I mean your *bargain* with him. Why do you think Quentin suddenly received a call to Ireland?"

Morag inhaled sharply. So Nicole did know . . . and then she realized what her cousin was implying. "But Maine didn't know he had gone! He . . . he said so."

Nicole gazed at her contemptuously. "And you believed him? You *are* an innocent! My dearest Cousin, not only did Maine send Quentin to Ireland, but he arranged for the ship to blow up at sea as well—" Morag's mouth dropped open. "—before you came to him with your little proposition."

Morag swallowed hard. "Why are you telling me this now?"

Nicole shrugged and strolled to the window. "Quentin escaped Maine's plot to kill him."

"He did?" Morag's heartbeat quickened.

"You're not disappointed, Cousin?" Nicole glanced at her shrewdly.

"Yes . . . no . . . well, I—"

"Well, it doesn't matter. I've just learned that Quentin is still with James. I'm going to Ireland to warn him."

"Warn him about what?"

"Oh, come. You don't think Maine is satisfied? Now that he knows the man is still alive, he's made other plans. Henri's to carry them out."

"But—"

"That dwarf hasn't been around the past week or so, has he?"

Morag shook her head. What Nicole said was true. She stood suddenly. "Let me go with you to Ireland."

"Why? So you can warn Henri? No, Cousin, you are at fault here!" Nicole turned swiftly and walked to the door. "Just tell me, Morag, why did you want d'Angeau murdered?"

She blanched; her green eyes seemed even greener in her pale skin. "I . . . I . . . I only wanted him to suffer for Maman's death. I . . ."

"*Mon Dieu*, Morag, you stupid child! Do you really think Quentin murdered your mother? The fool was going to marry her."

"But you . . . You said—"

Nicole smiled. "Cousin, you must learn not to believe everything people say." With that she was gone, leaving Morag stunned. Quentin hadn't murdered her mother? But . . . the locket and the ring, surely they were proof! But if Nicole were right, if he weren't at fault . . . She must go to him; she must explain. Nicole would be sure to tell him that Morag and Maine had collaborated . . . Not that she cared what d'Angeau thought of her, but if he was to suffer, she would be the one to inflict that suffering . . . not Maine, or, worse yet, Henri. Anyway, now that Nicole had raised a doubt that he was her mother's murderer, Morag had to speak to him herself.

She poured herself a brandy and began pacing the floor. Somehow, she must get to the coast, must get on a ship to Ireland. With the victory, James would probably remain there. Did that mean Quentin would stay too? Hastily, Morag crossed herself. She must reach him before Henri could carry out his evil deed.

Noise from downstairs and the sound of Maine's high-pitched voice reminded her that she still had the Duke to deal with. Desperately, she ran to her own rooms. She'd not suffer him to touch her again—she'd kill him first.

Her father's guns lay in their velvet bed as they had ever since Quentin had returned them to her that fateful day. Her heart skipped a beat, remembering. Quickly, she pushed the memory from her and picked up one of the pistols. With trembling hands, she loaded it. Next, she took the drawstring bag holding the ten thousand *pistoles* she'd saved and fastened it under her dress. Then, the gun hidden in her skirt, Morag returned to the drawing room to find Maine pacing the floor.

"Ah, there you are, my precious." He grinned, his thin mustache curling darkly against his painted face. His dark eyes glittered. "I've decided that I am in the mood for a romp before we set out for home. Besides"— he shrugged—"the streets are impossible now with all that wretched crowd about."

He saw the gun in her hand then. "What's this? You want me to whip you with that?" He smirked at her.

"I want . . ." Morag swallowed hard. "I want you to let me go. I also want to have you tell Henri you've changed your mind about killing the Marquis D'Angeau."

165

"My precious, think of what you are asking. Henri is a thousand miles from here. Besides, it is what you wanted, no?"

"No, it is what *you* wanted. You lied to me. You had it all planned even before I came to you. You—"

"My precious Morag." He advanced and she cocked the gun. He halted. "You hate the man. What should you care when he dies, or when I planned it?"

Morag swallowed hard. "I've changed my mind."

He shrugged. "It's too late."

"We'll see about that." She backed toward the door, keeping the gun on Maine, forgetting that he never entered a room alone if he could help it.

The burly dark-haired servant who had taken Henri's place blocked her way. Maine said, "My little friend is in sore need of some enjoyment, Verne. I think we will use the ropes."

Morag tried to dodge, but the huge man grabbed the pistol from her hand. "Give that back!" she cried.

"Don't worry, my precious, you'll get your father's pistol back—after I've pleasured you once more, but this time, I think I need not pay you."

Speechless, Morag shook her head. Trying to avoid Verne's grasp, she tripped backwards and fell into Maine's hands. . . .

Chapter Thirteen

THE HOT JULY air was stifling inside the coach. Morag fanned herself, keeping her eyes closed to blot out the sight of Maine, sprawled across the seat opposite, dozing. Could she possibly take off his sword without waking him? Unlikely. And the coach doors were locked, so she couldn't escape.

Peeking through the curtained window of the carriage as it rocked along, Morag was surprised to see that the road was not familiar to her. They were not, it seemed, traveling to court—or if they were, it was by a route she did not know. She clutched the side handle as the coach bounced about. God's blood but this road was rough!

At that moment, the coach lurched violently. Morag tried to keep herself from falling as the vehicle rolled sideways. She felt a sharp stab of pain as she hit her head and, after that, nothing . . .

It couldn't have been more than a few minutes before Morag regained consciousness. Gingerly, she moved her limbs. Thank goodness she appeared to be all right. Glancing around, she saw Maine sprawled unconscious. His mouth was open, and blood stained his hairless chest. Was he dead? Just then, the Duke groaned. No, that was too much to hope for.

Gently, Morag extracted herself from the wreckage, realizing that this was the answer to her prayers. One of the coach doors had broken open in the crash. If she didn't escape now, she might never get another chance.

The bright sun made her head ache and she blinked. When her eyes focused again, she saw the driver sprawled in the road. One glance at his crushed head told her he was dead. Swallowing her natural revulsion and praying that Maine would not recover and stop her, she stripped off the driver's breeches and jacket and put them on. It would be easier to evade Maine's pursuit in a man's clothing. Besides, the dress he had forced her to wear was immodest.

Without a backward glance, Morag began to run. She ran toward the sparkling Seine, toward the trees and the coast. Only after she had gone some distance, did she remember that she had no money—not a *pistole*. Maine had found the money she had hidden on herself and confiscated it—"for safe keeping." Well, somehow she must get to the channel, must get passage on a ship to Ireland, must reach Quentin.

She leaned against a tree, feeling the river breeze on her face. She would take one step at a time. She would manage . . . one step at a time.

The low moon shone through the branches of the trees where Morag stood on the outskirts of Brest. It had taken her nearly five days to reach the coastal town; longer than she had expected. Probably, it would have taken longer still, if a farmer had not given her a ride in his haycart. He had let her sleep there too.

From where she stood, Morag could see the masts of three ships in the harbor. Surely, one of these would be crossing to Ireland.

The long walk had given her time to think. She had decided that she could not face Quentin Sauvage. No, she did not wish to see him again—ever—but she did not want him to die either. Some of her hatred for him, she realized now, was due to the fact that he had taken her so easily that first night, that he had ruined her for the nunnery and had not made her feel loved in the process.

Her mother's death aside, Morag knew that it would be fatal for her to see the man again. She would have to be satisfied with letting Nicole warn him. She herself would go to London to find her father's family.

She stared down the path ahead. Did she dare go into the town? Why not? Probably, she tried to convince herself, Maine was not searching for her, but had just decided to let her go. Would *that* be too much to ask?

Glancing toward the cool sea lapping the beach, Morag decided to bathe before she went into town. She couldn't stand the dirt any more. She shed the jacket and the breeches. Shivering with the chill of the air, she quickly waded into the sea and crouched, letting the water wash over her.

She sighed as the waves caressed her. By tomorrow, if all went well, she would be aboard one of the ships in the harbor.

Returning to shore, Morag emerged slowly from the water. She could feel her hair dripping down her back and the breeze chilled her, but it was more than that: the night no longer felt as friendly as it had before.

Conscious of her nakedness, she quickly crossed the open beach to the tree where she had left her clothes.

They were gone!

"Lookin' for these, lass?"

Morag spun about to face a gruff-looking man in sailing scrubs. Flushing, she nodded and held out her hand.

"Yer a pretty one . . . did yer ma'm never tell ye t'be careful at night?"

"Aye, she did." With relief, Morag recognized the Scots brogue. "But the dirt was makin' me feel ill, mon."

"Were it now? Ye be walkin' long?"

"Five days."

"Five days, d'ye say? From Paris, ye be comin' then?"

Morag swallowed hard, nodding.

"And where is it ye be going to, m'good gurl?"

She inhaled sharply, wondering what his reaction would be. "London." Her voice was soft but firm.

"London is it now?" The man whistled through a hole between his teeth.

She nodded.

"I didna ken ye, lass. There be no one worth their grain of salt in London."

"My father's family is there." Then she stopped, realizing that he was staring at her.

"If they're true Scots, they'd be supportin' Jamie and not hankerin' after the Dutch. Yer sure yer not sent t'spy?"

"To spy?" Morag's eyes widened.

"Ye heard me, lass. There be word new come this mornin' from his French majesty. There be an English spy, a gurl, who'd be a comin' to the coast. Captain Josiah warned us again' her."

Morag felt the blood drain from her face. "Look here, mon, Morag Elliot's no spy."

The sailor gave a growl then and threw the jacket and breeches at her. "Dress yerself, lass. 'Tis not fittin' for the likes of ye, spy or no, t'be in the complete."

Hastily, Morag pulled the clothes on.

"I'm takin' ye t'Captain Josiah. He'll know what t'do with ye. An English spy frae the French court. Why, yer no bigger'n my thumb." He grabbed her arm roughly.

Morag realized it would be foolish to run—the man was three times her size. Her only hope now lay in convincing this Captain Josiah that she was not a spy.

The houses of the coastal village were still as they approached. No lights showed in the windows, and only an occasional puff of smoke from a chimney betrayed the fact that fires warmed the rooms where the villagers slept. Near the quay, however, the boisterous sounds from the inns and taverns told Morag that the sailors were a long way from settling down to sleep. Indeed, there were some engaged in the process of loading the ships with crates and barrels.

The sailor touched her warningly. "Ye'll remain here now, lass, or 'twill go bad frae ye. I'm t'find the captain."

As the sailor disappeared inside the tavern, Morag walked toward the nearest ship. A sailor heaved a tub onto his shoulder with a grunt as she approached.

"Are ye going t'Ireland, then?" Morag asked, careful to keep her brogue intact.

The man spun about. "Well, I'll be a jimmey goose. Don't ye scare me like that, lad. I ain't one t'hold m'temper when—"

He stopped at a sudden commotion behind her. Quickly, he put his burden down and came to attention.

Morag needed nothing more to tell her that Captain Josiah was approaching. She turned to face the accusing frown of the first sailor.

"Thought I tol' ye t'stay put, lass."

"Lass?" The second sailor's mouth opened and closed abruptly.

In the dim light of the moon, Morag could make out the high balding brow of the captain.

"This the girl?"

"Aye, captain."

It was Morag's turn to widen her eyes in surprise. The captain had not come out alone. A woman of approximately Morag's height was with him. Her blonde curls were unmistakable even in the moonlight; her crimson satin dress shimmered as she folded her arms across her breasts and eyed Morag with amusement.

"Well, girl? What have ye to say for yerself? Me mon tells me ye're London bound."

Morag swallowed hard. "Yes, sir."

He nodded toward the sailor who had found her. "He's told ye that we're t'look for a spy, has he not?"

Morag nodded, her eyes on the blonde woman. "Whatever you may think, captain, Morag Elliot is no spy. I . . . I do have family in London. I want to go with you across to . . . to see them."

"Do ye now?"

"I do. Ask her." Morag pointed.

The captain glanced back at the blonde in the crimson dress, whose favors he had obviously just enjoyed. "D'ye know the girl, Nicky?"

There was bitterness in Nicole's voice. "*Oui*, Ralph, I do. She's my cousin." Morag let out a sigh of relief. From the way Nicole had looked at her, Morag hadn't been too sure what she would say.

"She the spy?"

Nicole Le Martin laughed. "Not my little cousin. No, she is too stupid for that."

Morag's fists clenched. She should be grateful to Nicole for saving her, but . . .

The captain was watching her. Morag took a deep breath. "Please, sir, I should like to sail with you across the channel."

The high brow furrowed. "We're to Ireland, lass. They'll be no stoppin' afore that."

Nicole smiled at him and put a slender hand on his arm. "You could put her off near the English coast. You do have boats, don't you?"

"Aye, I could do that, but . . ."

Nicole's fingers strayed toward the man's wrist— stroking him. He licked his lips in obvious delight.

"Aye. All right." He nodded to Morag. "Get aboard." He turned to the sailors. "Ye'll say none o'this—neither of ye."

Numbly, Morag followed the sailors aboard the ship.

Chapter Fourteen

DAWN WAS BREAKING as the Marquis d'Angeau stood on the stone bridge above the Dublin castle. Glancing back toward the grim structure, he noted the signs of fires past, the jagged gaping holes, the gray walls. James II detested this castle, and no wonder. It was, Quentin thought, like the man's reign: an utter ruin.

He heard the raucous laughter of the courtesans, and his thoughts turned toward the ball he had just left. As such celebrations went, this one had been well-done. While not as lavish as the extravagances of the French court, it was certainly the equal of any wealthy nobleman's gathering. In many ways that's what James seemed to be—not a King in his own right but a Bourbon puppet.

Quentin turned toward the dirty swirling waters of the river. The smells here were the same as Paris, and the houses on the bridge and the narrow crooked streets reminded him of that city more than he liked. God, how he longed for the open spaces, the forests and rivers of the wilderness. When this war was done, when James had conquered—or had been conquered—

Quentin decided to ask the King's permission to return home to Canada. Grimacing, he turned back toward the castle; the end, he thought, would not be long now. William's forces had landed and were advancing, yet James played the noble host.

With the music of the ball floating toward him, Quentin scanned the city streets. Few were about because of the curfew. How the Irish must hate James! Even though the party was a birthday celebration for the absent Queen Mary, he wondered what the people must be thinking, and the soldiers, who were so hungry they chewed hides or gnawed at dried bread that would not rise because the flour had been stored in damp towers.

Quentin stiffened, aware of another's presence. He turned and made out a vague form in the early morning mist. From that distance, at first, it appeared to be Tyrconnel, but Quentin knew James' favorite would not dare venture out into the streets on a night such as this. Even with the war, the Earl was soft from a life of luxury. Therefore, trusting his instincts, Quentin moved forth to greet the only man it could be.

"Ho! Lucan!"

"Aye, Quentin, lad." The figure lit up a cheroot. "I didna want t'disturb yer thoughts, though I fancy they were much on the line of mine." Patrick Sarsfield, the Earl of Lucan, jerked his head back toward the noise across the river. "'Tis a shame, is it not? All that food and nary a bit for the soldiers. I've a fair t'middlin' bet that, sure as I'm Irish, Queen Mary would not appreciate what's being done."

"I doubt much that she knows. Mary's a good heart," d'Angeau said.

The men stepped aside for a cart passing over the bridge, then Lucan moved closer to d'Angeau.

"'Tis not going well, I hear."

Quentin merely nodded, glancing at the rising sun.

"'Twould be treason were Tyrconnel to hear us talk thus, but James is no more a King than his father was. God love him, though, for being a Catholic. Couldn't stand one of those turndown Protestants lording over me and my staff." Lucan paused. "'Twould be wise if James would forget the English and be content with the Irish. The people would love him, if only he'd give 'em some hope."

Again, Quentin nodded.

"Well, confound it, lad, yer uncle's as close as two peas in a pod to 'im. Can't he make 'm see any reason?"

D'Angeau shrugged, his cool gray eyes staring into the mist ahead. "James is more stubborn than one of the mules in your stable, my friend. I doubt that anything Lauzun could say or do would make much difference."

Lucan snorted and tossed his cheroot down the road. "Well, I'm away to my rooms for now. 'Twill be a soft morning—ya can see that from the mist." Lucan began to cross the bridge and stopped. "Well, will ya come, or go your own way?"

D'Angeau followed the Earl back over the river to Molesworth, near Saint Stephen's green. It was here that Lucan had an old high-gabled townhouse. Once, this district had been the finest in the city, but now the house, despite an elaborate staircase, was as dirty and wretched-looking as the rest of Dublin. Still and all, it was a roof over the head, which was more than most of James' soldiers had.

Catching up with his friend, Quentin put a hand out to stop the Earl. "Ho, man! Did you see that fellow we just passed?"

Lucan nodded. "As French as y'are, I'd guess by the fancy clothes."

"Yes," Quentin replied, puzzled and disturbed. He had recognized the man; it was Maine's valet, Henri. "Do you know if Louis has sent his son yet?"

"Which one?" Lucan's older eyes took in the other man's concern.

"The bastard—Maine."

Lucan shrugged. "Not that I've heard, but then yer uncle being in favor would make ya more privy to such things than I."

"Yes . . . you're right. I must ask Lauzun. He'll know if Maine has come, though I fancy if the Prince is here, he'll not show his face in battle."

"Cowardly, is he?"

Quentin shrugged. "Let's say he prefers to let others do the fighting for him when he can."

Lucan nodded, and the pair started up the townhouse staircase.

Quentin's confidence in the Irish was always restored when he breakfasted with Sarsfield. This man knew Ireland; this man *was* Ireland. After breakfast, exhausted from the night of dancing, Quentin accepted his host's offer of a bed, and was soon asleep.

He was awakened late in the day by Lord Lucan himself, and saw immediately by the troubled look on the Irishman's face that something had happened.

"What is it? What's amiss?" Quentin was on his feet instantly.

Silently, Lucan handed his friend a letter he was holding. It seemed to be from a man who had something of value to give Sarsfield regarding the coming battle with William.

"D'ya think it's a trick?" Lucan asked as d'Angeau finished reading the letter.

Quentin handed the parchment back to Sarsfield and shrugged. "It could be, but it could also be real. You did offer a reward to all who would desert to James, didn't you?"

The other nodded. "Will ya go with me to meet him?"

D'Angeau nodded without hesitation. He patted his dagger as he placed it inside his vest. If it were a trick, he and Lucan could manage. But as he completed dressing, his nerves were taut.

The thick mist coming in off the river cloaked the war-torn city in a premature shroud. The two nobles walked along in silence, feeling the tension and hearing the hisses as they passed the groups of Irish lounging about taverns which could no longer supply them with drink. The desolation, drizzle and smoky grayness of the sky made everything seem dirty.

Closer to the river, the streets were dark and crowded. The light here was dimmer by half. Quentin could still sense his friend beside him, but he was barely able to see him.

"Where was it we were to meet this man?"

"Butcher's Market . . . here on the quay," Lucan responded, glancing about. Though they had seen many Dubliners about earlier, this section of the city seemed deserted and silent.

D'Angeau touched Lucan's shoulder. "I believe we had best move on . . ."

Tension rippled through him. Though unspoken, the word "trap" seemed to vibrate in the air. Following his instincts, Quentin spun about, his stomach muscles tightening. Both men saw the advancing dozen then, walking through the fog like ghosts risen from the grave. Even in that pea-soup thickness, the clubs and sticks they carried were visible. The mist tunneled their vision so that Quentin was aware of the hatred in the eyes of the short man leading the group. No, it was not Henri, but as Quentin turned toward Lucan, he had no doubt that it was Maine's valet who had engineered this.

There was no time to dwell on that, as the small army of men advanced menacingly.

Quentin stood, waiting, legs apart. "We'll split up," he told Lucan. "If they are after both of us—"

"Of course they are after both of us! I'm no lily colleen, man." Lucan stood still, his dagger drawn.

D'Angeau nodded, peering into the fog. The men seemed to move in dreamlike isolation. A quick glance behind him revealed that they were standing up against a haycart.

"Move then," Quentin cried, pushing Sarsfield off to the side.

The Irish lord needed no further instruction to mount the pile of hay and tumble off down the other side, Quentin following. They ran, the sound of their nailed boots, striking cobblestones, echoing around them. Then a second group of attackers materialized at the end of the tunnel-like street.

"We'll crack them," Quentin told Lucan with stubborn determination. Bending his head as if about to run an Indian gauntlet, he braced himself for the blows. "Stay behind me."

Sarsfield grunted and the pair surged ahead, daggers out. They charged into their attackers, heads down, shoulders forward. The sticks flayed Quentin's skin, knocked against his skull, but he kept running until he was free of the pack. Breathless, Lucan caught up with him, and they paused to assess the situation. The packing-house, which Patrick Sarsfield now pointed to, was the only place they could hide.

Quentin nodded and jumped through the open doorway after Lucan. They slammed the door behind them. A moment later, their pursuers surged against it, banging the soft wood with their sticks.

"They mean t'kill us, lad," Sarsfield said. "I didna mean t'involve ya in this. 'Tis a personal battle, I'm sure." His breath was coming hard and fast, and Quentin realized that the sticks must have broken his friend's ribs.

"*Mon Dieu,* Patrick, this is not your fault! In fact, I was thinking that I involved you. I have many enemies in Dublin."

"Yet the letter came to me. No, 'tis I that—"

There was no time for futher argument. The wooden door splintered under the pounding, and the boots of two men were visible through the resulting gap.

"Will you swing with me?" Quentin indicated the empty meat hooks above them.

"Damned if I can, but I'll most certainly try. But ya'll not wait for me, lad. If ya can, go to it on yer own."

Grimly, Quentin nodded. He helped Lucan up, then hoisted himself up on the monkey ropes toward the top of the loft.

Lucan had just grabbed a hook when the door below splintered open.

"Go!" Quentin commanded. His breath rasping audibly, he led the way. Grasping his hook tightly, his boots properly aimed, he swung out through the open window.

It was the river on the other side. Lucan was gasping and struggling in the water beside him. Quentin locked an arm around the Irishman and quickly swam down-

THIS BITTER ECSTASY

stream with him. The curses of the men they had
eluded faded finally. Far enough away from the attackers, Quentin aimed for shore and assisted Lucan
out of the water.

"Thank Mary for yer strength, lad," Sarsfield
gasped, sprawled on the bank. Exhausted, Quentin
could only nod and sink down beside his friend. He
had no real idea of what happened; all he knew was
that it had been a well-planned attempt on his—or
Lucan's—life.

The older man's eyes were closed. Concerned,
Quentin took his wrist. Thank God, Lucan lived.

With a deep breath and a grunt, d'Angeau hoisted
the unconscious Earl to his back and slowly began the
walk back to Molesworth.

It was dark when Quentin mounted the steps to his
own rooms on Dawson Street. Once again, he stiffened
as he sensed an unseen presence. The perfume was
French—there was no mistaking that. Heart pounding,
dagger drawn, he kicked open his door.

A woman's scream rang out. The flame from a single
candle flared to reveal Nicole Le Martin, naked,
clutching a sheet from his bed about her.

Quentin let out a sigh of relief. "*Mon Dieu,* Nicky!
What in all the devils of hell are you doing here? I
might have killed you!"

With a cry, Nicole dropped the sheet and ran to him.
She touched the cuts on his face. "*Mon pauvre amour,*
I have come too late! My dreadful cousin's plan almost
succeeded."

He pulled away from her. "What plan is that?"

Nicole sobbed, clinging to him: "Morag . . ." She
wiped her eyes with the back of her hand, like a child.

181

"Oh, I should not be telling you this, Quentin, but she and Maine . . . oh, they will kill me if they discover I have told you!"

D'Angeau grimaced. "She and Maine have joined forces against me? Come now, Nicky, you'll have to do better than that." He strode across the room, ignoring her as he stripped and examined his wounds in the brass mirror by the candlelight. The blood had already dried on his left cheek and the gash there did not seem too deep. The swollen bruise above his left eye, however, looked bad.

Nicole came up behind him, her naked body reflected in the mirror as she reached up to put an arm about him.

"Oh, Quentin, *mon amour*, let me take care of your wounds." She stroked his cut cheek with her smooth hand. "Do not be angry with me. 'Tis not my fault that Morag is such a little fool."

He sighed and turned to face her. "Are you telling me that she has gone back to Maine? I don't believe it."

Nicole gave an expressive shrug. Her blonde curls bounced off the only thing she was wearing: a black velvet band about her neck. "You must believe it . . . it is true. She blames you for the death of her mother and—"

"What! What has happened to Marie Thérèse?"

Nicole blushed. "My aunt . . . is dead. Sh   she killed herself."

"Oh?"

"Well, that . . . that is what is commonly believed."

"But not by Morag, obviously," Quentin said dryly. "Why and how did Marie kill herself?"

" 'Twas poison, I believe."

"She had no reason to take her life. We were to be married."

"But . . . you had left her. She . . . she despaired of your return." Nicole swallowed hard. "What happened, I do not know. All I can tell you is that my aunt died suddenly and Morag blames you—"

"Go on." Quentin shook her none too gently when she paused.

"I cannot tell you much more. The next thing I knew, she announced to me that she would no longer be sharing my rooms, that she was returning to Maine."

Nicole glanced suggestively toward the bed. "I have missed you so, *mon amour*." Her fingers curled into the hairs on his chest. "You are the only man who can truly satisfy me. I have risked my life coming here . . . to warn you . . . and—"

In a soft but menacing tone, he said, "If you do not immediately tell me what has become of Morag, I will throw you out to the soldiers, Nicole."

Nicole's eyes widened. In a small voice, she told him: "My cousin made a deal with Maine . . . to be with him for three months. She wanted you . . . dead."

"I see. And where is she now. Still with Maine?"

Nicole stared at the wall ahead of her.

"Where is she, Nicky!"

Nicole sighed. "She found that Maine had lied to her. She . . . she is in England, I believe. She went to find her father's family."

"In England! That little idiot! Hasn't she heard about the wars? Where in England is she?"

Nicole shook her head. "I do not know. The Elliots are rather favorites of William." The tears that sparkled in her eyes were real now. "They have a London house, no doubt, and one in Kent, I believe."

Quentin began to dress quickly again.

"You are going after her?" Nicole said, incredulous.

"I am."

"But . . . what if you don't find her? What of the army? What of your commission?"

"I will find Morag, have no fear of that. As to the army, my uncle will manage quite well without me."

"And what of me?"

"Well, what of you?"

"I want to come with you, Quentin, *mon amour*. I want—"

"You made your way here without any problem. You can make your way back to Versailles." He scribbled a note. "Give this to my uncle. No doubt James will be happy to assist you—in every way—until you can return to France."

"But I do not want James! 'Tis you I want."

Quentin was fully dressed now and at the door. He stared at her a moment, then shrugged. "I will say this much to you, Nicole, my sweet. If you have lied to me about Morag, you will live to regret it."

As the door closed behind him, Nicole took a deep breath and said firmly: "And you will regret leaving me, d'Angeau. I have come for you and I shall have you. My cousin—if she still lives—will never claim you, Quentin Adam Sauvage. You are mine!"

Chapter Fifteen

THE WAVES WASHED over the sides of the small boat bouncing in the choppy sea off the English coast. Clinging to her seat in desperate fear, Morag watched the ship carrying Nicole and Captain Josiah to Ireland disappear in the distance.

With every moment, it became clearer that Morag's own craft was sinking. Had Nicole known the boat had a leak when she set her cousin off in it? She might be jealous, but Morag simply could not bring herself to believe her cousin capable of murder. Besides, Nicole had no reason to be jealous. She knew that Morag had no wish to see Quentin again. Yet, as Nicole's ship grew smaller and smaller on the horizon, Morag's boat went further and further under. More leaks had developed in the bottom, and there was no way to scoop the water out.

Desperately, Morag peered into the mist. How far was she from shore? Fear took hold as a wave swamped her. Soaked to the skin, Morag realized that she had only two choices: stay with the boat and most probably drown, or try to swim for shore.

Crossing herself, she slipped into the sea, watching the boat bob up momentarily as it was relieved of her weight. Water flooded over her again and she coughed up salty foam. Yet another wave struck her. She was going to die, she thought. No . . . she couldn't. Not until she knew that Quentin was safe.

Then she remembered that Nicole would warn him.

She struggled to stay afloat and, too late, saw the huge wave approaching. It crested, broke, knocking her into the side of the sinking boat. Quentin Sauvage's face seemed to flash before her as consciousness faded.

Hot afternoon sun beat down on Morag's head, and coarse sand rubbed against her cheek. She groaned and opened her eyes. Her head ached, but she sat up stiffly, amazed to be alive.

Blinking, she realized—as she stared through the heat haze into a grove of trees ahead—that she must have been swept ashore. She was in England. But where in England?

Moving gingerly, feeling the gritty sand fall from her clothes, Morag saw that she still wore the French blue naval jacket that Captain Josiah had given her just before ordering her into the boat. Torn now and encrusted with dirt, it nevertheless provided her with some protection from the burning sun.

She stood, swaying slowly, staring in surprise as a shaggy dog romped up to her—and pushed her back down with a thud. Stunned, she realized that the dog carried a man's homespun shirt in his teeth. Moments later, a man ran out of the forest.

"There you are, ye cur." He pointed an obviously loaded pistol at the dog, who now danced about Morag.

"Don't you hurt him!" Morag came to the dog's defense. "Put that gun down."

186

"An' 'ho might ye be, missy? You wi' that Froggie suit."

Morag blushed, glancing down at the naval jacket.

"Yer a spy, ain't ye? Commander'll be pleased to'see ye, Froggie."

Morag stood now, releasing the dog from her arms. "I am sorry to disappoint you, but I am not a spy."

"Then 'ho are ye? Tain't no people livin' here'bouts. Yer not an English lass—that much I'll say."

"And what makes you think I am not?"

The man cocked his gun. "Cuz ye talk too fine. Ye talk like one of them there Frenchies."

Her hands were on her hips now. "Well, I am not French. I am Scots."

"Scots, eh? That be the same as French. These blasted Scots'r right stubborn, fightin' fer the fool Catholic. Don' they know 'e's lost?"

"Lost?" Morag's eyes widened. She recalled the recent celebrations in Paris. "But . . . he defeated William . . . William *is* dead, is he not?"

"Naw, missy." The man snorted. "The King's much alive 'n' in Dublin." He laughed. "Much t' the distaste o'those fool Catholics. 'N' Jamie the Pretender is a runnin' fer 'is life."

The soldier stepped forward menacingly. The dog growled and flew through the air at him. The pair fell over, rolling on the ground as Morag watched helplessly. The shot startled Morag, just when it seemed the dog was about to sink his fangs into the soldier's jugular.

After a moment, she heard the man groan. "Damn dog!" He pushed the dead animal off him and stood.

Morag stared at the dog. "You killed him."

"That Oi' did, Missy. 'E would've killed me. 'Twas the same as wi' the other. If Oi 'adna killed 'im, 'e would've dun me.''He waved the pistol at her. "Twas why Oi were on the run, so t'speak, but now as Oi have ye, ye'll be me ticket back t'favor.''

"But I tell you, I am not a spy!''

The soldier shrugged. "Don't matter t'me none. 'Twill be fer Commander Dungan t'decide. Come on now, Oi've precious little time. Can't stay 'ere too long.''

Morag remained where she was. "What if I refuse to go with you? Will you kill me as well?''

The blow from the gun forced her to her knees.

" 'Odsfish, why do Oi always git the stubborn ones? Will, as yer on yer rump, wench. Oi might as well give ye a little pleasure.'' He grinned at her.

Morag stared back at him blankly.

"Go on now. Spread your legs, chit. Oi tol' ye, Oi got precious little time. 'Tis t'the capital we've t'go.''

"The capital? You mean, to London? Are we near it then?''

The soldier glared at her and bared yellow-stained teeth.

"Tis more n' a comfortable walk. 'Twill be less comfortable if ye don' do as Oi say. Now, will ye spread, or will Oi beat ye again?'' He made an ominous clicking sound with his teeth.

Reluctantly, Morag stood and removed the breeches she was wearing.

"Ah, now, that's more like it. Ye Frenchie women be the best.'' He grinned. "Lay yerself down now, missy, n' ye'll get a rare treat. Ye'll never forget 'enry Bucks . . .'' Nausea rose in Morag as she lay motionless, feeling the press of the man inside her. No, she vowed, she would never forget Henry Bucks.

* * *

If Morag had thought her trek from Paris to the French coast arduous, she did not think so after her third day with Mr. Bucks. Her hands bound in front of her, she trudged behind him, the thick sailor's rope bound about her waist jerking her forward up and down the hilly paths, over fallen trees, her face and arms scratched by the whipping branches of trees and brush.

She had no idea where they were, had seen no sign indicating that London was any closer than it had been the day she had landed. Never had the sun seemed so hot.

Although they passed several hamlets, Morag saw no one except an occasional shepherd in the distance. In general, Henry Bucks kept to the wooded areas. He seemed as much concerned about avoiding discovery as she had when fleeing Paris.

Whenever the urge came over him, he would order her to the ground and have his way. For the most part, he did not even bother to remove his outer garments.

By the fifth day, Morag knew that she could not stand it much longer. They seldom stopped, seldom ate, and never washed. She didn't know how the man could keep it up. Bucks gave only grudgingly of his water and hardtack, and nothing else. He would not stop to get any food at the farms. Again, Morag was struck by the way he purposely avoided any contact with the locals. It had to be, she reasoned, because of the killing he had boasted of on the beach that first day.

Lost in thought, she did not realize that he had stopped, and was then taken completely by surprise when he pushed her to the ground. The man was insatiable! Angry and sore, she scarcely noticed at first that this time he had dropped his dagger and pistol.

Her eyes focused on the weapons. She realized that even if her hands had been untied, the gun and knife were out of her reach. Yet . . . there had to be a way.

Above them, the sun went behind a cloud, darkening the path. For the first time in days, thunder rumbled ominously. It was a sign from Heaven, of that Morag was sure. Something had to happen.

Bucks mounted her in his usual style. "Will ye move, missy?" He slapped her behind, forcing her to cry out.

"How can I move with my hands tied as they are?"

He growled and raised up. "Ye kint do much anyway, yer a mote sore example of a woman, Frenchie." But he untied her wrists.

Morag stared at the red marks where the ropes had bound her, scarcely believing that her hands were free, as she felt him re-enter her. There was no pleasure, no pain, only numbness, but as he was coming closer to climax, she was moving closer to the dagger.

Heaving her hips upward, she moved her body forward. The dagger was against her foot now. Groaning as if she were enjoying it, she allowed her freed hands to roam the broad back above her.

One more time. One more time and the dagger would be hers. She felt the cold steel against her hand and closed her eyes for a moment.

"Oi knew ye'd enjoy it! Bucks ain't one t'leave a lady dissatisfied," he whispered hoarsely.

Morag merely grunted in response, intent on the dagger. Thunder rolled and lightening cracked the leaden skies, as the first drops of rain fell. Morag's fingers gripped the hilt.

As Bucks reached his climax, Morag plunged the weapon into his back.

"Kee-rist!" he cried, jumping up off of her, his eyes wide. "Bitch!" He tried to slap her, but his strength failed him and he dropped to the ground in a heap, hitting his head on a rock. He shivered, and lay still.

Hesitantly, Morag approached him. Yes, there was no doubt about it: he was dead.

Crossing herself, Morag stepped forward, took a deep breath and closed his eyelids. At least he'd not stare at her! She'd had to kill him, hadn't she? Wouldn't it have meant her own death otherwise? Hadn't what he'd done to her proved that he was an evil man?

She would have to bury him. Exhausted, she continued to sit and stare at the corpse. The rain veiled her vision and stood out in her mind shimmering like the problem before her. She realized that the long trek had drained her of all strength: her body would not obey her order to move. Curling into a small depression under the pine, her arms above her head and her legs drawn up, Morag promptly fell into a deathlike sleep.

She did not know how long she slept, but the rain was still falling when she opened her eyes again. Shivering, she realized that she was chilled through, that her clothes were caked with mud, and that her stomach was growling with hunger. She tried to sit up.

The body was still there—she had not dreamed it— but now the face was completely blue. Morag was glad that she had closed his eyes.

As she stood, feeling the sodden linsey-woolsey of the French sailor's breeches damp against her skin, Morag realized that the clothes did her no good. Her only choice was to put on Buck's breeches—a dead man's clothes! She had done that before, with Maine's driver, but that had been different: she hadn't killed him.

Gingerly, she tugged at the clothing, only to find that the body had already begun to stiffen. Finally, with great difficulty, she removed the breeches. They were several sizes too big for her, and she was forced to use the red sash from her French naval jacket as a belt. *Mon Dieu,* but it felt strange.

Recalling her previous mistake, she dug into Bucks' pockets. Her diligence was rewarded when she searched the sack he had carried. There was, besides English coins, several gold pieces. He must have robbed someone. The sack also contained dried beef, and bullets and powder for the gun.

Ravenously, she gnawed off a chunk of the jerky before she remembered that it might have to last for several days. Would the powder be any good, damp as it was? She wasn't sure, but decided to take the sack.

Picking up the pistol from where Bucks had dropped it earlier, Morag placed it in the sack too. Then, taking a deep breath, she seized the dagger and stabbed it into the ground to cleanse it of the blood.

For a moment, she wondered again if she should attempt to bury him. The idea sickened her, and she persuaded herself that Bucks would like as not remain undiscovered for months . . . maybe forever.

Dropping the French naval outfit over the body, Morag headed resolutely east, toward what she hoped would be London.

It rained again the following day, but not as long or as hard. The sun which followed caused sweat to drip down her brow, down the crevice between her breasts. Hot and uncomfortable, Morag trudged on.

Toward evening, she noticed a change in the coun-

tryside around her. The trees thinned out and gave way
to a landscape of soft rolling hills. Before long, Morag
could make out a gray church steeple against the bright
blue sky. She blinked.

The little village she approached was like an oasis
in the desert, its peacefulness reminding her of such
hamlets in France.

Yes, she decided, crossing a narrow stone bridge,
passing to watch the white ducks swim under it, she
would risk stopping here. She had to know how far
she was from London; she had to rest and get some
food. As she stood on the bridge, letting a light breeze
refresh her, Morag thought how wonderful it would
feel to sink into a soft feather bed again, to feel the
cleansing warmth of a soapy bath on her tired body.
She grasped Bucks' sack tightly. Surely, it contained
money enough to pay for those luxuries, and perhaps
a dress besides. It would not do for her to arrive at
her grandfather's house in London in Bucks' clothes.

She tried to recall something of her grandfather, but
she had only seen him once—when she was ten—and
then only briefly. Would he remember her? Would he
acknowledge her? She had not thought to bring proof
of her heritage, but she was her father's daughter—
there was no doubt about that.

A mobcapped matron carrying a basket stopped by
her. Morag remembered that she must not lapse into
French. For her own safety, she must remember that
she was in England and that she was English—not
Scots.

"'Ods, my life, sweetings, yer lookin' a bit lost. 'Tis
it such ye be?" the woman asked.

"No, I . . . that is . . . Could you please direct me
to the nearest inn?"

"There ain't but one. Cock's Head. Master Todd

owns it." She pointed that way, but her manner suddenly changed, becoming cool and distant. "But if it be business yer lookin' fer, ye'll not git it there. Master Todd's respectable, he is."

Unshed tears burned in Morag's throat. She wanted to explain to this woman that that "business" was the very last thing she wanted—ever. Indeed, Morag thought she had had enough of lovemaking to last her a lifetime. But, unable to speak, she merely nodded and turned in the direction of the inn.

Chapter Sixteen

CHARLES BONWELL SAT at a corner table in the private parlor of Cock's Head, at Crawford Pass. A large plate of macaroons was on the table before him. So were two empty glasses and a bottle of the landlord's best sherry. Next to him sat a tall awkward-looking girl with dark wispy hair piled about her head to make it look fuller. Her nose was sharp and long and her jaw more square than was pleasing, but to Bonwell she was beautiful because of the diamonds that glistened at her earlobes and the diamond pendant she wore about her narrow neck.

"Cynthia, my dearest," his hand covered hers, "you must meet this girl. 'Tis positively a shock . . . and a stroke of luck. Why, I could not believe that anyone such as she claims to be—an Elliot, no less—would appear dressed like that. I vow, 'twill be quite an interesting story." He grinned, "Can you imagine what Donald Elliot will do when he finds out? Can you imagine what Donald will say if she truly is Andrew Elliot's sprig?"

The older girl's eyes narrowed in suspicion. "Do you favor her, Charles?"

"Come now, sweetings, I fancy none but you. You know that. Yet will it not set Donald's teeth on grinders to learn what we have found?"

"What good will that do? I swear, Charlie, you get into such a bother over things which do not concern you."

"My heart, my heart!" the young man cried, popping two mácaroons into his mouth at once. "Do you not recall the big t'do of the Elliot's? 'Twas only a year ago, afore William took power. Do you not recall how the old man took off to that barbaric society with Robert, and how he declared to Donald that if Andrew—or any of Andrew's kin—should ever come around, the estate would be theirs? Do you not recall?"

"Aye, I do," Cynthia replied in a monotone. " 'Twill be a good laugh t'see Donald's eyes pop when you tell 'im. But what of the old lady? His mama did not go a-Puritaning. D'you think she'll welcome a granddaughter who stinks like a dog?"

"Little Miss Elliot will not stink like a dog when I am through with her."

Cynthia stiffened, seeing the glint in her lover's eyes. "I'll ask you again, Charles Bonwell, what do you get out of this? You'll not leave me for some heiress!"

He leaned over and kissed her nose. "What will I get out of it?" He shrugged his bony shoulders. "Precious little if I do not play my cards right, but more than enough if I do."

Cynthia eyed him while she nibbled a macaroon and sipped sherry. "Well, then, what's to do now, Charles?"

"Now? Now I shall off to get some decent clothes for our new little friend. Then we shall take her 'round to see Donald."

"But you have no credit." Cynthia whispered, so the landlord would not hear.

Bonwell shrugged. " 'Tis of no matter, sweetings. The Elliots have all the credit I need." He leaned over to kiss her cheek again. "I shall be back in a day or so. I trust you can entertain the child for that time."

"Faith, I know not what I'll do, but for you, Charlie, I shall manage."

He patted her rump lovingly and went off in search of a horse, while Cynthia watched the public room, hoping the landlord would not notice Bonwell's departure. 'Odsblud, she thought, it was difficult when you loved a man like Charles Bonwell.

Bare legs curled up under the voluminous brocaded dressing gown she wore, Morag sat on the velvet cushion of the library's bay window, staring out at the rain-drenched countryside. She could hear the burning wood crackle in the fireplace behind her and feel the heat of the flames on her hair, which was piled in a shimmering loose knot on top of her head.

'Twas hard to believe that it was barely two months since Charles Bonwell had brought her here to the Elliot country house in Kent. Morag often wondered what she would have done if she hadn't met Charles and had gone on to London, only to find the family gone to Kent for the summer.

Time had flown so swiftly these past weeks, and yet not swiftly enough. Her life was happy enough. Indeed, she had been pleasantly surprised at the warm greeting she had received from Lady Elliot, her father's mother. 'Twas a shame that her Uncle Donald had not seemed to be as happy to see her as Grandmama was. He seemed to resent her, though Morag could not fathom why. She was only glad that Lady Elliot, with her crisp March voice and commanding air, had instantly decided that Morag could be no one but Andrew's daughter.

Morag closed her eyes, listening to the rain against the window, and recalled that first day. Bonwell had insisted that they must meet Lady Elliot first—before Donald Elliot returned from his estate duties. It was almost as if Charles were protecting her from something . . .

"Sweetings! You're not ill! Methinks you are looking pale. I'll warrant you caught a chill on that ride this morn."

Morag opened her eyes. Charles Bonwell stood before her, his expression anxious. She had not heard him approach because of the thickness of the red carpet.

He bent to kiss her forehead. Morag smiled up at him tenderly. " 'Odsblud, my dearest heart, I do wish you'd take better care of yourself. You know how dear you are to me."

Morag, still smiling, nodded absent-mindedly. It was pleasant to be loved and cossetted in Charles' gentle way. It was nice to know that there were men who could be kind for kindness' sake and demand nothing in return. She wondered if it would shock him to know about her past with Maine, Bucks . . and with Quentin.

Her heart skipped a beat. God's death! If only she could get the Marquis out of her mind. He was in her thoughts night and day.

"S'life, I swear, my dove, that you are millions of miles away." Bonwell took her cold hand into his sweaty one. "I've a mind to send you to bed with a possett."

198

She looked up into his cornflower eyes. "Really, I'm fine, Charles. I was only thinking on . . . the future."

" 'Odslife, you needn't set your teeth to grinders on that." He kissed her again. It was a butterfly kiss, soft and undemanding, giving Morag a secure feeling, yet one of puzzling dissatisfaction.

She sighed. "Well, we are going to London soon for the season, are we not? I am worried about what will happen there."

"You needn't worry on that account, my little love." He paused. "You do know that I have already spoken to your grandmama?"

Morag stared at him. She had suspected as much, but now that it was said, she felt oddly uncomfortable. It was true that she enjoyed Charles' company and attentiveness. Yet somehow, she felt there should be something more.

"Say something, sweetings. Surely it does not come as a surprise to you?"

"No . . ." She hesitated. "But I thought . . . I mean . . . Cynthia said . . ."

"What did my dear Cousin Cynthia say?"

Morag shrugged. " 'Twas nothing definite, but last week, when we were out riding, I could have sworn that she spoke of you as if . . ."

"As if—what?"

"Well, as if she fancied herself in love with you. Was there not something understood between you before I came?"

Charles grimaced. "My heart, 'tis a fact that Cynthia and I did keep company at one time but"—he took Morag's hand and placed it near his heart— "you must believe that I did not attempt to mislead the child. I said nothing of marrying her—you can count on that. Indeed, on my life, you are the only one for me."

His hand stroked her cheek. For the first time, she wondered what kind of lover he would be.

Morag was breathless when she finished the coranto in Charles' arms, following close behind his Uncle Rochester and his partner. Her green eyes shone with mischief as she murmured to Charles, " 'Odsblud, my heart, you dance far better than William."

She glanced toward the royal dais, where a bored King William sat under a canopy with his fidgeting wife, Mary. It was evident that the little Queen wished to twirl her skirts along with the others, and that she was torn between her desire and her husband's disapproval.

Charles gave a low laugh. "I fear, sweetings, that is because William does not dance." He drew her away from his uncle. "And well you know that. Faith, Morag." he said, smiling at her. " 'tis good that you are in better spirits this night. Your headache is gone, I trust?"

She nodded as he escorted her back to her chair and the watchful eye of Lady Elliot. In truth, she had not wished to come this evening, but it had not been because of her headache. She had dreaded that this ball, the fourth she had attended this London season, would somehow be her undoing. Now, with the dancing nearly half over and the masks removed and nothing untoward having happened, Morag felt that she could relax.

Her spirits rose and she tapped her foot to the music. Tonight, she decided, she would give Charles his answer. She had kept him waiting long enough. There were worse fates than being wed to the nephew of Lord Rochester.

Startled by a light pinch on her bottom, she whirled about to find a little man with a face like a frog staring at her.

"You will dance the gavotte with me, Miss Elliot?" he asked, grinning.

"In faith, sir," Morag flushed, "my program is filled for the night. Is that not so, Charles?" she asked Bonwell, who approached with a glass of malmsey and some comfits for her.

" 'Tis the truth, Commander Dungan. Miss Elliot has been spoken for this night but, if she wishes, she may accommodate you."

Morag felt her stomach tighten. She forced herself to smile at Bucks' former commander. Did he know? He seemed ready, like the frog he resembled, to dart out his tongue and entrap her.

Fanning herself to cover her confusion, she said, "Mayhap ask me later, commander. For now, I could swear the heat in this room will kill me. I must sit this one out."

"I believe, Miss Elliot, that you are not as fragile as you appear, but at your request, I shall return later." Bowing low to take a peek at the tops of her breasts, which strained the top of the ice-blue taffeta gown, Dungan moved away, melting into the crowd and leaving Morag feeling uneasy.

Sipping the wine, she tried to regain her composure. That comment about her not being as fragile as she looked made her think that the man did know something. But, if so, wouldn't he have her arrested? She glanced at Charles, standing at her side. Would marriage to a crown favorite protect her?

" 'Odsfish, my love. You know you needn't confine

yourself to dancing with me if there are other partners you wish. I am confident of your heart." He smiled at her affectionately.

She shrugged, biting into a comfit. "Well, perhaps I shall . . . later."

Charles nodded, his hand resting on her shoulder. "I do not believe I have told you how very beautiful you are tonight. That gown suits you perfectly."

Before she could acknowledge the compliment, she saw Cynthia twirling toward them. The tall girl wore a gorgeous jeweled and lace-trimmed rose gown. She was partnered by the new Lord Clarendon. 'Twas positively disgusting, Morag thought, that William should present a title so close to James. Eyeing the fellow, she noted that he was far too old for Cynthia. Did Charles notice that too?

The music died then, and the men bowed to their partners. A hush suddenly fell over the room. Morag's heart leaped into her throat. The double doors had swept open and the dark panels framed a tall lithe figure. The newcomer wore knee-boots of gleaming leather, which were molded to the strong calves of his legs. The tan breeches above them were belted into a flat, athletic waist. A fine white holland shirt covered the man's broad chest and wide shoulders, but flaunting convention, he wore the neck of the shirt open, revealing a tawny-skinned throat. Morag took an unconscious step forward and saw the host of the evening, resplendent in a scarlet coat and canary-yellow small clothes, come forward to greet the Marquis d'Angeau.

Morag stared in amazement and shook her head. There had to be some mistake; it could not be . . . not Quentin, not at a ball applauding King William.

She stared past him at the stately blonde on his arm.

It was Lady Armstrong's niece, Amelia, a staunch supporter of William. Had the Marquis changed sides?

As she continued to stare at him, those piercing dark eyes met hers for a brief moment. Morag's fan fell noisily to the marble floor. There was no question that he recognized her too. She suddenly felt like an awkward child.

What was he doing here? She swallowed hard, blushing as she retrieved her fan from Charles, who was watching her closely.

" 'Odsfish, Morag! You're white as a ghost. What's amiss?"

"Noth . . . nothing. I . . . my head aches again, Charles. Can we please return to the house?"

"Tell me true, Morag, do you know that man?"

"Why do you ask? No. . . . no, I do not know him."

"You are positive?" Charles persisted. "I ask, my sweetings, only because the Marquis is French. He has come over to help William's forces. I thought you might have recognized him from your days at the French court. His reputation here is one of shame. Indeed, I am much surprised that Coldwater invited him. 'Tis said that Queen Mary—"

"Please, Charles, I do not care to hear about such a man. He is not even properly dressed. Look, he has no neckcloth, no jacket. Why, 'tis almost as if—savage that he is—he flaunts us for being more civilized than he."

Morag pressed her lips together, trying to control the tumult of emotions which raged within her. A liar and a spy! The odious creature. She wondered what William had paid him.

"I thought you knew nothing about him, my heart."

Morag forced herself to glance toward the Marquis again, and was relieved to see that he was apparently ignoring her. Even to her own ears, her voice sounded strange. "Well, I . . . I do recall hearing of him. But, Charles," she put her hand lovingly against his chest. "he is not one to concern us." She glanced up and her eyes met his as another coranto was begun. "My head does ache. I ought to return home."

Bonwell kissed her cheek. "I shall see to it, sweetings. But I do not think we can have the carriage before an hour. Your uncle has gone gaming elsewhere."

"An hour?" Alarmed, she saw Commander Dungan approaching out of the corner of her eye. Feeling trapped, she knew the choice before her was to dance with this horrid little man—his murry-colored silk with the gold buckles shining in the candlelight—or face a confrontation with Sauvage.

For her part, the former was at present more palatable. She turned her smile on Dungan.

"You are ready to dance, Miss Elliot?"

"But of course, commander. 'Twould be a pleasure."

They were halfway through the dance when she saw Quentin approaching. If he dared touch her . . . Noting the dangerous glitter in his eyes, Morag felt a stir of excitement, thinking how she would defy him.

To her astonishment, Commander Dungan made no objection, but released her to him.

"You are bold, sir. Am I not even to be allowed the privilege of being asked if I wish to dance with you?" Her green eyes flashed fire.

A cynical grin spread across his face. "Pardon me, Mademoiselle Elliot, I assumed you would be most happy to see me."

"Then you assumed wrong, sir," she hissed at him as he took her arm to whirl her about.

Quentin shrugged. "But here you are. As to my

being bold, I suggest you accept it. On the other hand, Miss Elliot, it might be wise to control your own boldness."

" 'Tis not I who must worry about being exposed as a rat."

"How so?" His eyes glinted. "I have nothing to hide." The rebuke in his cool tone made her even angrier. It was almost as if he knew her secret, as if he were threatening her.

"Is it true then? You're a spy for William?" Her eyes narrowed and she regarded him with disdain.

"And what of you, my dear little Morag? What are you doing here?" he responded, not answering her question.

"I have come to be with my family and . . . I plan to marry soon."

"Is that so?" The amusement in his voice drove her wild. If they had not been in so public a place, she would surely have slapped him. "It is Bonwell, I take it?"

She glared at him. "So you have been spying on me!"

He shrugged. "You flatter yourself. I only observe what is taking place about me here and listen to what people say." He spun her about again before she could regain her composure.

"What of James? What of your loyalty to your father's people?"

"What of it? They have given me up for dead. As"—he paused—"I believe you did."

She faltered a moment in her dancing. So he knew of her bargain with Maine! His tightening grip on her waist brought her back to the present. She was acutely relieved when the dance ended. He had no right to be there! No right to confuse her again and destroy her sense of security.

Bowing graciously from the waist, he said "I thank Mademoiselle for this dance." His smile was unnatural. "I trust I shall see you again."

Morag fanned herself indignantly. "And I trust you will not."

"*Mignonne*, you will have to go far if you intend to escape me."

"I shall—as far as necessary." She cursed him silently, seeking the safety of her corner seat. Damn him to hell!

Chapter Seventeen

IN DESPERATION, SHE glanced about for Charles, but he was nowhere to be seen. Was he dancing? No, he did not seem to be.

At that moment, much to her surprise, a note was pressed into her hand by a young page. "Is this for me?"

"You are Miss Elliot, are you not?" the boy asked.

Morag nodded, scanning the message. It seemed to be from Charles, but it was scrawled so hastily she could make out only half.

"So I am to follow you to a coach? What has become of the man who gave you this?"

The boy shrugged. "Don' know, miss. He went off with a gentleman, who said to see that you follow."

"Follow where?"

" 'Tis all I have been instructed, miss."

Her heart thumped loudly. Quentin was still dancing—with Lady Armstrong. Whatever this letter signified, Morag did not like the smell of it; but her curiosity won out.

"Very well. Let me get my cape."

"The gentleman at the door has it."

"Oh?" Morag glanced about and saw a lackey standing there, her cloak over his arm.

Outside, a cloudy moon sent pale beams of light into the shadows of the overhanging eaves as Morag followed the lackey. They had not walked far when a cloaked and hooded figure stepped out of the gloom and stopped them.

"Miss Morag Elliot?"

Morag nodded. "Yes . . . who are you? Where is Charles Bonwell?"

"You will find out in good time, miss. Will you enter, please?"

With a shrug of resignation, Morag entered the coach.

The hackney was surprisingly comfortable inside. She sat back as it clattered off, still clutching the note in her fingers as the coach rumbled along. A whiff of air through the window told her that they were passing Fish Street. What had Charles got himself into? Why had he been so insistent upon her following?

With a jerk, the hackney came to a halt. Morag felt the clammy touch of mist mingled with a slight drizzle on her cheeks. The sound of water slapping somewhere below reached her. She guessed, then, that she had been summoned on some government business, for they were standing at the secluded river stairs of Somerset House. Why was she wanted? Morag couldn't imagine.

A link boy appeared. His flaring torch guided her down the narrow steps to the platform at the water's edge, where a wherry waited. Gingerly, she and the two men with her settled themselves aboard. When they were seated, the boatman bent to his task, maneuvering the boat silently and smoothly out into the middle of the dark Thames. Behind them, the glimmer of the link boy's torch soon faded.

Closing her eyes, Morag tried to calm her fears. In the still air, she could hear the muffled BOOM, BOOM of the drum being beaten at Westminster Stairs to guide the boatman through the mist. The air was cool but fresh—a good deal fresher than the malodorous atmosphere of the London streets.

They drifted past the golden points of light from lanthorns dancing on the ripples of the running black water. Morag gazed up at the tall mass of Suffolk House and then York House, which loomed up behind the trees, then disappeared as they rounded the river bend.

Morag's heart beat faster. Glancing at the silent men sitting with her, she wondered if she would be returning to her grandmother's to tell of this night, or if she would disappear into the bowels of some dungeon.

As tall tiers rose out of the gloom to greet them, the boatman drew the wherry over to a solitary lantern. Arms reached out of the shadows and lifted Morag from the bobbing wherry, depositing her onto a small platform. A manservant bowed stiffly before her.

"Miss Morag Elliot?"

Morag nodded. "Yes, sir."

"I am the page of His Majesty's backstairs. You will follow me, please." Without a backward glance, the man turned.

Picking up her skirts, Morag followed the erect shadow up the steps. The wind flapped her cloak against her ankles as she caught up with the page.

"Please, sir. Can you tell me where . . . where I am?"

The man gave her a cool stare. "Why, you are at the private stair of Whitehall Palace, miss. Yonder," he indicated a row of tall leaded windows on the right looking out over the river, "lie Her Majesty's apartments."

Morag stared intently at the curtained windows. There was no sign of life, apart from a faint glimmer behind the thick hangings. Beyond sprawled the mass of buildings which housed the royal household.

"And why was I called?"

"Faith, I do not know, miss. 'Tis William Stewart, His Majesty's minister, who requested to see you."

"Oh." Morag could think of nothing else to say. She wrapped her cloak tighter around her, as if to shield herself from whatever faced her.

They had come to a spiral stair. Lifting her skirts, Morag followed the page to a tiny landing. Suddenly, the light was gone, and Morag realized she was alone in the darkness. As her eyes adjusted to the gloom, she saw a ray of light showing under a door in front of her. Silently, slowly, she fumbled for the latch, found it, and opened the door.

Light streamed out at her from a cozy well-lit room, richly-paneled in dark oak. An enormous Turkish carpet of rich red hues spread at her feet across the oak floorboards. Before her was a huge four-poster draped with carmine velvet, and embroidered in crimson and gold, with valances and curtains of gold cloth. Two embroidered armchairs and footstools stood in front of an enormous roaring fire. Beside a long seat in the window embrasure was a low table set with a glass serving-bottle, four silver-gilt cups and a tray of various cold meats.

As Morag slowly advanced into the chamber, her heart seemed to beat louder and louder.

"You are no doubt wondering where your beloved Mr. Bonwell is, are you not, Miss Elliot?"

Morag whirled about to discover, standing before a second chimney piece, a man of middle height and haughty mien. Under the broad forehead were centered two piercing eyes; the thin face appeared longer, owing to a short pointed beard and its accompanying mustache. Both were streaked with gray. Except that he lacked a sword, the man had all the appearance of a soldier. His buff boots with their slight coating of dust showed that he had recently been on horseback.

Taking a deep breath, Morag vowed silently not to let this man unnerve her into saying what she did not wish to say. "Indeed, sir, I am. I am also wondering why I have been brought here in this . . . this secretive manner."

Chuckling, the man stepped forward. "I like your spirit. We shall get on famously." He grinned, the ends of his mustache lifting. "Dungan, pour the young woman a glass of Rhenish. I believe she will need it afore long."

Morag turned, her heart hammering blood in her ears, to see the froglike Commander Dungan rise from one of the chairs by the fire.

"Well met, Miss Elliot." He smiled as he poured her a glass of wine. "Yoou will like this excellent Rhenish. I told Stewart that you would not be able to resist coming. No, I do not believe you to be the fragile little flower which you play at being." He handed her one of the silvergilt glasses.

Morag took it reluctantly, noting the sweat marks of his fingers on the gleaming stem.

Slowly, she took a sip. "Where is Charles?"

"Oh, you mean Bonwell?" Dungan asked. "You shall see him shortly—after we have spoken with you." He motioned for her to take the chair opposite him, as Stewart moved over to the fireplace to stand facing them.

Sipping her wine, Morag waited for them to begin. The silence of the room, the crackling of the fire, the eyes of the men upon her was becoming more than she could stand. They were testing her, she was sure, but . . . why? What did they want? Did they know about Bucks? God's blood, why didn't they speak?

It was Stewart who finally broke the silence.

"Tell me, Miss Elliot, what was it like, living in the decadance of Versailles?"

"I don't believe that the French are any more decadent than the English, sir. From what I've seen, they are about the same."

"No, girl, that's not a fact, but mayhap I should be more specific. What do you know of the French plans?"

Her fingers opened in innocent astonishment in her lap. Morag shook her head. "Truly, Mister Stewart, if 'tis a spy you want, you have chosen the wrong woman. I know nothing of the French plans. I—"

"You were mistress to that royal bastard, Maine; you must have learned something."

Morag blushed furiously. "Nothing that would be of value to you."

"That is for me to decide, my dear." He drank from his goblet. " 'Tis also for me to decide who will spy and who will not. You were born here, but you have lived in Paris and Versailles long enough to learn the ways of the French court. Indeed, you will suit me nicely."

The huge wooden clock against the wall loudly ticked away the seconds. Dungan smiled across at her in a way that made her shudder. She sipped her wine, swallowing hard, and waited for Stewart to continue.

"Tell me, what do you know of the Marquis d'Angeau?"

The question was so unexpected that Morag choked on her wine. Stewart moved quickly to assist her. His hands lingered on the smooth skin of her neck long after her coughing spasm subsided. Face flushed, tears in her eyes, she shook her head. "I know nothing of the man."

"Come, girl, he danced with you only this evening."

"I know nothing of him," she repeated, more firmly than before.

Stewart shrugged. "Your own body betrays the lie, but it does not matter what you know of his past, my dear Miss Elliot. That is immaterial to us for the moment. I wish to know why he has come to William's court. He fought with that Bourbon puppet, and now he turns up here, neat as you please."

Morag shrugged, trying to hold in her anger at the way Stewart spoke of King James. "Mayhap he had a change of heart. 'Tis not so unusual, I believe, these days."

Stewart shrugged and poured more wine for her. "It's true, I have only my suspicions. I need proof. God's death, I would dearly love to hang that fellow!"

To Morag's discomfort, he placed his hands on her shoulders. "Now, my pretty little French miss——"

"I am not French, sir, and well you should know that!"

He shrugged. "Indeed, I care not, only that you do what I say. I want information about d'Angeau."

Morag took a deep breath, feeling Stewart's fingers tracing the veins up and down her neck. "I want information, and you will get it for me."

She swallowed, but her throat was dry. "How? The man does not like me. He certainly does not trust me."

213

"That is your problem." Stewart's eyes glittered. "My dear Miss Elliot, you are no country virgin. How do most women get their information?"

"No! I shall not do it! There is nothing you can do that will make me." Morag glared at him defiantly.

"Is that so?" Stewart's hands continued to stroke the sides of her neck, giving her chills. "Dungan, fetch Bonwell and the girl."

Within moments, Dungan reappeared, a sheepish Bonwell following him. Charles was accompanied by Cynthia, who had linked her arm in his.

"Now, Mister Bonwell, you will describe how you first met Miss Elliot."

Charles began to shake his head as Morag stared at him. Then, weakly, he began to cry. " 'Twas not my fault, Morag, my sweet. They forced me—"

"They forced you with the promise of paying off your debts!" Cynthia said coldly, jerking his head up. "You thought to marry my Charles, did you, Morag? You thought to take him from me and be a lady of wealth. But Charlie had none of the money he pretended to have. Indeed no. Most of his funds he received from me."

Bonwell could not meet Morag's eyes, but stood staring down, his face as red as the carpet at his feet.

"When I met Miss Elliot, she . . . she was dressed as a common soldier."

"In these exact clothes, is that not so?" Dungan asked. He produced the bundle of Bucks' torn breeches and shirt. Morag gasped. Her head reeled. How had he got them? She had told the maid at the inn to burn them! Had Charles . . . or perhaps Cynthia . . .? She saw the triumphant smile on Dungan's face. Unconsciously, she reached for the wine again.

Bonwell glanced up, still avoiding Morag's eyes, and nodded.

"You have done well, Charles." Stewart patted Bonwell on the back. "You will be amply rewarded."

"When?"

"When you have wed me," Cynthia put in, smiling at Morag.

"Dungan, show the happy couple out," Stewart said. "When you have seen them safely off, we can continue our discussion with the fascinating Miss Elliot."

Morag took up her wine glass again and drained it, closing her eyes. She did not even care when the door closed behind Charles and Cynthia.

Aware of Stewart's eyes on her, she opened hers again. "Well? What does it matter what I was wearing? The things could have been given to me." She noted that Dungan had returned. He was grinning from ear to ear.

"Come now, Miss Elliot. Admit it. You murdered a soldier for his clothes."

"Nay!" Morag stood unsteadily. "I did not! It was self defense. He would have killed me. He told me himself that he had murdered others. He—" She sank back into the chair, realizing what she had done. *Ye great daftie,* she told herself.

"The circumstances do not concern me," Stewart said. "I know only that you are a murderess, and murderesses are usually hung."

Straightening up in the chair, Morag lifted her head bravely to meet Stewart's eyes, then glanced over at Dungan.

"You see, Stewart, it's as I told you." The little frog was grinning like a fiend. "The girl's got spunk. Anyone who could best a man like Henry Bucks must have it. She'll do well for what we want."

Morag leaned over and studiously poured more wine for herself. Taking a deep breath, she asked, "What if I refuse?"

Stewart's hand rested on her shoulder again. "If you do not do as I ask, my dear, that lovely neck of yours will be stretched to its limit. Of course, that would not happen immediately. Dungan and his men must be rewarded first for having tracked you down."

From under her lashes, Morag glanced at Dungan's grinning face. Her stomach turned and she shivered.

"Well, Miss Elliot? Does the commander here get his reward, or do you do as I ask?"

In a small voice, she responded: "I will try to get the information you want."

"Good. Lady Belmont is giving a party in two weeks' time. Your friend is to be a houseguest there— not only the daughter fancies him, I hear, but the old lady as well. I will see that you receive an invitation to spend the night."

"Grandmama does not like me to be away from home—"

"Lady Elliot will have no objection if I speak to her."

Morag glanced away, into the fire. She wished the sea had swallowed her. She wished she had never come to England.

Sighing, she said, "I will speak to Grandmama."

Chapter Eighteen

MORAG DRESSED WITH great care for Lady Belmont's party. She chose a green satin bodice, trimmed with point lace, which matched the green of her eyes and the green of the Elliot emeralds. The wide sleeves, she thought, were particularly fetching. Her skirts were black tabby. When she moved, the rich oriental watered-silk rustled.

Letting her auburn hair flow loose and free, with just a hint of curl over her white shoulders, she placed a lace cap on her head. Yes, she thought, looking into the mirror, the emeralds gave her eyes added sparkle. She was positive that she could not have looked better, yet her stomach knotted with uncertainty at the mere thought of seeing Quentin again. She had scarcely any idea what she would say to him—or, for that matter, what he would say to her . . . .

The ballroom at the Belmont's was already crowded when Morag and her grandmother alighted from their carriage and were duly announced. Soon separated from Lady Elliot, Morag moved to a corner of the room, where she could see the dancers and at the same time was hidden from view by thick velvet drapes

"Looking for me, *mignonne?*"

Morag clenched her fist, hating his arrogance, yet aware of how very handsome he looked in his dark blue brocade flared jacket, with matching breeches and white ruffled shirt. She was aware, too, just how much she wanted him to hold her.

She pushed the idea out of her mind, forced herself to concentrate on her dislike of the man, on what he was, on what he had done to her.

"You fool yourself if you presume to think that I was seeking you. 'Twould suit me just fine never to see you again. Bastard!"

His hand lashed out, grabbing her right wrist. "Do not goad me, *mignonne*, for I have a devilish temper— as well you know."

"Then may the Devil take you," she spat, her dislike of him overcoming her judgment.

Quentin regarded her silently a moment, then released her. Smiling, he reached out and gently drew a line along her jaw with his finger. "Come, dance with me. You look very fetching tonight. Come . . . let us show these English how the dance was meant to be done."

Reluctantly, remembering why she was there, Morag allowed him to lead her out onto the floor. Caught up in the music, she danced the gavotte as she had never danced it before, matching each of her steps perfectly with Quentin's. Or was it he who matched his with hers?

Her mind was still whirling with the joy and energy about her as she collapsed breathlessly into his arms, ending the round.

"Do you see how compatible we two can be?" he teased her.

Morag did not answer; she did not dare. She was aware of an aching desire that he never let her go. It wasn't fair that she should hate this man, yet want him so much.

"Shall we take up the dance again, my sweet?"

"No!" Morag snapped her fan shut abruptly, as the music began again. "I need some air. I am going into the garden."

"Very well then."

Seeing that he meant to follow, she shook her head. "No, leave me be. I don't want anyone with me."

Quentin shrugged. "As you wish," he said and turned away from her.

It was agony for her to see Lady Helena Belmont in his arms a moment later. But . . . what did it signify? He had no thoughts beyond gratifying his own pleasure. Morag would not—could not—concern herself with him.

Leaving the ballroom, Morag hesitated. Now might be the time to search Quentin's room, while he was occupied with Lady Belmont. With luck, she would find something to give Stewart and would be able to return to the ball without anyone missing her. Why, she might not even have to spend the night!

She paused in the empty hall for just a moment, getting her bearings. Stewart had given her specific directions about the location of Quentin's room. Her heart pounding, she lifted her skirts to climb the stairs.

To her relief, she located the room easily enough. Quickly, Morag slipped inside and waited for her eyes to accustom themselves to the darkness about her.

She would, she decided, begin with the desk. 'Twas, after all, the most logical place.

To Morag's ears, the loud squeaking as she pulled the drawer open was like thunder. She paused, waiting a bit, in case anyone might be outside the room. Of course, no one was; 'twas just her own silly fears. Quentin would never find her there, would never know she had been there. He was still downstairs making an ass of himself with Lady Belmont!

Touching papers in the drawer, she realized that to see which ones she needed for Stewart, she would have to have a light. Frowning, she felt gingerly along the smooth desk top, searching for a candle.

Just as she touched the object of her search, a hand clasped her wrist like a vise while, at the same time, a muscular arm encircled her waist. Morag gasped. 'Twas like one of those mythical snakes with coils everywhere!

"What a pleasant surprise, Morag. I did not think you desired my charms so much you would seek me here." D'Angeau's whisper in her ear caused shivers to run hot and cold up her spine.

"Let me go, Quentin!" She struggled, but ineffectually. "I must get back to the dance. Charles . . . Charles is waiting for me."

"Not so fast, my fair one. Why so hasty?" He pulled her close to him and, though she struggled, planted a kiss full on her mouth.

"Now, what is it you were looking for, Morag? Did you think I would be so foolish as to hide anything of merit in that desk? Who has put you up to this?"

Morag shook her head.

"Come . . . tell me. I'll warrant this was not your own idea."

"'Twas no idea. I was but looking for a candle. I . . . my skirt needed repair. How was I to know this was your room?"

"How indeed?"

He pulled her to him again, roughly, his fingers digging into her hair, tangling in the silky red softness. He lifted her face and his mouth met hers in a searching kiss.

For a moment, she was lost, abandoning herself to him. She was scarcely aware that his hands had dropped from her head and were on the curve of her soft breasts.

"Tell me, *mignonne*," he whispered, "is this what you came for?"

She pulled away sharply, slapping him. "You, sir, are a rake and a libertine. You think that every woman wants to bed you. You think—"

"Morag," his hand cupped her quivering chin firmly, "tell me why you are here."

"I told you! I came to mend my skirt!"

"Oh?" He lit the candle that was on the desk. Picking up her skirt and pretending to examine it, he said, "I see nothing at all wrong with your gown."

"'Tis true!" she protested. "There." Her trembling finger pointed to a spot she had just noticed.

But he had stopped playing games. Dropping her skirt, he said softly: "Tell me, *mignonne*, tell me of Henri . . . Tell me why you have come to my room."

She blanched. Henri! For a bewildered moment she thought he was asking about Henry Bucks. Then she remembered Maine's valet. Oh, what a world away that was! "There is nothing to tell. I do not understand what it is you wish to know." Her stomach curled into a tight knot. Damn the man, she had come to get information about him and he was questioning her!

"Morag," his hands were on her shoulders, "I know you. You rush into things, my dear, without due thought. It would be well for you to learn when to make concessions, and when to be on your guard. Now is the time for truth.''

She shrugged, glaring up into the gray eyes that were assessing her so coolly. ''Well, then, the truth is . . . my mother's death—'' she swallowed hard ''—I wish to know what hand you had in it.''

The candlelight flickered as he stared at her. Arms folded, he walked slowly about her, examining her as if she were on an auction block.

''Very well, *mignonne.*'' A slow smile crossed his face. ''I will tell you all that you wish to know, provided that you do something for me.''

In a small voice she answered, ''What is that?''

''You must undress for me, slowly, as you would have for Maine.''

''But, I . . . Charles—''

''We are past lies, Morag. Bonwell is not here and well you know it. In fact, if my information is correct, he is to marry the day after tomorrow, but the bride will not be you. Shall I go on?''

She shook her head. When she spoke, tears choked her. '''Tis Cynthia. Aye, I know. I was daft to think I could have his love.'' But it was not love of Charles but fear of Quentin that made her voice tremble.

''Morag . . . *mignonne.*'' He took her into his arms. She was amazed at how quickly he changed from enemy to lover. His hands undid the buttons at the back of her dress and slid the garment off her slender body. As he pulled her to him, she felt his hardness press against her, his kisses warm on her forehead.

''One has to take what one wants in life, Morag, and not be afraid to do it. Can we not love and enjoy each other and banish our cares for a while?'' She felt his hot breath on her shoulder. His hands slid over her, fondling her breasts. The flames rose within her so that she could think of nothing but him. Cupping her naked breasts, he bent to kiss them, devouring the pink tips as she groaned in response. There were tears in her eyes.

Morag quivered at his touch but did not struggle. When he lifted her into his arms, she heard the rustle of the dress as it settled on the floor. He blew out the candle and placed her gently on the bed. His touch was like fire.

The last thing she saw were his eyes—gray, intense, almost hypnotic—as his mouth closed on hers. A wave of warmth flooded her body and her soul stirred as though wakened from a deep sleep. The warmth spread through every part of her. Inside of her, she could feel his manhood bruising her, demanding a response. Her arms went about him. She cried out, not knowing if the sound that escaped her was one of joy or fear.

It was more than an hour later, with her head cradled on his hairy chest, her fingers trailing along his thigh, that she thought again to ask him of her mother.

"Was it true that you were planning to marry my mother?"

He kissed her forehead. "Yes, little love, as true as the fact that I am here with you now."

She stared up at him, her green eyes puzzled. "But . . . if you loved her, then why did you leave? Why did you go to Ireland? And why have you joined William now?"

"Joined William? What lies have you been hearing about me?"

"I . . . 'tis said that you deserted James in his hour of need. That you betrayed him."

223

Quentin gave a sour laugh. "Nay, I did not betray James—he betrayed himself."

"But you are here now. You have come—"

"To gain what information I can for my uncle's sake."

"Then you *are* spying for James?"

"What is it, *mignonne?*" He kissed her again. "Why so troubled? I should think that would be exactly what you want."

"It is." She responded to his kiss. The feeling of dullness in her heart was soon replaced by an intense hunger to feel Quentin's manliness within her again.

"Do you know," he laughed, as her hands fondled him, "I believe you missed your calling, *ma petite*. You would have made an excellent courtesan."

She shook her head. Passion for him flooded her as he entered her again. At the moment, she thought of nothing but him.

Morag did not know if it was the light of the moon or the coldness from his side of the bed which woke her. But she opened her eyes to a sense of desolation: he was gone!

The house about her was silent. The ball must have ended long ago. Where had Quentin disappeared to? Lady Belmont's room, no doubt, she thought bitterly. She did not doubt that he had gone to another—as he had gone to Nicole that first time—and she hated herself for having given in to him so easily.

She had the information now that the Stewart wanted. Had Quentin not admitted that he was a spy? But while she could repeat what he said, she had no proof. Slipping from the empty bed, Morag crossed the room, intent upon checking the desk once more.

But, passing the window, she glimpsed a figure in the garden below. So that was where he was. Pausing to watch, she soon realized that he was not alone, and there was no doubt in her mind that the caped and hooded figure standing with him was a woman.

At that moment, the hood fell. The blonde curls were unmistakable. So, Nicole had come to claim him as she had promised she would. Morag's heart tore in half. Once again, her cousin had won.

Turning away, dressing quickly in her crumpled gown, Morag left Quentin's room without another thought for the proof Stewart had asked her to obtain.

Morag remained in her room all the next day, debating what she should do. Sooner or later, if she did not come to him, Stewart would come to her. Yet, while she had the information he wanted, she still was not certain what she should tell him.

After all, she reasoned, she had only Quentin's word that he was a spy for James. For all she knew, he might have said it only to bed her.

A knock on the door startled her.

"Yes?"

"'Tis Annie, Miss. 'Er ladyship do want t'see ya in the drawing room fer tea. . 'Tis a gentleman here as called t'see ya."

Fear clutched at Morag's throat. Stewart had come! Could the man not give her a moment's peace? Wondering what to tell Grandmama, she dressed hurriedly in a cool cotton gown and ran down the stairs. Breathless, she made her entrance into the drawing room, only to see Lady Elliot pouring tea for Quentin!

Morag stood there with her mouth open; then she

225

forgot herself completely. "What the devil . . .? A pox on your soul! Can you not leave me be?"

Her grandmother stared at her in shock. "Morag! Is that any way to talk to the Marquis? He has come to call upon you and pay his respects."

Glaring at him, Morag came on into the room and took a cup of tea from the old lady. "Pray forgive me, Grandmama. 'Tis only that I am surprised to see him. I had . . . rather expected someone else."

"My poor little one," Lady Elliot cooed. "You will get over Charles, never fear. 'Tis well that you had not given him an answer. But that part of your life is over, chicken. I vow you will forget Charles when you hear what the Marquis d'Angeau has to say to you."

Morag glanced sharply at the man. "And what has he come to say to me?"

"'Tis your marriage we speak of, child," her grandmother told her.

"What marriage? I have given my pledge to no one."

"Child, you must realize that in English society, one's reputation is of the utmost importance. You were seen coming out of the Marquis' room at a rather late hour yesterday and, while I have no doubt that, as he says, it was all perfectly innocent—that you went with him to speak of your mother and of France—'tis not right for you to have met alone with him." Lady Elliot noted her granddaughter's raised chin and stiff neck. "His lordship has graciously volunteered to wed you, to save your reputation."

"No! I'll not have it." Morag stood abruptly, spilling the tea on her gown.

"Morag, you will do as I say! Such conduct may be permissible at the vile court of Versailles, but 'tis not acceptable here, among the best families of England. Go to your room and change for supper. The Marquis has agreed to move his things here, since you will be wed before the week's out."

Fire in her eyes, Morag glared at Quentin. Then, picking up her skirts, she stormed from the room. She was no fool; 'twas plain to her the man intended to wed her to silence her. After all, once they were wed, any word about her husband's activities would mean very little. Damn the man!

Slamming the door to her room, she shed the tea-stained dress. Ringing for the maid, she flung herself down on the bed to cry. Yes, she wanted to marry—she most definitely wanted to marry someone, to have children —but she wanted a man who would love her, who would cherish her. Not the Marquis, who was willing to wed her only to silence her.

She did not hear the door opening. Only when he bent over her did she realize that the man had had the audacity to enter her room!

"How dare you!" she cried, glaring up into those gray eyes. "How dare you enter my room without permission! Get out! Or I shall scream!"

Quentin shrugged. "Then scream, my dear. I do not think anyone will pay attention. Your grandmother has given me leave to speak to you privately."

"Oh, of course, since my reputation is already in ruins."

He made a face, but there was laughter in his eyes. "That is not my fault, *mignonne*. I did not ask you to come to my room."

"No, but you did not have to seduce me."

He was by her side again. "Come now, Morag. I did not have to do too much to persuade you." He kissed her nose. "When will you admit that you enjoy my caresses?"

"Never!"

Quentin leaned over her. His lips grazed her neck, moved to her ear. He took her into his arms and began to kiss her, exciting her. Suddenly, she found herself straining against him, returning his kisses.

"Tell me you will marry me," he whispered, biting her ear gently, driving her mad.

"No!"

"*Mon Dieu,* Morag. You are a stubborn little wench. 'Tis no disgrace to love a man. Say that you want me."

"You are a fiend and a blackmailer!" she cried, as his fingers continued to inflame her, as the waves of warmth swept over her and she gasped for breath.

Morag closed her eyes, hating this man. "I . . . I want you."

"Excellent." He laughed softly as she mewed like a kitten in sore need of attention. "Now, say that you will marry me."

"I . . . yes! Oh, damn you for a devil," she cried. "Yes! I will marry you!"

His kiss was her answer as his mounting brought her to a fiery climax. Finally, satisfied, she curled up against him, feeling the warm protectiveness of his arms, forgetting her hatred of him . . . forgetting her plans to destroy him.

Chapter Nineteen

WITHIN THE WEEK, the season had suddenly turned inexplicably cold for a London autumn. In contrast, Morag found herself thinking warmer and warmer thoughts about the man she was to marry. Indeed, not one day had passed since he moved his things into the Elliot townhouse, that they did not make love. Each time, Morag would struggle against her desires, but each time, Quentin would stir such a fire within her that she felt she would go mad if it were not quenched. The man had become like a drug to her.

The more time she spent with him, the more her confusion grew. He could be domineering one moment and gentle and tender the next, silently holding her when she needed to be held. He could almost read her mind; he instinctively knew what she needed. Could it be that she was falling in love with him?

She contemplated what it would be like to be the Marquise d'Angeau. No doubt he would continue his wenching. A pang of jealousy stabbed her heart. No, she did not love him . . . how could she love one who would be so careless of her feelings?

Dressing for tea, she wondered how her grandmama had been so completely won over by the man. Despite the swiftness of the arrangements, she had been amazed to learn that they would be married at Saint George's and that King William himself would attend the ceremony!

Reaching the first floor, Morag saw that the door to the drawing room was partly closed. Was something amiss? Then she became aware of the butler standing just to the left of the door.

"Is there not some task you have at the moment, Tims?"

"No, miss, but I do have something for you." He handed her a sealed note with the royal stamp on it.

A chill of foreboding ran up Morag's spine. Until that moment, she had managed to put William Stewart out of her mind. Now, staring at the smooth parchment, she knew it was a summons from the minister.

Tims added, "It was hand-delivered, miss. The gentleman asked that you receive it personally."

"Thank you, Tims," she said, stuffing the note into her pocket. She brushed past him to enter the drawing room, and saw Quentin sitting with her Uncle Donald and Lady Elliot. Morag was amazed to see her uncle smiling for a change.

Supper was over that day before Morag recalled the note in her pocket. Going quickly to the hall, on the pretext of fetching a book, she opened the sealed letter. Her hands trembled as she read the command that she be ready to meet Stewart that evening. She glanced at the clock in the hall; the coach would be along to fetch her in less than an hour! What excuse could she possibly give her grandmother? What excuse could she give Quentin, who had scarcely allowed her out of his sight all week long?

THIS BITTER ECSTASY

Biting her lower lip, she stared at the note. She could ignore it altogether, but she did not think that would be wise. In truth, though, she had little to tell Stewart. Other than that one indiscretion, Quentin had said nothing to her of James or William. She supposed, were she truly a spy, she should have asked or at least searched his things once more. But, she acknowledged to herself, she had not really wanted to know.

"You are pale, *mignonne*." Quentin suddenly came up behind her. Hastily, she stuffed the letter into her pocket.

"'Tis nothing. I believe I ate too much this night, or mayhap it is nerves. Do not forget that I am to be wed tomorrow."

Quentin smiled gently. "No, Morag, I do not forget that, though I see no cause for worry there. You'll have no complaints of me as a husband."

She shook her head and shrugged. "Whatever will happen, will happen." She bit her lip. "I will not fault you if you turn to another. Indeed, it seems most husbands do."

His eyes narrowed and he regarded her thoughtfully. "Something has come over you, Morag. Has someone stolen your heart from me?"

"My heart was never yours," she snapped.

His hand cupped her chin. "Well, if not your heart than your body was, or else you are a damned good actress."

She quivered at his touch and hoped that she would be a good actress this night when she saw Stewart. He would have to believe that she knew nothing of Quentin's plans.

Suddenly, her throat ached with unshed tears. God's death! This was no time to be weak, but she would have given her all for Quentin to take her in his arms lovingly, for him to know that—no matter what happened between her and Stewart this night—she loved him. But she dared not say it, nor even think of it. Quentin would only laugh. Besides, it was not love—it was merely her body betraying her.

Picking her skirts up, she freed herself from him. "You will excuse me, Monsieur, but my head aches greatly. I think, for this night, I shall take a draught to be sure that I sleep quite soundly."

He seemed to stare through her with those cold gray eyes, making her shiver. "As you wish, my dear. I trust you will feel better in the morning."

Morag merely nodded, not daring to speak, then turned and fled up the stairs.

Locking the door to her room behind her, Morag changed into a dark cotton gown. From below, she heard the clock in the hall chime. God's death! How was she to get out of the house without being seen?

She glanced at the window. No, the roof was too steep; it was too dangerous. Going to Stewart's might mean her death, but she'd not hasten it. Nervously, she paced the floor, wondering just what she could tell the man. Would he believe that she had learned nothing?

Clenching and unclenching her fist, Morag decided that it would be best to leave now, while Grandmama and Quentin and Uncle Donald were in the salon. Ringing for her maid, Annie, she unlocked the door and pulled the girl inside the room quickly.

"'Tis of utmost importance that I go out, and I want no one in here while I am gone."

"Yes, miss.' Annie curtsyed, not understanding.

"If anyone comes to the door, you will tell them that I am asleep."

The maid's eyes opened wide. "Ya mean, I'm t'stay here meself?"

Morag nodded. "With the door locked until you hear a stone thrown at the window." The girl's eyes continued to dilate in surprise. "That will be me signaling you to come down and open the door for me. Do you understand?"

"Aye, miss, I think so. But . . . ya'll not be gone long, will ya?"

Morag took a deep breath. "I pray not."

Creeping down the stairs, pattens in hand, Morag held her breath, listening. Yes, there were voices coming from the drawing room where the family were no doubt having their cocoa and that vile new brew, coffee.

Her heart pounded and the blood rushed to her ears, but she had reached the front door and, seconds later, was safely out.

Shivering, and not just from the cold, she drew her cape tighter about her and peered into the darkness. Mayhap she should expose Quentin for the spy he was! Yet, despite the man's arrogance, she did not think she could do it. Would it be so terrible if she married him on the morrow? Whether they loved or not, a married matron definitely had advantages in society which a single girl did not.

Morag was still debating what course to take when the hooded lackey approached her out of the darkness.

"Miss Elliot?"

She nodded and followed him to where the coach waited.

As they drove through the silent streets, Morag realized that they were headed not toward the palace but to the city proper. She longed to call up and ask the driver where they were going, but was afraid. She closed her eyes as the coach rumbled on, her stomach lurching with each jolting movement.

By the time the coach stopped, she was in a state of anxiety. Nearly vomiting from the stench of the city, she saw the dark form of the Tower looming over her as she alighted from the coach. God's blood, was Stewart going to put her away without even a hearing?

The lackey, who had ridden with the driver, now motioned for her to follow him. Morag could hear the ships in the harbor behind them, creaking noisily in the wind. The area here was so desolate she was glad to hurry her steps, walking close behind her guide.

The spiral stair they entered was cold and damp and dark. Morag touched the sides, feeling the slimy moss that grew there, as they made their way up. She was breathing heavily when they reached the landing. Feeling dizzy, she glanced out of the narrow window. There was nothing to see except the river shining below in the moonlight.

With relief, she entered a room at the top of the stairs, glad to see the fire roaring in the grate. Morag looked around the modestly furnished, yet comfortable, suite.

Stewart was seated, quill in hand, at a narrow oak desk. The candlelight playing on his face gave him an eerie, evil look. He paid her no attention at first. Finally, he glanced up, acknowledging her presence.

"I owe you my congratulations, I believe."

"Congratulations . . .?"

"On your coming marriage, my dear. All of London is talking about how you sank your hook into the—I am told—most eligible bachelor on both sides of the Atlantic."

Morag shrugged. "'Twas not any of my doing."

"No? As I understand it, he proposed to save your reputation. I wonder how you came to be in the Marquis d'Angeau's room?" The amusement in his voice was unmistakable.

"You know exactly what I was doing there—what I was attempting to do." She stared down at the floor.

"What is your definition of 'attempting,' Miss Elliot? Did you not accomplish your mission?"

Morag shook her head.

"I do not believe you.

"Believe it or not, 'tis true. He came upon me before I could discover anything." Her eyes flashed and she struggled to control her hatred for this creature. "Would you have had me tell him, or would you have had me follow your advice and bed him?"

"And then? Do you mean to say you have discovered nothing at all to assist me during this past week?"

"No, sir. I have not." She swallowed hard.

He pounded his fist on the table, shaking the ink and causing the candle flame to waver. "Do you take me for a fool? You must have learned something, or he would not now be marrying you."

"My reputation—"

"Hang your reputation! 'Tis to silence you, of that I am certain." He glared at her. "Tell me what you have learned."

"Nothing!" Her voice was hoarse. "He was suspicious of me. There was no opportunity for me to search his papers, he . . . he carries them on his person at all times, but . . . but I do not think he is the spy you seek."

"Do you know what my plans are for you, Miss Elliot?"

Morag swallowed hard. "You made that clear at our

first meeting, but I told you then, I am not by nature a spy." She stood stoically, waiting for his response, while inside she trembled.

He smiled grimly at her.

"Enjoy your life as the Marquise, Miss Elliot, for it will be short. On the morrow, shortly after you are wed, your husband will be arrested for the French spy he is."

Morag swallowed hard. "Who . . . who has told you such tales?"

"Does it matter? What signifies is that I believe her. She has shown me the proof I needed. The King will have no doubts that his favorite has betrayed him."

He sat down at his desk, not looking at her. "Shut the door after you, Miss Elliot."

"I'm free to go? You'll not keep me?" Morag could not believe it.

"I will not keep you. I've no use for a dunderling such as you. Besides, as you probably suspected, your Grandmama would scarcely allow me to take you into custody. So, you see, you really had nothing to fear after all."

"Do you mean that you tricked me?" She slammed her hand down on his desk.

"Miss Elliot, I suggest you leave—now. You are not completely beyond my reach."

Swallowing rage and injured pride, Morag turned toward the door.

"And I would not advise warning the Marquis," Stewart added. If you warn him, you will have to tell him how it is you know. Think about that, my dear. Think what his reaction would be."

Morag stared at the man, realizing that he was right. Quentin would hate her. She could not tell him. Numbly, she followed Stewart's lackey from the room and down the stairs to the waiting coach. As the vehicle moved off, Morag pressed her nose against the window. She supposed she should be grateful that Stewart had not carried through with his threat, but . . . what was she to do now? How could she allow Quentin to be captured? She could not warn him without revealing her own part in the sorry business, yet somehow she must save him.

The carriage stopped at the end of Saint James Square, and Morag slipped out to walk the rest of the way. The house was dark. Loose pebbles in hand, Morag threw them at her window. Within a moment, Annie's round head popped out.

Moments later, the door was opened and Morag slipped into the dark hall. "No! Don't light a candle!" she warned the girl. "I shall go up without it. There were no problems, were there?"

"No, miss . . ." Annie's answering whisper assured her.

"The Marquis did not question you?"

"Yes, miss, but I told 'im ya were asleep."

"Thank you, Annie," she whispered, starting up the stairs.

Reaching the top of the landing, Morag paused for a moment. The silence of the sleeping house pressed around her. Holding her breath, she slipped quickly into her room. Turning to lock the door, she stiffened, suddenly aware that she was not alone.

"I trust you are only sleepwalking, *mignonne*." Quentin finished locking the door and drew her into his arms, kissing her expertly on the mouth.

Pulling away, Morag snapped, "What are you doing here?"

"Your little ruse might have worked had not your

maid slammed the window down so hard." He grinned at her. "Naturally, I wondered what that was about."

She remained standing near the door, removing her cape and placing it over an overstuffed chair. "I wanted to . . . get some air—I could not sleep—so I went for a walk."

Quentin's eyes narrowed. "That is strange, my love. I could swear your maid told me you were fast asleep not an hour ago."

Morag blushed and stammered: "I . . . I *was* asleep. I woke—I told you. I am nervous about . . . about tomorrow. I—"

He tilted her head back, forcing her to look into his eyes. "Morag, my pet, I have told you—you have nothing to fear. When we are married, you will have nothing to worry you."

Tears welled up in her eyes; she could not stop them. Gently, he kissed them away as he lifted her up, carrying her to the huge four-poster bed.

As they made love, slowly and with a sweet harmony, Morag was suddenly filled with sadness. She would never experience this again unless . . . unless she told him what she had learned from Stewart. Perhaps, on the morrow, she would. Yes, she decided, just before the flame climaxed within her, she would tell him in the morning, before the wedding. She must, she thought, snuggling up against him. In a moment, she was fast asleep.

Morag awoke to the sound of a door slamming below. Her heart hammered as she sat up in bed, startled. Beside her, Quentin was still asleep.

"Get up!" she said, shaking him.

His eyes opened and for a moment he just stared at

her. Then he heard the voice of William Stewart ordering his men to search the house, find the Marquis and arrest him. Quentin looked at her with sudden comprehension.

"By my faith, Morag! I did not think you had it in you! Do you hate me so very much?"

She tried to shake her head; she wanted to tell him that this was not her doing, but no words would come. She had meant to warn him, yet now she could not speak.

"Very well, my little love." He yanked her from the bed. "Two can play that game. If they take me, you will be taken as well. Your pretty little neck will mean nothing with a knife through it."

Morag tried again to shake her head, to speak . . . explain. Tears blinded her as the door to the room crashed open. Behind her, Quentin pulled her arms to her back, holding her as a shield.

"And I thought you were a man, D'Angeau!" Stewart sneered. He entered the room, holding high a candelabrum.

Blinking in the light, Morag heard the minister order Quentin to let her go.

"Why should I? If you want her, come and get her, though I'll warrant you've already had your fill of her, have you not, Stewart?"

Morag swallowed hard, praying that the minister would tell Quentin that she had not been the one to betray him. But the look in Stewart's eyes told her that he was enjoying her discomfort.

She found her voice then and, unthinking, asked "Why have you come tonight? You said—"

"I said I would take the man when I would. 'Tis a pity you believe everything you are told, Miss Elliot. I do regret that you will not be a Marquise."

"Oh, she will yet, have no fear of that, Stewart!" D'Angeau laughed as he grabbed Morag's cape with one hand and draped it about the both of them. "My little Morag would not let such a prize slip so easily from her hands, would you, *chérie?*" he asked, squeezing her so tightly as he edged her toward the stairs that she could not answer.

Out on the landing, she tried to free herself, tried to push him forward, hoping he would run, while she somehow distracted the soldiers. But Quentin didn't understand and only pulled her tighter to him.

Morag saw the soldiers approaching, swords drawn, before Quentin did. She screamed, trying to warn him, but again, he misunderstood. Abruptly, he released her and turned to defend himself. Strong as he was, d'Angeau could not best six armed men. As he was dragged down the steps, he shouted: "Morag Elliot, you shall rue the day you laid eyes on me!"

She shook her head in despair, having no answer for him.

"*Mignonne,* you have not done with me yet. I shall have my revenge!"

Morag choked back the tears which threatened to overwhelm her. She did not realize that Stewart was at her side until she heard him say, "Well done, my girl," loud enough for the prisoner to hear.

Morag glared at him. Then, unable to bear it any longer, she ran up the stairs to her room, threw herself down on the bed and cried her heart out. This time there was no hope—he would die. It didn't matter that she had not betrayed him; she had done nothing to help him.

"Oh, Quentin!" she cried. "Quentin, my darling, you must forgive me! I love you . . ."

Chapter Twenty

MORAG SANK INTO a deep depression. Since d'Angeau's arrest, she had eaten little, slept little and prayed much. Daily she waited, hoping for some word of him, yet dreading to hear it.

Finally, two months after his arrest, news came. He would be hung on Queen Mary's birthday, along with three other spies. Fainting when she heard it, Morag recovered to find herself in her room with her grandmother's doctor hovering over her.

"What is amiss, sir?" She saw the gray-haired gentleman frowning.

She sat up in bed, her heart pounding as she stared anxiously at the doctor.

"You are pregnant, my dear. Two months at least, I would say."

"But . . . I can't be! I . . . I'm not married."

The man blinked. "Nor were you when you slept with your young man. There is no such law, as you French should know, that one must marry to have a child."

Suddenly lightheaded, Morag sank back against the

pillows. Only vaguely did she hear the doctor ask her if she would tell Lady Elliot.

"Yes," she responded distantly, "I suppose I shall."

Would her grandmother understand, or would Morag be banished somewhere to the country? She could not bear to leave London while the Marquis was still alive, or to think of losing the family she had found so recently. In truth, she thought grimly, Quentin was having a most excellent revenge.

As Morag feared, her grandmother was not pleased with her.

"'Tis not an uncommon thing, however, especially with a man as handsome as the Marquis about. I fear, though, that we shall have to deal with it rather quickly."

"I will not destroy it, if that is what you mean, Grandmama. I want this child."

"Sweetings, 'tis not a matter of want. You are an unmarried woman. We shall never find you a husband if this leaks out."

"Then I shall go elsewhere."

"And what of the babe when it is born? What will you do with it?"

"I . . . I will keep it." Morag was amazed at the question. No alternative was possible; the bairn was hers.

"Morag, the man is a spy!"

Morag clenched her fist tightly. "Grandmama, I—"

She swallowed hard and sank back into her bed-pillows. "Grandmama, I do not wish to speak of it now."

"Do not worry, my dear." The old lady patted her hand. "There is time yet to talk and make our plans."

"Then, you will not send me away?"

Lady Elliot hesitated. "Well, 'tis true that Donald spoke on the matter, but I disapprove of his ideas. Whatever happens, you are still my Andrew's child." She gave a heavy sigh. "Spy or no, the man was handsome as the Devil."

Morag bit her lip. "Please, Grandmama, do not say 'was'. The Marquis lives until after the New Year."

Lady Elliot eyed her granddaughter speculatively. "You say that as if you loved the worthless creature, my pet."

Morag shook her head fervently. "No. I do not love him, I . . . just do not want him to die!" Tears sparkled in her eyes.

"Well," Lady Elliot shrugged. "die he will, unless some miracle occurs and he is transported. 'Tis said William was furious to learn that his new favorite had betrayed him. Aye," she patted Morag's hand. "do not dwell on it, lass. You must rest. I will have Annie bring your tea now."

The pale winter afternoon cloaked the city in mist. Despite the fire in the room, the air was cold and clammy, the dampness penetrating the closed windows. Morag moodily regarded the tray before her. Eyeing the teapot, Morag wondered: the tea had tasted strange, but was that not usual during pregnancy? Surely, Lady Elliot would not be so cruel as to drug her? No, 'twas just her imagination.

She rose and, moving to the window, stood staring down at the square below. Mayhap some fresh air would help. She had hardly ventured out since the day of Quentin's arrest, but tonight the townhouse seemed to stifle her. Putting on a dark wool dress and a warm cloak, she slipped downstairs and out of the house before Tims or Lady Elliot could see and stop her.

Without much thought, she began to walk in the direction of the city. Later, when her legs were beginning to ache, Morag realized that she had walked all the way to the Tower. Her heart hammered. Did they have Quentin there? If so, could he see her? If only she could get a letter to him; if only she could tell him of the babe. Mayhap he would forgive her then.

Morag became aware that her head ached dreadfully and her vision was blurring. Fear gripped her as she bent over with the first pain. Stepping forward, she tumbled headlong over a stone. Crying out with the suddenness of her agony, she stood quickly as terrible stabbing pains cut into her stomach. Breathless, she sank to the ground again, hot tears running down her cheeks. No! It could not be, she could not be losing his child!

Somehow she managed to signal a wherry and instruct the man to take her to Whitehall. 'Twas only her Scottish luck that her auburn hair was recognized by a passerby when the puzzled boatman pulled the unconscious girl from his craft near the palace steps.

Morag woke to daylight in her own bed. Her head pounded, but that was nothing compared to the emptiness she felt within her. Glancing up, she met the troubled eyes of her grandmother's doctor.

"You were a fool, Miss Elliot, to take that walk. It ruined your chances for now. Faith, I wonder if you will ever be able to have a child after this."

"Then I have lost this one?"

The doctor nodded. "You'll be in bed for several days, but at least you'll not have to worry about bearing a child without a husband."

"No," She turned her head away. "That is something I'll have no worries on." Burying her face in her pillow, she let the tears fall. No, she'd not voice her suspicions to her grandmother. What was done, was done. Indeed, if Lady Elliot did drug the tea, Morag could not fault her. Still, the tears continued to choke her. She supposed she was better for having lost the babe, but she knew it would be some time before the ache in her heart would heal.

The prison stank of the foulest odors. The large room the guard threw Quentin into was crammed with men barely alive, standing, swaying and moaning. They blinked, crying aloud with pain, as the unaccustomed light hit their eyes. Quentin, inwardly appalled but outwardly expressionless, turned to the guard.

"I am a Marquis, sir. I expect better than this."

"'Spect better, Frenchie? Ya'll get better." The guard laughed, ramming Quentin backwards so that he lost his footing and sprawled in the slimy filth on the cell floor. Still laughing, the guard slammed the door and locked it.

During the next few weeks, Quentin Sauvage's Indian training served him well. He managed to satisfy his hunger with a few crusts of the stale bread the guards tossed into the cell periodically, but he drank none of the putrid water, noting that those who did eventually took the fever. For the most part, he spent the time leaning against the wall, meditating on his future, wondering at Morag's betrayal, plotting revenge.

He was preoccupied in this fashion one day when the same guard who had brought him there entered the cell.

"You there! Frenchie!"

D'Angeau glanced about, then back at the guard. "Could you possibly mean me, sir?" he asked with mock humility. "Am I being released?"

"Released?" The man laughed. "Nay, the only release ya'll have is at the end o'yer rope. Jist be a good boy 'n' come 'long now."

D'Angeau shrugged. Whatever it was, it could not be any worse than what he had endured these past weeks. Without another word, he made his way through the crush of prisoners.

They were crossing a courtyard when Quentin spoke to the guard again.

"Where is it you're taking me?"

The guard spat on the broken stone pavement. "It seems ya got a friend."

"Oh? And who might that be?"

"Says she's yer cousin." The man gave a hoarse laugh, spitting again. "Don' say as I believe it, but she paid plenty fer ya t'ave a private chamber. Must say she's a pretty little thing."

"Is that a fact?" Had Morag done this out of guilt? Well, it would do her no good. He would still have his revenge. The thought of it was what kept him alive these days, though, he admitted grudgingly, it wasn't only vengeance he thought on. It was also that soft supple body, that smooth skin and the innocent wonder in her green eyes when they made love. He could not get the girl out of his mind. Yes, by God, he would

have her again—and he would make her beg for his
forgiveness.

The private parlor on the opposite side of the courtyard was nearly half the size of the room he had been
incarcerated in these past weeks. A chair and a table,
complete with inkstand and paper, stood in a corner;
the left side of the room had a narrow hay mattress on
a rope bed. It would not be as comfortable as feather
mattresses in the court of Versailles, but it was certainly better than the earthen floor, slick with human
waste, that was his bed these days.

Turning about from his cursory appraisal, he saw
that the guard had left him, and then he heard light
quick footsteps coming his way.

"Quentin?" The low, honey-smooth voice startled
him, and then a blonde girl entered.

"*Sang de Dieu!* Nicole!"

"You look surprised, *mon amour*. Whom did you
expect to see? My cousin?"

His gray eyes narrowed. "What is it you want, Nicole?"

"You know what I want." She licked her lips.
"But"—she wrinkled her tiny nose—"I shall have to
order a bath for you first. *Mon Dieu!* These guards
gouge you for the slightest thing!" She stared at him
with guileless blue eyes. "Why do you look at me so?
Are you disappointed that I am not the fool who betrayed you to Stewart?"

He continued to stare at her with unwavering gray
eyes. The girl shifted her weight uncomfortably. Finally, he said, "I will deal with Morag in my own time
and my own way, Nicole."

"Will you now? Will you indeed!" Nicole's voice

rose shrewishly for just a moment. With obvious effort, she said sweetly, "Quentin, love, I do not think you realize your position. You are to be hung until you are near death and then . . ." she paused for dramatic effect, "then you are to be drawn and quartered."

"Am I now?" he drawled.

His indifference irked her. "Most certainly, unless . . . unless I help you."

A cynical smile showed on his face. "Are you offering your services?"

Nicole paced toward the room's narrow window and back, coming only just so close because of his smell. "You know I will help you. I am not the idiot my cousin is. I can arrange for you to be chosen for transport."

"Oh?" His eyebrows rose. "And how will you do that?"

Seeing her blue eyes flash, Quentin was shocked at the family resemblance between this cold, hard blonde girl and the soft, innocent red-haired Morag.

"Must you know? *Mon amour*, be content with knowing that I will do my utmost to save your life."

"I am content," Quentin said. "Do you wish your reward now or later, my dear?"

Nicole wrinkled her nose. "I will arrange for your bath, then I will return for my reward—after I have taken care of my cousin."

"Nicole! I forbid you to go near Morag. Leave that to me."

The blonde shrugged. "Very well, *mon amour*. I will leave her to your revenge." She smiled and licked her lips seductively. "I will return shortly for my reward."

Morag remained in bed for several weeks after her miscarriage, feeling even worse than she had during her pregnancy. Even with Stewart's assurance that the Marquis would hang, she lived in fear of Quentin. She could not help wondering how he would engineer her ruin—for ruin her he most certainly would.

She was sitting by the fire in her bedroom, wrapped in her dressing gown, staring alternately into the flames and out the window at the sodden gray sky. It was almost four months now since Quentin had been arrested, and no word of his execution.

A knock on the door roused her.

"Yes?" She did not look up when the door opened, expecting it to be Annie with her tea. But it wasn't; it was Donald Elliot.

"Uncle!" Morag jumped up from her place by the fire. "I .. . . I am not seeing visitors."

"Dear Niece, I hardly count myself a visitor, and there are matters we must speak of, which I do not want my mother to overhear."

"Oh?" Her heart was hammering.

"'Tis about your father." He sat down opposite her. "Sit down, my dear."

Morag sank down in the chair she had occupied before and waited, watching her uncle's face. What in heaven's name was there to speak of? Her thoughts flew to her father's last duel, to the earlier happy days when he and Maman were so much in love. Tears filled her eyes and she turned her head away, staring into the fire.

"What is it that you have to say about Papa, Uncle? If you are going to condemn him, I do not want to hear it."

Donald Elliot smiled coldly. "That is not for you to decide, Morag, whether it is a condemnation or not. The fact is, Andrew was not your father."

"What!" Her green eyes widened in shock.

"Let me phrase that differently. Andrew never married Marie Thérèse Le Martin, and it is a well-known fact that afore he chose to throw in his lot with her, she whored around."

"How dare you say that about Maman!" Morag leaped to her feet, clenching her fists. "You are daft, mon. She loved my father!"

Donald continued to smile. "Love does not enter into this conversation, Niece—if you are, in truth, my niece, and I do not believe you are. That is the crux of the matter, whether you are an Elliot or not."

Even as he spoke, Morag's mind went back. She recalled those days when Maman was with others, days when Papa would go off and Morag would hear Marie Thérèse's high laughter from beyond the walls of her bedroom.

Tears sparkled in her eyes. "I am his daughter! I am the daughter of Andrew Elliot." She saw her uncle's startled look. He obviously had not expected such strong resistance. "'Tis no matter what you tell me, or whether they married or not. He was my father! I am his daughter! That is not something one can hide."

Donald Elliot's eyes narrowed. "Daughter or not," he shrugged, "your mama and papa were not married. Of that I am certain. That means that you are a bastard."

Morag stared at him. She refused to believe it. A bastard! Just like Quentin! *Mon Dieu!*

"There is a ship sailing to the New World colonies in two weeks. Mayhap you heard my mama or Andrew speak of Robert, my brother? He and Papa went Puritan and sailed to the New World with their co-religionists. At first they lived at Plymouth, but now they have moved to a place called Latimer, New York. Robert writes that it is a quite comfortable little town."

The pain and tears were impossible to hide now. "Do you suppose he will want a bastard niece—any more than you do?"

Donald shrugged. "If you do as I say, my dear, they need never know you are a bastard. Nor must they know of your recent shame. Your passage is arranged on the *Blessed Queen Mary*, due to sail in two weeks' time."

"I will tell Grandmama about this!"

"Lady Elliot is in accord with my wishes to see you safely off to the colonies. 'Tis best for everyone concerned."

"And what will you tell her if I refuse to go?"

Donald shrugged. "I believe Mister Stewart has some unfinished business with you. No doubt he will be happy to learn that you are no longer under the Elliot protection."

She stared at him. What choice did she have? The word "bastard" seemed to echo in her head as she stood there. She knew that, in two week's time, she would sail on the *Blessed Queen Mary*.

Nicole's blonde hair mingled with Quentin's matted dark chest hairs as she lay beside him.

"You were superb as always, *mon amour*. In faith, I do not know how Morag could have been so stupid as to have betrayed you."

She felt him stiffen and raised her head to peer up at him. "I have told you, Nicky, I do not want that girl spoken of."

Nicole sat up and shrugged. "Well, you needn't worry about her much longer."

"No?" He adjusted the single sheet about her shoulders and turned her to face him. "What have you done to her, Nicky?"

A sly smile played on the pretty little face. "'Tis nothing I have done to her, 'tis what I have done for you."

"I am not to be drawn and quartered, I take it?" He stared at the half-stubble of the candle, which barely lit his private cell. Indeed, Nicole had done much these past few weeks to make his life bearable.

"Did you think I could let that happen? *Mon Dieu,* Quentin, what do you take me for?" Nicole breathed into his ear. "No, do not answer. I will tell you. I have arranged for you to be transported to the colonies."

"Oh? When will this take place?"

Nicole smiled. "Two weeks hence. But that is only the beginning. At sea, you will meet up with Jean Baptiste's ship and—"

"He will rescue me from the English." He eyed her speculatively. "You will await me with Jean Baptiste? Eh?"

"Yes, of course! Do you think I want to stay here without you?"

"Tell me," he asked, just before mounting her, "what is the name of the English ship?"

Nicole gave a small moan of pleasure before answering: "I believe it's called the *Blessed Queen Mary.*"

Chapter Twenty-one

PULLING HER FUR cloak closer about her, Morag tried to protect herself from the cold clammy air that seeped into the coach and made the leather seats feel damp to the touch. Fog hopelessly obstructed any view, but even if it had been clear, she probably would have noticed very little.

It was still impossible for her to believe what her uncle had told her only weeks before. Her father had loved her mother. Surely he would have wed her. But if Donald Elliot had proof . . .? Morag sighed and wondered what her fate would have been had she refused to leave England. As it was, the ship was two weeks late in sailing.

As they approached Bristol Harbor, she glanced around at her surroundings with growing dread. Passing the jail, its stocks empty for the moment, she cringed. The New Year had passed with no word of the Marquis' execution. Surely, her grandmother would have told her of any reprieve, wouldn't she? Morag swallowed the painful lump in her throat. Probably the deed had long been done, and Grandmama had not wanted to upset her with the knowledge.

Dead or alive, Quentin Adam Sauvage had vowed revenge, and the man was influential enough to have worked some mischief where she was concerned even while in prison. Mayhap his fellow tribesmen would attack her in the New World, or mayhap his revenge was of the "other" world. After all, didn't the heathen have influence with the Devil? Morag shivered, recalling the bloody ring and the locket in that haunted clearing in France.

The coach pulled to an abrupt halt. Before Morag could compose herself, the door was flung open.

"Well, mistress, we are here," the driver announced.

She nodded silently, taking the man's hand, and allowed him to assist her out of the carriage. Squinting into the grayness, she made out the towering masts of the ship, rising like a giant gallows above her.

Shivering, she asked, "Pray, sir, is that the *Blessed Queen Mary?*"

"Aye! It is."

She glanced at the man, feeling suddenly frightened of the vessel that would be her home for the next months. "When is she to sail?"

"On tonight's tide, mistress. 'Tis our good luck to have made it to port with only a few hours to spare."

"Yes." She sighed. Obviously, Donald Elliot had paid the man handsomely to see her safely aboard the ship.

"Shall we board? Your uncle, no doubt, would wish you to become acquainted with the captain."

Morag glanced about her. The servant had already unloaded her trunks. Indeed, there seemed no reason to linger.

254

But as she stepped on the ship's gangplank, an unnatural chill assailed her. As she hesitated, a vision of fire passed before her. Was it her death? Was it her immortal soul in purgatory? Whatever it was, Morag could not move. She knew that this ship was not good for her.

"Mistress Elliot? Is something the matter?"

Morag continued to stare ahead at the main mast of the *Blessed Queen Mary* rising above the fog.

"What?" Morag turned to the driver then, still in a daze. The fearful vision had faded. At her feet, the waves lapped the sides of the ship. A gull screeched overhead and, indeed, all seemed quite normal.

"Tell me, is there not another ship sailing for the New World?"

"Nay, mistress. Not for a month more yet! 'Tis only chance that this one be headed ter the southern ports. M'lord says ye'll be able to change ships in Virginia."

"Oh?" Morag frowned. "Well, would it not be better for me to wait for a ship that was going directly to New York?"

The driver shrugged. "'Tis but a small difference, miss, and a great difference in the time you'd lose. Why, handled right by Captain Robin Townsend, this ship'll make the voyage in six weeks, stopping and all. Captain's got a real way with the winds." The man licked his lips.

Morag searched her mind for some other excuse. "What other women will be traveling with me? I mean, I have no companion, no maid. I—"

"'Twill be provided, mistress, I'm assured. 'Twill be provided. 'Tis nothing improper that old Gregs does. Yer a lady of quality. 'Tis not fittin' fer ye t'sail alone."

Sighing, Morag could think of no other excuse to

delay. Raising her wool skirts, she moved up the ramp. But near the top she stopped once more, seized by dread. It was no vision this time; it was a sound, like that of a dying man gurgling his last. She clutched at Gregs.

"What is that?" she whispered, her heart in her mouth.

"What is . . . what?" the man asked. But he had heard it, too; his face was as white as Morag's.

"That noise! What is it?" The groaning seemed to be even louder. Morag, now on deck, turned and peered into the fog, but she could distinguish nothing.

Then, as suddenly as they had begun, the groans ceased. Morag shuddered and shook her head. Was she going daft? Or was it an omen?

A door flew open with a mighty slam and a tall gaunt man emerged from below. By the gold braid on his bright blue jacket, he could be none other than Captain Robin Townsend.

Morag stared at him. A ragged beard half-concealed cadaverous cheeks; lank hair was tied in a queue with a ribbon. A black patch covered what must be an empty eye socket. Morag felt a sudden apprehension, as he walked toward her with tigerish grace. Forcing herself to appear calm, she took the hand he extended.

"Mistress Elliot, I trust you will enjoy the voyage. I have made every effort to arrange for your comfort, but you will understand that we are not a luxury vessel."

She nodded, feeling the pressure of his fingers. "Yes, I understand. Thank you."

"Would you like me to see you to your cabin now?"

"I—"she broke off. There it was again—the moaning . . . louder now. Morag swallowed hard. "If you please, captain, tell me. Do my ears deceive me, or are those groans I hear?''

Townsend smiled, looking rather pleased with himself. "No, Mistress Elliot, your ears do not deceive you. Those groans are from the prisoners. They must be brought into line.''

"Prisoners?''

"Yes, mistress. Men I've acquired from the jails to man this ship—with my own men overseeing them, of course. You need have no fear. They will be watched at all times, and my men know well how to handle them. Naturally, I'd advise you not to walk in certain areas of the ship, but there's no fear of mutiny. Once we reach port again, they will be sold for their passage.''

"You mean, they are being transported?'' she asked, just as a group of prisoners, ragged and filthy, came into view on shore.

Townsend shrugged. "One might call it that, though they are better off for the food and exercise this way than they would be if transported as common criminals.''

The fear that had taken hold of her subsided. "These are not common criminals then?'' Out of the corner of her eye, she watched the men file past the ramp as their guards waited for orders from the captain. Indeed, poor creatures, they seemed harmless.

"No, mistress. These are political prisoners. But come, let me take you below to your cabin. 'Tis not a pretty sight, these stinking creatures.''

Morag nodded, resigned. If her vision was an omen of death, well, so be it. She would just have to place her trust in God.

"Yes, captain,'' she responded. "I would very much like to see the cabin.''

"Good." He placed his arm on hers, turning her slightly.

Pain stabbed through Morag's chest and she inhaled sharply. More prisoners had been herded forward. Standing just below her, his arms bound behind him but his head held high, was the Marquis d'Angeau. There was no mistaking that craggy profile. Dear God, had the man seen her?

"Faith, what's amiss, mistress? You look as though you have seen a ghost."

She took a hesitant step forward, but the shock of seeing Quentin was too much. She fainted, the captain catching her in his bony arms before she could hit the deck.

Morag awoke in a dark stuffy cabin, furnished only with a narrow bunk and a square iron table bolted to the floor. As she stirred, blood pounding in her ears, she realized from the sound of creaking boards that the vessel was moving. How far had they gone?

Sitting up slowly, she had trouble at first recalling what had happened. When memory returned, her heart began to pound. God's death! It could not have been Quentin that she had seen! They had hung, drawn and quartered him—they must have!

Of course they had. Mayhap, indeed, 'twas his ghost haunting her. Marry, she had best rid herself of that notion. Was not the only ghost that of the Holy Spirit?

The ship creaked beneath her, swaying ever so gently. Morag forced herself up and out of the bed. She stared at her trunk and then at the small table, which held a pewter mug, and a pitcher and basin for washing. Yes, 'twas only her wild imagination. She had best find the captain, and apologize for her strange

258

behavior. She would also like to make the acquaintance of the other women aboard the ship.

Timing her motions with the gentle rocking of the vessel, she managed to dress in an emerald green wool, plainly-tailored yet unable to hide the smallness of her waist and the delicate swell of her bosom. Topping her outfit with a new paisley shawl, she left the close confines of the cabin.

Reaching the deck, Morag felt a cool gust of air in her face. The sky was rosy with the rising sun and she realized that England's shore was still to be seen. Breathing deeply, letting the fresh sea air fill her lungs, she watched the gulls glide and listened to them squawk as they played about the ship, waiting for the remains of the crew's breakfast.

Yes, she felt calmer now. At the stern end of the ship, she could see some of the prisoners, obviously washed and wearing clean uniforms. She saw, with relief, that Quentin was not among them. Of course not; her fears had been groundless imaginings.

Turning toward the captain's cabin, Morag paused. She would wait until later in the morning to approach him and ask about a maid. She had always been an early riser, and no doubt the other women aboard were still asleep. For now, she had best return to her cabin.

It was late afternoon before Morag saw Captain Townsend. By then she had already determined, to her chagrin, that she was the only female aboard the ship. A fact that made her uneasy.

"Why ever should that matter, my dear Mistress Elliot?" Captain Townsend asked when she confronted him. "The men, I have told you, will not harm you. Indeed, if one of them so much as gives you an improper look, you need but tell me and I will deal with him.''

"And how would you deal with him, captain?"

The gaunt cheeks fattened with a smile and his eyes lit up with pleasure. "Why, he would be flogged until his back was in ribbons, until he could no longer stand. It would make anyone witnessing it most reluctant to approach you.''

Morag's stomach turned at the man's description. "Yes, no doubt it would," she said weakly.

The next few days proved monotonous. Morag ate most of her meals in the cramped quarters of her cabin, going up on deck only when she felt reasonably certain Townsend would not be about.

She was there one twilight, gazing out at the ocean, thinking that she could understand why sailors felt an almost mystical attraction to the sea. Her shawl about her shoulders, she stood with the seaspray caressing her face, the dying sun flaming in her auburn hair.

"You should be careful, *mignonne*. That delicate skin might burn."

Morag whirled about to face the man she most feared.

Cool gray eyes studied her. "Come, come, Morag. I have not risen from the dead, *ma petite,* like Lazarus. I am as much flesh and blood as you.''

"But . . . I thought—" Her voice cracked and she swallowed hard.

"You thought they hanged me?" His hand went to her shoulder and she froze at his touch, trembling within. "You should know me better than that. If Maine could not kill me, then most certainly these English fools will not.''

Morag continued to stare at him, wishing he would

not stand so close, wishing she could not feel the warmth of his body.

"Come, *mignonne*, did you not miss me?"

Abruptly, she turned away. Her heart beat as conflicting emotions swirled within her. His hands gripped her arms, turning her about. Before she could react, he bent her head back with the hard pressure of his mouth. Morag felt her desire for him and knew his own for her. When he moved, as if to draw away, Morag realized suddenly that her arms had locked about his neck.

She looked up and saw the contempt in his eyes. Furious at her own response, she dropped her arms. Her voice was hoarse when she spoke, answering his question with one of her own. "Did you plan this? Did you know I was to be on this ship?"

"No, Morag, 'twas not by my design. I thought it was yours. If not—" he shrugged—"the fates are playing games with us."

Looking at him, Morag decided that the time in prison had done his looks no harm. Slowly, she shook her head. "'Twas not my idea to take this ship. I—" she stopped. No, she would not tell him about her uncle, her disgrace. She would not speak of the lost babe. "I . . . I decided to go to my Uncle Robert in New Amsterdam."

"Oh? Has Stewart no more use for you then?"

She blushed but held her head high. She refused to answer him; instead she said: "I do not think it wise for you to be seen with me. Captain Townsend has said he will take the whip to any man who dares touch me."

"Is that so?" There was laughter in his voice as he quickly bent to kiss her once more. God's death! How she hated this man . . . and how she wanted him! But it was she who drew away first this time. "Yes, Monsieur, that is so."

"And how will he know?" The gray eyes shone, obviously delighted with the knowledge that he could still excite her.

"Because . . . because I shall tell him."

Quentin shrugged. "Then I had best leave you for now." He turned and was gone before she could say another word.

For a moment, she remained where she was, trying to calm herself. She could certainly report him to Townsend, but she would not. No, there was little she could do aboard ship other than try to avoid him.

Damn the man! She clenched her fist. She knew she should not have boarded this ship. She also knew that when they reached port, she would try to get her uncle's help to set Quentin free.

For the first time in a long while, she smiled. If Uncle Robert Elliot bought Quentin's papers, that would make her his mistress—though hardly the way he would want.

Chapter Twenty-two

IT WAS ALMOST two weeks before she saw Quentin again.

The morning had started out with a hazy red sun. Morag had been aboard ship long enough to know that this boded no good; by evening, the wind had churned up the promise of a storm. Small confined whitecaps seemed to leap up, as the sun settled on the horizon. Gray storm clouds covered the sun and the wind rose threateningly.

A young boy, on the orders of the captain, raced up the mainmast to the topsail. Morag could see the wind blowing his blond hair. The wind was gale force now as the boy inched slowly along the spar. Morag held her breath as the ship yawed violently. At that fateful moment, the boy seized the sail; it unfurled rapidly, catching him unawares. He cried out, grabbed a rope, and hung suspended above the angry waters.

The other sailors stood watching the lad struggle to reach the safety of the mast.

"Aren't you going to send someone up to save him?" Morag shouted to Townsend.

"Why should I? He chose his job. He knew the dangers."

"Captain, he's but a child. I—"

"Mistress Elliot, you are a guest aboard my ship. If you cannot tolerate the way I treat my men, then I suggest you go below."

The boy, now frantic, was calling out for help, as the ship keeled over once more.

"Captain! Please—!"

" 'Tis a fearful storm we are coming into, mistress," Townsend said. "I've no men or time to waste on a mere lad." He turned and began shouting orders to his crew.

Morag's stomach dived with the ship's motion. She glanced up again at the struggling lad. He could not stay up there much longer. Tying her skirts up, Morag began to cross the deck.

The wind took up the boy's cries. The ship lurched violently, forcing Morag off her feet. She skidded to the side, nearly going overboard. Strong arms, circling her, saved her from a watery grave. She glanced up gratefully—and looked into a pair of piercing gray eyes.

"Get below, you little fool! Don't you know it's dangerous up here?"

"'I don't care!' she shouted, the wind carrying her words away. "Someone has to help that boy."

Quentin glanced up at the mast where the child still struggled, then over at Townsend. "And how did you plan to help him? Were you going to climb the mast?"

"That was my intention."

"What a little idiot you are. Do you think you could keep your balance on that pole?" Even as he said it, the ship rolled again and the rain, which had been holding off, began to pour down.

"If I do not do it, no one will. Look—" Morag

pointed above. "He's ready to fall." She broke away from the Marquis, only to have him grasp her again.

"Morag, I tell you once more—get below!" He glanced up at the mast. "I will take care of the boy."

He gave her a shove toward the hatchway and headed for the mast. Morag did not move. Rooted to the spot, she watched in amazement as he shinnied up the pole.

The terrified boy was in no condition to help himself, so Sauvage inched out on the spar, seizing him in one arm. Their combined weight was too much. A loud, snapping sound rose above the wind; the mast was splitting.

Morag bit her lip, crossing herself as she watched, paralyzed. "Dear Lord," she prayed fervently, "save his life just once more. He did this for me. 'Tis a Christian deed. Please, dear Lord, save Quentin's life."

Quentin and the boy had reached the halfway point on the mast now. Morag prayed silently. Please, God . . .! Her heart leaped with joy when Quentin, carrying his burden, reached the deck safely moments later.

Unable to stop what she had started, Morag rushed toward Townsend, who was giving orders for Quentin and the lad—Toby—to be lashed to the breaking mast for the duration of the storm, to be flogged as soon as the storm was over.

"Sir, you will not punish them!" Morag had to shout above the wind.

"Don't bother me, chit! Can't you see that I'm busy?"

"Busy as pig's feet!" she shouted. "I said, you will not punish them. The man rescued the child because I asked him. Besides, you need all hands available in this storm."

Townsend glowered at her. "Why did I ever take you on? I shall have Donald's head for this! Oh, well—Untie those men!" he screamed. "Get them to work. We head east by northeast."

"Thank you, captain," she responded, watching as Quentin was freed of his bonds. Then, seeing the man's angry look, she decided to retreat to her cabin.

Morag remained in her cabin while the tempest raged above. The air was damp, foul, and she dared not light a candle for fear it would fall over and start a fire. She lay on the bunk in the dark. It seemed to her that the undulating motion of the ship would never stop, that she would never go back on deck again. But after two days and two nights, the storm at last subsided.

To Morag's amazement, it did not take long to clear up the storm's destruction. Except for the broken mast, which was neatly sawed off and laid along one side of the ship, one could not see any damage.

"Will the lack of sail hamper our voyage, captain?" she asked Townsend.

"Nary a bit, mistress. You are anxious?"

Morag shrugged, not wanting the man to know how desperately she wished to get off this ship. "Only to see my relations and . . . I believe there was a vessel sighted a day or so ago?"

"If you're worrying about pirates, mistress, my ship is well prepared. Indeed, that vessel you speak of was unidentified—it disappeared afore we could determine its origin—but I'll wager it's one of those scurvy Frogs."

"A French ship, you mean? Along?" Her heartbeat quickened. How he could have managed it in prison,

Morag did not know, but somehow she felt the mysterious ship had something to do with the Marquis.

"You fear the Frenchies, mistress? Bah!" Townsend mistook her sudden paleness for fear. "Frogs or pirates, you need not worry."

Morag swallowed hard. "That is good to know." She picked up her skirts and moved to leave him.

"One moment, Mistress Elliot. I would be pleased if you would dine with me tonight in my quarters."

"Dine with you? Alone?"

The captain smirked. "Is it your reputation you fear for, mistress? My men will say nary a word. Though I tell you now, you have nothing to fear. We shall be accompanied by my first mate, Paterson, and my serving boy, Toby. You are acquainted with the lad."

If Toby would be there, and the first mate, what could be the harm? Smiling to hide her hesitation, she nodded. "Yes, captain, you may tell the cook I shall be happy to dine with you."

Back in her small cabin, Morag washed herself with the water in her pewter pitcher, then flung open her trunk and chose a peach silk dress that did not too badly show the wrinkles. The lace and ribbon trailing down the skirt and bodice showed her narrow waist and shapely bosom to perfection. Brushing her hair, she arranged it so it fell over her white shoulders.

Fan in hand, Morag proceeded toward the captain's quarters. Toby stood at attention by the door. His mouth gaped open when he saw her. "You . . . you look lovely, mistress. Faith, I did not think 'twould be you when the captain said he had a special guest for dinner."

Morag shrugged. "I would not have accepted Captain Townsend's invitation if he had not assured me that both you and the first mate would be present."

"He said that?" Toby's face registered surprise.

She paused, feeling a twinge of apprehension. "Did he say nothing of it to you?"

"Nay, mistress, he did not."

"Well, then," she took the lad's hand, "let us enter together and ask him."

"Nay, mistress." He drew his hand away. "I cannot do that! He would punish me."

"Come . . . I will protect you."

He hesitated, swallowing nervously. "I do not think you can, but I will follow you—for your sake, miss."

Morag opened the door. She stood there in awe. The captain's quarters were far larger and more luxurious than she had imagined. While the whole room obviously served for his apartment, there was room in a wainscotted halfparlor for a medium-sized table set with lace cloth and tableware. Candlelight from a multi-tiered chandelier glimmered on the plates as Captain Townsend, resplendent in a royal blue and gold braid outfit, came forward to greet her.

"Ah, Mistress Elliot. I see you have brought young Toby." He nodded curtly to the boy.

Morag was looking at the table. "But there are only two place settings, captain. Did you not say, sir, that Toby and your first mate would be joining us?"

"That I did." Townsend smiled his death's head smile. "But, unfortunately, my mate had other duties to attend to. However, if you wish, Toby may eat at the corner table."

Morag glanced at the boy, seeing the fear in his eyes. "Yes, I would like that."

Captain Townsend shrugged. "It matters not to me. Toby will do the serving. He often serves me—right, boy?"

"Yes . . . y . . . yes . . . sir."

"Right then." Townsend pulled a chair out for Morag. "I must say, you look fetching tonight, mistress. Dare I hope it is to please me that you dressed so?"

Morag sucked in her lower lip. "'Tis the custom to dress when one is invited to dine with the captain, is it not? I do but observe custom."

Taking his seat across the table, Townsend continued to stare at her. He seemed oblivious even when Toby brought the soup. The breeze coming through the open cabin door felt good on Morag's back.

They had but finished the first course when Townsend ordered Toby to the galley to fetch a salt cellar. There was none on the table, so Morag could find no fault with the move, but she was vastly relieved that the door remained open.

"Come, while we wait for the salt, let me show you my collection of coins." The captain moved over to his desk. Reluctantly, Morag followed.

But the collection was fascinating. Absorbed by the various shapes and sizes, Morag did not notice that Townsend was no longer at her side—not until she heard the door shut and locked, and looked up to see him standing with his back to the door, smiling that ghastly smile.

"What is the meaning of this, captain?" She glared at him.

"The meaning of what, my dear Mistress Elliot? Surely, you knew what my intentions were when you accepted my invitation."

"No, sir, I did not." Fear uncoiled in her stomach and her hands were sweaty. "Therefore, open that door and allow me to return to my cabin. I will be most happy to dine with you another night—when others are present."

The captain gave a short laugh and took a step forward. "I do not think you understand, mistress." He began to unbutton his tunic. "The fact is, I desire you. I want you, and I shall have you."

Slowly, Morag shook her head, backing to the wall.

"Ah, got you now, you pretty thing!" The bony arms bound her tight. Morag screamed as the cadaverous head tried to kiss her. Lashing out, she managed to kick his leg as he shoved her to the floor.

Again, she screamed. Townsend laughed. "Go on, slut! Scream all you want. Not a soul will help you." He reached for the fabric of her peach dress.

Morag kicked out again, hearing his cry of pain as she hit his groin. Swearing, he struck her. For a moment, she was aware of nothing but the sound of the slap in her ears. Then she realized that he lay on top of her, pinning her hands. She had opened her mouth to scream again, when there came a pounding at the door.

"Captain, 'tis a mutiny. Open the door and help us put down the men!" The voice sounded frightened.

Morag inhaled sharply as, cursing, Townsend rolled off her and stood. Quickly, she scrambled to her feet. His wiry hand grasped her wrist painfully. "You'll stay here, mistress. You'll be safe here."

Morag could only nod, stunned by the turn of events.

Townsend flung open the door. Quentin, sword in hand, bounded into the cabin. One quick glance from those keen gray eyes assessed the situation quickly.

Morag wondered where he had obtained the sword or how he had known where she was. Then she saw Toby behind him in the shadows.

The captain had made his own assessment. "So, swine! There is no mutiny, I take it."

"Oh, but there is, captain. Morag, get to your cabin."

Townsend, furious at having been frustrated in his pleasure, at being fooled, glared at him. "The girl stays here, Frenchie, and you will feel more than the lash on your bare back. Harvard! Alton!"

"Your men will not come, *Monsier le Capitaine*. I have already had a nice talk with them. As to my punishment," Quentin shrugged, "a slave has no other road but miserable obedience. I, for one, shall seek Heaven first." He flicked his sword.

"So, you wish to fight? Very well, I shall give you a fight, my man." Townsend selected a rapier from the weapons on his wall. "This is a man's weapon, Frenchie. 'Tis meant for killing. I don't know where you obtained that toy you carry, but know that this"— he lunged at Quentin, who leaped away—"will be your last fight."

He rushed at Quentin with vicious intensity, but the Marquis stood his ground and parried the thrust. Then Quentin swung his blade into attack. The English captain was no neophyte; their blades clashed again. Quentin made a quick quartet of attacks, and a small gap appeared in the dark blue tunic Townsend had hastily put on. The captain growled fiercely, realizing that his opponent was not going to be easily defeated.

Parrying a lunge and responding with a quick riposte, the captain glanced over at Morag, who had moved out of the candlelight. It was foolish of Townsend; it opened the way for Quentin to draw blood from the captain's shoulder.

Both hands gripping his weapon, Townsend sliced the air. The point of the rapier nicked Quentin's cheek, and he jumped back just in time to escape a wicked

271

slash at his stomach. He lunged before Townsend could fully recover and parry.

Morag cringed, seeing the blood dripping from Quentin's cheek. God's death, she felt so helpless!

Suddenly, Quentin stuck his blade into the wall; it snapped in two, flying across the room. He stood armed only with the weapon's handle and a blade stub. Townsend lunged, seizing his moment, as Morag screamed.

Quentin's knees came up. He propelled himself forward against his opponent, connecting with the captain's groin as Morag had earlier. Cursing and dropping to the ground, Townsend was ill-prepared for Quentin's blows. With stiffened fingers, Sauvage rammed the Englishman's head back. Retrieving the captain's dropped rapier, without looking at Morag, Quentin ordered: "Get to the stern of the ship, *mignonne*."

"But—"

"Go, you little fool!"

She hesitated no longer. As she left the cabin, she heard Townsend groan. Had Quentin murdered the man? She did not want to know. Indeed, there was no time to think about it, for now Quentin was beside her, running as he grasped her hand.

"Where—where are we going?" she gasped.

"For a swim, my dear. 'Tis a pleasant night for it, is it not?"

Morag's eyes widened in fear.

"Do not worry, *mignonne*. 'Twill be only a short distance. Jean Baptiste awaits us with his ship."

So she had been right. "But I . . ." She swallowed hard, hearing a growing commotion behind her. "Quentin, I do not swim. I am afraid."

The sounds of pursuit behind them were louder now. Had the captain survived Quentin's blows after all?

"Don't be afraid. Strip off your clothes. Hurry!"

In no mood for argument, he grasped her dress, ripping it off with one swift movement. While she stood stunned, he undressed quickly, then grabbing her around the waist, plunged over the side.

The splash was hard and painful. Water filled her mouth, eyes, ears. She sputtered and struggled to free herself.

"Be still," Quentin ordered. He raised her head above the water, keeping one arm securely about her.

With much misgiving, Morag forced herself to relax. Blinking furiously to clear her eyes, she saw that Toby was in the water with them.

From above, she could hear the *Blessed Queen Mary's* guns firing. Only then did she realize that the other ship was closing the distance to them. She gasped, swallowing water and coughing furiously.

Cannons continued to fire back and forth as the two ships battled. No sooner had the trio been pulled from the water to safety aboard the French ship when the *Blessed Queen Mary* burst into flames.

Morag stared in horror, crossing herself instinctively. This was the vision she had seen. She turned away, sickened, hearing the screams of the trapped men, seeing the flames leap about the two remaining masts. Quentin stood behind her with a cloak. As he slipped it around her, she looked around and saw Nicole.

Her cousin stared frostily at them. "What is she doing here, Quentin? We didn't agree to this! 'Tis she who would have had you hanged. I want her off this ship. I—"

D'Angeau silenced her with a look. "Be quiet, Nicky. We will speak of this later." He put a hand on the blonde's shoulder. "Now, be a good girl and fetch the three of us some clothing."

He turned to Toby. "Can you help man the guns?" The boy nodded.

"Good. I will tell Jean Baptiste that we sail for the islands, but first, Morag, I must get you to a cabin afore you catch a chill."

Dazed, she cast one last look at the flaming ship; then, shivering, she allowed the Marquis to lead her below.

Chapter Twenty-three

THE SOFT WHITE clouds racing over the island seemed to herald the approach of the magnificent vessel gliding effortlessly over the blue-green glass sea. Morag, standing on the veranda of Quentin's island home, thought she had never seen a sight so lovely as the ship's sail against the azure sky.

A breeze gently combed her auburn curls, allowing the sun to drench them with coppery highlights. She turned her attention idly toward the natural bay below, now filled with every type of craft. Brigs, barks, sloops, snows and schooners—all lay at anchor alongside frigates and privateers.

A sigh escaped her. She had been here for over a month, and still nothing had been settled about her future. It was not that Morag did not enjoy the peaceful island ways, but she did long to know what Quentin planned to do with her. But he had only recently recovered enough from his illness to join them at meals. It hurt her to think that the wound which had brought on his fever was her doing. Had he not, after all, received it while fighting for her honor?

She glanced toward the house. At least young Toby was happy here. It was evident that he worshiped Quentin. During the Marquis' illness, the boy had spent almost as much time in the sick room, caring for him, as she had. Did Quentin realize they'd been there? Probably not. He had been delirious much of the time, speaking in his native Indian tongue. Once or twice, he had called out Marie Thérèse's name.

While d'Angeau lay delirious, Nicole had dallied with Jean Baptiste and his cousin, Armand, who had also been aboard the French ship. Now that Quentin was awake and alert, she catered to him as if she had been at his side all along.

Approaching the house, Morag sniffed appreciatively and smiled. Eustasis, the Creole girl, was making her specialty, turtle soup. Mellow light glinted from the windows. Inside, a Negro youth was touching a flaming taper to the candles in a candelabrum.

Opening the screen door to the kitchen, Morag greeted Eustasis. "I take it that Monsieur Sauvage is awake and well?" It seemed strange calling him that. In the past, she had always used the name to taunt him, but here Quentin had no wish to use his title.

"That he is, mistress," Eustasis responded, tight-lipped. "*She's* with him . . . Or she were earlier."

Morag felt a stab of jealousy. Glancing at Eustasis, she knew the girl was reproaching her for letting Nicole take over, for letting Nicole pretend that she had nursed him all during his illness.

"He is well now, Eustasis, that is all that matters." Morag said.

"It isn't right. It is no use to say it is." She saw Morag frown. "Oh, very well. I'll say no more, but 'tis a damn shame." She paused, her hands on her hips. "When you goin' to let me read your hand? I feel the spirit within me."

Morag sighed. "Tonight. Are they in the parlor?"

The smooth coffee-colored shoulders shrugged. "There or the bedroom."

Morag winced. "Well, I'll change and be down shortly."

In the large airy room she had been given, Morag went to the white wood armoire. All of the clothes she had brought with her from England had gone down with the *Blessed Queen Mary,* but one of Quentin's last orders, before the fever had overtaken him, had been to outfit her with a new wardrobe. Choosing a cool lace and linen gown of palest green, she rang for Sally, Eustasis' daughter, to help her button up.

Morag had been reluctant to force herself on Quentin. Besides, having been an English spy, willingly or no, she could—as Nicole so often took the opportunity to point out to her—be considered a prisoner of war: a slave to be sold to the highest bidder.

All too vividly, Nicole had painted Morag's possible future for her. No, she was just as well off not to remind Quentin of her presence. She wondered if he would sell Toby too. Somehow she doubted that; he did not hate Toby.

Quentin and Nicole were nowhere in sight when Morag entered the long hall. Returning to the kitchen, she allowed Eustasis, now finished with the dinner preparations, to take her palm.

"Mammy says I'm good at this. Hold still now," the girl told Morag, who was squirming in her seat, bothered by the number of mosquitoes flying around.

Eustasis gripped Morag's hands tightly, studying

both palms, her brown eyes huge. The silence stretched on and on, and Morag was beginning to feel impatient, when Eustasis began to speak; the voice did not sound like hers, but was deeper and fuller than Morag had ever heard it before: "I see a strange break in your life. There are woods. Lots of trees and a river. It's cold. Very, very cold. Something in the woods will change your life. There is death. Much death follows you. Your journey . . . is not at an end."

Hesitant and fearful, Morag asked: "When and where will my journey end?"

In the same monotone, Eustasis continued: "I see 'tis years before your journey will end. There is an oldish man . . . and a child—"

Abruptly, Morag pulled her hand away. Eustasis blinked rapidly, coming out of her trance. "Why have you broken, mistress?"

Morag flushed. Mention of the child had brought to mind the babe she had lost.

"I . . . I'm sorry, Eustasis. Please go on." She offered her hand again, but the woman shook her head.

"It's no use now, mistress. The spirit done left me for now. I'll let you know when he come again. I tell you something that I do not need your hand for: Beware of *her!*"

"Her? You mean Nicky?" Morag's eyes were wide. "Oh, don't be silly, Eustasis. Nicky is my cousin. She might be jealous, but she would never truly harm me . . . would she?"

The Creole girl stared into space, as if in another trance. "I say again— *beware of her*. That's all I say."

Unnerved by her session with Eustasis, Morag left the kitchen. She glanced up the stairs, wondering, with pain in her heart, if Nicky were still abed with Quentin.

278

Despite the bugs, Morag decided to sit on the veranda. Mayhap later she would walk to the water. The softly lapping waves always seemed to calm her.

As she put her hand on the front door, she heard: "Just where are you going now, Morag?"

Spinning about, she faced the Marquis, standing in the study door. So he was not upstairs with her cousin.

She flushed. "To sit outside a bit until dinner is ready." She hesitated, but her curiosity could not be contained. "Is . . . is Nicky with you in there?"

"Nicole? Faith, no. I have not seen your cousin since early afternoon. I have been cloistered with my books. Much has happened here with my father's property since I have been away." He paused, staring at her.

"But I am not so busy that I cannot set aside a few moments for you. I am sure Eustasis will call us for dinner the moment Nicole reappears from whoever's bedroom she has gone to now."

So he knew that her cousin slept with the others. The lump in Morag's throat grew. If he acknowledged Nicky's faults and still wanted her, then it must be that he loved her. Reluctantly, she followed him into the study, noting that he closed the door.

She walked over to the small bookcase that stood next to the fireplace. When he had been ill, she had spent most of her time here, though since his recovery she seldom ventured in.

Morag was suddenly aware of him behind her, of the warm vibrations she always received when he was near her, but she did not turn. She pretended to read the titles of the books.

Finally, Quentin spoke, his voice seeming to boom out: "Why have you been avoiding me, Morag? I can understand your having no desire to be with me during my illness, but since I have recovered, you have purposely arranged things so you do not have to be alone with me."

Morag stifled a protest. Not be with him during his illness! Why, she had been with him day and night, except for those hours when young Toby had sat for her so she might sleep or get some fresh air. What lies had he been told, she wondered? As to her never being alone with him since, 'twas none of her doing, but Nicole's. If he could not see that, if the man was too daft or too in love with her cousin to see her tricks, well, then, 'twas not up to Morag to set him right.

His hand tightened its grip on her shoulder. "I have asked you a question, Morag."

She did not look at him for fear her true feelings would show. "And I, sir, have chosen not to answer it."

"Look at me, Morag."

She refused to turn, and was not really surprised when he forced her to. His lips met hers briefly. She tried to steel her heart from responding, but it was no use. Just his nearness set her whole body quivering and her nerves tingling with unbearable longing.

How gentle he was! How deceptive! Did he forgive her then for the betrayal, which was not her fault? Neither of them had yet spoken of it—nor of his promised revenge. Was it his plan to make her love him and then betray her, as he felt she had betrayed him? You are being a daft fool, she told herself. Tell him that you had nothing to do with Stewart's capture of him. Tell him that you love him! But the words would not come.

As he once more bent to kiss her, she felt herself melt into his arms. Closing her eyes, she stretched her arms up and pressed herself toward him.

"It's been a long time, eh?" He nibbled her ear, sending delicious shiverings through her.

"Too long," she whispered, unable to believe that it was she talking. "Oh, Quentin, I—"

The dinner bell rang just then.

His fingers touched her chin. "We will finish this later. Yes? I may come to your room tonight?"

Morag nodded happily.

When dinner was over, Morag excused herself as soon as possible. Once in her room, she lit a sweet candle that Eustasis had given her, to increase fertility, she had said. The doctor had told Morag after her miscarriage that she most likely would never bear any children, yet in her heart she did not believe it. And if she was to have a babe, she wanted it to be Quentin's.

Glancing in the mirror, she realized how her thoughts had changed. Since coming to the knowledge that she too was a bastard, it did not matter so much to her that her child be born within a marriage.

She heard the clock downstairs striking. Half-past ten. Was he still at his books? She knew that he had gone back to the study after dinner, but Nicole had disappeared as well. Morag would not put it past her cousin to confiscate his affections for the night.

With a tired sigh, she continued to brush her hair. She said out loud, "'Tis no good fretting, ye great daftie. Why did ye no tell him yer thoughts this afternoon?"

"Tell him what?"

"Quentin!" She spun about on her chair, dropping the brush. It unnerved her, his silent way of entering a room.

Embarrassment flooded her. "'Tis nothing . . . something I wished young Toby to do."

"Oh?" His hands on her shoulders gave her shivers as he bent over her and blew out the candle. She put her arms up to meet him and his lips caressed her neck, lighting the flames within her.

Lost in the pleasure of his touch, she was only vaguely aware that they were heading for the bed. Only with Quentin did she feel complete and truly alive. With the heady scent of the sweet candle in her nostrils, she climaxed—not once but three times.

Morag awoke to find herself alone in bed, and shortly afterward, she heard Quentin's voice—and Nicole's—on the terrace below her window. She could not make out what they were saying, but when she ran to the window, she saw them disappearing around the corner, hand in hand. She did not see either of them for the remainder of the day. Quentin did not come to dinner, sending down word that he was busy in his study, and would like his meal sent up to him. Nicole, also, excused herself from dinner, pleading a headache.

That evening, curled up by the fireplace trying to read a treatise by Bishop Laval and wondering all the while if Quentin would come to her that night, Morag became aware of her cousin standing before her with a tray of coffee and chocolate.

"I have brought you some evening refreshment, Cousin."

"Oh?" Morag straightened in her chair. "I understood that you had a headache, Nicole."

"True, and chocolate always seems to help my headaches. I thought that you would like some too."

"How considerate of you," Morag said warily, accepting a cup from her cousin.

Nicole stood watching her taste the chocolate. "Well, Cousin, it seems you are not to be sold as a slave after all. Quentin tells me there is a ship in the harbor bound for New York, and that he's going to offer to pay your passage to your relatives there."

"How generous of him!" Morag said quickly, forgetting to whom she was speaking. She took a deep sip of the sweet brown chocolate. "But, truly, Nicole, I am frightened of the New World. I would rather stay here, if Quentin will let me." Her voice betrayed the confidence she felt that Quentin would be glad to have her stay.

"Oh, come. There is nothing to be afraid of." Nicole poured more chocolate for Morag and for herself, drinking her own very slowly.

Reluctant to move from her comfortable position, Morag took up her cup again. Why was she suddenly having trouble thinking? She dribbled some chocolate on her dress but, oddly enough, did not care.

"You look very tired, Cousin. Let me take you upstairs."

Morag tried to shake her head, but Nicole had already put her arms about her and was lifting her from the chair. The pair began to walk then, and an odd feeling of floating enveloped Morag.

"But . . . are . . . we not . . . going up the stairs?"

"No, dear heart." Nicole's laughter seemed far away. "We are not." They were outdoors now. Vaguely, swaying on her feet, Morag saw a hooded figure on horseback approaching.

"What . . . is . . . happening?"

The hooded figure leaned down and swung her onto the horse.

"What is happening, Cousin, is that you are, after all, going to New York. 'Tis too bad that you would not go willingly. I have told you many times, Morag: Quentin is mine, mine alone."

Tears rolling down her cheeks, Morag realized that she was in no position to struggle. The arms which held her were too strong. She tried to speak, but her voice failed her. As horse and rider rode away with their burden, Morag heard Nicole's laughter echoing into the night.

Chapter Twenty-four

MORAG WOKE THE next morning to the creaking of ship's boards. Sitting up too quickly, she was overcome by nausea.

"Here, *chérie*, let me assist you."

Strong hands held her. Focusing her eyes with difficulty, she at last recognized her companion.

"*Bon Sang*, Armand! Did Nicky trick you too?"

The young man sighed deeply. "*Non*, Morag, I almost wish she had. 'Tis I who brought you here to the *Joseph*."

"You! You were the man on the horse?"

He nodded. "Forgive me. I feared Nicole would do you more harm if I did not do as she asked."

"But why you?"

The large brown eyes were sad. Armand gave an expressive shrug. "'Tis my misfortune to love Mademoiselle Le Martin. I will do whatever she asks."

A sharp pain stabbed Morag's chest. "Would that include murder?"

"*Non!* That I would not do, but Nicky . . . she is desperate for the Marquis. She will tire of him, as she

285

has tired of others, and then I will claim her. Then she will know where her heart lies."

"Oh, Armand . . ." Morag regarded him sadly, wishing she could be as sure. "I am sorry for you."

"*Sacre!* You are strange. I have just helped to take you from your lover and you are sorry for me."

Morag sighed, leaning back against the pillows, "I am afraid, Armand, that my love is not as steadfast as yours. If he does not come after me, then I shall . . . I shall just have to forget him."

The young man looked away, unable to meet her eyes. "Yes, you had best do that." He glanced toward the door. "I will go now and get you some food. It will make you feel better."

Silently, she watched him go, wondering how long it would be before they reached New York.

On their second day out, Armand took a fever. Dutifully, Morag cared for him with the same compassion she had shown Quentin. Armand was her last link with the past, and the only one who could tell Quentin what had truly transpired and where she had gone. As he thrashed about in delirium, moaning for Nicole, Morag listened with growing fear—and pity.

On the fifth day, Armand's fever peaked. Morag had slept little since he had fallen ill. At dawn that day, she sat holding his sweaty hands. With glazed eyes, he stared at her.

"Tell . . . tell Nicky . . . I loved her."

His hand went limp in hers. In a moment of utter stillness, the glaze left his eyes and a smile touched his parched lips.

With a heavy heart, Morag closed his eyes and covered him. She did not want to leave the cabin; she did not want to leave him alone, but she knew the captain must be informed.

It was only after the sea had taken Armand's body that Morag became aware her monthly courses had come. She had not, after all, conceived. Crying bitterly, she flung herself down on the narrow bunk, sobbing her heart out . . . for Quentin, for Armand, for the babe she had lost and for the bairn she had hoped to have.

The town of New York—made up mainly of neat little houses of wood or red brick, some of which had been there since the Dutch settled the town and called it New Amsterdam—was not large, but it was probably as big as any Morag would find in that savage land.

To Morag's surprise, there was no customs house, no place where she could inquire about settlers in the colony and begin her quest for her Uncle Robert. Distressed, she rented a room from an elderly Dutch couple, the Van Der Dooncks, and at their urging wrote to her uncle using the simple direction, Latimer, New York. Donald had said Latimer was a small town, and perhaps no street address was necessary.

She soon learned that to get along in this new land she had best hide the fact that she had lived a while in France and danced at Saint Germain with James. Frenchmen, especially those who had settled in neighboring Canada, were hated and feared, because of the raids on settlements they encouraged their Indian friends to carry out. Morag was horrified to learn of whole towns burned, their peaceful citizens murdered.

"It is not just the killings that they do," her landlady said. "It is what they do to the captives. Those bacon and pea-soupers are more devilish than the red skins.

They incite them, they do. Papists! Bah!'' The woman spat tobacco juice on the ground. Morag felt uneasy with all the intolerance around her. What if her Uncle Robert had been murdered or taken captive? What would she do?

The days passed slowly for Morag as she waited, wondering if this day would bring an answer to her. To pass the time and with her New World future in mind, Morag set herself to learn housekeeping, candlemaking and soapmaking, things she had never thought on before. So much was involved in keeping a house going. Mrs. Van der Dooncks was a patient, but exacting teacher. The home on King Street always looked neat and fresh.

In her free time, Morag liked to explore the city. One afternoon, two months after her arrival in New York, she walked down to the river and stood staring out across the water, wondering if Quentin ever thought of her, if she would ever see him again. 'Twas best, she tried to tell herself, to forget him. Nicky must have told him that Morag had left voluntarily, and if the daftie believed that, it must be what he wanted to believe. If he loved her, he'd have followed her to the New World. Most likely, her cousin Nicole had already wed him and the pair were on their way back to France.

When she entered the hall, inhaling the tart apple pie baking in the big bread ovens, she heard voices coming from the front parlor. A visitor! He had to be someone special for the Van der Dooncks to open up the front parlor.

Curiosity overwhelming her, Morag paused by the parlor door, as yet unseen. She saw an elderly man with pewter-gray hair and dark scowling eyes. He was not ugly, but s'life, he would have been far handsomer had he not had such heavy square jowls, which seemed to hang down over his dull gray coat.

It was the visitor who saw her first. His dark eyes seemed to pierce her soul. "Art thou Mistress Elliot? Morag Elliot?"

Stunned, she nodded, and stepped into the room. "Are you my uncle?" Somehow she could not quite believe it. "Or . . . or my grandfather?"

"Nay, I am Peter Alden." He paused to loosen the neckcloth he wore. "But I have come from thy uncle. He bids me welcome thee and bring thee to him. Your grandfather died in Plymouth, but Robert is well, praise the Lord."

"If you are welcoming me, then why are you staring at me so?"

The man blushed. "'Tis thy hair, mistress. A sinful color. Red is the work of the Devil. Hast thou lain with the Devil?"

"Mon Dieu!" Morag whispered, forgetting herself.

"What is that, mistress? Do thee speak the Devil's own tongue?"

Morag flushed. "Nay, sir, I speak a word or two of French, my mother's language."

The thick brows met a moment in dismay. "Pray, mistress, fetch a bonnet for thy hair and refrain from ever speaking that devilish tongue again."

"You mean, we are leaving now?" Morag felt a pang of fear.

"I do not see why not. The Elliots are desirous of meeting thee, and thou wishes to see thy family, is that not so?"

Morag nodded. "Yes, but I have packing to do. Besides, I—'twould be unseemly for me to travel alone with a man to whom I am not wed."

"Aye, methinks there is a soul there to be saved.

Yet, verily, I understand thy concern. Thou needst not fear, Mistress Elliot. My daughter, Sara, will accompany us. Sara!'' He turned slightly in his chair. ''Sara?''

It was then that Morag noticed the child playing behind the curtains. As the little girl emerged to stand obediently before her father, Morag stared. The child was small, with light curly hair that escaped from beneath a white cap. Her gentle gray eyes stared blankly at Morag, who stood smiling encouragingly at her. In that moment, Morag knew: Sara was ''slow.''

''Aye, mistress. 'Tis my cross,'' Peter Alden said, seeing she understood. ''Thou wilt not be alone on the journey with me.''

Morag hesitated, then said: ''I would take it kindly, sir, if we could leave with first light on the morrow. Do you not have some business in town?''

''Verily.'' He stood, and Morag realized that he was not much taller than she. ''I will occupy myself for the remainder of the day and prepare to leave on the morrow if thee will see to Sara.''

''Yes . . . yes, of course.'' Morag held out her hand. The girl took it unquestioningly, taking Morag's heart as well. If there were any doubts about her going, they were dispersed by the child's bright and eager smile.

After dinner that evening, Morag put little Sara to bed and returned to the kitchen. She saw the sadness in her landlady's face.

''I shall be most sorry to see you go, Morag.''

''I know.'' Morag said, feeling a twinge of regret. ''But it is something I must do. Don't you understand? I must know my family.''

''It will not be an easy life for you.''

Morag sighed. ''Life has never been easy for me.''

* * *

They left with dawn's first light as Morag had asked. The open wagon swayed, sometimes violently, as Peter guided his two nags along the rutted Bowery Road out of town.

Not speaking, they drove on, pausing for morning refreshment at the pleasant little village of Niew Haarlem. At noon, they stopped in Breukelen, now called Brooklyn by the English who lived there. The church there was small and ugly, but Morag felt compelled to step inside to pray for guidance in her coming life.

They slept that night and the next few with Morag and Sara curled up in the wagon—using some of Morag's clothes to cover them—and with Peter Alden on the ground beneath it, his hand on his gun. The majority of their meals along the way were what Peter himself shot or caught—woodchuck, partridge, rabbit, bass—and what she and Sara gathered of the fruits and berries. Morag was sensitive to the fact that Peter catered to her needs first, then to his daughter's, and last, to his own. Despite his bulk and heavy smell, Morag did not find him an unpleasant companion.

As they drove through the countryside, Morag noted the fine lands near the town of Albany. She could understand why no one who had not been in the country for three years was allowed to settle here.

The road now was a fine sandy one, leading through a wood of nothing but beautiful evergreens and fir trees. Even to her inexperienced eyes, she could see that the flats were exceedingly rich land.

"'Tis Mohawk land, this," Peter told her. "The Indians are a puzzle to some. I would not trust them and I would not like burying thee . . . as I buried my dear wife."

Morag nodded, but she glanced about, unbelieving.

"'Tis a warning well taken, Mr. Alden. I shall have care."

Robert Elliot, her uncle, was not at all what she expected. Tall and thin, towering over her, he reminded her briefly of Townsend with his gauntness, yet he did have the Elliot green eyes. His hair, once a light brown probably, was now sparse and gray; his face was worn and wrinkled with care.

"'Twas the sickness," he told her. "It took my father, and my good first wife as well. That is why I moved from Plymouth. I could not take the roughness there and needed a somewhat milder clime."

"But why did you not return to England?"

"Nay, that was not possible. I signed all my worldly goods over to Donald and to Andrew's heirs, should they ever come." Morag stared at him. So that was it! She should have guessed. "I take it, lass, that Donald did not tell thee of thy fortune?"

She shook her head, numbly, then shrugged. " 'Twould not have mattered, I . . . I did not belong there."

"Nor did I." The bony shoulders lifted expressively and Morag felt immediate compassion for this man, her father's brother, who had been driven from his home as she had.

"Of Andrew we shall speak later." His warm dry hand covered hers. "Just know that we are thankful thou hast come to us, Morag."

She nodded, hoping fervently that this would be the family she longed for. But her joy was soon dimmed by Patience, her uncle's second wife.

Goodwife Elliot was as hefty as Robert was slim. She lost no time telling Morag that they had a front pew in the church and that Mr. Elliot was an elder. Morag supposed that was a warning that she not embarrass him.

Her aunt showed Morag up the ladder to the screened-off loft area where she would be sleeping. Indeed, Morag thought, taking off her gray bonnet and shaking her heavy red hair free, the bed was not the feather mattress she had had at the Van Der Dooncks, but it would be welcome, for she was weary from the journey.

The scream pierced Morag's very soul. Frightened for her life, she spun about to see her aunt pointing a sausage-like finger at her.

"Sinful! Robert! Robert! Thou must come and save me from the Devil's child!" She screamed again. Morag stood there, stunned, as her uncle bounded up the ladder to the loft.

"What is the matter, Patience? What has happened?"

"'Tis the Devil's spawn, Robert! Look! Look!" She waved her finger again, pointing at Morag. "That red hair! 'Tis the Devil's doing! And look—look at these clothes, Robert. These laces, silks, satins, ribbons!" She spat on the hay-covered floor. "All spun with the hands of the Devil."

Morag started to shake her head, open her mouth to protest, but Robert's eyes warned her to be silent.

He turned to his wife. "Quiet, woman! Morag is no Devil's child—she is the daughter of my dearest brother. 'Tis none of her doing that her hair be the color it is. Though verily"—he turned to Morag—"I do believe 'twould be more modest if thou wert to keep it covered."

"Yes, Uncle," Morag responded, a bit intimidated, and hurriedly replaced her gray bonnet.

"As to thy clothes, thou cannot go to meeting dressed like a frivolous maiden."

"But these are all I have."

"Thou wilt make over some of my first wife's clothes. Thou canst take a needle, can thou not?"

Morag nodded, swallowing hard.

"Good. Rachel, our Indian girl, will help thee."

"She is to stay then, Robert?" Patience asked her husband, her voice registering dismay.

"Woman, she is my kin. She will stay."

Patience sighed. With one last pained glance at Morag, she turned away. As she watched her aunt make her way down the ladder, Morag knew Goodwife Elliot was now her enemy.

Chapter Twenty-five

MORAG HAD TROUBLE settling into the community.
Though she attended all the meetings with her aunt
and uncle, keeping her hair modestly covered and
wearing the gray or brown dresses she had made over,
she knew that everyone regarded her with disapproval,
some even with open dislike.

And she had to admit that she found the life there
dull and sometimes fearsome, with the ceaseless self-
examination and accusations, and the hushed voices
whispering incessant prayers. How sorely she longed
for the gaiety of the court life she had once detested.
Surely, there must be a happy medium!

Her Aunt Elliot made it clear that she was there only
because of her uncle's goodness, and pushed Morag
to all manner of work—from hauling water and wood
and scrubbing floors, to ceaseless mending, sewing,
carding of wool and knitting. Most of it, Morag was
unaccustomed to and did poorly. Goodwife Elliot did
not hesitate to expose her failures to her uncle, who
merely shrugged.

Soon Morag grew to hate the house at the edge of

town. It was small by all standards she had known, though, in truth, others in the town were smaller. Robert Elliot's house was comparatively spacious, with its three downstairs rooms, loft and lean-to. The furniture was crudely made, but serviceable. The flock beds were hard and uncomfortable. Morag could not help but smile when Peter, on his first visit, made a point of telling her that he had feather mattresses. The men here had strange ways of courting a woman!

Aunt Elliot was not her only problem. Reverend John Alden, Peter's half-brother and the community's charismatic minister, made it clear that he did not approve of her. Often, during the sermons, he would stare full down upon her just as he came to speak of damnation.

"Sinners! Repent!" he would cry from the pulpit, directing his gaze at Morag. "Women who incite men to lustful thoughts are objects of the Devil!"

Morag avoided the minister as best she could. She feared him and felt his accusations were the result of their first meeting, when his hand had brushed her own and she had abruptly drawn away.

Between them, the Reverend Alden and her aunt made life most uncomfortable for her. It was no wonder that, as often as she could, she sought the sanctuary of woods and stream, just beyond the town, and that despite Peter's warnings she went alone.

One day, the beginning of her third month there, with the air shimmering with heat about her, Morag again escaped the confines of the house. She had just learned that her aunt was expecting a child, though it scarcely seemed possible that her uncle would lie with the woman. The unsmiling firm mouth Morag knew would become even more unsmiling as time went on, for Patience did not like the idea of being pregnant. It also meant that Morag would have even more chores to do. In addition, her aunt had already mentioned that Morag would share the loft with the infant.

Carrying a berry bucket to excuse her absence from the house, Morag walked quickly. At last, in the solitude of the forest, she sighed and quickly unbound her hair, the auburn curls cascading down her back like the rush of white water before her. Ah, much better; gratefully, she massaged her scalp.

Removing her shoes and hot woolen socks, Morag slid her toes into the cool water. God's death, she wished she knew what to do.

She had thought Peter would have made her an offer by now, but he had not. Though he often visited the Elliot home, he had said nothing about marriage. Faith, she did not love him, but at least it would mean escape from her aunt.

Leaning back upon the rocks, she hitched up her brown linen skirt and tied up her shift, exposing her white legs to the sun. Yes, that felt wonderful. At peace and relaxed, lying there listening to the chirping of the birds, she could almost forget Aunt Elliot and the Reverend Alden.

Unable to resist the lure of the murmuring stream, Morag stood. She was hidden by the tall evergreens; it was safe. She stripped off her clothes. Only for a brief moment, as she entered the soothing waters for the first real bath she had had since coming to Latimer, did she think about her nakedness. Then, as the water beaded on her smooth skin, she began to make some hesitant swimming motions. Quentin would be proud of her, she thought, remembering their escape from the *Blessed Queen Mary*. God's death! Why must she always think of the man!

After her bath, Morag dressed quickly and pulled on

the heavy socks. Tying up her hair, she covered it again with her bonnet. The townspeople, when not discussing the Bible, talked only of the Indians and the wild Canadians—those bacon and pea-soupers—who incited the savages. 'Twas no wonder the French were considered to be devils here; Morag did not think she wished to meet up with one of them.

She bent to pick up the berry bucket. There was a meeting this afternoon and she must be present . . . if she did not want to find herself in the stocks.

It was a sermon morning, the third Tuesday of the month, when the Reverend John Alden, standing above them all on his tall wooden pulpit, once more directed his baleful gaze at Morag.

"My friends, evil lurks everywhere among us, though many of us do not recognize it. It masks itself as witches are known to do—and calls itself a wholesome maiden."

There was a sudden hush in the room.

"Stand up, Mistress Elliot."

Stunned, Morag stared up at him, not moving. Her green eyes were wide with surprise. What had she done this time? She could recall no disgrace. She swallowed hard, blushing.

"I said, stand up, Mistress Elliot."

Everyone was silent, watching her. She felt a chill but, boldly meeting his eyes, her chin up, head high, in what she knew would be regarded as the sin of pride, Morag stood.

She regarded him steadily, but he would not meet her eyes.

"Thou hast sinned, hast thou not?" His voice boomed from the pulpit.

"In what way have I sinned, Reverend Alden?" Her voice rang out as clear and firm as his.

She was challenging him! It was unheard of, she knew, but she could not help it. She had been passive too long.

"Hast thou no pride, mistress? Must I expose thy wantonness afore the whole community? Nay, I feel thou hast too much pride—but in the wrong direction."

"Wantonness, sir?" She stared directly at him. "I have shown no wantonness. If you believe I have, then you must have wanton feelings too."

A horrified gasp came from the church members. Morag knew she was treading on dangerous ground.

There was no telling what might have happened next if Peter had not stood up in the men's section. His bulk overwhelmed those about him.

"Reverend Alden," he addressed his brother respectfully, "thou art no doubt correct as always, but I humbly suggest if good Mistress Elliot seems wanton, it may only be because she knows not our ways."

"Knows not our ways, Brother? Surely, the girl is a Christian!"

"Minister Alden," Peter continued, "I humbly suggest that while Elder Elliot and Goodwife Elliot are most dutiful and wondrous Christians, they may not have the necessary patience for one who has led such a wandering life as Mistress Elliot has."

"Are you saying, Brother, that you have that patience? Patience to fight the very Devil? Verily, Brother, thou needs more than patience in such a struggle." The thunder from Reverend Alden was truly frightening to hear.

"Aye, I am suggesting that I do have what is needed. I will wed Mistress Elliot. My little Sara needs a mother and—"

"He is bewitched!" Goodwife Calton cried out. "She is a witch! We must burn her!"

Morag glanced at the woman with pity. The goodwife seemed to wither under the "witchlike" stare. She remembered, then, hearing that Goodwife Calton, a widow, had set her cap for Peter Alden and he had rejected her.

Peter continued humbly: "With proper guidance, Mistress Elliot shall learn our ways. Verily, I do believe this."

The silence in the meeting house then was almost unbearable. Morag glanced from the Reverend, furious that his brother had foiled whatever punishment he had thought to inflict on her, to Peter. Her heart beat quickly with fear.

"Well, Mistress Elliot, what say you?"

Morag swallowed hard. She had hoped for Peter's proposal, but not this way, not before the whole community; yet she knew that if she refused him, the Reverend would punish her with a vengeance, perhaps even have her tried for witchcraft!

In the stillness of the meeting house, Morag's voice rang out: "Aye, I will wed Mr. Alden and be a mother to his child."

Chapter Twenty-six

MORAG HAD BEEN married to Peter Alden for two years.

The first winter had been difficult, but not as difficult as she had feared. She did not think that Peter, for all her lack of housekeeping skills, had any reason to be dissatisfied with his choice of a wife. Indeed, she had increased the storage area twofold with extra strips of wrinkled red peppers, dried pumpkin rings and feathery branches of herbs, which she had hung from the ceiling and was learning to use in ways she had never thought possible.

"Mo—ther!" Sara approached, smiling, a hornbook in hand. "Read."

Morag smiled at the girl. The pair had made much progress with Sara's reading skills, despite the child's slowness. It pleased Morag too, that Sara called her Mother, that the gray eyes lit up with pleasure whenever Morag approached her, or took her hand. The child's presence had more than made her marriage a tolerable one.

Even the nights she spent in Peter's bed had not

been as difficult as she had expected. He was, by all standards she knew, a dull lover, but he did at least try to see that she was not unhappy.

Life was not, however, without its problems. Reverend Alden still had his eye on her, still spoke of sinners as he stared down at her in meeting, though no mention was made of witchcraft.

Looking down at Sara, asleep at last, Morag had decided that tomorrow she would go back to the river if she could find a free moment. It was too cold to bathe now, but she needed to go there from time to time to calm herself, to be alone with her thoughts. 'Twas like another world there with the murmuring river and the soft hum of insects and the chirping birds . . . 'twas her world.

Her chance came after she put Sara to bed for a midmorning nap. When she reached the riverbank, Morag lay down on the rocks, motionless. It was only here that she managed to find some semblance of the freedom which her soul and body longed for, which she could not find as Goodwife Alden . . .

Morag awoke several hours later. She hurriedly started back for the farm, running nearly all the way. How angry Peter would be when he returned from the fields for lunch and discovered her missing!

As soon as she reached the house, Morag knew something was wrong. The front door was wide open; Morag remembered having closed it before she left, and Peter was not a careless man. Perhaps little Sara had awakened from her nap and . . .?

Morag ran quickly up the steps to her stepdaughter's bedroom. A terrible sight met her eyes there. Peter's body lay on the floor, gouts of blood oozing from his hairless scalp. On the bed lay Sara, her small legs still curled up on the quilt as when Morag had left her, but her skull was split open and gore was strewn all over her pillow. In the midst of the gore was a bloody object. Shuddering with horror, Morag realized it was a tomahawk.

Indians! Quickly, Morag raced out of the house, headed toward the town. There was nothing she could do for her husband and stepchild now—God rest their souls—but she must warn the others. She must find her Uncle Robert—before it was too late.

Morag had only just reached Robert Elliot's house when the Mohawk war-cry rent the air. Frozen in her tracks, she watched horrified as the Indians, already inside the loosely-guarded gates, set fire to the meeting house and then to one of the markets. The sight jerked Morag out of her trance. She pounded on her uncle's door, crying to be let in.

Quickly, the door opened and Robert Elliot pulled his niece inside. He was not swift enough though. Before he could shut the door again, the Indians, having advanced through the streets more swiftly and silently than anyone in Latimer could have imagined, glided into the house. Patience Elliot screamed as an arrow pierced her husband's heart. Her screams were cut short by a tomahawk slicing through her neck.

Blood spurted everywhere. Morag, eyes wide, stomach turning, ducked the arrow which flew toward her and fled the house.

The screams, war-cries, flames and death were all about her. Fear gave way to panic and wings seemed to grow on Morag's feet, propelling her forward faster than she would have thought possible. Behind her, the whole town now seemed to be up in flames. Morag hastily crossed herself as she reached a path relatively free of fleeing townsfolk.

She ran for her life through the woods, not knowing where she went. She had not gone far, however when a burly man stepped out of the woods and blocked her path.

"And where do you theenk you are goeeng, mees?" he asked in heavily-accented English. Morag recognized the accent at once; he was French. She answered him with a torrent of French curses.

The Frenchman's eyes widened. "*Sacre!* I do not believe this. How is it that you speak French so well?"

Morag's eyes flashed with anger as she snapped, "If you must know, Monsieur, I am half French. I lived at Versailles—"

"When? When did you live at Versailles?"

She flushed. Well, it did not matter now what the townspeople learned of her.

" 'Twas with King James, afore he went to Ireland and for a time after."

"Mademoiselle—"

"It is not Mademoiselle, it is Madame—Madame Alden."

"Very well, Madame Alden, did you know the Marquis d'Angeau at Versailles, perhaps?"

Morag's eyes widened. "Aye." Her voice was subdued. "I knew him."

The Frenchman studied her thoughtfully. "Madame, I believe that you had best accompany me."

Morag swallowed hard. "Where, Monsieur?"

"We go to Ville Marie," the Frenchman informed her.

"Canada?" Morag asked, astonished.

"Canada," the Frenchman responded.

Chapter Twenty-seven

MORAG STARED AT the burly Frenchman, wondering at his mention of Quentin. Did this man know him? Was he a friend or an enemy of the Marquis? Had her admission helped or hurt her chances of survival?

"Is the Marquis d'Angeau in Ville Marie?" she asked her captor.

"That is not your affair," he answered. "You are my prisoner." He removed a ball of twine from his coat pocket, and, though she tried to struggle, quickly tied Morag's arms and feet to a tree. "You will wait here," he told her in French, "while I return to the town to take other prisoners."

Hour after hour passed, until finally, when the rosy sky gave an indication of dawn, the Frenchman returned. With him were a dozen of his compatriots, two dozen Indians, and about twenty-five of the towns-people. They were the sole survivors of the raid; the rest of the townsfolk had been butchered, either in their beds or on the streets, or subjected to horrendous tortures. How many of the women and girls Morag had sat through meeting with had been raped? How many people would survive in agony for a few more hours, uncared for? As the Frenchman untied her bonds, Morag said a silent Our Father for the repose of the souls of all the dead, and for a merciful quick end for those still lingering on.

They were forced to march all that day—and the next and the next. Their brief meals consisted of some dried beef and bread, provisions that had been stolen from the town. At night, Morag and the other captives were tied to sturdy trees. Faith, she did not think a one of them had the energy to escape, let alone fight their French and Indian captors. Already, the number of the prisoners had dwindled to nineteen.

For three days they trudged on. Once Morag stumbled, nearly falling. A tomahawk loomed over her for a brief moment. Quickly, she straightened and heard the Indian commanded to move away. Whatever the reason for the Frenchman's protection, she was grateful, but she feared that it could not last.

When they stopped again for the night, a welcome fire was lit. Were they that far from the English settlements now? Would there be no rescue by the brave soldiers of King William? One of the Indians had killed a deer, and while the food was not appetizing to her, Morg knew she must eat the meat she was given, or she could not go on.

After two more days of constant walking Morag felt she could endure no more. It would seem to her that she had been walking all of her life. Mayhap death would be preferable, she thought as she tripped on a root and fell sprawling to the ground. Let them scalp me, she thought, I don't care.

But, her survival instinct was not yet spent, and she

had risen to her knees when a hand touched her. "Come get up afore they tomahawk you," a familiar voice said.

Morag, dazed, took the outstretched arm. "God's death! Toby! How came you here? Have they captured you too?"

Toby flushed. He was, she saw, no longer a boy, but a gangling youth.

"So it *is* you, Mistress Elliot! The report was right!"

"Report? Toby, I do not understand. Surely, you are not—"

"Aye, Mistress. I come with the French. I owe no allegiance to the English. I was forced onto that ship as a boy. Your coming aboard was the best thing that ever happened to me."

Morag, confused, dizzy with hunger, still could not comprehend, "But how . . .?"

"I come with the Marquis, mistress. Faith, he will be happy to see you."

She swallowed hard against the sudden dryness in her throat. "So, he is here then?" She glanced about.

"Nay, not here. Wildcat will meet us later. He could scarce believe you had been found."

"Wildcat?"

Toby grinned. "This is his Mohawk name. Takojkowa—the Wildcat. Magnificent, is it not?"

Morag nodded. Yes, the name was quite fitting for Quentin Adam Sauvage. "Do you mean to say that he—he searched for me?"

Toby shrugged. "He told the commanders of this mission to keep a sharp eye out for a French-speaking woman with red hair and green eyes. When we heard that a 'Madame Alden' answering that description was among the captives, he sent me ahead to see if it might be you. Faith, he did not expect to find you wed."

Numbly, Morag said, "Aye, wed and widowed." She hesitated, then asked, "The Marquis . . . he is not wed?"

"Nay, though Mistress Le Martin might like it so. She has gone to Quebec City, to wait, as she says, for the Marquis to return to his senses and leave the savages." Toby grinned. "But come, we will talk later." He took her arm to lead her back to the captives' line.

Toby was nowhere to be seen when they started off again the following morning. Nor did she see him the next day or the next.

On the eleventh day of the forced trek, when death and illness had decimated the group by nearly half, the first Frenchman—Jacques Boucher, Morag had learned his name was— approached her.

"We are dividing," he said simply.

"Why?" Morag asked, wishing Toby were there and wondering again what had happened to him.

The Frenchman shrugged. "It is better this way. It is easier for us."

"You mean, it is easier for the English soldiers, who are following you, to lose our trail," she said.

Jacques threw back his head, laughing. Morag saw a deep scar in his thick neck. "You think the cowardly English will come after you? *Non,* they will not. Do not fool yourself, *ma petite.* We are dividing because I say so. It is easier for our Indian friends to house you."

Morag's eyes widened. "We are going to their village, then?"

"*Oui,* to the Mohawk village up the river."

"But you said you were taking us to Canada!"

"I do not care what I said," Jacques snapped. "We

do not want sniveling English dogs in Canada. You will be tested at the village. If you survive that—" he smiled pitilessly "—then we will go to Canada. If not"—Shrugging, he walked away.

Four women, including Morag, and four men, were in the group that Boucher decided to take with him. Morag stared at Boucher's broad back as the group started off. Had he had word from Quentin or Toby? Was he, as she somehow felt, taking them farther afield so the pair would not find them? Glancing about at the Indians who accompanied them, Morag felt sure that escape was next to impossible. No, they would just have to go on.

For a brief moment then, the bright afternoon sun shining in her eyes, she trudged along thinking of Quentin . . . and of how it would be to see him again.

Boucher's group walked for another two days. Morag had no idea where they were or where they were headed, but it did puzzle her that Jacques refused to light a fire. Surely, there were no English nearby now to see it.

The morning of the fourteenth day of their captivity, they reached the Indian camp. Morag was amazed that she was still alive.

The Mohawks gave their war-cry upon entering the village, crying out eight times, once for each of the prisoners they had brought back. As if by magic, the empty streets of the Indian village were filled with old women bearing staves and younger women carrying heavy clubs. Youths held knives and tomahawks, and even half-naked children, who seemed oblivious to the cold, held sharp stones.

The lines of Indians undulated as the people strained

to see their brave warriors and the bleeding scalps of the English, which they carried. Each warrior stepped forward, proudly bearing some trophy, while the women sang songs of praise.

The prisoners, grouped together, were now singled out to begin the fearful trial. A Mohawk approached to sever their bonds. The pain made Morag gasp as blood rushed to her wrists and hands.

"Goodwife Alden," one of the male prisoners whispered, "what will happen to us?"

She swallowed hard, shaking her head. "I know not, Master Standish. I imagine that we must run the gauntlet." She stared at the vicious old women, their weapons ready. "'Tis what Quentin once told me prisoners must do."

"Quentin?"

She licked her lips. "'Tis not important." Indeed, it was not, for it seemed that before he or Toby would find her, she would be dead.

Inhaling deeply, she tried to steady herself against a tree as the first of their number, Elder Mitchell, a man about her Uncle Robert's age, was prodded forward and began to run. The Indians jeered and screamed at him, laughing and hooting as he tried unsuccessfully to dodge their blows, crying out to Jesus to save him. Halfway down the line, he stumbled, the blows raining down on him as he fell, never to rise again.

The body was dragged away. Fear in his eyes, another prisoner, a mere boy, began the run, followed by his father. The boy made it safely to the lodge post at the end of the run, breathless and bleeding, but his father tripped three-fourths of the way, dying as a club struck his head.

"Lord Jesus, help me," the man who had spoken

to Morag prayed hoarsely. Much to Morag's surprise, he finished the gauntlet. Breathless but alive he clung to the lodge post, blood streaming from his wounds. The women continued to hoot and jeer, but Morag could see that the Indians approved of the prisoners who had survived the first ordeal.

Nervously, she waited, wondering what her fate would be, while Master Standish and the young boy were bound to separate posts. She did not have long to wait. Each female captive now was led to a post. Morag glanced about, wondering where Boucher was. She did not see him. Well, no doubt his authority here was useless. Whatever would happen, would happen.

Grimacing, she stood, head high, already immune to the cold, while ropes were placed firmly above her shoulders and then her knees to prevent her from sinking down. Morag wet her lips with anguish when the first female prisoner was approached. The braves each took a tomahawk and threw it, stepping closer each time. Vomit rose in Morag when she saw how many times the girl was cut. Could she stand up to that? She did not think she could. She prayed that if she must die, for that seemed inevitable, she would do so bravely.

The girl was now barely alive, and the Indians approached Morag.

She sucked in her breath and stood straighter, a small defiant candle daring the wind to blow her out. The first tomahawk whizzed past her ear. She did not flinch, though she was positive she would faint.

Swallowing hard, she watched the Indian step closer for another throw. It would be now, she was sure of that. Holy Mary, Mother of God, she pleaded silently help me.

The warrior grinned at her as he raised his weapon

again. But as his arm came back and his weapon began its flight, there came the crack of a musket shot ricocheting off the tomahawk, driving it off course. Furious, the Indian whirled to see who was responsible.

"Takojkowa!" he cried.

Morag's knees seemed to turn to water. Quentin Sauvage was riding into the camp on a black horse, followed by Toby and a Frenchman with a barrel-chest and muscular arms and legs. Tanned from days in the snow and sun, lean and muscular as ever, his glossy dark hair braided Indian-style down his back, the sight of the Marquis made Morag's heart beat quicker than it had moments before when death had been so near.

D'Angeau dismounted in one smooth motion, his look taking in the two dead men, the sobbing tortured girl, Standish and the boy. His eyes lingered briefly on Morag.

A fat round-faced Indian stepped forward and all the young warriors looked reverently toward him. He was wearing a full-length beaver cloak, and leggings and moccasins of deerskin embroidered with delicate porcupine quills.

Morag understood nothing of what was said now, but apparently Quentin did, for he responded in the same tongue. The big round face was creased by an apparently good-natured smile, and then grew serious. Walking quickly back and forth, with just the hint of a waddle, the beaver cloak bunched up over his belly now, Round Face glanced toward Morag.

Before another word could be said, a strikingly lovely Indian girl, with smooth black hair and the most astonishing blue eyes, broke through the crowds. With a cry of joy, ignoring the chief, she ran into Quentin's arms, hugging him fiercely, kissing him and laughing with relief that he was safe.

D'Angeau was obviously pleased and, in front of the whole tribe, returned her kiss.

Morag's heart sank into her stomach. She wished now that the Indian's tomahawk had killed her. 'Twas no wonder that the man did not want to wed Nicole when he had a maiden lovely as this waiting for him.

Scarcely aware that one of the warriors had cut her bonds, Morag sank down dizzily, losing her balance, catching herself but not quite before she felt Quentin's strong arms around her.

"Are you all right, *mignonne?* Have you been hurt much?"

Morag, struggling to free herself, scarcely heard the words.

The girl who had run up to Quentin now stood before Morag. "I am Winter Blue Eyes. You are to come with me." To Morag's surprise, she spoke English.

"With you?" She glanced toward Quentin, who was speaking with the chief.

The girl nodded. "We will rub your wounds with salve and the medicine man will come to see you."

Morag was bewildered. Surely, Quentin would not have her share the same tent with him and his Indian wife? Dizziness again assailed her, as the days of hunger and exhaustion caught up with her. There was no longer any need for her to fight, she thought vaguely, as once again she felt Quentin's arms encircle her. She had no more strength . . . not even to struggle against him.

Chapter Twenty-eight

MORAG LAY LISTLESSLY on a mat near the fire. After nearly two weeks, she was getting slowly better. But the medicine man, Winter Blue Eyes told her, said it would be at least another week before she would be permitted to rise. Then, if she so desired, she could be adopted into the tribe.

Morag did not much care what happened to her. There were times, lying on her mat, when she wished that the fever had taken her. It would be tolerable to have Quentin married to Nicole and far away, but to have him here, to see him daily, wed to such a sweet thing as Winter Blue Eyes, that was more agony than she could bear.

"You are crying, Hair Like Rising Sun!"

Morag looked up to see a concerned Winter Blue Eyes beside her, holding a bowl. She shuddered: probably some more of the medicine man's horrid herbal concoction. Swallowing hard, Morag thought ironically that she could not very well tell Winter Blue Eyes she was crying because she wanted the girl's husband.

"Would you not cry if you had lost your home, your husband, your child?"

"There is a heavy grief on your heart, but it will heal."

Morag shrugged and pushed away the bowl.

"You refuse to drink? But why? You are still so weak."

Morag turned her face away, reveling in her misery.

"You will not drink?" the girl asked again.

Morag's eyes flooded. "Nay! I told you. I . . . I appreciate what you do, Winter Blue Eyes, but I . . . I wish to be left alone. Please."

The girl shrugged, saying nothing and, still holding the bowl, withdrew.

Morag stared after her. Actually, she was rather surprised to have got her way so easily. With a disappointed sigh, she turned her head and closed her eyes.

It seemed scarcely a moment later that Morag sensed another presence in the lodge. Without opening her eyes, she said, "I want nothing. Please . . . won't you leave me alone?"

"Not when you are obviously determined not to do what is best for you—as usual."

Quentin! Morag's eyes shot open. She shuffled about quickly to face him, wishing that her hair were cleaner and that she smelled of rosewater and not of greasy salves. She stared at him a moment, and then at the bowl in his hand.

"I will not drink that. 'Tis vile. I . . . I am sure I will recover without it."

Shrugging, he set the bowl on the ground next to her. Warily, she watched him as he sat down cross-legged at her side.

Morag turned her back, not wishing to look at him, knowing that his gray-eyed stare would soon break her down. Yet feeling his eyes upon her back was no more comfortable.

It seemed an age; he did not move. Then, finally, she felt his hand on her hair. She did not shrug him off, though she stiffened slightly at his touch. Then his hand moved to her brow. How comforting it was, God's death! Sick as she was, she wanted him.

"Morag, *mignonne*," his voice was low, "you still have a fever you know."

"Aye."

"Is it that you're homesick? If so, I promise to see you safely back to the English settlers if you will drink the potion and get well."

Her heart was in her throat. She did not look at him. So, he wanted to be rid of her.

"What if . . . what if I do not want to go back?"

"Why would you not?"

She shrugged, still not turning. "I have no family there. My uncle, my stepdaughter, my husband . . . all dead."

"Your husband? Dead?"

Morag blushed. "Aye, scalped back in Latimer. But what has become of my fellow prisoners?"

"The boy has been adopted into the tribe. The man is gone—ransomed by the English. And the women are, by now, safely with the Ursulines in Quebec."

"Oh! Then . . . then I am alone."

"*Non,*" his eyes looked directly into hers, "you are not alone."

She swallowed hard, feeling lightheaded and strange. He took her in his arms, and she let her head rest against his chest.

"My daughter, Winter Blue Eyes, tells me—"

"Your . . . daughter?" Morag stared at him then.

With sudden comprehension, Quentin laughed. "Who

did you think she was? I do not seduce children, little one. No matter what else you might think of me."

"But . . . she is your daughter?"

"*Oui*, she is mine. I was young—no more than ten and six. Morning Flower, her mother, was murdered by a roving band of English." His voice hardened.

Morag did not trust herself to speak.

"You are trembling, *chérie*. I believe it is your fever."

She shook her head, unable to speak, feeling his lips brush her brow.

"Come little one. Take your medicine like a good girl. I promise you will go wherever you wish to go."

Morag took a deep breath. Winter Blue Eyes was his daughter—not his wife. Yet he still wanted to be rid of her! Well, this time she would not leave him so easily!

"I will drink that vile stuff but . . . there is nowhere I wish to go. I think I should like to be adopted into the tribe. I . . . I have no other home now."

Taking up the bowl, she swallowed the dark, bitter concoction, nearly gagging.

He accepted the empty bowl from her. "You are sure you want to stay here? 'Tis not the life of the French court, nor the English one, for that matter. The women work hard—"

She flushed with anger. "Think you that I have lived in luxury these past months?" Morag held out her once smooth white hands to show him the broken nails and reddened skin. "I have been a farmer's wife, Monsieur. Think you I cannot learn to do what must be done?"

Quentin gave a laugh; his eyes seemed to glitter in the firelight. He stroked her cheek gently. "You have not changed, *mignonne*. You are still a little cat." He leaned over quickly, kissing her forehead before she could protest. "Rest now. We shall talk more of this tomorrow."

He left then. Morag was already feeling drowsy from the potion. Joyously, she thought: He is not wed! He is not yet wed . . . and I am a widow!

It was several more weeks before the subject of Morag's adoption into the tribe was brought up again. Meanwhile, she had recovered sufficiently to do things about the lodge. It fascinated her to see how Winter Blue Eyes made the dyes for the porcupine quills and did embroidery with them and how the skins were prepared. Indeed, while there was a freedom among these people that did not exist in New England, the work was much the same—preparing means, making clothing, taking care of children and the home.

Toby, who had been adopted into the tribe as Quentin's son and was called Standing Pine, was often with her these days, assisting her. Morag was grateful for his companionship.

But one thing bothered her. Sitting before the fire one evening, doing embroidery work on a pair of moccasins, Morag asked Winter Blue Eyes, "Who will adopt me when the council fire is held next week? I mean, I know no one but you, Standing Pine and Wildcat."

"There is a man who has said that he would like to take you to his lodge—if it would be agreeable to you."

"As his daughter?"

Winter Blue Eyes shook her head. "As his wife."

Morag swallowed nervously. She did not like the idea of living with another man when Quentin was so close. "Is . . . is this man young or old? What does he look like?"

"I do not think his looks would disappoint you. As to his age—" Winter Blue Eyes shrugged. "To me, he is old but then I am young. To you, he may not seem so."

"But . . . who is he?" Morag tried to recall all the warriors who had passed through the lodge these past weeks, to call on Winter Blue Eyes or Gray Eagle, her grandmother, or Quentin, who often spent his evenings with them.

"I cannot tell you that. The evil spirits would be angry if I mentioned his name to you before the time of the fire."

Morag wondered why the girl was smiling to herself. It would be just like Quentin, she thought, to marry her off to some old man. If Quentin no longer wanted her . . . She bit her lip. Well, she would not demean herself and go begging to him.

"You are thinking of your husband again?" Winter Blue Eyes asked.

Morag nodded. "Aye, the one I had and the one who will take his place."

The day of the council fire was the warmest so far. Morag was astonished at how quickly winter seemed to depart here. There were a few lingering signs of it yet, but spring was well on its way. Soon the hunters would go off on their first trip, and the shaman would make "medicine" to bring them luck.

The town was filled with Indian dignitaries—major and minor sachems—from all the surrounding tribes. Despite her own anxiety, Morag felt the excitement about her, the festive air in the village. Winter Blue

Eyes returned to the lodge that afternoon, her eyes shining. "I believe Two Deers will offer my father for me very soon."

The girl often spoke of this young warrior. Morag wished her well. She had come to look on Winter Blue Eyes like a younger sister; she would miss her. 'Twas a shame that while the girl often poured out her heart to her, Morag dared say nothing about her own true feelings. On the nights when Quentin shared their fire, Morag wondered if there was another Indian maiden, not his daughter, whom he loved. Those cool gray eyes told her nothing.

Brushing her newly-washed hair with the tail of a porcupine, Morag parted it and began to braid it, the way she had seen Winter Blue eyes do.

"Here let me do that, Rising Sun. When you are wed, your husband will have the honor of caring for you, but for now, I shall assist you and then you will assist me."

Morag sighed and nodded. "Must you paint me and smear my body with bear grease too?"

"It is the custom," Winter Blue Eyes said solemnly.

As the girl worked over her, Morag wanted to laugh out loud. If the elders of Latimer could see her now! They would indeed believe she was a witch.

The songs and dancing had already begun when Morag took her place, at the fire, sitting cross-legged beside Winter Blue Eyes. Across the leaping flames, she saw Wise One, the chief, and then Wildcat, looking as much like an Indian as the rest of them. Behind him sat Toby.

The sun had gone down now, in a blaze of crimson and gold. The glowing colors danced and gleamed across the river and among the tree tops. As the shadows deepened within the forest and cool air stole over the camp, the hunters' dance concluded.

Now was the time. Silence fell among the crowd. Nervously, Morag tugged at her short deerskin skirt.

"Do not worry," Winter Blue Eyes whispered. "All will go well. Grandmother will stand for you."

"You mean, she is going to adopt me?"

"Nay, Rising Sun. I did not say that. Wait." The girl smiled and Morag wondered what was making her look so happy. Then she remembered Two Deers.

Aye, that must be it. Gray Eagle stood to address the council. Morag's heart seemed to skip a beat.

"Oh, Wise One, Chief of all Mohawks . . . Grandest of the sachems . . . brave chiefs, hear me out. There is a young woman who wishes to live with our tribe, to become one of us. She was taken from the English, but she has shown her merit. She did not flinch from the tomahawk. Our mighty medicine has brought her back from death, and now she wishes to remain with us. Oh, Great Wise One, this girl's heart is that of a true Mohawk woman. If she is allowed to remain, she will make happy the heart of some warrior."

Morag, who understood a little but by no means all of this, saw the fat chief nod solemnly as Gray Eagle sat down. "Let this woman rise and come forward."

Morag stared, paralyzed for a moment, until Winter Blue Eyes pushed her: "Go on!"

Stumbling slightly, Morag quickly straightened and, head high, she walked into the center of the circle. The firelight flickered on her auburn curls. All eyes were upon her. Her heart hammered and she could feel the sweat on her brow and her palms.

"Is it true that you wish to become a Mohawk woman?"

"Aye, it is." Her voice rang out clear and sweet.

She struggled to keep her eyes cast downward, as Winter Blue Eyes had advised.

"What is the Indian name you have taken?"

"Rising Sun."

"And why is it that you wish to stay? Have you no other home or place that you wish to go?"

"Nay, there is none. This village is now my home and Winter Blue Eyes is my sister. My past is dead. I wish only the present—to be here."

The chief nodded. "Gray Eagle."

The old woman was standing again.

"Know you one who will protect and care for this girl, who will bring her corn to crush and plant, skins to dry? Who will give her children when the time comes right?"

Morag glanced at Gray Eagle out of the corner of her eye. "It is true, Wise One, that I cannot continue to care for her. My hope is that some good family who had a daughter or a wife lost, or a warrior who is lonely, will take pity and claim her."

Gray Eagle stepped back then. Morag felt the blood pounding in her ears. Time seemed interminable. The silence about her continued so that she was aware of the buzzing of the insects. She had forgotten about the patience of the Indians.

"Is there no one—warrior or family—who desires to adopt this girl? To care for her as daughter, sister or wife?"

Still, no one rose. Morag waited, head still high, wondering if this was some test. Wondering if . . . Quentin unfolded arms and legs, and stood in one smooth motion.

"I will adopt Rising Sun." His voice boomed out over the gathering. "If she agrees."

"How will you adopt her, my son? As daughter, as sister, or as wife?"

Across the flames, his eyes seeemd to bore directly into hers. Was he doing this out of pity for her, because someone else had changed his mind? What would happen to her if she did not accept him? Confused, she barely heard his answer.

"'Tis my misfortune, oh, Wise One, to have no woman now. I will ask Rising Sun, once she has accustomed herself, to be my wife."

Morag continued to stare at him. Behind her, she heard Winter Blue Eyes giggle. What was the girl thinking?

"Well, daughter? Do you accept Wildcat's offer?"

She took a deep breath. Did he truly want her? Was it from the heart, or was it pity he felt for her; offering for her again as he had once before. If only she could know.

The chief was waiting for her answer. She took another deep breath. Once again, her voice rang out. "Aye, I will go with him."

As she took a step forward, he came to meet her. His hand touched hers. She felt the same shock she always did when they touched. Beyond him, she saw Toby grinning, and suddenly she knew that Quentin had planned to offer for her all along. Hesitantly, she glanced up into his face. The gray eyes were smiling.

"Come, *mignonne*. I will help you to move your things to the new lodge I have built for you. Then we will return to the festivities."

She wanted desperately to ask if he would share the lodge with her, as she followed him out of the circle of light.

Chapter Twenty-nine

THE FIRELIGHT PLAYED on the stony planes of Quentin's face as he sat beside Morag, emphasizing the firm square jaw, the long straight nose, the determined line of his mouth. From under her lashes, Morag stared at him.

It had been six months now since her adoption. She had gone to him that first night and he had seemed pleased, had made love to her as tenderly and passionately as ever. At the end of the week, when he had announced that he must go to Quebec City, she had been sure that he was going to see his Jesuit friend, Père Raoul, to ask him to marry them in a proper Christian service.

But Quentin had returned from his journey looking pensive, troubled. He refused to tell Morag what his business there had been, and suddenly she was afraid. Perhaps he had gone to Quebec to visit Nicole—Toby had said she lived there—and not to see Father Raoul at all. Of course, that was it. He had adopted her out of pity, but now that he had her, he did not want her; it was Nicole he loved. For though he made love to her eagerly every night, he never told her he loved her, and his expression seemed to grow sadder with each passing day.

After returning from a week-long hunting expedition, Quentin suddenly announced that he must go to Quebec City again. "I must see the governor on a matter of extreme importance," he explained.

Morag was instantly suspicious. The governor . . . or Nicole? But Quentin wanted her to go with him.

"You are sure you wish me to accompany you?" she asked dubiously. Perhaps he intended to surprise her with a wedding after all!

"*Oui,* will you come or no?"

She swallowed hard. "Aye, I will come with you."

The Marquis nodded. "I will inform Wise One. We will leave at sunrise."

The journey to Quebec City, it seemed, would be easier than the one from Latimer to the village. Though she detested the smell of bear grease, Morag agreed with Quentin that it was best to smear it on, to keep the insects from biting.

"Mind," he said, as he lifted her onto her horse, "'tis not rosewater, but it does have its uses."

She watched him pack a bundle of furs behind her. "Will you be selling those?"

"Yes, there will be a fair in Ville Marie, near my home, in a few months. We will reach Quebec City in time for me to speak to the governor, and then go to my home near Mount Royal."

As he doused the fire, he turned about. "Now where is that boy?"

"Toby is going with us?"

"I cannot leave him behind. Besides, I have promised him an introduction to the great Frontenac."

Morag stared at him. "And will I also be introduced?"

Quentin averted his eyes and didn't answer. Morag felt a sudden fear then, and as she prepared for the journey her heart was heavy.

Their canoe glided down the smooth river, Quentin and Toby paddling in unison, as if they had always worked as a team. Morag smiled at Toby. The boy flushed and turned his head away.

By evening of the third day, the river had the dank, rich smell of rotting leaves and rain-bruised fern. The forest animals, Morag noticed, were much scarcer here. They could not be too far from their goal.

"How soon will we reach your home?" she asked Quentin.

He glanced at her. "We go to Quebec City first, *mignonne*. I told you." His expression was sad. "We will be there in a day or so."

"Is that why you are unhappy?"

"*Non,* Morag."

"Then," she stretched out, her hand touching his gently, "tell me what it is. Mayhap I can help."

He gave her a quick smile. "There is nothing you can do, *mignonne*." He helped her from the canoe. "We will set up camp here. I will help you."

Morag glanced at him sharply. Something was wrong, she felt it in her bones. Always before he had let her set up the camp while he and Toby went off in search of their dinner. Why then, this night, was he staying with her?

Finally, in desperation, she cornered Toby. "Am I a great daftie, or is Quentin strange this night?"

"Aye, he is strange," Toby responded. "'Tis he who is daft. Were I he—"

"Were you he—what?" she demanded. "You know something, Toby. Please . . . you must tell me. I'll be crazed afore morn if you do not."

Toby glanced at her with something like pity. Then he looked back over his shoulder to where Quentin sat by the fire. "Nay, Morag, I love you most, but I love him too. 'Tis from him you must hear it." He turned then, to return to the fire, leaving Morag by the river, thoroughly bewildered.

What was it? Was it possible that he *had* married Nicole on that first trip to Quebec City, and now could not bring himself to tell her? She swallowed hard, staring over at him. Well, she would be his mistress then. Having once lost him, she had learned that she could not live without him.

With a heavy heart, she completed her washing and returned to the fire. Quentin glanced up, giving her a smile, motioning for her to come sit beside him. Was that the gesture of a man who did not want her? Nay, it could not be.

"Quentin "

"Hush, little one." He put his arm about her, drawing her close. "Let us enjoy this time of peace."

"But, Quentin, something is wrong. I must know. I—"

He silenced her with a kiss to which she responded avidly. Aye, there was no man like Quentin Adam Sauvage. Oh, if she could only make him love her, then he would never leave her.

* * *

By afternoon of the next day, they had reached breathtaking Montmercy Falls. Morag knew they were nearing the city proper. She glanced at Quentin, but he said nothing. As they paddled on, signs of habitation increased, until there were houses lined up all along the riverside. Up ahead, Morag could see the castlelike structure of the governor's mansion, perched high above the Saint Lawrence and the city, a proud edifice, as proud as the governor, General Frontenac, was said to be.

Absorbed in the sights about her after having been so long in the wilderness, Morag scarcely noticed that they were approaching the landing. It was an open place of middling size and irregular shape, nothing like the docks of New York. Steep steps led from the river landing to the Upper Town.

"Come, *mignonne*." Quentin took her arm.

"Where are we going?" she demanded. "You plan to leave me somewhere . . . don't you think it's time for me to know?"

His gray eyes studied her face; she hoped it did not reveal the emotions she was feeling.

"*Oui*, 'tis time I told you." He cupped her chin with his hand. "I have . . . a great deal of affection for you, little one, but—" He paused as if expecting some reaction from her, but she would not give him the satisfaction of knowing how much he had hurt her. Affection. Was that all he felt for her? What a fool she had been to give herself so completely to him. She might have known that this half-breed had no heart.

"But—what?" she asked, trembling inside.

"But I have no right to be your husband." He gently brushed away a curl that had fallen into her eyes. Tears began to form, but she blinked them back. "I am taking you to the nuns, the Ursulines in the Upper Town. They are good folk . . . you will like them. I believe at one time you were most anxious to join a convent?"

"Aye." She felt numb. "At one time I was." She took a deep breath. "But what if I do not care to stay there now? My life has changed much since . . . since Versailles."

"Indeed it has." He sighed. "*Mignonne*, I have come to love you so much these past few months—no, I think I always loved you . . . from the first."

Her heart leaped for joy and she opened her mouth to speak, but he silenced her with a gesture.

"No, *mignonne*, let me finish. I could not help but think how much you have suffered on my account, how you would have been spared this suffering if I had only heeded your plea to speak to the Queen about letting you take the veil. I did not want you to become a nun then, *ma petite*—I wanted you for myself. But you have only suffered . . ."

She interrupted him then. "But Quentin, we are past all that. I assure you, I have never been so happy as since the night you adopted me and I came to live with you as your wife."

He shook his head. "*Non, ma petite*, I have done you a great wrong. When I went to Quebec that first time, it was to speak to Père Raoul, my confessor. I told him I wished to marry you, but was not sure I had the right. I told him the whole story, *mignonne*, including your wish to become a nun. He was very thoughtful then, and said a vocation is from God and should not be interfered with. But he also said that a mere desire to become a nun might spring from causes other than a true vocation, and that I should not act hastily. He thought perhaps you might have conceived a child, in which case the best thing would be for us to marry. If not, he said, perhaps you ought to test your vocation, by trying the life of a nun for a while.''

"But I don't wish to try it!" Morag cried. "I wish to stay with you."

Quentin shook his head sorrowfully. *"Hélas*, Morag, it cannot be. I wanted so much to marry you that I waited these months in the hope that you would conceive, prayed every time we made love that you would get pregnant. This was not what Père Raoul advised me, but I could not bear to let you go. Only now I see that it is not the Lord's will, and truly, *mignonne*, I think you must test your vocation."

Did not this great daftie realize that she wished only to marry him? But she could tell by the set of his jaw that there was no use trying to change his mind. Perhaps he was lying to her. Perhaps it was that he loved Nicole after all, and was only trying to get rid of her. Perhaps he wanted children, and feared she could never give him any. He might be right at that—the doctor in England had warned her. If Nicole could bear him children and make him happy, did she have any right to stand in his way? If he were sincere in what he said about loving her—well, no matter. Whether he loved her or Nicole, Morag loved him—loved him enough to let him go. She would not grieve him with her barrenness.

"Perhaps you are right," she said meekly. "Perhaps I am intended to be a nun after all. And if you should wish to marry someone else—"

"Do not speak of that," he said quickly, and her suspicions were ignited. So it was Nicole, it had to be. Well, she would not let him know how much he had hurt her.

At the convent gate he paused, putting his hands on

her shoulders. "*Mignonne*, will you not kiss me one last time?"

She glanced toward the convent. "That would be most improper. I am sorry, Monsieur le Marquis." She opened the gate to the small courtyard.

"You are right," he said, a sudden sadness in his voice. "It was wrong of me to ask. Come, I will introduce you to the sisters . . ."

Chapter Thirty

A MONTH AND a half after coming to the convent, a month and a half since she had last seen Quentin, it came to Morag during evening meditation that she had not seen her courses yet. Well, they would come, she assured herself, praying even harder to the blessed Virgin. It was too late for her to be pregnant now— Quentin must already have wed Nicole.

But two weeks later, there was still no sign. Not even a special petition to the order's foundress, the Blessed Marie de l'Incarnation had helped. No, Morag had to admit that, despite what her grandmother's physician had said, she was once again pregnant, and by the same man.

Pacing her small room, from the bed to the wall and back again, she wondered what to do. Would she be allowed to stay at the convent? If not, where would she go? She could not ask Quentin; that was a fact. She was sure he had either married Nicole already or was about to.

She paused a moment, picking up her Bible. Silence would soon be starting, but she had time. Walking swiftly through the cool corridors, the gray cotton dress the nuns had supplied her rustling about her feet, Morag let herself into the church and then into the chamber housing the tomb of the Blessed Marie de l'Incarnation.

Crossing herself, Morag knelt beside the tomb. "Help me, please, Blessed Marie. I want this babe and I want that man, and I also want a life of holiness. I know not where to go nor what to do." Tears rose in her eyes.

A bell rang. Was it time for silence already? She did not think she had been there that long. As she got to her feet, she saw one of the nuns, Sister Joseph, at the door.

The nun smiled at her. "Madame Alden, I have come to tell you that you have a caller."

"A caller? This late?"

"*Oui*, he says it is most important that he speak to you. I told him silence would soon begin and that you would not want to be disturbed, but he was insistent. I have put him in the common room."

Quentin? Dare she hope? Heart pounding, Morag glanced back at the tomb. If so, the Blessed Marie had worked a fast miracle. With a bowed head, she followed the sister to the common room. She wished there were time to freshen up.

The heavy oak door creaked open to the common room and Sister Joseph stood aside.

Morag entered, barely hearing the door close behind her as the nun withdrew. The room seemed empty, then, she saw her caller standing against the wall.

"Toby!" She ran to him. "Oh, Toby, 'tis good to see you." She kissed him on the cheek impulsively. "My how you've grown! It's been scarce two months, yet you seem so much more the man."

"Do I?" He blushed, obviously pleased. "You
. . . you look beautiful. Even that plain dress cannot
hide it. Your eyes glow."

Morag glanced away for a moment; her eyes glowed
with unshed tears. "Thank you." Her throat hurt.
"How have you been? I have missed you."

The boy nodded. "I have missed you, too, and so
has he. Morag, he loves you."

"I do not believe it. Why would he send me away,
put me here? Nay, Toby, he told me 'twas for the best.
He has not even come to see me once since I have
been here."

"The Marquis is troubled."

Morag paled. "What sort of trouble? Is he in danger?"

"Nay, it is nothing like that, but he does stand to
lose his lands and his title."

"How so? I heard from the sisters that he is something of a hero here."

"Aye, but it is also a fact that New France wishes
to have its settlements increased, and has made it a
law that all bachelors must be wed within thirty days
of the arrival of the girls."

The girls, Morag knew, were the "King's Daugh-
ters," so called because Louis supplied the dowry for
many of those peasant women who came here to marry
and settle in New France. The Ursulines themselves
took charge of some of the girls until husbands could
be found for them. Most were wed within two weeks
of their arrival.

Toby continued. "So far, Quentin has escaped.
After all, there were so few women and so many men,
but now it seems the intendant—who has become quite
friendly with your cousin Nicole—insists that the Mar-

quis is a criminal, and that if he does not marry within the next thirty days, all honors should be denied him.''

Morag pursed her lips. "So? Let him marry Nicole." She could hardly believe he hadn't done so already.

"'Tis exactly what she wishes, but I did not think to find it your wish.''

"Nae, mon, my wishes do not count. Quentin had his chance to wed me. I'll not—" she paused, realizing that her voice was rising. "Oh, what nonsense you tell me.'' Could Quentin really love her after all?

"You can go to him. You have not yet pledged yourself to the Church.''

"Nae, but Toby, lad—''

"Hear me out, Morag. I have a plan. If the governor knows that Quentin plans to wed, he will not lose his title nor his money. I am sure that if you accompany me to Quentin's seigniory and tell him that you still love him, that you are not, after all, suited to the convent, he will agree to marry you.''

"He will agree!" Morag said indignantly. "I shall not ask him to do me the favor, Toby.''

The lad sighed. "Morag, I would not advise it if I did not know it is what he wants. The Marquis, as you know, is a proud man. He is convinced that you no longer love him, that you wish to spend your life with the nuns. He tells himself that if you loved him still, you would have written to him, or made your way to him. He forgets that you are also proud.''

Morag flushed. "In truth, Toby, I had almost begun to think I had best remain here. The sisters are good women, and I have felt renewed by the quiet and holiness of the place. But—" She broke off abruptly. Should she tell the lad that she was pregnant?

"But what, Morag?" he urged her.

Mayhap it was the Lord's will that she should marry

Quentin after all; mayhap He had sent Toby to expedite the affair. After all, she was carrying the man's child, wasn't she? Blushing, she told Toby: "I no longer have any doubts; I am carrying Quentin's child."

Toby seemed elated by the news. "'Tis a confirmation!" he said. "Morag, you must go to him at once."

She shook her head. "Nae, let him come to me. I'll nae beg to be made his wife."

Toby threw up his hands in exasperation. "Morag, you don't understand. There is no time to lose. Mademoiselle Le Martin is living at the seigniory. She is Quentin's housekeeper."

"His housekeeper!" Morag exploded. "His mistress!"

The youth averted his eyes. "Well, Morag, he is a man, after all. But 'tis only because he thinks you don't want any part of him, that you have found your true life here with the sisters. One word from you—"

"Nae, Toby, he is doubtless married to her already. Did you not say she had incited the intendant to pressure him into marriage."

"Aye, but he has resisted. Indeed, Morag, I do not trust your cousin; it is for that I am come, because I fear she will not be content to wait the thirty days."

"Toby, is there something you are withholding from me?" Morag demanded, green eyes flashing.

He began to pace the room. "Aye, Morag, I was ashamed to tell you what I have done, but I see I must."

"What you have done?" she echoed, bewildered.

"The fact is, I have long been suspicious of Mademoiselle Le Martin. She is an evil woman, one who will stop at nothing. One night, when she was with Quentin," he flushed, "I searched her room. I found this." He withdrew a small leather-bound volume from his coat pocket. "Her diary."

Morag's huge eyes widened. "Oh, Toby!"

"Aye, I took it, but I'm glad I did. She reveals here that she hopes to trick the Marquis into marriage. She will tell him that she is with child, but the fact is she is barren. She was told so by a doctor in Paris, when she hoped to entrap the Marquis earlier."

"But will he believe her?" Morag asked.

Toby shrugged. "Your cousin is clever, as well as ruthless. I don't know if I should tell you this, Morag, but the diary is full of schemes against you and your mother."

"My mother?" Morag exclaimed. "Then it was Nicole—"

"—who poisoned her, aye," Toby finished. "And she has plotted against you as well. One of the early entries tells how she cut the reins of your horse, another how she tried to drown you at sea. And that is not all, Morag. She was the spy who betrayed the Marquis to Stewart. She—"

"What?" Morag could hardly believe it. "Oh, but Toby, why have you not showed that little book to Quentin? Surely, he would not stay with her another moment if—"

"Aye, I will show it to him. But I want you to be with me. As soon as I took the book from your cousin's room, I knew it was not safe for me to remain at Ville Marie. But if you will come with me, Morag, if we confront the Marquis together—"

"Say no more, Toby. I am ready. I must go to the Reverend Mother, but when I tell her the whole story, when she knows I am with child, I am sure she will give permission for me to accompany you."

"I will wait," Toby said quietly. "But we must leave

today. 'Tis a journey of several days, and we have not a moment to lose.''

As Morag foresaw, the mother superior gave her blessing. "The Blessed Marie knows this the right path for you," the nun assured her. "The Marquis needs a good woman like you to keep his faith true. Marriage is an honorable vocation, my dear. And it seems to be the one our blessed Savior has destined you for."

Morag knew in her heart that Reverend Mother was right; to be Quentin's wife was her destiny. If only he had not yet married Nicole. The absence of her diary and Toby's departure would be sure to arouse her cousin's suspicions.

Four and a half days after their departure from Quebec City, the canoe bearing Toby and Morag neared Mount Royal and its coastal city. "There is no time to lose," Toby reminded her, as they set off for Quentin's manor house in Ville Marie. "I left Quentin a note saying he should by no means marry before my return, but knowing Mademoiselle Le Martin, I have doubts that my letter reached him—or if it did, maybe she will trick him into marrying her anyway."

But Morag, exhausted by the long days of strenuous paddling, suddenly felt a sharp warning pain in her womb. "Toby! The bairn! I lost the first one he left me," she blinked back tears, "and if I should lose this one . . ."

"You will not lose it," Toby said grimly. "Lie down, Morag and rest."

"But . . . how can you paddle on your own?"

"I can and I will. Do as I say now."

Within a few hours, twilight was upon them. The

spasms—Morag thanked the Blessed Marie—had passed.

"Keep up your prayers," Toby told her. "We are nearly there."

"Are we truly?" She raised up slightly and saw lights on shore. "Oh, Toby we are! I hope we're not too late, that they are not wed—"

"Don't think that." He steered the canoe toward the river bank.

"Come! Hurry!" Toby grounded the canoe and grabbed her hand. Together they ran to the private chapel. At the door, the pair paused.

"Mademoiselle Le Martin!" Toby called out. He withdrew the leather-bound volume from his coat and brandished it menacingly.

Nicole, standing at the altar in a white satin gown, her blonde curls demurely covered by a gauze veil, turned, saw the book, and screamed. Her eyes met Morag's for a moment, and she stared at her cousin in disbelief, then she stared again at Toby and the little book that he held aloft. Before anyone could stop her, Nicole had grabbed Quentin's pistol, which he was wearing at his side. Quickly she fired at Toby, hitting him in the heart, and would have shot Morag as well, but Quentin knocked the pistol from her hand.

"Nicole!" he shouted. "Have you lost your senses?" She did not answer, but raced to Toby's body, which had fallen into one of the pews, and retrieved the incriminating diary. She faced Morag, her blue eyes ablaze. "No! You cannot have him. He is mine—mine at last! You will pay for this," she threatened, then lunged toward the terrified Morag.

The strain of the journey, the fear of losing her baby, and now this, were too much for Morag. She swayed dizzily, clutching at the back of a pew as her knees gave way. Nicole was on top of her instantly, her small hands tightening around Morag's throat.

But the Marquis had anticipated Nicole's movements, and raced after her to Morag. His strong muscular arms pulled at Nicole's tiny fingers, releasing their deathhold on Morag, and in one expansive gesture, he flung Nicole across the pew toward the altar. Without looking to see where Nicky had landed, he bent tenderly over Morag. His long dark hair hung over his shoulders, curled in the current style of the court and the gentlemen of New France, and he wore a coat of hunter's green and a fine white holland shirt frothed with lace at the wrists and neck. Morag hardly recognized him as the same half-breed who had left her at the convent. But he was—in all the many guises she had seen him in—the man she loved. That, at last, she knew for a certainty.

"Quentin!" Morag clung to him. "Please . . . see to Toby!"

He held her tight. "Nay, do not look, my sweet. He is dead."

"Oh, Quentin." She began to sob

A woman screamed: "Mademoiselle! *Non—!*" It was Nicole's maid.

Morag and Quentin turned, but before either of them could move, Nicole had plunged a knife into her breast.

When they reached her, blood had stained the white satin bodice of Nicole's gown red.

"Oh, Nicky! Nicky, why did you do that?" Morag cried, sinking down beside her.

"You have . . . won, Cousin, but you cannot say . . . I did not try."

"But, Nicky, was it worth dying for?" Morag's tears could not be stopped now. She did not know if she

340

were crying for her cousin, for Toby, for her mother, for Armand . . . Peter . . . Sara   Eustasis had been right: death followed her.

"I . . . wanted you . . . Quentin." Nicole coughed blood. "Oh, how much I wanted you, but   " She closed her eyes.

"Toby knew. And you, Morag . . . I have wronged you both . . . Marie Thérèse . . . I am sorry. There . . . is no baby, Quentin. I . . . lied."

Numbly, Morag stood there. All the things her cousin had done to her—all the ways she had tried to win Quentin—passed through her mind. Then she thought of Eustasis again: Was her journey really over? Were her troubles at an end??

Nicole did not speak again. The Marquis gave orders for her body and Toby's to be removed and prepared for burial before turning to Morag.

"By my faith, *mignonne*," his arm went about her, "I never thought to see you again. Nicole had me convinced that—well, let us not talk of that now. How is it that you returned? That Toby was with you" His voice shook with emotion and she saw the sorrow and regret in his eyes. Aye, he had loved the lad too.

She stared up at him. "Oh, Quentin, I am so sorry!"

"Then come." He took her hand and drew her to his side. "Show me how sorry you are. Father Raoul will join us now, afore you escape me again."

"Now? As I am?" She looked down at her plain gray dress, much the worse for her harrowing journey.

"Does the gown matter so much, *mignonne?* Do you not know that I love you, no matter what?"

She smiled at him as, tenderly, he wiped a dirt

smudge from her cheek. "The dress does not matter." She squeezed his hand. "I love you, Quentin Adam Sauvage, and I will be with you forever."

"And I love you," he responded, his arms about her. "With God's help, nothing shall separate us again."

Romance & Adventure

New and exciting romantic fiction—passionate and strong-willed characters with deep feelings making crucial decisions in every situation imaginable—each more thrilling than the last.

Read these dramatic and colorful novels—from Pocket Books/Richard Gallen Publications

_____83164	ROSEWOOD, Petra Leigh	$2.50
_____83165	THE ENCHANTRESS, Katherine Yorke	$2.50
_____83233	REAP THE WILD HARVEST, Elizabeth Bright	$2.75
_____83216	BURNING SECRETS, Susanna Good	$2.75
_____83331	THE MOONKISSED, Barbara Faith	$2.50
_____83332	A FEAST OF PASSIONS, Carol Norris	$2.50
_____83445	THIS RAGING FLOWER, Lynn Erickson	$2.50
_____83446	FAN THE WANTON FLAME, Clarissa Ross	$2.50

Dear Reader:

Would you take a few moments to fill out this questionnaire and mail it to:

Richard Gallen Books/Questionnaire
8-10 West 36th St., New York, N.Y. 10018

1. What rating would you give THIS BITTER ECSTASY?
   ☐ excellent ☐ very good ☐ fair ☐ poor

2. What prompted you to buy this book? ☐ title
   ☐ front cover ☐ back cover ☐ friend's recom-
   mendation ☐ other (please specify) _____

3. Check off the elements you liked best:
   ☐ hero ☐ heroine ☐ other characters ☐ story
   ☐ setting ☐ ending ☐ love scenes

4. Were the love scenes ☐ too explicit
   ☐ not explicit enough ☐ just right

5. Any additional comments about the book?

   _____

6. Would you recommend this book to friends?
   ☐ yes ☐ no

7. Have you read other Richard Gallen
   romances? ☐ yes ☐ no

8. Do you plan to buy other Richard Gallen
   romances? ☐ yes ☐ no

9. What kind of romances do you enjoy reading?
   ☐ historical romance ☐ contemporary romance
   ☐ Regency romance ☐ light modern romance
   ☐ Gothic romance

10. Please check your general age group:
    ☐ under 25 ☐ 25-35 ☐ 35-45 ☐ 45-55 ☐ over 55

11. If you would like to receive a romance
    newsletter please fill in your name and
    address:

    _____

    _____

    _____